What's more irr
sexy man? Wha
sexy guy and

Two lucky women

THEIR BABY GIRL...?

Two bestselling authors deliver two compelling, emotional stories.

THEIR BABY GIRL...?

The Baby Mission
MARIE FERRARELLA

Her Baby Secret
VICTORIA PADE

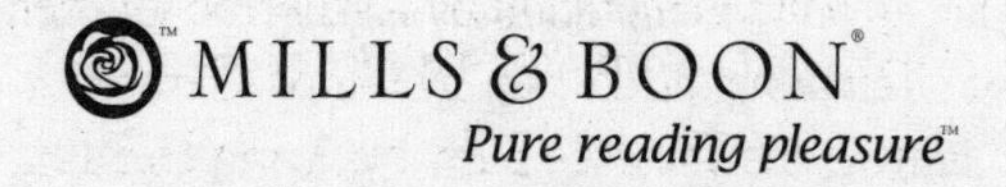

This collection is first published in Great Britain 2008.
Harlequin Mills & Boon Limited,
Eton House, 18-24 Paradise Road, Richmond, Surrey TW9 1SR

ISBN: 978 0 263 86109 9

064-0908

Printed and bound in Spain
by Litografia Rosés S.A., Barcelona

The Baby Mission

MARIE
FERRARELLA

MARIE FERRARELLA

earned a master's degree in Shakespearean comedy, and, perhaps as a result, her writing is distinguished by humour and natural dialogue. This RITA® Award-winning author's goal is to entertain and to make people laugh and feel good. Her romances are beloved by fans worldwide and have been translated into Spanish, Italian, German, Russian, Polish, Japanese and Korean.

To
Patience Smith
and our bonding process

Prologue

She was back. He'd seen her. Seen Claire.

Held her.

Her eyes were closed now, but she knew it was him. He knew she knew. Because Claire was his.

Now and forever.

He'd been away for three long, aching years and when he'd finally been allowed to return, he was afraid that he'd never see her again. That she would be gone.

But he had found her, found Claire. No one else would ever have her again. Would ever touch her again.

There were no words to do justice to the emotions that were skittering through him. Elation, joy, empowerment, those were all good words, but not really good enough. Not nearly good enough to begin to describe what it was he was experiencing right at this moment, just looking at her lying here on the grass.

He sifted a strand of her hair through his fingers. Bending down, he closed his eyes for a moment and inhaled deeply.

Her hair smelled of something herbal. Something nice.

Silky blond hair.

Hair that would continue to grow even though she no longer would. She wouldn't have the promise of another sunrise, another star-filled night.

He sat back on his heels and looked at her.

She looked so beautiful.

In his other hand, he held a rose. A single, perfect red rose. A rose as perfect as the young woman who lay here before him.

There were bruises on her throat, which marred that perfection. But he had hidden them. Nobody would ever see.

Carefully he placed the single red rose in her hand, then arranged the fingers of her other hand around the stem. He sat back and studied his handiwork.

She looked as if she was sleeping.

Perfect.

The pressure in his chest was gone. It felt good to be back.

To have Claire again.

Because he loved her.

Chapter 1

"Guess who's back?"

Special Agent Chris Jones, C.J. to her friends, looked up from her desk, the same desk that had kept her a virtual prisoner in the Southern California office for the past two months. She struggled against a very strong inclination to frown.

By the tone of her partner's voice, her completely free-to-work-in-the-field-while-she-withered-on-the-vine-in-the-office partner, Special Agent Byron Warrick was either going to give her more paperwork to cope with, or worse, he had something going on in the field that she was barred from. The powers that be didn't think a pregnant woman belonged out there.

Bracing herself, she tossed her long, straight, blond hair over her shoulder and asked, "Who?"

Warrick perched on the edge of C.J.'s desk and looked down at her. All of her. He hadn't seen her in nearly a week, and every time he was away from her, he had to admit it was a shock when he first saw her again.

He wasn't accustomed to seeing her this way. When they had first been teamed up, she'd weighed scarcely more than his equipment bag for the pee-wee softball team he used to coach. The last couple of months had certainly taken their toll on his partner.

He shook his head. She dressed well, and there was a certain amount of camouflage involved, but there was no way she could hide what was going on.

Warrick stole a peppermint from her desk and began to remove the cellophane. "You know, C.J., I can't remember what you looked like when you weren't pregnant."

Why was it that men felt compelled to bury affection in a sea of banter, barbs and teasing? There were times when Warrick acted just like one of her brothers.

"Very funny." C.J. sighed, then admitted, "Neither can I." She pushed the keyboard back on her desk. Something was clearly up. "Okay, what has you so all-fired chipper this morning?"

"Not chipper, C.J." Under the circumstances, that was rather a disrespectful word to apply to the situation, but then, she didn't know yet. "Just energized."

He played out the moment, reeling C.J. in. He felt

bad for her, knowing how she felt about being stuck behind a desk. But he also felt relieved. Her reflexes had to have slowed down in this condition, and he didn't want to have to be worried about something happening to her if she tried to go about business as usual. Business was definitely *not* as usual.

"Remember our old friend, the Sleeping Beauty Killer?"

Recall was instant. C.J. stiffened. The Sleeping Beauty Killer was the name she had dubbed the serial killer who had killed twelve women over the space of two years. All his victims were blue-eyed blondes, all between the ages of twenty and thirty. The name had been given him not for any missives the killer had left in his wake, but for the way he had arranged all the bodies postmortem. He strangled his victims, put a costume jewelry choker on them to hide the marks on their necks and then lyrically placed them on the ground with their hands folded around a single long-stemmed, perfect red rose. The women all appeared as if they were just sleeping, waiting for their prince to come and wake them up with a kiss.

Except that no kiss could undo what he had done to them.

Ordinarily, since all the murders had taken place in the vicinity of Orange County, the FBI wouldn't have gotten involved unless requested to do so by the local authorities. But victim number two had been found in the parking lot of the federal court building. That made it a federal case and gave the

Bureau primary jurisdiction. She'd been the first to come aboard.

Capturing the Sleeping Beauty Killer had been C.J.'s own personal crusade, one that had gone unfulfilled. The killings had abruptly stopped three years ago and the trail had gone completely dry.

The drudgery of the morning with its data inputting was forgotten. C.J.'s eyes brightened as she looked up at Warrick.

"Are you sure?" She made no attempt to hide the eagerness in her voice. If the serial killer was back, that instantly increased their chances of finally getting him for all the murders. "As far as anyone knows, he's been out of commission for three years."

The unofficial theory was that someone had turned the tables on the Sleeping Beauty Killer and killed him. Serial killers rarely lost the blood lust, so the abrupt termination hadn't been voluntary. C.J. had spent countless hours scouring the crime databases herself, looking for any murders that had been committed using a similar MO. But none had come to light. Eventually C.J. decided, with no small relief, that although she wasn't the one to bring him to justice, chances were that the Sleeping Beauty Killer was answering to a higher power for his crimes.

Obviously, relief had been premature, she thought.

"Take a look at what just came in." Separating the photograph from the rest of the folder he was carrying, Warrick tossed it on her desk.

C.J.'s stomach tightened. She found herself looking down at an angelic face that was all but devoid of makeup. The Sleeping Beauty Killer liked them fresh, untouched by anything but death.

The girl in the photograph couldn't have been more than twenty. Her whole life ahead of her, and now it was gone. With effort C.J. pushed down the anger that rose up within her.

She took the photograph in her hands, studying it. The girl was holding a single red rose in her hands. It was too eerily similar. But there were the three years to consider.

C.J. raised her eyes to Warrick's face. "Copycat?" Not that that was a cause for celebration. Copycat or original, the girl was still dead.

"Maybe." But somehow Warrick doubted it. He tapped the folder. "But he got it right, down to the last detail. Including the polished pink nails."

It was the one detail they'd withheld from the public when the story had broken. The Sleeping Beauty Killer liked to give the women he strangled a manicure, also postmortem. He used the same shade of nail polish every time, a shade too common to be useful in their search.

C.J. shivered. "Sick bastard," she muttered under her breath. In an unguarded moment, her hand slipped down over her belly in the eternal protective movement of expectant mothers everywhere, as if trying to shield her baby from this kind of horror. *It's not the best place I'm bringing you into, baby.* She let the photograph drop back on her desk. "I guess he isn't rotting in hell the way he was supposed to be.''

Warrick tucked the photograph back into the folder. ''Guess not.''

C.J.'s eyes were drawn back to the photograph. They had to catch this killer before he struck again. She tried not to think about how many other times she'd thought the same thing. ''Okay, what have we got on this?''

There was that word again, Warrick thought. *We.* They weren't a ''we'' at the moment. And they wouldn't be until after her baby was born. She made things hard on both of them by not remembering that fact.

''Information's just coming in, C.J.'' Looking at her, he could read her mind the way only some members of her family could. They'd been partners for six years now, covered each other's backs on the job and offered silent support outside the job's perimeters when the situation called for it. ''Hey, this isn't a signal to leap out from behind your desk.'' His green eyes swept over her considerable bulk as a hint of a smile played on his lips. ''Not that leaping appears to be in your repertoire at the moment.''

''Thanks a bunch.'' C.J. shifted in her seat, wishing she could get comfortable, knowing it was a futile effort. These days *comfortable* was only a word in the dictionary. ''I wasn't about to leap, just walk out with as much dignity as a pregnant elephant can muster.''

He'd crossed the line and hurt her feelings, Warrick realized. So he backtracked a little. "I wouldn't say elephant."

"Not verbally," C.J. countered, knowing she had him and skewering him just a little. Because he owed it to her. "But I can see what you're thinking in your eyes. I always could, you know."

He liked being able to read her, but he didn't like being transparent himself. "What I'm thinking is that any normal woman would have already gone on maternity leave by now."

She'd been over this subject ad nauseum, with both Warrick and her family. Four brothers, two parents and a partner, all of whom thought they knew better than she did what was best for her.

"We both know I don't fall into that category," C.J. reminded him. "And we superwomen have an image to maintain."

He grinned. It was the kind of grin that raised women's blood pressures and lowered their resistance. At times, C.J. mused, it was hard to remember that she thought of him as another brother and was thus immune to him. He did have one hell of a smile. Lately she kept finding herself attracted to her partner at very odd moments. For some reason, Warrick had been looking sexier and sexier to her. Had to be the hormones, she decided. They were completely out of kilter. She was usually better at keeping a tight rein on her thoughts.

"Superwoman, huh?" Warrick nodded at her stomach. "I don't exactly picture you flying around right about now."

She eyed the folder in his hands. It was like waving a piece of ham in front of a starving dog. "Did you just come in here with this to torture me?"

Following her eyes, he tucked the folder under his arm. "No, but it was our case. I thought you'd want to be in the loop."

Impatient, she shifted in her chair again. It creaked its protest over the change of position. C.J. frowned. "These days I feel like the whole damn loop."

One more month, she thought, squelching a note of desperation. One more month like this and then it'd be over. One more month and she'd have this baby so she could try to get her life back on track again. It was going to be a lot better when she could finally hold her baby in her arms instead of carrying it around like a leaden weight.

She tried not to let her mind drift. There was time enough for maternal feelings *after* the baby arrived, healthy and strong. Until then, she was determined to keep her emotions under tight wrap.

That wasn't going very well right now.

C.J. noted where her partner's eyes were resting. On her abdomen. Annoyance rose up three flights.

"Don't look at me like that. I've got my whole family watching my stomach as if it's a pot about to boil, and I don't need my partner doing the same thing."

Warrick straightened. "The person you should have watching your stomach is—"

She shut her eyes, searching for a vein of strength. They'd been down this road before, too. Too often.

"Don't start, War. I know what you're going to say and I don't want to hear it."

"Don't want to hear what?" He meant to make his question sound innocent. It sounded heated instead. But he wasn't exactly impartial when it came to the FBI special agent who, until seven months ago, had a prominent place in his partner's life—a partner he was extremely fond of. If he felt anything else toward her, well, that was something that wasn't going to be explored in the light of day. It couldn't be. Never mind that, pregnant or not, C.J. was the hottest-looking woman he'd ever come across. "That your insignificant other should at least be around to lend you some emotional support?"

They'd already been through this, she and Warrick. Why couldn't he get this through his thick black Irish head? "He's not my 'other' anything, War."

The hell the man wasn't. He had no idea what the attraction had been, but it was obviously hot enough to get her in this condition. Hot enough for her to want to keep the baby instead of going another route.

Restless, Warrick got up. "I just think that after he got you pregnant—"

C.J. took instant offense. From the moment she'd first opened her eyes on the world, despite the fact that she had a warm, loving family, she'd been her own person. She resented the implication, even for a moment, that she wasn't.

"Nobody *got* me anything. We took precautions, they didn't work. The pregnancy was an accident."

Again her hand went over her belly, as if to block out any hurtful words the baby might hear. ''It happens, okay? Now if you don't mind, Special Agent Warrick, let's drop the subject.''

She watched the deep frown take root on his face and tried to tell herself she appreciated where he was coming from. He just cared about her, the way she did about him. Cared the way she had when his wife of two years had left him three years ago because she couldn't stand the instability of the life he led.

''Don't talk to me like that, C.J., as if we're two characters out of the *X-Files,* calling to each other by our titles. It's not natural. And neither,'' he added vehemently, ''is walking away from a woman you're supposed to be in love with.''

He'd never liked Tom Thorndyke, hadn't liked him from the first moment the man had stared unabashedly at C.J. But he'd made concessions because C.J. obviously cared about the jerk. He hated to see her hurt and abandoned. For two cents proper, he'd make the man eat his perfect teeth. If he could get to him. The man had taken an assignment out of the state right after he'd told C.J. that they were better off going their separate ways.

Which was right after she'd told him she was pregnant.

''Forget about Tom Thorndyke and tell me who's been assigned to the case.'' C.J. shrugged. She'd made up her mind to only look ahead and not back. Looking back never got you anywhere, anyway.

Because he knew they weren't going to get anywhere waltzing over old ground, Warrick backed off and told her what she wanted to know. ''Rodriguez, Culpepper...''

The two other special agents who had been on the original task force. A flutter of unfounded hope passed through her. ''And?''

''Me.''

C.J. knew what he was telling her. Disappointment jabbed her with a sharp, extra-long knitting needle. ''But not me.''

He'd gone to bat to get her on the team over the assistant director's reservations. On the team safely.

''Unofficially.'' Warrick pointed to the computer. ''You can cross-check information for us, go through the files, things like that.''

It wasn't what she wanted to hear. ''I've got too much seniority to be a grunt, Warrick, and I'm not old enough to be stuck behind a computer.''

He looked at her for a long moment. She should never have gotten involved with that character. For once it seemed as if her keen instincts had completely failed her. ''Should have thought of that before you tripped the light fantastic with old shoot-and-scoot.''

She'd never been long on patience. Pregnancy had cut her lag time in half. She struggled to hold on to her temper. ''Don't you think it's about time you stopped with the cute references?''

''I'll stop when he materializes out of the Bermuda Triangle to live up to his end of it.'' He looked at her long and hard. ''And there's nothing 'cute' about a man who ducks out on his responsibilities.''

She'd given the matter a great deal of thought

even before she'd told Thorndyke about the baby she was carrying. She'd found herself drawing up a list of the man's pros and cons. Disgusted, she'd crumpled them up. Love and marriage was not decided by a safe, sane list of pros and cons, but on a gut feeling, a lack of breath and an X-factor that defied description. None of the latter applied to Tom Thorndyke. The relationship, short as it was, had been a mistake. A misjudgment on her part because she'd been lonely, and she took full responsibility for it.

She just wished Warrick would let it drop. ''The worst thing in the world would have been for Thorndyke and me to get married.''

Part of him felt that way, too. But he wasn't about to tell her that. ''If you felt that way, why did you sleep with him?''

Very simply because she hadn't thought about any consequences arising from the liaison. For once in her life, impulse had guided her. But once she'd discovered she was pregnant, changes in her outlook followed. She saw Tom's true colors. And maternal instincts came out of nowhere. She never once doubted that she wanted this baby. But even so, she refused to allow herself the luxury of making plans. Plans had a way of falling through, dragging disappointment in their wake.

She looked at Warrick. ''Since when do I owe you any explanations?''

Holding the folder in one hand, he opened his arms wide and shrugged. ''You don't.'' With that, he turned away.

Annoyed at him and herself, C.J. called after him. "You can have a serving of ice cream without wanting to marry the ice cream vat." Warrick stopped and looked at her over his shoulder. She shrugged. "Besides, it was just one of those things that happened. It would be a mistake to have three people pay for one night of passion." And a birth control method that had failed, she added silently.

He crossed back to her slowly. "I guess that makes sense."

She'd known all along that Warrick hadn't liked Tom. Maybe, in some perverse way, that might have even spurred her on, although she couldn't have actually explained why. In any event, as far as she was concerned that was all behind her.

"Okay, enough atonement, Father Warrick." She put her hand out for the folder. "Give me the information. Do we know who the victim is?"

He nodded. There'd been no mystery here. "Same as always." Warrick handed her the folder. "There was a wallet. He doesn't get his jollies challenging us."

As far as serial killers went, the Sleeping Beauty Killer wasn't unduly cruel. He'd always made a point of making sure that the victim could be readily identified, that her next of kin, if there were any, could easily be contacted and informed of the person's death. The only secrecy was his identity. And why he killed in the first place.

C.J. glanced at the information. She felt heartsick for the family. No one should have to put up with this kind of thing happening.

"A serial killer with heart. How lovely. Damn it, Warrick." She slapped the folder down on her desk. "I want this guy in the worst way." Emotions weren't going to catch the killer. Only cold, hard, deliberate investigation would do it. And a great deal of luck. "What do you think made him stop for so long?"

He perched on her desk again. She was wearing a different perfume, he noted. It was sexier. He couldn't help wondering if she was trying to compensate for her present state. At a different time...

He caught his thoughts before they could slip off to somewhere they shouldn't.

"Maybe he didn't. Maybe he just shifted his base of operations," he theorized. "Maybe our guy discovered that the world is a hell of a lot larger than just Orange County in California."

It was a theory, but not one she subscribed to. Not after all the hours she'd logged in, looking for the Sleeping Beauty Killer's pattern and coming up empty. "I don't think so. No other murders matched this particular, meticulous MO. No, something made him stop. How do you crawl into the head of someone like this?" she wondered out loud.

He looked at her. There was a danger in that. "Careful that once you crawl in, you don't forget how to crawl out again."

She laughed, knowing exactly what he was referring to. "Been watching Al Pacino in *Cruising* again?" Though he denied it, the award-winning actor was clearly one of Warrick's favorites.

"Hey, things like that happen," he protested.

"You become one with the criminal and forget where you end off and he starts."

She shivered. "Never happen. There's no way I would ever mentally bond with this character. He gives me the creeps." Just touching the folder made her skin crawl. He had to get these women to trust him, played on their vulnerability and then struck. He was a loathsome creature of the lowest order.

Warrick was more concerned about her right now than the Sleeping Beauty Killer. "Why don't you knock it off for a while?" He glanced at his watch. It was close to two. If he didn't miss his guess, she hadn't left her desk, except for bathroom runs, since she'd come in this morning. "Want to pick up some late lunch?"

She tilted her head, studying his face, suppressing a grin. "You buying?"

"No way." Warrick laughed shortly. "I've seen the way you eat lately. We'll go Dutch." He moved behind her. "I will, however, help you out of your chair."

Another crack, however veiled, about her weight. She could do without that, even though she'd gained a good twenty-eight pounds in the past two months. Before then, she'd stayed rail thin, actually losing weight because of an extra-long bout of morning sickness.

"Forever the gentleman. Thanks," she waved him away, "but I'll pass." She opened the folder and spread it out on her desk. "I want to go through this file."

Serial killers were not something a woman about

to give birth should be concentrating on. Maybe that made him old-fashioned, he mused.

"You know, you could start thinking about decorating that spare bedroom of yours." He knew from her brothers that she still hadn't bought a single thing to reflect her pending motherhood.

C.J. looked at him sharply. Not him, too. He was the last one she would have thought would bother her about this. "Bad luck."

He shook his head. "I never took you to be the superstitious type."

Her shoulders rose and fell in a vague gesture. "We're all superstitious in our own way." It had taken her time to come to terms with this phase of her life, but now she wanted this baby, wanted it badly. And was afraid of wanting it. "I don't like counting on anything unless it's right there in front of me."

Her comment surprised him. It wasn't like her. "I thought I was supposed to be the cynical one."

Her smile went straight to his inner core. It never failed to amaze him how connected he and this woman were. Even more so than he and his wife had been. As a rule he wasn't given to close relationships, always keeping a part of himself in reserve. But there was something about C.J. that transcended that rule.

"Spend six years with someone," she told him, "some bad habits are bound to rub off. But if you must know, you didn't have anything to do with this one. My mother's four aunts did a number on me once the cat was out of the bag." Aided and abetted by her enduring trim figure, it had taken her five months to tell her family about her condition. They'd been wonderfully supportive, and ever so slightly annoyingly intrusive. "They had a dozen stories about miscarriages to tell me. Each."

He leaned over the desk. A strand of her hair hung in her face, and he tucked it behind her ear. In typical obstinate behavior, she shook her head, causing it to come loose again. He wondered why he found that so damn attractive. He shouldn't.

"You're eight months along and the doctor gave you a clean bill of health. I don't think you have to worry about miscarrying. Just about how to make the spineless wonder pay his fair share."

Warrick was definitely too close—and making odd things happen inside her. C.J. pushed herself away from the desk—and her partner. "Warrick, I know that in your own twisted little way, you care about me. But get this through that thick head of yours. I don't want anything from Tom Thorndyke. As far as I am concerned, this is my baby and only *my* baby."

He crossed his arms before his chest. "Another case of the immaculate conception?"

Her temper was dangerously close to going over to the dark side. "Byron—"

He winced at the sound of his first name. One of these days, when he got a chance to get around to it, he was going to have it legally changed. Lord Byron had been his mother's favorite poet while she was carrying him, but there was no reason that he had to suffer because of that.

"Okay, I'll back off."

"Thank you."

He started to head for the door. "Want me to bring you back anything?"

She glanced at the folder on her desk. "Just the Sleeping Beauty Killer's head on a platter."

He laughed, shaking his head. "Afraid that's not the special of the day." Warrick paused for a moment longer, looking at her. There was affection in his eyes, as well as concern. "Take some personal time."

She just waved him off, then watched appreciatively as he walked away. The man had one hell of a tight butt.

"Damn hormones," she muttered to herself as she began to pore over the folder he had given her.

Her hands braced on the arms of her office chair, C.J. pushed herself up to her feet. It was late, but she wasn't finished yet. Time for her hourly sojourn to the bathroom.

She hated this lumbering girth that had become hers. In top condition since the age of ten when she'd picked up her first free weight to brain her older brother, Brian—an occurrence her father had prevented at the last moment—C.J. hated physical restrictions of any kind. The last two months of her pregnancy had forced her to assume a lifestyle she disliked intensely.

The only thing that made it bearable was knowing that she was doing it for her baby's good. But it was rough being noble, especially as she watched Warrick team up with other people, handling cases she wanted to be handling. She'd never been one to sit on the sidelines and it was killing her.

"Ah, I see you're ready to go."

Turning around, C.J. saw Diane Jones coming toward her. She didn't remember making any arrangements to meet her mother at the office. "What are you doing here?"

"Is that any way to greet your mother?" Diane pressed a quick kiss to her daughter's temple. "Ethan had a deposition to take not far from here. He dropped me off." She tapped her wristwatch. "Chris, your Lamaze class starts in half an hour. At this time of day, it might take us that long to get there. Let's go."

She'd only gotten halfway through the details in the reports. Besides, she wasn't in the mood to stretch and lie on the floor. Class wasn't as much fun now that Sherry and Joanna were gone, each having given birth.

"I was thinking of not going," she told her mother.

Protests had never gotten in Diane's way. She hooked her arm through her daughter's, tugging her in the direction of the door.

"Fine. And you can continue thinking about it on the way there." She used her "mom" voice, the one that had allowed her to govern four energetic boys and a daughter whose energy level went off the charts. "Let's go, Chris. Don't make me get Warrick in here to convince you."

Funny how much a part of her family her partner had become. ''He's out in the field.''

Diane picked up on her daughter's tone. ''You'll be out there, giving me heart failure, soon enough.'' She gave C.J.'s arm another tug. ''Now let's go.''

Resigned, C.J., sighed and got her purse from the bottom desk drawer. ''Yes, Mother.''

Diane nodded, pleased at the capitulation. ''Well, it could be a little more cheerful, but I'll take what I can get.''

So saying, she gently pushed her daughter out the door.

''We have to stop at the bathroom,'' C.J. told her.

Diane's smile didn't fade. ''I never doubted it for a minute.''

Chapter 2

"I've got a surprise for you," Lamaze instructor Lori O'Neill whispered to C.J. as the class began breaking up.

Handing her pillow to her mother, C.J. looked at the perky, rather pregnant blond instructor. The session had run a little long tonight. All C.J. wanted to do was drop her mother off at her house and go home herself.

She'd been preoccupied throughout the entire session, her mind constantly reverting to some stray piece of information about one or another of the Sleeping Beauty Killer's victims. Twice her mother'd had to tap her on her shoulder to get her to pay attention to what was going on in class.

This was a far cry from the way the classes normally used to go, Lori thought. It wasn't all that long ago that she, Lori, Sherry Campbell and Joanna Prescott would go out together after class to a local, old-fashioned ice cream parlor where they would indulge their insatiable craving for sweets. But Sherry and Joanna were no longer part of the class, or the inner clique Lori had pulled together and whimsically dubbed the Mom Squad. Sherry and Joanna had each given birth and with new men in their lives as well, were on their way to no longer being single mothers.

C.J. shook her head. "I don't think—"

On a mission of mercy, Lori was not about to take no for an answer. "You've been looking a little down these last two sessions, so I called up Sherry and Joanna and invited them out for the evening. They're waiting for us at the ice cream parlor."

She really didn't need the extra calories. Even so, C.J. could feel her taste buds getting into gear. Still, she felt she needed to review the personal notes she'd kept at home dealing with the serial killer's various victims. There just had to be *something* she was missing.

C.J. grasped at a plausible excuse. "But I've got to drop off my mother—"

The excuse died quickly. "Not another word about it," Diane protested. She was already digging her cell phone out of her purse. "I'll just call your father and he can come to pick me up." Her blue eyes sparkled lustily as she grinned at her only daughter. "Did I ever tell you about the first time he picked me up?" She sighed dramatically. "Your father was the handsomest thing on two legs, and I would have followed him to the ends of the earth.'' She winked at Lori. ''Luckily, I didn't have to. His apartment was right around the corner.''

C.J. had grown up hearing the story in its various forms, originally amended because of her age, then updated on every occasion. In its time, it had made a wonderful bedtime story, but not tonight. She cut her mother off before she could get rolling. ''You don't mind calling him?''

Diane pressed a single number on the cell's keypad. ''Not in the slightest.'' Her eyes took on a glow as a male voice echoed in her ear. ''James? Chris can't drop me off, would you mind coming to get me?'' Catching her daughter's eye, she shook her head tolerantly. ''No, she's not going out in the field.'' Diane covered the cell phone with a well-manicured hand. ''He worries about his little girl,'' she confided to Lori.

C.J. rolled her eyes. ''I'm probably the only FBI agent who has to look over her shoulder to make sure her father isn't trailing after her.'' Her father would have been a great deal happier with her if she'd put her law degree to use and followed him into the firm, as her three older brothers had. Even Jamie, the youngest, was studying law. She was the only maverick in the family—and she liked it that way.

Lori laughed, slipping an arm around C.J.'s shoulders. ''Hey, it's nice having a family care about you. I'd give anything to have my dad trailing after me.'' Both of her parents were gone now. The only family Lori had left was her late husband's older brother.

Diane flipped her phone shut. ''There, all settled.'' She tucked the cell phone into her purse. ''Your father'll be here in fifteen minutes.'' She shooed the women off. ''Go, have an ice cream for me.'' She looked down at a figure that was still trim by anyone's standards except her own and sighed. ''Anything I eat goes right to my hips. No passing go, no collecting two hundred dollars, just directly to my hips.''

Lori gave C.J. a quizzical look. C.J. was quick to provide an explanation. ''Mom's a Monopoly enthusiast.''

Diane leaned in and confided to Lori. ''She'd say 'freak' if I wasn't here.'' The look she gave her daughter spoke volumes. ''We all have our little obsessions.''

Her mind on other things, C.J. couldn't help thinking about the Sleeping Beauty Killer and the women he had singled out to eliminate. ''Yes,'' she agreed quietly, ''we do.''

The ice cream parlor, with its quaint booths and small tables, looked as if it belonged to another era, nestled in another century. C.J. felt completely at ease here. There was something soothing about the decor. It spoke of innocence and simplicity, something she found herself longing for.

By the time she and Lori arrived, Sherry and Joanna, both now enviably slim, were already seated at a booth. Sherry waved to them the moment they walked in.

There was no need to place an order. The instant

the waitress saw the four of them, she began making notations on her pad. The women's choice almost never varied.

"I'm really glad you called," Sherry told Lori as she settled back with her hot-fudge sundae. "I've been meaning to get in touch." Her eyes swept over the faces of the other two women. "With all of you." Leaving her spoon buried deep within the mountain of French vanilla ice cream, she dug into her purse and pulled out three official-looking ivory envelopes. She handed one to each of them. "I'm not economizing on stamps," she explained. "I just thought the personal touch was nicer."

Taking a generous spoonful of ice cream, Sherry savored the taste as she watched her three friends open up the lacy envelopes.

The tearing of paper was followed by squeals of enthusiasm and mutual joy.

C.J. was the first to collect herself and say something closer to a level pitch. "You're getting married."

Sherry grinned. If anyone had told her three months ago that she would be marrying one of the richest men in the country, not to mention one of the best looking, she would have told them they were crazy. But here she was, wildly in love and engaged. Life had a funny way of working things out with excellent results. "Yeah, I know."

Joanna tucked the invitation away into her purse and began sipping her strawberry ice cream soda in earnest. "Talk about the lengths that a journalist is willing to go to in order to get an exclusive interview...''

A reporter for the *Bedford World News,* Sherry's assignment had begun as a challenge. To get a background story on an elusive, successful corporate raider dubbed Darth Vader. Things had gotten tangled up when she'd suddenly gone into labor at his mountain hideaway. St. John Adair had wound up delivering her baby. From there, everything had just escalated.

Sherry looked at her friends. They all knew her story. She'd become as close to them as she was to her own family.

''*Exclusive* is definitely the key word here.'' Sherry sighed, temporarily forgetting about the sinful dessert. ''I've never felt this way about anyone before.'' Her grin widened. ''Part of me feels that it's got to be illegal to feel this happy.''

Reaching over the table, C.J. squeezed her hand. ''Enjoy it while you can. As far as I know, they haven't passed a law against that yet.''

Since her sundae was beginning to drip a little around the edges, Sherry's attention reverted back to her dessert. ''I tried to time the ceremony so that it didn't interfere with either of your due dates.'' She looked at the two pregnant women. ''You will come, won't you?''

She could use a little happy diversion in her life, C.J. thought. ''Try and stop me.''

Lori patted her stomach affectionately. ''Count me in. This little darling'll be out and smiling in time for you to exchange your vows.''

''Babies don't smile until they're at least six months old,'' C.J. contradicted. She saw Lori begin to protest. ''Those funny little expressions you see on their faces is just gas.''

''Don't you believe it,'' Joanna interjected with all the confidence of a new first-time mother delving through the mysteries of babies. ''My baby smiles at me all the time. And at Rick.''

''That's not surprising,'' Sherry commented. ''A stone would smile at Rick.'' Her eyes shifted toward C.J. The FBI special agent was the next one due and had plied both her and Joanna with questions about what giving birth actually felt like. ''So, are you getting excited?''

C.J. had gone from excited to nervous to feeling twinges of encroaching panic. With the big event less than a month away, she was now banking down any and all thoughts regarding the pending experience. It was easier getting through the day that way.

''I'm trying not to think about it.'' She took a long sip of her mint chocolate-chip shake and let the coolness slide down her throat before continuing. ''I'm not much on anticipating pain.''

Or dealing with the fear that had descended over her, she added silently. For probably the first time in her life, she found herself afraid of the unknown. Afraid of what she *did* know about the unknown. Afraid of what came after, as well. Because, despite the support of her family and friends, she was afraid of screwing up.

Joanna waved away the comment. ''That's just a

small part of it,'' she assured C.J. ''It's true what they say, you know. You do forget.''

C.J. curled her lip cynically. ''Probably because it hurts so much, you black out.''

Lori looked at her in surprise. ''I've never heard you sound so negative before.'' She studied her for a second. ''Anything wrong?''

C.J. sighed, pushing her straw into a glob of ice cream. ''Just feeling sorry for myself, I guess.'' She saw the others were waiting for a more detailed explanation. ''My partner's out in the field, tracking down a serial killer.''

Sherry was the first to break the silence. ''Serial-killer envy.'' Exchanging looks with the others, she laughed incredulously. ''Boy, that's definitely not my thing.'' And then she became serious. ''You're a mom-to-be, C.J. You're supposed to be agonizing over what shade of blue or pink to paint the nursery, not about wanting to go chasing after the bad guys with a gun strapped to the inside of your maternity bra.''

They didn't understand, C.J. thought. Though she gave the appearance of being flamboyant and quick to act, deep down, she felt a strong commitment to her work. She defined herself by it. There was this overwhelming need within her to put ''the bad guys,'' as Sherry called them, away.

''Speaking of nursery,'' Joanna, ever the peacemaker, interjected, ''*have* you decided to finally let us give you baby presents?''

It was a sore point with everyone, C.J. sensed. Even her brothers were commenting on it. Warrick's crack this afternoon had made it unanimous. She shook her head, a curiously shy smile creeping along her lips. "There's no need to give me presents."

"Yes, there is," Sherry insisted. She waved her hand around the table, taking them all in. "It's part of the bonding process."

Sherry thought back to when they had all initially gotten together. She knew as far as she went, talking with the women had gone a long way toward helping her remain calm about the challenges that were ahead of her. She had her parents, whom she loved dearly, but there was something infinitely comforting about being able to turn to women who were in the exact same rocky boat as she was and be able to talk out the fears that plagued her.

"We're all in this together, so to speak," Sherry pointed out. "C'mon, C.J., why won't you let us give you anything?"

"After," C.J. told them. "Once he or she is here."

This time it was Joanna's turn to shake her head. "I can't believe that you're the only one of the four of us who had an amniocentesis done and you didn't ask the doctor to tell you what you were having."

She had her reasons. "I always liked opening up my gifts at the end of the day, not the beginning."

C.J. didn't add that she was afraid if she knew the sex of the baby, she'd start thinking of it as a real person. This way, if something unforeseeable did happened and she lost the baby, she could still mentally divorce herself from it somehow.

Just the way she had from Tom.

All her protests to Warrick and her family notwithstanding, when Tom told her that he thought it was best if they just stopped seeing each other, she'd felt cruelly disappointed. She'd honestly thought that for once, she'd found someone she could count on. Someone who felt as strongly about her as she did about him.

That was what happened when you expected too much, she told herself. You wound up with too little. Or, in this case, with almost nothing at all.

But she was determined that no one would suspect how she really felt. It didn't go with the image of herself she wanted to project.

Wanting to change the direction of the conversation, she looked at Joanna. "So, your turn. How are things going with you?"

Joanna's eyes glowed. She pushed aside her almost depleted dish of dessert, wiping off the area in front of her. "I thought you'd never ask."

Digging deeply into her purse, she pulled out a small white album that was almost bursting at the seams. It was crammed full of brand-new photographs of her brand-new baby.

Sherry laughed as she dug into her own purse. "I'll meet your stack—" she plunked down her own album "—and raise you five pictures."

"You're on," Joanna declared.

Lori exchanged looks with C.J. "I think we're about to get babied to death."

"Bring them on," C.J. encouraged. "I can't think of a sweeter way to go."

* * *

Last night had been nice break, but it felt good to get back to work, C.J. thought as she sat, reading over the folder that Warrick had left with her yesterday. She was reviewing it for the umpteenth time.

The office was empty, except for her. There were times she welcomed the quiet.

She enjoyed getting together with the other women. That in itself was a constant source of surprise to her. Apart from her mother, she'd been raised in a world of men. With three older brothers and one younger one, C.J. found that she had a difficult time relating to other women.

But Lori, Sherry and Joanna were different. Maybe because, for different reasons, they had all found themselves approaching motherhood while in a single status. Facing the biggest event in their lives without a life partner beside them had given them all something in common.

Something in common.

What did these thirteen women have in common? she wondered, staring down at the photographs spread out on her desk. Beyond the obvious, of course. If you looked quickly, and myopically, they almost looked like photographs of the same person.

Of her, she thought grimly. Because she bore the same eerily similar physical features as the dead women. She was a blue-eyed blonde within the age range that the Sleeping Beauty Killer gravitated toward.

There but for the grace of God…

C.J. shifted uncomfortably in her seat. She didn't

know if it was the thought or the unnerving twinges she kept feeling that was getting to her.

What had made the Sleeping Beauty Killer snuff out these women's lives, executing them politely but firmly? Why them? Why not green-eyed redheads or brown-eyed brunettes?

There had to be a reason. Something.

One by one she held up the photographs of the young women, taken while they were still alive, and examined them closely. Did they represent some kind of fantasy woman to the killer? Someone in his life who had been unattainable to him? Who perhaps had spurned him?

Or was there some kind of other reason behind his choice?

She just didn't know, and not knowing frustrated her to the nth degree. Muttering an oath, she tossed down the last photograph, taken of the last victim. A Bedford University sophomore named Nora Adams.

''Did you know him, Nora? Did you talk to him? Smile at him? Or did you not even see him?''

''Don't you have a home to go to?''

Startled, C.J. almost jumped. It took a moment for her heart to stop slamming against her rib cage. Turning around, she saw that Warrick was standing not five feet away from her. She hadn't even heard him come in.

C.J. took a deep breath and gathered the photographs together again. ''Since when did you decide to become my keeper?''

As if that was possible. "It's a dirty job, but someone has to do it."

This pending motherhood with all its emotional baggage was getting her too jumpy, she thought disparagingly. Her nerves felt scattered and dangerously close to the surface. She just wished she didn't ache so. "How's the investigation going?"

He'd been on his way home when he'd decided to take a detour and stop at the field office. He had a hunch C.J. would still be here. There were times, such as these, when he felt that his partner didn't have the common sense of a flea. Not when it came to herself, anyway.

Warrick shoved his hands into his pockets. The case was as frustrating to him as it was to her. There were dead ends as far as the eye could see. Just like the last time.

"No more dead girls, if that's what you're asking. No more clues, either. No fingerprints, no bodily fluids, no sloppy anything left in his wake." He laughed shortly. "It's like the guy's a ghost."

He'd put into words the thought she'd just been entertaining. "Maybe he is."

Warrick looked at her sharply. "What do you mean, like Casper?"

"No." He knew she didn't mean that, C.J. thought in exasperation. "Like someone nobody notices. One of those people who pass through our lives who we never take any note of." Caught up in a fast-paced existence, she was as guilty as everyone else. "The kid bagging your groceries, the toll booth guy making change. The postal worker who weighs your package. People we see every day without really seeing them at all.''

She could be on to something. That could explain why no one ever noticed anyone out of the ordinary hanging around, Warrick reasoned. ''That doesn't mean he won't make a mistake.''

She sighed, flipping the folder closed. She shifted again. Her back was aching in the worst way. She tried to remember if she'd done something to strain it. ''He hasn't until now.''

''And odds are, he won't tonight.''

She looked at Warrick quizzically. What was that supposed to mean? Had he heard something? ''Tonight?''

''Yes.'' Pulling her chair back from her desk, he turned it around to face him and leaned over her. ''Go home, C.J. You look tired.''

Feet planted on the floor, she scooted back. ''Bad lighting.''

There was no such thing as bad lighting as far as C.J. was concerned. She looked good in shadow and in sunlight. Rousing his thoughts, he waved around the office. ''Everyone else is gone.''

She raised her chin defiantly, knowing she was baiting him and enjoying it. ''You're not.''

''That's because I'm checking in on you.'' He stopped, knowing this was going to go nowhere. With C.J. it never did unless she wanted it to. ''God, but you are a stubborn woman.''

She pulled up another program on her computer. Maybe a fresh perspective would help. ''Wouldn't have lasted all this time with you if I wasn't.''

"Hey, the only reason we're together is because I'm the patient one. You're the one who's always running off half-cocked."

The ache began to sear through her body. "No running tonight," she muttered.

He gave it one more try. "C'mon, C.J., let me take you home."

She splayed her hand over her chest. "Why, Warrick, this is so sudden."

Not really. The small voice in his head came out of nowhere, implying things it had no business implying. Damn it, what had gotten into him tonight?

He raised a brow at the wordplay. "Your home, not mine, partner."

It was late and she didn't know how much longer her energy would last. Maybe something she came up with here would ultimately save someone. "Later."

He felt the edge of his temper sharpening. "Now."

C.J. looked away from her screen, fluttering her eyelashes at him. "You're not the boss of me, Warrick."

He gave up. Drop-dead gorgeous or not, she was stubborn as a smelly mule. "Fine, sound like a two-year-old. You'll be good company for that baby of yours."

She knew he meant well, but so did she. There was a man out there killing women because they looked like real-live versions of Barbie, and she had to put a stop to it. "I don't feel like going home, War. There's a stack of dirty dishes in the sink waiting for me, and a pile of laundry held over from the Spanish Civil War. If I'm here, I don't feel guilty about not cleaning.''

She had to be the most contrary woman he'd ever met. Nothing about her went by the book. ''Aren't you supposed to be in the nesting mode by now?''

She hated that term. ''In case you haven't noticed, I'm a woman, not a bird.''

''You're a walking contradiction of terms is what you are.'' Surrendering, Warrick sighed. ''Never could get you to listen to reason.''

She spared him a look and grinned. ''Right, why start now?''

Why indeed. There was a cold beer in his refrigerator with his name on it. It was time to start the reunion. ''Good night, C.J.''

''Uh-huh.'' Her attention was already fastened to the reports she knew almost by heart.

Warrick had crossed the room and was about to pass the threshold when he heard a strange little gasp behind him.

''Warrick?''

There was something in her voice that made the hair on the back of his neck rise up. He swung around to look at her. C.J. was still sitting at her desk, but there was an odd expression on her face.

''What?''

Oh, God. Her words came out measured. ''How close would you say we were?''

That was a hell of an odd question for one partner to ask another. ''Pretty close, I guess.'' He looked at her more intently. ''Why?''

She caught her lower lip between her teeth a second before answering. "I think we're about to get a lot closer."

Like a man feeling his way along a tightrope, Warrick slowly made his way back into the room, staring at C.J. as he came. "What are you talking about?"

Very deliberately C.J. closed the folder on her desk. The pain shot through her again. She fisted her hands against it, but it didn't help. Her knuckles felt as if they were going to break through her skin.

It matched the sensation going on in other parts of her.

She looked up at him, telling herself not to panic. "I'm in labor."

Warrick's eyes widened in disbelief. C.J. was given to practical jokes. This had to be one of them, although it went beyond the pale as far as he was concerned. "The hell you're not."

She caught her breath, trying to keep her voice steady. From everything she'd been able to pull out of Joanna and Sherry, this was definitely the real thing. Her skirt was damp and that could only mean one thing. Her water had broken.

"The hell I am."

Chapter 3

"This isn't funny, Jones," Warrick snapped as a wave of uneasiness all but drowned him. He couldn't remember any incident in his career, recent or otherwise, that had ever had him feeling this unprepared.

The pain found her and began twisting her in two. C.J. tried to fill her lungs with air, but even that hurt. "I don't think any stand-up comic ever gave birth for laughs."

He didn't like the edgy note in her voice. The hope that this was just a bad joke on her part faded. "You're serious."

She pressed her lips together as she looked at him. She felt fear taking a strong toehold. *Don't panic, don't panic.* "Deadly."

"You're really in labor." Somehow, maybe because he didn't want it to, the thought just refused to penetrate his mind.

She nodded her head. Damn, this was *really* beginning to hurt. "Like a prisoner at Devil's Island."

Why was she still just sitting there, gripping both armrests as if she expected the chair to somehow launch her? "Well, damn it, what are you waiting for?" He put his hand on her arm. "Let's go."

She didn't budge. She was afraid to. Afraid to even move. C.J. raised her eyes to his. "That's just the problem, Warrick, all systems *are* go."

Then why wasn't she getting up? This wasn't making any sense. Maybe it *was* a practical joke after all. He'd seen her deadpan her way through more than one joke before. He gave her arm another tug, surprised at how tightly she continued clinging to the armrests.

"Quit fooling around, C.J. The faster we get you to a hospital, the better."

Biting down on her lower lip, C.J. pushed herself upright and immediately sank down in the chair again. Her legs had buckled, giving way beneath her. She couldn't walk, couldn't move.

She looked up at Warrick. "New plan."

Impatience waltzed with nerves. "What?"

She shook her head, shrugging his hand off her arm. "We need a new plan. I can't walk."

This was bad, he thought, becoming really concerned. C.J. just wasn't the frail, damsel-in-distress type. She'd been shot once and had almost snapped off his head when he'd tried to help her up off the ground.

His mind scrambled to make sense of this new input. ''Okay, okay, I'll carry you—''

''No!'' With a sweeping motion, C.J. batted away his hands and then grabbed onto the arms of the chair again. It was either that or rip his arms out of their sockets. The pain was back and it had brought friends. ''You don't understand. It's too late for that.''

Did labor enfeeble a woman's brain? She was talking nonsense. ''Too late for carrying?''

Breathing and talking at the same time suddenly became a challenge. ''Too late...for...anything. I'm having this...bay-BEE.''

The sudden crescendo echoed in his head, hurting his ears. ''Yes, I know—''

Her efforts to the contrary, panic was definitely taking hold. C.J. looked at him. Did she have to explain everything?

''Now, Warrick...I'm having...it *now.*''

He stared at her, numb. ''What do you mean 'now'?'' She couldn't possibly mean what he thought she was saying. ''As in this minute?''

The wave of pain ebbed back a few inches, letting her catch her breath. Perspiration was beginning to drench her. ''I knew...if...you...sounded out the... letters, you'd...get...it.''

Feeling a little weak himself, Warrick sank down on his knees beside the chair, holding on to one armrest. ''C.J., you can't be having this baby now.''

''That's...not...what the...baby...thinks. It's breaking...*OUT.*'' This time, C.J. did grab Warrick's hand. Wrapping her fingers around it tightly, she squeezed and held on for all she was worth. "Oh...God...Warrick, I think...I'm having...an... exorcism."

He felt completely powerless and lost. This was not covered in any FBI handbook he'd ever read. "What do you want me to do?"

C.J.'s answer came without hesitation. "Kill me."

Unequal to what was happening, Warrick dragged his hand through his hair, momentarily at a loss. "Damn it, C.J., this would have never happened if you had better taste in men."

It was lessening, the pain was lessening. C.J. took a breath and hoped her heart wouldn't pop out of her chest. She spared her partner an annoyed look. "What...you saying? A better...class of man... wouldn't...have slept...with me?"

"No." Warrick shot her a look. She knew better than that. She knew he thought she was too good for the likes of Thorndyke, even if he hadn't told her. "I don't know what I'm saying."

He dragged his hand through his hair again, trying to think. Nothing came. He didn't know the first thing to do in this case, other than to keep her from panicking. But it wasn't easy, not when he felt like panicking himself.

"I've got a law degree, C.J., not a degree in babies. I don't know what to do." He took a couple of deep breaths, trying to gather his thoughts together. A small bud of hope began to bloom. "Maybe you're just having false labor."

She felt as if someone had taken a carving knife

to her. ‘‘If this is…false…labor, I don’t…want…to be around…for the real…thing.’’

Comfortable, he had to get her comfortable. The thought was almost laughable, seeing the situation. Warrick stripped off his jacket and threw it on the floor. She could lie down on that.

Unbuttoning his sleeves, he pushed them up his forearms. ‘‘Okay, let’s get you in a better position.’’

C.J. pressed her lips together, struggling hard not to give in to the waves of panic that were surfing atop waves of pain. ‘‘I bet you…say that…to all…the girls.’’

Determined to muster a small ounce of dignity, she tried to get out of the chair herself. Dignity took a holiday. C.J. all but slid out of the chair in a single fluid motion, landing on his jacket on the floor.

Warrick gave his jacket a couple of tugs, trying to get it flat beneath her and make her more comfortable. It was a futile effort. He knew C.J. wasn’t going to be anywhere near comfortable until this baby had made its appearance in the world.

He was in over his head.

Warrick pulled out his cell phone. ‘‘I’m calling security—’’

Her hand went around his wrist like a steel band. She didn’t want some stranger gawking at her while she writhed in pain. She wanted Warrick.

‘‘No…no security.’’ She gave his wrist another tug. ‘‘Just…you.’’

She had entirely too much faith in him, he thought. ‘‘C.J., I don’t think I can—’’

She wouldn’t let him finish. Her eyes, filled with

pain, pinned him. "You're...my best friend...Warrick. You've got...to help me.... You can...do this."

Entirely too much faith. Surrendering, Warrick flipped the phone closed. "Yeah, you've got the tough part." He tucked the cell phone back into his pocket and drew closer to her. His voice was calmer when he spoke. If she could have that much faith in him, the least he could do was come through for her. "Okay, C.J., this is all supposed to be natural. What's your body telling you to do?"

She grit her teeth together. "Run...like...hell." And then her eyes opened wide like two huge sunflowers. "I've got...to...push!"

He knew very little about the birth process, but what he did know was that things were happening much too soon. "Are you supposed to do that yet?"

"Dilated," she suddenly remembered. "I'm...supposed to...be...dilated."

Warrick had heard the term in reference to childbirth before, but for the life of him, he wasn't sure what that actually meant. "C.J.?"

The look on his face told her everything. "I'm supposed...to be...fully...opened."

That didn't help very much. Warrick sat back on his heels and looked at her. "I don't know what you look like fully closed, C.J."

Her head ached. It was hard remembering everything that Lori had told them in class. Hard to think at all. Her brain felt as if it was winking in and out. What were the words Lori had used?

"You're...supposed to see...the crown...of...the baby's head." That was it. Crowning. Lori had called it crowning.

A sinking feeling was taking up residence in the pit of his stomach. "Where?"

She stared at Warrick incredulously. When she needed him most, he'd become a complete idiot. "Where...do you...think?"

He knew exactly where he was supposed to look, he'd just been hoping against hope that he was wrong. They'd shared thoughts, feelings, almost everything over the past six years, and he would have been lying if he'd said that the thought of being intimate with her hadn't crossed his mind more than once. But this wasn't the way he wanted to see her nude.

"Oh, God."

The groan escaped before he could prevent it.

The next moment he got a hold of himself. He was all she had right now and he knew it.

In its own way, this was really no different from him having her back when they were out in the field on a dangerous assignment. C.J. was putting her life in his hands and he had to keep her safe—her and this baby of hers who obviously didn't have any respect for due dates.

He offered her what he hoped was an encouraging smile. "You know, when they first put us together, I used to wonder what it would be like if I'd met you on the outside." His smile broadened a little. "This wasn't what I had in mind."

This was no time for them to go to places they couldn't afford to go to. "War—rick."

He took a deep breath, then stated the obvious because he needed to get it out in the open and out of the way. This wasn't going to be easy for either one of them. "It's going to have to get personal."

Damn it, didn't he think she knew that? They weren't waiting for the baby to come COD by parcel post. "Warrick...do what...you...have to do...before... I start ripping off...pieces...of your body...along... with mine."

He grinned this time. "Nice to know you haven't lost your winsome ways. Hang in there, champ."

As delicately as possible, Warrick lifted her skirt and removed her underwear. The moment he did, she raised her hips off the floor, crying out as another contraction, the biggest one so far, seized her in its jaws, tightening around her so hard she thought she was going to snap in two.

She wasn't fooling around, he thought. She was really going to give birth. It was really happening right here on the seventh floor of the federal building.

"I think this is it," he told her, his voice slightly in awe.

"That's...what...I've been...trying...to tell...you!" She twisted and turned, desperately trying to maneuver beyond the pain, and failing. She began to pant hard, not knowing what else to do. The urge to push was overwhelming, and Lori had promised she couldn't pant and push at the same time.

She was panting. What did that mean? Warrick called up every relevant medical program he'd ever watched, trying his best to fathom his next step. The first aid course he'd taken as a teenager had completely faded from his memory banks.

Instincts took over. Needing to reassure her that it was going to be all right, he made his voice become deadly calm. "On the count of three, C.J., I want you to push. One—two—"

She wasn't about to wait on any lousy numbers. She couldn't pant anymore. Sitting bolt upright, she squeezed her eyes shut and bore down.

"Now!" she cried.

Ready or not, she was pushing, he realized. "Damn it, C.J., you never could take instructions." Mentally he counted off the numbers until he reached eight, then looked up at her. Her face beet red, she looked as if she was going to pass out. "Okay, stop, C.J., stop!"

Like a rag doll whose stuffing had been yanked out, C.J. collapsed in a heap on the floor, panting. She felt as if she'd just run one leg of a marathon. Without securing the baton.

Maybe she was wrong. Maybe she'd pushed the baby out and just didn't know it. "Is it—"

"No, not yet."

And then another contraction came, again threatening to tear her in two. She didn't know if she could take much more of this.

She heard the sound of Warrick's voice and strained to make out the words.

"Ready?" he asked. She was breathing hard, as

if she just couldn't pull enough air into her lungs. He glanced up to see if she'd heard him. She was nodding. Just barely. "From the top, C.J. One, two, three."

This time she waited until the last number was uttered, then bore down as hard as she could, pushing with all her strength.

She thought her eyes were going to pop out of her head when she heard him yelling at her.

"Stop, stop."

Gasping, C.J. fell back on the floor again. She was sucking in air, and her head was spinning badly. She was afraid she was going to pass out at any moment, and struggled to hold on to the world around her.

"It's...not...working...is...it?"

How many times did it take to push out a baby? he wondered. One look at C.J. told him that she couldn't take very much more of this.

He took it one step at a time. And lied. "One more time."

But she knew better. He could fool everyone else, but not her.

"You're...lying." Tears and sweat were mingling in her eyes, sliding down her cheeks, pooling beneath her back. "I...can't do...this...Warrick. I'm...not...cut out...for...this...kind of thing." Each word felt like a boulder she was trying to push up a hill.

There was no giving up now. He couldn't let her. "Yes, you are." His voice was fierce. "You're the toughest woman I know. Now c'mon, one more time." Abandoning his post at her nether end, he brought his face up close to hers and implored, "C.J., one more time. Just one more time."

Damn it, why didn't he just let her die? "I...hate...to see you...beg." With superhuman strength, she drew her elbows in to her sides and pushed herself up again. Her head was spinning worse than a top that was out of control. "Okay...let's get...this watermelon...out...of me!"

Warrick strengthened his resolve. "Let's get serious now. Ready, C.J.?"

She wasn't ready, would probably never be ready again. Probably would never be able to breathe right again, either. But there was no postponing this and coming back tomorrow, refreshed and braced. She was in all the way.

It was now or never.

Sucking in one more breath to fortify her, she nodded at Warrick. C.J. screwed her eyes shut and bore down with every last fiber in her body. It felt like forever. She could swear she felt her blood boiling in her veins.

An eternity later C.J. fell back against the floor, hardly aware of what she was doing. Only aware that there was some kind of noise buzzing in her head. No, outside her head. A wailing sound that could have been coming from somewhere else. Or maybe even from her. She wasn't sure.

Wonder was filtering through him. He was supporting an infant's head in the palm of his hand. The emotion was almost indescribable. Warrick looked up at C.J. For a second it looked as if she wasn't moving. "C.J., don't pass out on me now, you're almost finished."

A lot he knew. She had no idea where the strength came from to form the words. "I...*am*... finished."

"No, a little more," he coaxed, infinitely grateful that God hadn't made him a woman. There was no way he could have gone through this, he thought. "You have to push out the baby's shoulders."

There was no energy left to breathe, much less to push. "Can't...you...just...pull?"

"C.J., push," he ordered.

Swirling through her head was the vague thought that she was going to hold Sherry and Joanna accountable for not telling her that giving birth was like trying to expel a giant bowling ball through her nose and that everything inside her body felt as if it was being ripped apart by a pair of giant hands.

"C.J., you have to push!"

She had to die was what she had to do, C.J. thought in despair. No, a faraway voice echoed in her head, the baby, the baby needs you. Your baby. You can't quit now.

"Now!"

Hating Warrick, C.J. propped herself up one last time. She knew in her heart that if the baby didn't completely come out with this effort, she was going to die this way, midpush.

She glared at Warrick. "Count," she gasped angrily.

If looks could kill, he'd be dead right now, Warrick thought. "One—two—three. Push!"

Glancing at her face just before he gave the command, Warrick saw the sweat pouring down into her eyes, saw the look of complete exhaustion on her face. If he could have, he would have changed places with her.

Just like he would have been willing to take a bullet for her any day of the week. She was his partner, his friend, and the person who knew him better than anyone, warts and all. He cared about her more than he cared about anyone else in the world.

The next moment, he was holding her daughter in his hands.

The wailing increased. Was something wrong? Was there something wrong with her baby? *Oh, please let the baby be all right.* C.J. was lying in a heap on the floor. There wasn't a single part of her that didn't ache and wasn't all but smothered in utter exhaustion. It took all she had to raise her head.

"What—"

He grinned, making sure the baby's passageways were all clear. That much he remembered from his training. She was breathing. The life he held against his chest was breathing. He couldn't describe the feeling going on *in* his chest. "A girl."

A girl. She had a daughter. She felt like crying. "What…what does she…look like?"

"A guppy in Jell-O. A beautiful guppy," he qualified, looking up at C.J.

Something very strange was going on inside of him. There was relief because it was over and because C.J. was still alive. He could afford to admit to himself now that he had been laboring under the very real fear that something could have gone wrong during the childbirth. Something could *always* go wrong.

But there was also something else, another feeling that he couldn't readily identify. Something he was unfamiliar with.

It felt as if there were suddenly a rainbow inside of him. A rainbow that seemed to be also raining sunshine.

Quickly he did a tally of the baby's fingers and toes. All were accounted for. He looked up at C.J. "Want to see her?"

She barely had enough strength to form the word. "Please."

Holding the moments-old infant against him, Warrick moved on his knees until he was level with C.J.'s face. But as he began to transfer the baby into her arms, he looked down at the small face. The infant had ceased crying and was simply looking up at him, her eyes as wide as spring flowers sunning themselves.

He felt as if she was looking right into him, right into his heart. Which only seemed fair since it was already hers.

"This is your mother," he whispered to the infant. "Be kind, honey, she's still a work in progress."

He was surprised the words came out at all. It felt as if his throat was constricting. For all the different experiences he had gone through in his life, he had never had a moment quite like this before and he wasn't altogether sure what to make of it.

Amid the waves of exhaustion washing over C.J. was a sense of elation. It spread out, covering her completely as Warrick tucked the baby into her arms.

She was here, C.J. thought, her baby was finally here. Her impatience, her fears, everything she'd lived with all these months were fading into the mists as if they hadn't really existed.

Without a hand to wipe them away, C.J. blinked back her tears.

Her baby was finally here.

"Hi, baby," she said softly to the infant warming her breast. "That was just Warrick. Don't let him scare you." And then she raised her eyes to her partner's face. There really were no words that seemed adequate enough. "Thank you."

He grinned, rocking back on his heels. "It's not as if the two of you left me much choice."

The two of them. It had a nice ring to it, C.J. thought.

Her heart swelling, she tightened her arms around the baby.

Chapter 4

The paramedics arrived ten minutes after he called them.

It occurred to Warrick, as he rode down in the elevator with C.J., the baby and the attendants, that had he gotten on the phone and dialed 911 to begin with, he would have been spared all the trauma he'd just gone through.

And missed out on what was probably the greatest experience of his life.

He smiled to himself as they all got out and he hurried behind the gurney. It made him glad that for once he had been slow to follow through on his original instincts.

Warrick stepped out of the way to allow the paramedics to slide C.J.'s gurney into the ambulance. At that moment, as he watched, she looked very vulnerable. It placed her in an entirely new light for him. She'd probably punch him out if she knew what he was thinking, he thought. But that didn't change the fact that he had an overwhelming desire to be there for her, to somehow shield her, although from what he hadn't the vaguest idea.

Had to be the high he was still running on because of the delivery, he decided.

With the gurney secured in place, Warrick started to climb into the ambulance.

The paramedic beside C.J. placed a hand out to block his entrance. "Only relatives ride in the back with the patient." He cocked his head, scrutinizing him. "You her husband, buddy?"

"That's Special Agent Buddy," C.J. informed him. "And he's my partner."

Unconvinced as to the propriety of all this, the attendant raised his brow. "Like a life partner?"

Warrick glanced toward C.J. and saw that she was looking at him, amusement highlighting her exhausted features. That she could smile after what she'd just been through amazed him.

"Maybe as in life sentence," he cracked. "We work together."

That settled it for the attendant. He reached for the doors, ready to pull them shut. "Sorry, then you've got to follow behind in your car."

Warrick was quick to get his hand up, blocking the doors before they closed. He looked at C.J. Hers was the only opinion that mattered in this. "You want me in the ambulance?"

Under normal circumstances, her answer would

have been flippant. But these weren't normal circumstances. She was feeling elated and teary and a hundred other things. She needed someone there with her to run interference until she could pull herself together. ''Yes.''

Warrick looked meaningfully at the paramedic. ''Then, it's settled.''

The paramedic raised his hands, surrendering and backing off. ''Sorry, just stating company policy, Special Agent.''

''I'll take it up with your boss,'' Warrick said, climbing on.

The trip to Blair Memorial Hospital took just long enough for Warrick to make the necessary call to her parents. He left it up to Diane to notify the others, knowing it would probably take a matter of seconds.

He was right. C.J.'s family converged on the hospital less than ten minutes after the front desk had found a room for her on the maternity floor.

The six-foot-two nurse with the kindly smile had no sooner helped C.J. slip into bed than Warrick was knocking on the door. He peered into the room just as she said, ''Come in.''

Some of C.J.'s color was returning, he noted. She was beginning to look like her old self again. Feisty and contrary. He felt relieved. ''Got some people out here who for reasons beyond me seem to be awfully anxious to see you. Can they come in?''

As independent of ties as she liked to pretend to be, C.J. had to admit that it felt good to know that she had family close by who cared about her. "I guess we can't keep them out, can we?"

"You just try, sweetheart," her father said, pushing past Warrick as he sailed into the room. Nodding at the nurse who was a shade taller than he was, James Jones elbowed his way next to the bed and took one of his daughter's hands into both of his. His blue eyes crinkled, barely disguising the concern etched on his face. "How are you, darlin'?"

"Tired." C.J. tried to rally, summoning what energy she could. Her brothers surrounded her bed, leaving a space for her mother directly opposite her father. "How did you all manage to get here so fast?"

"Dad broke a few speed limits," Diane told her, attempting to look annoyed but not quite pulling it off. "What are you doing, having this baby without me? I thought I was supposed to be your coach."

C.J. glanced at Warrick who was standing at the foot of her bed behind one of her brothers. "I had to settle for second best."

Diane turned her attention to the man she had taken aside and charged with her daughter's care the very first time she'd met him. "Thank God you were there to help her, Byron."

C.J.'s eyes shifted toward her partner. As ever, the use of his given name didn't seem to faze him when her mother called him by it. It still amazed her. She supposed he more or less considered her family to be his own. Her brothers were his friends, and her mother and father were like a second set of parents to him.

Or maybe even a first set from the little she'd managed to get out of him about his childhood. Warrick had been an only child. An accident of nature was the way he had put it once. His parents had kept him, much the way a customer keeps an item they'd accidentally broken in a shop and were forced to pay for. The relationship was that sterile.

There was no mention of love, of affection existing in his past, even remotely. He rarely spoke about them, even when she asked him direct questions. His father had died some years back and his mother had remarried and was living out of the country. Even that had not come firsthand to her. Warrick had told her mother one rainy Sunday afternoon after watching a football game on TV with the male contingent of her family.

It amazed C.J. how much information her mother could get out of her closemouthed partner. There were times when she honestly thought her mother had missed her calling, although, to hear Diane Jones tell it, being the wife of a prominent criminal lawyer and the mother of three more, plus another potential up-and-coming barrister as well as an FBI agent, was more than satisfying enough for her.

That her mother added her as an addendum was just a trademark of her sense of humor. C.J. knew that her mother doted so much on her that it was difficult for the woman not to show it.

Warrick shrugged carelessly at her mother's comment. "C.J. did most of the work."

"*Most* of it?" C.J. hooted. "Ha! I did all of it."

"Knowing C.J., you're lucky to have come out

of the ordeal alive,'' Brian, her oldest brother, said to Warrick.

Warrick poked his tongue into his cheek. ''She did get a little testy.''

''Spoken like a typical man,'' C.J. countered. ''You try pushing out an elephant through a keyhole, see how cheerful you stay.''

Ever the referee even after her children were grown, Diane held up her hands, waving all involved parties into silence.

''Enough. The bottom line is that the baby's here, Chris is all right, and we're all together.'' She laced her arm through her husband's, glowing with contentment. ''So, have you decided what my new granddaughter's name is?''

C.J. shook her head. Ever mindful of the possibility that something might go wrong, she had refused to think of any names for either sex while she was pregnant. ''No, not yet.''

Her father looked at her, his disappointment apparent. ''Not even one name? Oh, Christmas, you even put that off?''

C.J. shut her eyes. Christmas Morgan were her official given names, laid on her by an act of whimsy on her father's part because she'd been born on Christmas morning.

When she opened her eyes again, it was to look at the guilty party. ''Well, when I do come up with a name, it's going to be a hell of a lot better than 'Christmas,' I can promise you that.''

Warrick grinned. He knew this was a really sensitive topic for her. ''What's the matter with being called Christmas? Although I have to admit, it doesn't exactly suit you.''

''And just exactly what is that supposed to mean?'' she wanted to know.

Ethan nudged Jamie, the baby of the family. ''Nice to see that the miracle of birth hasn't changed you any, Chris.''

She was feeling better already. Having her family here was the best medicine of all. ''Maybe growing up in a houseful of boys had something to do with that,'' she pointed out. ''I had to be twice as good as each of you just to hold my own.''

''Your own what?'' Jamie cracked. As the youngest, he was forever struggling to find his own place in a family of overachievers. The fact that at six-five, he towered over all of them helped to help balance things out.

''Her own everything,'' Wayne said. With two brothers born before him and a sister and brother born after, Wayne was the most even tempered of the family, given to thinking twice before speaking once. It was a trait his mother often wished out loud had been spread out amid her other children. Moving forward, Wayne brushed a kiss on his sister's forehead. ''Get some rest, kid. You look like hell.''

''Thanks.'' Her eyes met her brother's. ''You always did know what to say to perk a girl right up.''

''Why don't we all leave and let Chris get some well-deserved rest?'' Diane suggested.

''Which way's the nursery?'' Brian wanted to know.

''Can we see the baby?'' Ethan chimed in.

''Do they have her in an incubator?'' Jamie wanted to know.

''No.'' C.J. finally managed to get in a word. ''She weighed in just over five pounds. The doctor said she's strong and healthy.

''Of course she is,'' her father said. ''She's my granddaughter.''

''Yes, dear,'' Diane patted his face. ''You deserve all the credit here.'' Turning her head, she winked at her daughter.

One by one her family filed by, kissing her and taking their leave. Diane waited for them at the door, making sure her brood made it into the hallway. But when Warrick moved to follow, she shook her head.

''Why don't you stick around a little while longer, Byron? She might like the company. Maybe even get around to apologizing for being so testy with you earlier as you put it.''

Warrick glanced over his shoulder toward C.J. She nodded. ''Okay, just for a few more minutes.''

Diane paused at the door, the men in her life waiting for her to join them in the hall. Placing a hand on Warrick's shoulder, she raised herself up on her toes and brushed her lips against his cheek. ''Thank you for being there for her.''

His smile was almost shy. ''Just a matter of being in the right place at the right time.''

''I'm glad it was you.'' She turned toward her daughter, beaming. Her baby had had a baby. ''You did good, honey. I'll see you in the morning. And don't forget, think of some names.''

C.J. nodded. Warrick let the door close and then crossed to her. ''You really don't have any names?''

She shrugged her shoulders. The hospital gown slipped off one, and she tugged it back into place. ''Not a one.''

He shook his head. She had been damned determined not to allow her pregnancy to interfere with her work. No one knew until it was absolutely necessary. The only reason he'd found out before the others was because he'd stumbled onto her condition completely by accident. While on a stakeout, she would periodically bolt out of the car and dash for the closest bathroom. It didn't take him long to figure out she wasn't battling food poisoning but morning sickness.

Warrick leaned against the wall, studying her. ''Never knew you to be this unprepared before, Jones.''

She offered him a wan smile, her mind half a world away. This was supposed to have been a happy time. Instead she'd just joined the ranks of single motherhood with all its scary ramifications. Served her right for veering from her course and thinking that maybe she'd been one of the lucky ones to find someone special. What had led her down this primrose path was that her parents seemed so happy together. It had made her believe that marriages, if not made in heaven, certainly created one of their own. Well, Thorndyke had certainly set her straight about that.

''Some things,'' she murmured, ''you're never prepared for.''

Something inside of his gut tightened. He knew she was thinking about Thorndyke. Warrick could feel his blood pressure going up several notches at the very thought of the man and his emotional abandonment of C.J. This time he kept his comment to himself. She'd been through hell, and he didn't want to agitate her right now with any negative comments about the poster boy for slime. Thorndyke had obviously made her happy once and whatever did that was okay with him.

At least, he tried to tell himself that, although how she could be happy, even for a moment, with that shallow pretty boy was beyond him. If he didn't know better, he would have said he was experiencing a bout of jealousy. But he did know better.

Rather than use the chair beside her, Warrick sat down on the bed and looked at C.J. for a long moment. That strange, funny feeling he'd gotten the moment he'd held her daughter in his hands hadn't completely dissipated. On the contrary, alone with C.J. like this, it seemed to take on more depth and breadth. He still couldn't put a name to it. Maybe it was better that way.

He looked at her pointedly. "He should know."

She'd expected another put-down of her ex-lover. She certainly didn't think Warrick was going to push for any sort of contact. C.J. raised her chin defensively. "He knows."

"You called him?" There hadn't been any time, unless she'd done it while he was filling out her insurance papers at the registration desk.

C.J. looked away, in no mood for a lecture. "I

told him I was pregnant, A baby is usually the end result of that condition.''

Cupping her face, he made her look at him. ''You weren't that sure,'' he reminded her.

She pulled her head back. So he was Tom's champion now? ''I don't count.''

A very soft smile curved Warrick's mouth as he said quietly, ''Yes, you do.'' And then he straightened. ''Thorndyke doesn't know he has a daughter.''

Their last conversation together, the one that was littered with words like, ''no strings'' and ''hey, how I do I know it's even mine?'' played itself over in her head. She'd hated Thorndyke for that, hated him for making what they'd shared seem tawdry and cheap. The one time she'd let her guard down and it had to be with the wrong man.

And now her partner was just making things worse. ''He doesn't *want* to know.'' She raised her voice. ''Will you leave it alone, Warrick? He's like you. No strings.''

Warrick's brows narrowed over stormy eyes. There was no way he'd allow himself to be compared to the other man. ''He's *not* like me. I'd want to know. I wouldn't have left you to begin with.''

The tightly reined-in emotion in his voice surprised her. ''You didn't,'' she told him.

He'd almost lost it just then. Maybe this whole baby thing had him more wound up than he thought. Warrick cleared his throat. ''Yeah, I know. Do you want me to find him?''

Did he really think she didn't know where her baby's father was? "No need."

Warrick looked into her eyes. He was the detail person and she was the one who went in like gangbusters, but it was stupid of him to think for a second that she wouldn't keep tabs on Thorndyke, if only to make sure there was space between them.

"You know where he is, don't you?"

"He's in D.C.," she told him crisply, and then added, "And if you get in contact with him in any way, I'll rip your heart out."

He laughed softly, letting the matter go. After all, it was her life. And maybe he was even a little relieved that she *didn't* want to see Thorndyke, though there was no way he would ever have admitted to that.

"Always the delicate lady."

A little of the luster returned to her eyes. "And don't you forget it." There had been only one detail about her pregnancy that she'd planned. "Now, are you going to be the baby's godfather?"

The request, coming out of the blue, almost rendered him speechless. It took him a second to recover. "I'd be honored."

She shrugged, trying not to let him see how much it meant to her to have him agree to be her baby's godfather. "Just be there. Otherwise I'd have to substitute one of my brothers and that's like putting a double whammy on the baby. Grossly unfair."

"Wouldn't want that." He rose. It was time to go. There were only five hours until morning. "So, you want me to draw up a list for you?"

The question caught her off guard. She thought of the case she'd been poring over when this had all started. "Of suspects?"

"Of possible names." She was unbelievable. "Damn it, C.J., you just gave birth. How can you be thinking about serial killers at a time like this?"

He didn't understand, did he? Now it was personal. "*Because* I just gave birth to a little girl not unlike thirteen other little girls, that's why I can be thinking about bringing this scum in. Each one of these thirteen victims had a first day, Warrick, just like my baby. Each one of them was someone's little girl."

He understood where she was coming from, but he was shooting for something far less complex. Leaning over her bed, he tucked the blanket up around her waist. "Stop being an FBI agent for a few minutes, C.J. Just for tonight, be little what's-its-name's mom."

He had no idea what she was experiencing, C.J. thought. How hard it was to keep the tears from forming in her eyes. Maybe it was just her hormones, running amok, but she was filled with so much love, so much *everything* that it was a miracle she was even able to draw a breath in. It felt so crowded inside of her.

But there was no way anyone, not even Warrick, was ever going to see just how vulnerable she actually could be. Weakness was always exploited, intentionally or otherwise.

"Okay," she finally allowed somewhat cavalierly. ''But promise me you'll keep me posted about the case.''

''Right.'' There was no way one word about the case was going to reach her ears from his lips until she was back to active duty, he thought, smiling at her. ''I'll call if there's any breakthrough.''

That was too easy. She knew him better than that. ''I'm not kidding.''

''I know.'' Warrick took her hands into his and looked into her eyes, his expression softening just a little. Until a few hours ago he would have said that he was as close to C.J. as he was ever going to get. He'd been wrong.

Maybe it was just the excess of emotions he was feeling, he thought, searching for a reason for what was going on inside of him. ''Don't you ever relax?''

C.J. pressed her lips together. ''The last time I relaxed, I wound up pregnant.'' She instantly regretted the confession, but as she watched his eyes, she realized with relief that Warrick was being sympathetic.

He shook his head. ''I know this is a new concept for you, Jones, but try for middle ground.'' He bent over the bed, intending to brush a kiss on her cheek. Caught off guard, she turned her head. Her lips made contact with his. It was hard to say who was more surprised.

Something that had all the markings of an electric current snaked its way through her at lightning speed, making every hair on her body stand on end. She knew it was only a matter of extreme exhaustion mingled with being emotionally overwrought, but the end effect was still the same.

Her heart was pounding almost as hard as it had when she was struggling to give birth.

Very slowly Warrick lifted his head. His eyes held hers for a beat before he took a step back. He was as unsure of what had just transpired here as he had been about the feeling that had taken hold of him in the field office.

"You missed your target entirely," she said quietly, struggling for a fragment of composure. She felt as if she was going to shatter into a million pieces if he so much as blew in her direction. "I think you'd better get back on the firing range."

Warrick laughed then and ran his thumb along her bottom lip, wiping off the imprint of his lips. "Don't worry about my ability to shoot straight. I can handle my own. See you tomorrow, Mommy."

That term was reserved for her daughter when she learned to talk. C.J. loathed couples who referred to one another that way. "Don't call me that."

He paused. "'Daddy' doesn't seem to fit, even if you do wear the pants most of the time."

She didn't want him thinking of her any differently. Not because of the baby. And not because of what had just accidentally happened here. "I'm still C.J.," she insisted.

"Yeah," he agreed. His eyes swept over her. "You're still C.J. But as of two hours ago, you're now a hell of a lot more."

He winked at her and left.

Chapter 5

That old familiar feeling came over her. The one where she felt as if she was in the right place, where she was meant to be.

After completing three weeks of her maternity leave, C.J. absorbed her surroundings as she made her way from the elevator and down the hall. The last time she'd been here, she'd been done in by exhaustion, flat on her back and strapped to a gurney on the way to the hospital with a minutes-old baby in her arms.

God it felt good to be back.

She took a moment to gather herself together outside the office she shared with Rodriguez, Culpepper and Warrick, then pushed open the door.

Culpepper was the first to see her. Portly, with a

layer of muscle beneath the fat, he rose to his feet and came forward.

"Hey, looks who's here, Rodriguez. How's it going, Mommy?"

Tossing her purse on her desk, she glanced toward her partner. "Warrick, did you warn these people about calling me that?"

"Hey, I can't help it if they all have the attention spans of baby gnats." Their desks butted up against each other. He rounded his and came to stand by hers. "Speaking of baby, why aren't you with yours?"

She took a deep breath. Slightly stale air, lemon floor polish and Rodriguez's ever-present jar of peanut butter. It even smelled good to be back here.

"The doctor gave me a clean bill of health, said I was fit to report back for duty." C.J. had left the appropriate papers down at personnel on her way up here. "She actually thought I would be a nicer person if I went off to work every day."

That was because even despite the work a new baby required, C.J. found herself going stir-crazy. The ability to multitask with speed was not always a good thing. It left her with too much time on her hands. She needed to fill that time with her job. Besides, ever since she'd become a mother herself, she had this overwhelming need to make the world around her a safer place to be for her daughter. She was doing it the only way she knew how.

"Besides," C.J. continued, "My daughter's actually got the semblance of a sleeping schedule down, and I've been kept in the dark long enough."

She looked at Warrick pointedly, then turned her attention to the other two men who were part of the Sleeping Beauty Killer's task force. ''Can either one of you two fill me in?'' She nodded toward Warrick. ''My partner here refused to say a word about the case to me. Every time I asked, he kept changing the subject so much, I began thinking that maybe Warrick was the Artful Dodger come to life.''

''Artful anything doesn't sound like Warrick,'' Ralph Culpepper hooted.

''Never mind that.'' She sat down at the edge of her seat, as if poised to leap up at any second, Warrick noticed. Same old C.J. ''I need input,'' she told them. ''Someone brief me.''

George Rodriguez raised and lowered his wide shoulders. At six-five, everything he did was big. ''Nothing to brief, C.J., our boy's laying low again. Maybe we'll get lucky and it'll be another three-year reprieve.''

That wasn't the way she saw it. ''We'll get lucky when we nail the son of a bitch.'' As long as the serial killer wasn't off the streets, he could always strike again. ''So nothing's been happening while I've been out of touch?'' C.J. underscored the final word, sending an accusing glance Warrick's way.

''Well, Rodriguez, here, got engaged.'' Culpepper slapped his partner on the back. Sitting, Rodriguez was almost as tall as Culpepper was standing.

She hadn't even known he was seeing anyone. ''Is that true?'' Squirming ever so slightly in his seat, Rodriguez nodded. ''Who is she?''

Culpepper answered for him. A new grandfather,

he looked upon his partner as a son. He was accustomed to doing most of the talking. ''You know that cute little receptionist on the second floor?''

C.J. thought a minute. Her eyes widened as she realized who Culpepper was talking about. ''You mean that little-bitty dark-haired one who looks like she wears size-one clothes?''

Culpepper grinned at Rodriguez, who was taking a considerable interest in the file he was holding open in his hands. ''That's the one.''

Talk about the long and the short of it. ''What are you going to do, Rodriguez,'' C.J. asked, ''carry her around in your pocket?''

''For starters,'' Culpepper laughed, nudging his partner and winking broadly.

Rodriguez had only been at the Bureau for three and a half years. She still thought of him as ''the new guy.'' ''Well, I'm very happy for you, Rodriguez. Don't forget to let me know when the wedding is.''

Culpepper sat down and leaned back in his chair. ''Hey, talking about weddings, I hear there's a rash of those going on. Any of you remember Tom Thorndyke, that tall dude who used to work down the hall?'' He looked from Warrick to his partner and then at C.J. ''You went out with him, didn't you C.J.?''

Damn it, why did her heart just skip a beat? She thought she'd drummed that bastard out of her system. ''Once or twice,'' she allowed. She congratulated herself for keeping her smile in place. ''What about him?''

Warrick slanted a look at C.J. There was no way he could prevent the conversation from continuing without alerting the other two men that something was wrong. No one else knew that the absent special agent was the father of C.J.'s baby.

Culpepper's chair creaked. "Word is he's getting married."

"Married?" The word tasted like dried cardboard in her mouth. She struggled to sound only mildly interested. Anger mingled with surprise. "Really? To who?"

Culpepper scrubbed his hand over his face, thinking. He prided himself on always getting his facts right. "Somebody he met while on the job. One of the bean counters." Every organization had them. Even the Bureau. "She moved out with him when he transferred. Got the story from the guy who used to be his partner." He glanced at C.J. "All these weddings, must be something in the water, eh, C.J.?"

"Must be."

She knew that Culpepper wasn't trying to be insensitive. The oldest of them by twenty years, it was probably his fatherly way of suggesting that she herself find someone to marry, to give her baby a proper father. He had no way of knowing that he'd struck a bad chord.

Picking up her purse, she pretended to look through it. "I think I left something back in the car." Dropping the purse, she rose to her feet, keys in hand. "I'll be right back."

"Pictures of the baby, I'll bet," Culpepper chuckled. He looked at Rodriguez. ''They've always got pictures.''

Warrick hurried after C.J. She'd managed to get far ahead of him in the hall. He lengthened his stride.

''Hey, Jones, wait up. Didn't the doctor tell you not to start jogging the same day you went back to work?'' Catching up to her, he took hold of her arm, bringing her to a halt. ''C'mon, C.J., stop for a minute and talk to me.''

She didn't want to talk to anybody. She wanted to kick something, break something. Vent. But because Warrick had placed himself in the line of fire, she took it out on him.

''Did you know?'' she demanded.

He didn't know if she was hurt or about to spit fire. With C.J. it was hard to tell. ''I—''

Her eyes narrowed accusingly. ''Did you know?''

He made it a point not to lie. Especially not to a friend. The closest he came was to omit mentioning things. But there was no space for that here.

Warrick threw his hands up. ''Hell, C.J. what do you want me to tell you? Yes, I knew. I heard via the grapevine last week just like blabbermouth in there.'' He silently cursed Culpepper. Why couldn't the man have been out of the office when she came back?

''And you didn't tell me.'' How could he? she demanded silently. How could he have known and not told her?

''Why should I?'' He hadn't told her because he didn't want to reopen any wounds that might have been healing. ''You said you moved on, remember? You told me in the hospital that you didn't want to get in contact with him—ever.''

''I didn't. I don't.'' Confusion was running riot through her. She honestly thought she was over the man. But if so, why this sudden onslaught of pain? What the hell was wrong with her? ''It's just that...'' Anger creased her brow as she looked up at him. ''Damn it, War, here I thought he didn't want to get involved and it was that he just didn't want to get involved with me.'' And being rejected stung. ''I guess it just hurts my pride, that's all.''

He bracketed her shoulders with his hands. Wanting to protect her. Knowing she'd bite off his head if he even hinted at it. ''Just goes to prove how stupid the guy really was, letting someone like you go. Look, I didn't tell you because I didn't want you reacting this way. He's not worth it, C.J. You know it, I know it. End of story.''

''Yeah, end of story,'' she echoed, then thought of her daughter and how hard it had been to leave her this morning. She'd never known she could fall in love so completely and with such little effort. But she had. And if not for Thorndyke, Joy wouldn't have existed. And all that love C.J. felt within her at this moment wouldn't have even materialized. ''I guess I got the best part of him anyway.''

He'd been out in the field for the last week and hadn't had time to drop by to visit C.J. ''Speaking of which, how's my future goddaughter doing?''

C.J. thought of the way she felt walking to her

car after dropping the infant off. Empty, as if a part of her was suddenly missing.

"A lot better than me. I left her the center of attention at my mother's house." She'd never realized just how much her mother had wanted to be a grandmother. "My parents have more baby furniture and toys for Joy than I do." This despite the impromptu shower the Mom Squad had thrown her when she'd come home from the hospital.

He saw nothing surprising about that. "Why not? They had five kids—and an attic." He crossed his arms before his chest. "So I take it she didn't have any—what do they call it?—separation anxiety?"

C.J. laughed shortly. "She didn't. I did." Even now she couldn't help wondering what her baby was doing. Did she realize C.J. wasn't around? Or was Mommy just another face to look up at? God, but she was getting mushy. How long before hormones adjusted themselves back into place? And then she looked at Warrick in wonder. "How do you know about separation anxiety, anyway?"

He was the methodical one. "I thought that since I'm supposed to be her godfather, I should bone up on these things." He looked at his partner pointedly. "I should also insist that she have a middle name to go with the first name. You can't just call her Joy Jones."

She saw nothing wrong with that. "Why not?"

"Do you want people to call her 'J.J.'?

"I don't just want her to have any old middle name. I want the whole name to be special. To fit her."

Time was running out, Warrick thought. The christening was set for next week. ‘‘Okay, what d’you say I come over tonight after work with a book of baby names, and we’ll start tossing out names at her? One of them is bound to stick.’’

‘‘Sounds like a plan.’’

He cocked his head and peered at her, the teasing note gone from his voice. ‘‘You going to be okay?’’

She tossed her hair over her shoulder, raising her chin. He was familiar with that move. It was her ‘‘the world can go to hell’’ gesture. ‘‘I’m already okay. Just took the wind out of my sails, that’s all. Worse things could have happened, right?’’

‘‘Right. You could be marrying the guy.’’ They began to walk back down the hall when he stopped her again. ‘‘Hey, have you got any pictures of the baby with you?’’

She thought that was an odd question, coming from him. ‘‘In my purse. Brian’s been snapping his camera so much around her, she’s probably debating getting a career as a model right now. Why?’’

‘‘Because Culpepper’s expecting you to come back with pictures.’’ He didn’t want the other man quizzing her and having his suspicions raised. Culpepper might come off as a busybody, but there was nothing wrong with his deductive reasoning. ‘‘He thinks that’s what you went to get from your car.’’

‘‘I’ll just tell him I made a mistake.’’ But as they started to walk again, she placed a hand on his arm. She had to ask. ‘‘War, does anyone else know? About Thorndyke and me?’’

Warrick shook his head. ‘‘Not unless Thorndyke

told them, and considering how fast he put in for a transfer to another field office after you told him, I really don't think he did.''

''Good.'' Despite the fact that she was outgoing, C.J. hated having her business plastered all over the office.

She supposed that gave her something in common with Warrick.

''It was good to go back to work, but it's even better to come back to you,'' C.J. told her baby as she let herself into her house. ''I forgot how long days could feel.''

Still holding Joy in her infant seat, C.J. kicked off her shoes and wiggled her toes. The rug felt good beneath her feet.

Despite her mother's protests and her offer to make dinner, C.J. had opted to come home to snare a little peace and quiet, or a reasonable facsimile thereof. The day had been deadly dull and overly long, at least it seemed that way. Their investigation was going nowhere—slowly. At times it felt as if every minute was being individually held hostage, doubling in size before it was released.

She supposed that missing her daughter had something to do with that. At twenty-eight, she was surprised to find out something new about herself.

C.J. rotated her neck, trying to ease away some of the tension. She looked down into the car seat. Joy's eyes were shut, long black lashes creating dark crescents along her cheeks.

''Oh, honey, are you asleep already? I thought I'd

get in a little quality time with you.'' She banked down her disappointment. ''I guess not.'' She smiled to herself. ''With my luck, you'll probably want quality time at two in the morning.''

Carrying the infant seat over to a safe, flat surface, C.J. placed it on the dining room table. Careful not to wake the baby, she unbuckled the restraining straps one at a time.

''Well, don't get used to being a dictator. Once you figure this language of ours out and can understand me, there are going to be lines to toe, young lady, and hoops to jump through.'' She laughed, nuzzling her daughter as she picked her up out of the infant seat. ''Yeah, and I'll probably be the one doing the toeing and the leaping. Just don't tell anyone your mom's a softie, okay? It'll be our little secret.''

Holding her daughter in the crook of her arm, C.J. looked down at the perfect little face. ''Slept right through that, didn't you? Next you'll be telling me I'm boring.'' She thought of the news about Thorndyke and his wedding. ''Maybe I am at that. Okay, enough pity. Let's get you into bed, my love.''

The baby made no protest.

After making sure the baby monitor, with its multiple receiving units that she'd placed in each room, was turned on, C.J. gently closed the nursery door.

The doorbell rang.

She sighed. Now what?

Training had her glancing at her holstered gun on the hall table before approaching the front door. The weapon was in easy reach, just in case. "Who is it?" she called out.

"Rumpelstiltskin. Who do you think? Open the door, C.J."

Warrick. Their conversation in the hallway came back to her. She'd completely forgotten.

About to appeal to his better nature and beg off, C.J. opened the door. She didn't get the opportunity to say the words. Warrick walked in, juggling a large pizza box in one hand and a couple of books in the other. He held the latter aloft.

"I come bearing pizza and not *one* baby name book, but two." He tossed the books on the sofa as he came into the living room. "I couldn't decide between the two and thought I'd splurge. I figured, Murphy's Law, the one I didn't buy would have the name that appealed to you." The coffee table was littered with papers. She was the only one he knew who was a worse housekeeper than he was. "Where do you want this?" He indicated the pizza. "It's hot."

Walking ahead of him, she moved the infant seat off the table and put it on the floor in the corner. "You didn't have to bring that."

He was already opening the box. The smell of pepperoni and three kinds of cheeses filled the air. "Hey, I've got to eat, too."

C.J. went to the kitchen and reached into the cupboard for a couple of plates. "I could always have rustled up something."

He shivered at the thought. "No offense but I'd rather eat my shoes." He took a plate from her.

"You're a woman of many talents, C.J. Cooking is not one of them." He held up the first slice, offering it to her. "My dog cooks better than you."

She slid the slice onto her plate and sat down at the table. "You don't have a dog."

He took a slice for himself. "If I did, he'd cook better than you." He sank his teeth into the slice and savored the taste. It had taken him almost four years to find the right pizza place. It wasn't just about tossing the right ingredients onto dough, it was about care and timing and crust. Though his body gave no indication of it, Warrick loved his food. "And I'm thinking about getting one."

She stopped midbite. "You?"

He could just hear her mocking him. "Is that so hard to imagine?"

"Yes. I can't see you getting attached to anything." His marriage and its disastrous termination testified to that.

"Who says I'm the one getting attached? Dogs are supposed to be the loyal ones, the ones that stand by the door, waiting for you to come home." He had to admit, he kind of liked the thought of having something there to greet him. Though he enjoyed his solitude, there were times when there was too much of it.

"Good luck with that." She took another bite, then looked at him. "And since when do you care about those kinds of things, anyway?"

He wasn't about to admit to having a real need. "Seems like the right thing to do. Then my goddaughter would have something to play with whenever she came over to visit.''

''My daughter's coming over to your house? When did this happen?''

''Well, not right now.'' Polishing off the slice, he helped himself to another. ''I mean later. When she can walk and talk and stuff. I haven't even got the dog yet,'' he pointed out.

C.J. laughed and shook her head. Getting up, she went to get a couple of napkins.

''If you ask me, I came back from maternity leave just in time.'' She tossed several napkins on the table between them. ''You sound like you're losing your mind.''

He had to admit he'd missed having her around. ''Rodriguez and Culpepper aren't exactly next week's contestants for Jeopardy.'' At least not as far as day-to-day conversations went. ''All Culpepper wants to talk about is that gopher he's been battling since the beginning of time, and Rodriguez keeps getting that goofy look on his face whenever he thinks about his fiancée.''

''How can you tell the difference? He always looks goofy.''

Warrick laughed. ''Goofier.'' He realized he needed something to drink. ''I didn't bring beer, I didn't know if you were, um, you know.''

''No, I'm not, um, you know.'' Getting up, she went to the refrigerator and fetched a bottle of beer for him and a can of diet soda for herself. ''The baby's pediatrician said she needs a special formula. Seems that she's allergic—''

Warrick held up his hand. ''Too much information.'' He felt this was getting into a realm he had no business being in. ''That's violating doctor-patient privilege.''

''How much privilege are we talking about?'' C.J. laughed, then looked at her partner. Was that a pink hue she saw creeping up his cheek? Warrick? This was a man who'd busted a prostitution ring and walked in on two naked women without blinking an eye. ''Pink is not your color, Warrick.''

He pushed the box toward her. ''Why don't you just finish eating so we can get down to business?''

She helped herself to a second slice. ''Okay, but I warn you,'' her eyes indicated the books, ''this might not work.''

''Every known name in the world is in these books. If you can't find a middle name here, you're going to have to make one up.''

She hadn't thought of that. The idea was not without its appeal. ''There's an idea.''

Warrick was sorry he'd said anything. ''Let's just leave it on the back burner until we've gone through this.''

''Whatever you say.''

He gave her a dubious look. ''Now there's something I never thought I'd hear from you.''

The sound of her laughter enveloped him. He'd missed that, too, Warrick thought as he got up to get the books.

Chapter 6

Warrick shook his head as he got up from the living room sofa. It was getting late and they had more than done justice to the pizza, if not to the quest for a suitable middle name for C.J.'s daughter.

The latter was not for his lack of trying. He glanced at the books on the coffee table. They looked as if they'd been run through the wringer. "You know, you're impossible."

C.J. rose, as well. She stretched before rounding the table to join him.

"No," she said, "I'm selective."

She wasn't any happier about the situation than he sounded, but she was determined not to rush this process. Her daughter's full name had to be absolutely right for her.

Warrick had another word for it, but kept it to himself.

"It's just a middle name. Just pick one."

She glanced back at the books. "I don't know, maybe I went through them too fast, but none of the names I looked at 'feel' right for my daughter." She frowned.

Why did he even bother trying to win an argument with her? "You know, rather than Christmas, your parents should have named you Mary. Like in that nursery rhyme— 'Mary, Mary quite contrary.'" He took a closer look at her. There were shadows beneath her eyes. He hoped her daughter would let her get a few hours rest. "Do you have to disagree with everything I say?"

"I don't have to..." C.J. let her voice trail off. The further it went, the wider her grin became.

Warrick surrendered with a symbolic throwing up of his hands. He had to be getting home. There were a few things he wanted to check into before he went to bed. "You win. I give up."

C.J. picked up the two books he'd brought and held them out to him, but he shook his head.

"You keep these and see if a name does 'feel right' to you." He moved his hands around like a wizard conjuring up a spell.

C.J. put the books back down. "You'll be the first to know," she promised. She walked him to the door and opened it, then lingered a moment in the doorway. "Thanks for the pizza and the books."

He pointed toward them behind her, a headmaster

giving a pupil an assignment. ''You've a week, Jones.''

She sighed. That did limit her time, she thought. ''I know, I know.''

''Hey,'' he leaned his arm on the doorjamb just above her head, ''different strokes for different folks. It's what makes the world go around.'' He moved back a hair that was in her face. Her pupils looked as if they widened just a touch. He felt that same funny stirring in his gut. Again he locked it away. ''You're entitled to be a little strange once in a while.''

Warrick wasn't sure just what made him do what he did next. He supposed it was a natural by-product of a good evening spent in the company of a good friend, although he'd never brushed a kiss on the cheek of any of the guys he'd interacted with on the basketball court, no matter how good a game had been played.

Whatever the reason behind it, the bottom line was that he leaned over and touched his lips to her cheek, as he'd done in the hospital.

This time it didn't stun her. It didn't even register because just then a cat unleashed a wild screech that sounded as if it was being vivisected somewhere in the vicinity. The unearthly noise startled her, and she jerked, turning her head, just as before.

But this time when their lips met, neither one of them sprang back. Instead they drew together. And allowed the unintentional meeting of two pairs of lips to instantly flower into something a great deal more lethal, a great deal hotter than simply skin against skin.

And a great deal more pleasurable.

He didn't remember doing it. Didn't remember taking hold of C.J.'s shoulders and drawing her up a little higher, a little closer, helping her along as she rose on her toes. Didn't remember deepening the kiss, even though he did.

What he did remember was thinking that now he finally knew what it felt like to be kicked by a mule. Because something sure had found him where he lived and given him a swift, sound kick right to his gut.

Damn, for someone with just a tart tongue, she tasted sweet.

This wasn't happening, it couldn't be happening, she thought. But she was so glad it was.

For one long, everlasting moment, C.J. felt as if her connections to the real world had all been short-circuited and severed. There was no sky above, no ground below, no walls around to contain her. She was free-falling into an abyss, a wild swirling surging in her chest.

Warrick?

This was Warrick?

How the hell could this be Warrick? She'd worked alongside him for more than six years. Possibly, once or twice in an off moment, she'd fantasized what it might be like to be with him in some capacity other than his partner, but nothing that had momentarily traveled through her brain had been remotely close to this.

This was something she didn't know how to begin to describe.

Was that her pulse vibrating so fast? Could he tell? What the hell was happening to her? She was melting all over him.

Limp, she felt limp.

No! No way this was happening to her, not here, not now. Not again.

The next moment, contact was broken. Whether she pushed him back or he'd done it of his own accord, she didn't know. But the sky, the ground and the walls all made a return appearance.

It took all she had to remain standing where she was and not grasp the doorjamb for support.

Very slowly Warrick let out his breath. What he really wanted to do was gulp air in to replenish the lack of it in his lungs and maybe, just maybe, squelch this erratic hammering of his heart.

He looked at her, striving for the nonchalance that was one of the cornerstones of their partnership, hoping his voice didn't give him away. ''You've got to learn to stop turning your head at the wrong moment.''

She looked at him in surprise. Wrong moment? Did it feel like a wrong moment to him? It felt like a right one to her.

Careful, C.J. you're vulnerable. This is what got you in trouble before. Think, *don't feel.*

She clenched her hands at her sides, pressing her nails into the palms of her hand.

''Maybe if you stop going at my cheek like some hungry chicken pecking at scattered corn, there wouldn't be any wrong moments.'' One hand squarely against his chest, she pushed him over the threshold as she grabbed the door with her other one. ''Thanks for the books, see you tomorrow. Bye.''

Warrick found himself looking at the closed door before he could utter a single word in response or defense. Just as well.

He drew in the air he so badly needed, then turned away and walked to his car on legs that were a little less solid than they had been when he'd made the walk to her front door.

C.J. stood leaning against the door, her mind numb. Which was fine. It went along with the rest of her body. Numb mind, numb body—it was a set.

Like someone waking up from a dream, not quite sure what was real and what wasn't, she walked very slowly to the sofa.

And then collapsed as if every single bone in her body had just been pulled out.

''You're here already.''

The sound of Warrick's voice behind her had C.J. straightening slightly. She turned away from one of several bulletin boards covered with various pieces of the investigation, determined not to let him suspect that he was partially to blame for her getting only three hours sleep last night.

''Where else would I be?'' Was it just her, or did her voice sound a little too high? Where was this nervousness, this uncertainty coming from? This was just Warrick, for heaven's sake. A Warrick who had completely blown her out of the water last night.

She cleared her throat. ''We've got a serial killer on the prowl and we're partners on the task force, remember?''

Feeling suddenly awkward, C.J. offered the box of doughnuts she'd stopped to pick up by pushing them toward him on the new appropriated conference table. ''Care for a sugar high?''

Warrick made his selection without really looking, then took his prize to the coffeemaker. He'd already had a strong cup of coffee but he felt as if he needed another one. Even stronger this time.

Damn if he could explain why the sight of her alone in the room they had commandeered for their task force made him feel as if he needed to fortify himself somehow.

But it did.

She watched him pick up the mug that had once been white and start pouring. ''You know, you really should wash that out once in a while. Bacteria breeds in cleaner places than that. Your mug must seem like Disneyland to them.''

''Adds to the taste of the coffee,'' he muttered. Warrick took his coffee without compromise: black and hot.

She picked up her own half-empty coffee mug, now cooled to the point that it practically looked solid, and stared into it, thinking. The fluorescent lights overhead danced along the surface, adding to the trance.

She blew out a long breath. They could skirt around this, pretend it wasn't there and it would continue to gain depth and breadth, like some white elephant in the living room no one wanted to acknowledge. Or they could address this while it was still in its infancy, clear the air and move on.

She'd always been one to grab the bull by the horns instead of leap over the fence, out of harm's way.

C.J. set her mug down with a small thud, catching his attention. "We've got to talk about it."

Warrick raised one eyebrow. "The case?" He broke off a piece of the doughnut and popped it into his mouth. A small shower of white powder rained down to the floor. "That's why we're here."

He was playing games. "You know what I mean. What happened last night."

Warrick looked at her pointedly. "Nothing happened last night. I was feeling a little protective, like a big brother I guess, and you turned your head at the wrong moment. We established that fact, remember?" He shrugged, washing the doughnut down with a sip of coffee. "If you'd turned it the other way, I would have gotten a mouthful of hair instead of a mouthful of lip."

She scowled. "If I turned it the 'other' way, it would have probably been part of an exorcism because that would have meant my head was turned at a 180-degree angle."

He knew better than that, she thought, exasperated. Why was he pretending that they hadn't really kissed, not like partners, certainly not like a brother and sister, but like a man and a woman who wanted each other? They both knew they had.

He gave a short laugh and put a little distance

between them, just for good measure. ''There you go again, being contradictory. Arguing.'' His eyes held hers, his voice lowering, underscoring his words, his feelings. He wanted this buried. ''Well, I don't feel like arguing, okay? Let's just do what we're being paid to do.''

Warrick gestured at the main bulletin board, the one that displayed photographs of the victims, both before death had found them and after. Below each young woman was a list of statistics: name, age, height, weight, what the victim did for a living and where the body was found. So far none of that or any of the other endless pages of data they'd collected was giving them any clues that went anywhere.

The next moment, before she could answer him, they were no longer alone. Whatever was to have been said had to be set aside for now.

Culpepper poked his head into the room. ''Was that the sound of raised voices I heard?'' He walked into the room. ''Back one day and you two are at it already, C.J.?'' And then he looked at the conference table. His eyes lit up. ''Ah, doughnuts.''

He reached for one, but C.J. pulled the box away from him. He looked at her accusingly.

''Uh-uh, if you're going to insult me, you can't have any. I brought them.''

Culpepper folded his hands together, palms touching and held them up before her. ''A thousand pardons, oh wisest of the wise. That was just my sugar-deprived brain, running off with my mouth. If you were arguing, it was only because Warrick was provoking you."

C.J. laughed and pushed the box toward the heavyset man again. "Better."

"No one was doing anything to anyone," Warrick told the other agent firmly. He slanted a look at C.J. to get his point across. "Now feed your habit, Culpepper, and let's get to work on this."

C.J. tossed her hair over her shoulder, ready to do battle. "Fine with me. Let's nail this son of a bitch once and for all before he finds another victim."

C.J. glanced at Warrick's profile, then lowered her eyes to her keyboard as he turned in her direction. Her fingers flew over the keys, drawing up screens she had already looked at a hundred times if not more.

She didn't know which was driving her crazier: the fact that after a few days the murder investigation seemed to have ground to a halt again—this despite phone calls coming in all hours of the day and night from helpful and not-so-helpful citizens who gave information that only led to dead ends, if they led anywhere at all—or that there was this restless tension intermittently buzzing through her. A restless tension that seemed to rear its head every time she and Warrick were near one another.

C.J. flipped to another screen, scrolling down. She knew this was stupid. Warrick was right, she argued with herself, absolutely right. Nothing had happened. After all, it wasn't as if he had actually *tried* to kiss her. It was a brotherly peck gone awry, that's all.

She hit the keys harder. She saw Warrick giving her a curious look. Damn it all, no brother she knew had ever kissed his sister like that.

Quietly C.J. took a deep breath. She had to get a grip on herself and let this die a natural death. After all, what was the big deal? Okay, so they had reacted to each other like a man and a woman. She hadn't been kissed by a man in almost nine months and he reacted like—well, like a man. All men took advantage of a situation if given the opportunity, some just less than others.

The kiss and her reaction had been an aberration, a freak of nature, like a thunderstorm in the wrong season, that's all.

Why was she letting it creep into each night and snare a toehold on each day?

C.J. looked over to the main bulletin board. Her eyes swept over the faces of the women there, women whose likeness were imprinted on her heart. Rising, she crossed to it.

She had no business even thinking about something so petty as a kiss at a time like this. Warrick was her partner, her backup, her friend, and she was his. That's all.

And that was enough.

Warrick looked at her over his computer. Her hands were clasped behind her back and she was studying the board intently.

''You're being quiet again,'' he observed. ''It's

not like you. You make me nervous when you're quiet.''

''Why, because you're afraid I'll pounce?'' Not waiting for an answer, she turned from the board. ''Just trying to get into the killer's head.''

She looked over her shoulder, back at the board. Missing were the photographs of gruesome deaths, of savage beatings or stabbings. That wasn't the Sleeping Beauty Killer's style. Each victim was tenderly, perhaps even lovingly arranged. The latest victims even wore makeup that appeared to have been applied postmortem. They looked just like princesses waiting for their princes to come and wake them up. She chewed on her lips and looked at Warrick.

''You think he's a mousy man? You know, someone who yearns after the unattainable?''

He had never been able to crawl into a murderer's mind, maybe because he couldn't begin to identify with the kind of person who would willingly, sometimes even joyously take another human being's life. He marveled that C.J. could do it.

''Profiling's your department, not mine.'' Warrick moved over to the bulletin board with the map of Orange County on it. Each small pin designated a site where the victim was found. He wondered if there were going to be more pins before they caught the killer. ''I just think he's one sick bastard.'' He looked at the blown-up photograph of the latest victim's nails. ''Someone who obviously has a nail polish fetish.''

Standing next to him, she studied the photograph

herself. ''Maybe not a fetish. Maybe he's just trying to do something nice for them.''

He caught a whiff of her perfume. Light, stirring. He wished she wouldn't wear it. Abruptly he directed his thoughts back to the conversation. ''Not strangling them would have been nice.''

Half aware of what she was doing, C.J. waved her hand at him, asking for silence. She was piecing this together as she went. ''I mean like the kind of thing a guy would do for his girlfriend.''

Culpepper came over to join them. ''No guy I know paints women's fingernails.''

C.J. frowned at the other man. ''That's because every guy you know has just learned how to walk upright without scraping their knuckles on the ground.''

''Hey,'' Rodriguez protested, walking into the room in time to catch the tail end of C.J.'s comment, ''I take exception to that.''

C.J. inclined her head toward the youngest member of their team. ''Present company excepted, of course.'' She became serious again. ''But what I'm talking about is when a guy tries to pamper a woman.''

She looked from one man's face to the other and knew that as far as they were concerned, she was speaking a foreign language. She turned her focus on Rodriguez. After all, he was the one who was getting married and should be informed about this kind of thing. Her guess was that he was generally ignorant of the little niceties that women craved.

''You know, draw her bath, wash her hair for her

in the sink, do her nails.'' Nothing. Rodriguez's face was still blank, and Culpepper was laughing. She threw up her hands. ''What am I, speaking in tongues here? Haven't any of you guys ever heard of pampering a woman?''

Culpepper stopped laughing. ''That kind of thing really turns women on?''

She patted his chest. ''Try it tonight on Adele and see.''

He snorted, waving away the suggestion. ''If I try washing her hair, she'll probably think I was trying to drown her.''

''You're not supposed to drag her by her hair to the sink,'' C.J. pointed out, then shook her head as she looked at Warrick. ''See what I mean? Neanderthal. I rest my case.''

Warrick had the impression she was saying more to him than the actual words conveyed. But then he told himself to knock it off, he was starting to babble in his head.

Wanting to kiss a woman did that to a man.

He shut his mind down.

Culpepper regarded her with blatant curiosity in his eyes. C.J. thought for a second that perhaps she had a convert. ''How about you, Jones? Does that kind of thing turn you on?''

She might have known better. This was getting a bit too personal. ''Solving murders turns me on.''

''Oh, tough lady,'' Culpepper deadpanned.

''Yes, and don't you forget it,'' she cracked, returning to her desk. She wondered if another canvass of the area where the last victim was found would yield anything. Maybe someone remembered something they hadn't mentioned the first time around.

She felt as if they were going in circles.

"Hey, Jones," Rodriguez called. "I almost forgot. It's your turn to field the crank calls."

She groaned, rising again. The more time that passed since the murder, the higher the ratio of crank calls to actual informative ones. "What are they down to? A hundred a day?"

Rodriguez sat down at his own desk. "Give or take."

She groaned louder as she walked into the adjacent room.

Chapter 7

"How about Hannah? Are you a Hannah?"

C.J. looked down at her daughter, trying out yet another name on her. The christening had been postponed because Father Gannon had suddenly been called away on personal business. His aged mother in Ireland was ill and not expected to recover. She could, of course, go with another priest, but she had her heart set on Father Gannon. She could wait. And while she waited, she continued searching for that elusive middle name.

Wide blue eyes looked back at her. Picking the baby up, C.J. patted the small, dry bottom.

"No, huh? How about Annie? Annie do anything for you?" She held the baby away from her, peering at the almost perfect face, trying to envision her daughter responding to the name. "Nothing." C.J.

tucked her against her left hip. ''Okay, Desiree, how about that one? No, you're right, it's all wrong. Napoleon's mistress after Josephine, what are we trying to say here, right?'' She sighed. ''Let's forget about this name game for now and get you some breakfast, Joy.''

C.J. hummed softly to herself as she walked back into the kitchen, the baby nestled against her hip. Outside, the world was dressed in dreary shades of gray, a rainstorm threatening to become a reality at any moment. But it was Saturday and she wasn't going into work today. She intended to make the most of it and spend the day bonding with her daughter.

It amazed her how quickly this little person had become such an integral part of her life. She couldn't begin to imagine life without her now.

The baby seemed to be growing a little each day right in front of her eyes. Each stage filled C.J. with wonder, but made her feel nostalgic, as well, something she would never have thought she'd experience. Nostalgic for the precious, small person she'd held against her breast, even though it had only been two short months since she was born.

Looking at her daughter, C.J. laughed softly to herself. ''I don't know, Baby, I've turned into a real marshmallow when it comes to you.'' She opened the refrigerator and took out a bottle of milk, then placed it on the counter. Maybe she'd just name her Babe and be done with it. Naw. ''If I feel this way now, what am I going to do when you want to start dating? Hanging out to the wee hours of the morning with who knows what kind of characters. And all they'll want is—''

C.J. stopped abruptly. Something akin to a revelation came to her. What she was feeling had been felt by mothers since the beginning of time. What her own mother must have gone through with her. She'd been more than a handful, determined to stay out as late as her brothers had, eschewing curfews.

Wow. Her poor mother. ''Omigod, honey, I think I owe your grandmother a great big apology.''

With the baby still tucked against her hip, C.J. picked up the telephone and dialed her parents' phone number with the same hand. She'd discovered she had an aptitude for doing a great many things with just one hand if she needed to, the other being recruited for far more precious work. Necessity was truly the mother of invention.

She heard her mother's voice on the other end of the line. ''Hello?''

''I'm sorry.''

There was a slight pause on the other end. ''Chris, is that you?'' Concern filled her mother's voice. ''Honey, what's wrong?''

''Yes, it's me.'' She hadn't meant to scare her mother. ''Nothing's wrong, Mom. I just wanted to call you to say I'm sorry.''

A note of confusion entered Diane's voice, even as the concern lingered.

''Why, what did you do? Chris, are you sure you're all right?'' Her voice began to escalate as countless scenarios occurred to her. ''You're not in any hostage situation are you? God, I wanted you to go into your father's firm instead of this cloak-and-dagger business. Why wouldn't you listen to me for just once in your life? You were always too independent—''

C.J. found her opening as her mother took a breath. ''Mom, slow down. I'm not in any hostage situation. I'm standing right here in my kitchen with the baby on my hip and—''

''She's not a rag doll, C.J.'' her mother admonished. ''Use both hands.''

C.J. rolled her eyes. ''Mom, can I just get this out, please?'' She said the words in a rush before the next interruption could occur. ''I'm sorry for everything I put you through while I was growing up.''

''You're forgiven.'' Her mother's concern took another direction. ''You're not ill or anything, are you, Chris? Should I come over?'' Not waiting for a response, she obviously made up her mind. ''Give me a minute, I'll just turn off your father's breakfast and—''

''Mom,'' C.J. raised her voice. ''Mom, stop letting your imagination run away with you. I'm fine, the baby's fine, I just suddenly had momlike feelings, and I realized what you must have gone through all these years with all of us. With me,'' she added after a beat. ''And I just wanted to tell you that I'm sorry for the grief I gave you.''

''Well.'' She heard her mother sighing a sigh she'd obviously kept in for years. ''I'm glad I lived to see the day.'' There was no pause whatsoever as she asked, ''Now, does she have a middle name yet?''

Time to retreat, C.J. thought. ''I've got to go, Mom, there's a call coming in on the other line. Talk to you later, bye.''

She heard her mother sigh, murmur goodbye and then hang up.

''Okay, young lady, we were about to get you some breakfast before I had that unprecedented qualm of conscience.'' She cocked her head, looking at her daughter again. ''Are you a Joy Michelle? No, that's not right, either.''

With a sigh she opened the microwave door and reached for the bottle. The phone rang. Now what?

''This'll just take a minute,'' she promised her daughter. Picking up the receiver, she wedged it against her head and shoulder as she returned to the microwave. ''Hello?''

Warrick was on the other end. His voice was grim. ''There's been another murder, C.J.''

She didn't have to ask if this concerned their killer. Her stomach instantly tightened.

Letting out a breath, she punched in one minute, three seconds and pushed the start button. ''Where?''

''In Santa Barbara.''

She frowned. That didn't sound right. ''Santa Barbara? Is our boy spreading out?'' God, she hoped not. C.J. shivered.

''That's what I'm going up there to find out.''

Where was this coming from? ''Not without me you're not.''

"This is just a courtesy call, C.J. I figured you'd want to know. Stay home and take care of your baby."

C.J. frowned. This was getting old. Ever since she'd returned to work, Warrick had been treating her differently. Not as an equal, but like someone who needed protecting. She didn't know if it was because of the kiss that shimmered between them like a silent entity, or because of the baby, but either way, she didn't like it and she wasn't about to stand for it.

"Warrick, this is my case just as much as it is yours. Now just give me a few minutes to get some things together so I can take the baby over to my mother's. I can be there in—" she realized she didn't have enough information to make a time estimate "—where are you?"

"I'm still at the field office. But C.J., there's no need—"

The microwave bell went off. She opened the door, then drew out the arm that was supporting her baby just far enough to test the temperature of the milk on her wrist. Perfect. Unlike this conversation.

"Yes, there is a need," she insisted. "I have a need." Moving the chair away from the table with her foot, she sat down, then shifted the baby onto her lap. Cradling her daughter to her, she began feeding the infant, all the while never losing an ounce of her indignation. "Damn it, Warrick, I'm still the same partner you always had."

"No, you're not." His voice was low, steely. Unmovable. "You're someone's mother now."

That didn't warrant the preferential treatment. ''And as someone's mother, I want to catch this bastard before he robs some other mother of her child.'' She smiled at her daughter, keeping her own voice calm so as not to frighten the baby. But it wasn't easy when her temper was flaring this way. ''Now stop treating me as if I was made of porcelain and give me the courtesy of waiting for me to get there.''

Soft tone or not, he knew C.J. well enough to know she was mad as the proverbial wet hen. ''I'm not sure I want to do that now. You sound like you're breathing fire.''

''You bet I'm breathing fire,'' she said between clenched teeth, her smile never wavering. ''I worked long and hard to get here and I'm not about to give it up because you suddenly feel the need to treat me with kid gloves. I wouldn't treat you any differently if you had a baby.''

She heard him laugh. Even though she was angry, the sound rippled against her ear, undulating through her. Did postpartum syndrome include hallucinations?

''If I had a baby, the *world* would treat me differently.''

The baby was chugging away at the bottle, draining it like a trouper. At this rate, C.J. estimated, she would double her size in no time.

''Very funny. Now let me get off the phone and do what I have to do. And you'd better be waiting for me when I get there or I swear I will fillet your skin off your body when I get my hands on you.''

She heard him laugh again. ''Love it when you

talk dirty like that. Okay, I'll wait. Just don't take too long.''

C.J. hung up. The bottle was empty. She put the baby over her shoulder and just before she began burping her, she hit the speed dial to call her mother and switched to speakerphone. Multitasking had become a way of life for her.

She heard the phone being picked up. ''Mom? Guess what—''

Thirty-five minutes later, C.J. was dashing off the federal building elevator and into the task force room.

Warrick was the only one in there. He looked up as she entered. ''You look winded.''

She was winded. There had been no need to pack up anything, her mother had spares of all the necessary items for the baby. She'd made the trip from her house to her mother's in record time. For once, every light was with her. The hardest part was leaving the baby. You'd think it would get easier with each day, she thought, but it didn't. Some days it just got harder.

Still, C.J. waved away his observation. She was eager for news. ''Never mind my wind, what have we got?''

He handed her a picture that had come in over the fax less than an hour ago. ''Sally Albrecht, twenty-three, blond, blue-eyed, strangled, poetically arranged, pink nail polish.''

She nodded grimly, taking the photograph from him. This wasn't the kind of thing any of them welcomed hearing. She studied it for a moment. Like all the others, the latest victim appeared as if she were sleeping.

"Sounds like our boy's gotten tired of the local area and is making his way up the coast." Putting the fax down on her desk, she crossed to the map that had a tight little circle of pins on it. She'd been hoping that they could keep narrowing the circle, not widen it. Usually, serial killer victims were all over the map. This was supposed to make it easier for them. It didn't.

When she turned back from the map, she was frowning. "I don't like it. This blows the whole theory to pieces that he's a local guy."

"I know." He'd signed out a Bureau vehicle in the last half hour. Ready to go, Warrick gave her one last chance to change her mind. "You sure you don't want to stay home?"

He was just trying to be kind, she told herself. She had to remember that and stop taking offense where none was intended. There was no doubt in her mind that if he had some personal reason impeding him, she'd be trying to get him to stay behind.

C.J. nodded. "I'm sure. After my mother finished complaining that the Bureau doesn't let me have a life, she was thrilled to have to watch the baby."

"I've got a company car waiting downstairs. Let's go."

Walking through the office door first, Warrick didn't bother holding it open. C.J. put her hand out in time to keep it from shutting on her. "Hey!"

Warrick looked at her innocently. ''You said not to treat you any differently from any of the other guys, remember?''

She strode past him to the elevator and punched the down button. ''I don't recall you slamming the door in any of their faces.''

''No slamming,'' he pointed out. ''Just every man for himself.''

''Person,'' she corrected as the elevator arrived and opened its doors. C.J. walked in ahead of him. ''Every person for themselves.''

Warrick followed her in and sighed. He pressed for the first floor. ''I got a feeling this is going to be a long road trip.''

Santa Barbara was approximately 150 miles north of the county that had previously been the Sleeping Beauty Killer's stomping grounds. Ordinarily C.J. loved driving up the coast, but the unexpected rain with its gloom made the trip dreary.

They'd flipped a coin, and Warrick had lost the toss. Taking the keys, he'd gotten behind the wheel of the midsize vehicle the Bureau had provided.

C.J. settled back in her seat and stared straight ahead. The rain was almost mesmerizingly hypnotic, causing everything farther than twenty feet away to appear surreal.

''You know, it's funny, but I miss her.'' She glanced at Warrick to see if he was laughing. He wasn't. ''When I'm on the job, I find myself missing her, and when I'm home, my mind keeps going back to the case.''

That was the complaint of more than one special agent. He could feel the car beginning to climb. Warrick swallowed to relieve the pressure in his ears. ''Welcome to the world of parenthood.''

She laughed shortly, shifting in her seat. Rain made her restless. Or maybe it was this case. ''How would you know?''

He shrugged. ''I read a lot.'' Moving with the curve in the road, Warrick spared her a glance. ''You know, Rodriguez could just as easily have come with me.''

C.J. thought the man was a good agent, but he liked his weekends to himself. ''Rodriguez is still in love. Leave him with his fiancée.''

Driving was getting a little trickier. Warrick slowed their speed down to a careful thirty-five miles an hour. ''Well, Culpepper isn't in love.'' Not the way the man liked to complain about his wife, although Warrick suspected that there was a measure of affection in the grousing. ''I know he would have been more than happy to make the trip to Santa Barbara.''

C.J. looked at him incredulously. ''You telling me that you'd rather have Culpepper sitting here next to you than me?''

For an optimistic woman, she had a habit of twisting his words to give them a darker meaning. ''No, I'm telling you that it would have been okay for you to sit this one out.''

C.J. wished he'd stop trying to make things easy on her. How could she feel like his equal if he kept insisting on spreading out his cloak for her so she could walk over the puddles without getting her shoes dirty?

"No," she told him quietly, firmly, "it wouldn't have."

"C.J. you're a new mother—"

Not that again. "Not so new," she contradicted. "Sure, I'm a mother now, but I'm also a special agent with the FBI." And that was very important to her. She'd had to buck not just her mother, but her father as well to get to where she was. And that didn't begin to take in the male agents along the way who resented having a woman on equal footing with them. In many ways it was still a man's world. "It's who I am and I'm damn proud of it. I've just got to find the proper balance to this combination, that's all. And you throwing up roadblocks all the time isn't exactly helping."

What was the use? thought Warrick. Mules had nothing on C.J. He slowed down more as a car, traveling in the opposite direction, its tires plowing through large puddles, sent an even heavier shower of water their way. For a second the windshield was obscured. Rain brought out the nutcases, he thought, all driving as if they had something to prove.

"I'm not throwing up roadblocks," he told her. "And I thought I was helping."

"Think again."

They needed a break. His eyes on the road, Warrick switched on the radio. He wanted some music to take the place of their voices.

She frowned at his selection and changed the station.

He switched it back, then batted away her hand when she reached for the dial again. "I'm driving, I get to pick the music."

"I'm driving on the way back."

He didn't bother looking her way. "Deal."

Crossing her arms in front of her, C.J. settled back in her seat again and watched the rain fight an endless skirmish with the windshield wipers.

She could never get used to it, C.J. thought. The smell of the bleak, dismal area where the Medical Examiner did his gruesome work permeated her senses even as she tried to breathe through her mouth.

The victim's body had been taken to the morgue. The local coroner had held off on the mandatory autopsy until the FBI special agents could get there. The moment they'd gone to the sheriff's office, the man had brought them here.

C.J. tried to divorce herself from the fact that the body on the table had been a person with aspirations and dreams under a day ago. Someone's daughter, someone's sister. She succeeded only marginally. Glancing at Warrick's profile, she saw that it remained stoic. Didn't he have any feelings?

Steeling herself, she approached the table.

"When was the time of death?" Warrick asked the heavyset man in the white lab coat.

The M.E., a Dr. Hal Edwards, glanced at the notes on his clipboard before answering.

"As near as I can place it, about fifteen hours ago." He flipped the pages back in place, retiring the clipboard to a desk. ''I hate to tell you this,'' he looked from one to the other, ''but you've probably figured it out already. Most of the clues have been washed away. It's been raining steadily here for the past few hours.''

''Who found the body?'' C.J. asked. She resisted the desire to brush back the victim's hair. There were no signs that the woman had suffered. She supposed that was some consolation to the victim's family, although not much.

''A jogger running for cover stumbled over her in the park. Called the police.''

''Man?'' Warrick wanted to know. It was not unheard of to have a killer take a life then pretend to be the first one on the scene to try to avoid suspicion.

''Woman. They had to give her a sedative to calm her down.''

C.J. couldn't take her eyes off the girl's face. ''God, she looks like a kid.''

''We've got a positive I.D.'' the M.E. told her. ''She was older than she looked.'' This time he didn't refer to his notes. The facts were still fresh. ''Waitress in a local restaurant. No priors, decent girl. Engaged to be married. She looked like she fit the description of the Sleeping Beauty Killer's victims, so we called you.'' He recited the similarities. ''Bruising around the neck, died of asphyxiation, pink nail polish.''

C.J. carefully circled the girl, moving away from the M.E. The marks around the girl's neck were dark, ugly. She could almost feel the killer's hands around her own throat, literally choking the life out of her. C.J. shivered, looking down at the girl's hand. Something nagged at her. She picked it up to examine it.

The polish looked darker than the others had been. She looked closer.

Putting the lifeless hand down again, C.J. raised her eyes to the other two occupants in the room. Both men were looking at her. "This isn't his work."

The M.E took exception. He gestured toward the body. "The MO matches."

Warrick always teased her about her hunches, but 75 percent of the time C.J. was right. He'd learned to take her seriously. "You think someone else killed her?" C.J. nodded.

"She was found the same way," the M.E. pointed out. "On her back, hands folded around a rose. Choker around her neck."

That was it, she realized, what had bothered her when she looked at the fax the police had sent. "What kind of choker was it again?"

Edwards referred to his clipboard, scanning through two pages before answering. "Cameo."

Warrick shook his head. "Our boy uses cheap costume jewelry. Pearls." He glanced at C.J. "What made you realize this wasn't our serial killer?"

She held up the victim's hand. "I think the nail polish is just a coincidence. It's the wrong shade. More important than that, it's chipped. Our killer puts it on after they're dead." Her expression was grim. "Not much chance of chipping then."

Placing the hand respectfully beside the body, she moved around to the victim's feet. C.J. raised the sheet. "And also, it matches her toes. None of the others had painted toenails." She draped the sheet back over the victim's feet and looked up at the coroner. "I'm afraid it looks like you've got yourself an independent copycat murder, Dr. Edwards."

Chapter 8

The rain was coming down harder, beating down on all sides of the car.

C.J. looked at her partner as he carefully guided the vehicle. ''Think whoever killed that girl is a groupie?''

They'd gone back to the sheriff's office after leaving the coroner and told the man their findings. Signing off on the case, they'd gotten back on the road within the hour, stopping only long enough to get something to go from a fast-food restaurant. The crumpled-up wrappers were now tucked inside the greasy paper bag on the floor behind her.

Warrick's hands tightened on the steering wheel. Despite their earlier agreement about C.J. driving back, she had deferred to him. Much as it pained her to admit it, of the two of them, he was the better driver.

It wasn't easy holding his own against the weather, Warrick thought. The roads were tough to negotiate and getting tougher by the minute. Rather than let up as the weatherman had predicted, the rain was coming down progressively harder.

''Maybe, maybe not.'' There were a lot of reasons to make the murders appear similar. ''Maybe just someone looking to kill Sally and throw the blame somewhere else.'' He figured that was the most likely reason. The car kept swerving as the wind picked up. Keeping in his lane had become a monumental challenge. The lines were all but obliterated by the rain. ''What I do think is that we'd better get ourselves an ark or get off this damn road. This stuff doesn't look like it's going to stop coming down.''

C.J. frowned. Visibility was getting worse and worse as the windshield wipers, set on high, were clearly losing their battle with the rain. Except for precious single moments right after a pass, the rain had all but obscured the windshield.

To back up his suggestion, he added, ''I remember passing a motel just on the outskirts of the city. After that, there's nothing for miles.'' He looked at her. It was their only alternative, but he left it up to her. ''What do you want to do?''

''What I *want* to do is get home.'' C.J. pressed her lips together, frustrated. There was no way they were going to make it tonight. ''But the sensible thing to do, I guess, is get a couple of rooms for the night and get an early start in the morning.''

He nodded. He had slowed down considerably. The vehicle was barely crawling as it was. At this rate the trip would take more than twice the time.

"The rain might not let up by morning, but at least there'll be some light to help us see something." Warrick slanted a quick glance at her before gluing his eyes back on the windshield. Not that it helped all that much. "No sense tempting fate."

They'd already avoided one near accident just after the fast-food restaurant. A big rig, going the opposite way, had swerved, taking up too much of the road. They'd had to quickly scramble to the side, into what would have been a dirt shoulder. Because of the rain, it had almost become a river of oozing mud. Her heart was still trying to recover from the scare.

But weren't they tempting fate in a different way, stopping at a motel like this?

C.J. squelched her uneasiness. There was clearly no other sane choice. Besides, they were both adults, both sensible. In addition, they'd be in separate rooms. No reason to worry.

A smear of lights broke across the right corner of the windshield. C.J. squinted.

"There it is," she said, "that's the motel—I think." At this point it was difficult to identify anything positively.

"I see it."

Warrick slowed the vehicle even more, practically inching his way over as he searched for the entrance to the motel's parking lot. Finding it, he traveled approximately two feet before abruptly stopping the car.

"What's wrong?" C.J. asked.

"Is it me, or is that parking lot a lake?" From what he could make out, the center of the lot appeared to be underwater. "I think we'd better stop right here." Warrick pulled the vehicle over to the side as far as he could.

C.J. realized they had no choice but to get out and make a run for it to the rental office which, according to a neon sign, was directly beneath an arrow and off to one side.

She shook her head. "This is just getting better and better."

"We could spend the night in the car."

C.J. looked at him. The quarters were much too close for comfort of any kind, mental or physical. "You're kidding, right?"

"Right." Warrick put his hand on the door handle. "I'm beginning to appreciate the title *A River Runs through It.*" He looked at her. "Ready?"

She braced herself, then nodded and swung open her own door. The wind nearly pushed it closed again. Shoving, she made it out of the car. A gust of wind, pregnant with rain, hit her square in the face the moment she was out. Her ankles were instantly submerged in dirty water. The parking lot was rising.

Was the area prone to flash floods? She had no idea.

Her heart hammering, C.J. began to fight her way to the walkway that ran along the perimeter of the motel. The water tugged at her shoes. She tugged back with each step she took. Losing her footing, she slid and suddenly found herself meeting what would have been the ground if it hadn't been submerged.

The next second she was being pulled back up to her feet by her arm.

"Stay behind me," Warrick shouted to her over the howl of the wind. For once, he noted, she offered no resistance, no rebuttal. Using his body as a shield, he held her by the hand, keeping her well behind him as he made his way to the rental office and shelter.

Pulling the door opened, he pushed C.J. in ahead of him and shoved the door shut. They took a second to catch their breaths and get their bearings.

The dank smell of wet wood assaulted their noses. There was limited light in the office, coming from the yellowed fluorescent fixture overhead. Comprised of three long bulbs, the two closest to the door were out. There was an ancient TV set perched on a tall crate in the back. The blurry image of a sitcom was scattering itself all over the screen. The set had dials.

The small, thin clerk slowly uncurled himself from his position on the chair in front of the set and made his way over to the front desk. His eyes slid over C.J. slowly before he spoke.

"What can I do for you folks?" He was smirking as he asked the question.

"We'd like a couple of rooms," Warrick told him.

The man shook his bald head. ''Sorry, no can do. All's I got is one left.'' He winked broadly at Warrick. ''This *is* Saturday night, you know. Busiest night of the week.''

''On a night like this?'' The wind rattled the window to underscore C.J.'s point.

The man's smile was smarmy. ''Hey, nothin' stands in the path of grabbing a little true love for an hour or two.'' Small, dark eyes moved from one to the other like little black marbles. ''But then, I don't have to tell you two that, do I? I mean you're here, aren't you?''

''Not by choice,'' C.J. muttered.

Warrick sighed and took out his wallet. He put a fifty-dollar bill on the counter, keeping his fingertips solidly on the edge of it in case the man had any ideas about just grabbing the money.

''You sure there's only one room?''

The clerk's eyes were fastened to the bill. ''I'm sure. If you want two, put another Franklin down on top of that one and I'll let you have my room for the night.''

Warrick looked at C.J. ''What do you want to do?''

There was nothing else *to* do. She was positive that the clerk's room probably had to be disinfected before it was inhabitable. She blew out a breath. ''Give us the room.''

The clerk cackled. ''That's it, honey, you play hard to get. Men like a challenge, long as you don't make it too hard.'' He winked. ''If you know what I mean.''

Warrick saw C.J. clenching her fists at her sides. He felt like punching the clerk himself. The weather and circumstances had made him irritable.

"Just give us the key and spare us the philosophy," he ordered.

The clerk put his smudged fingers on the other end of the bill and waited. Warrick released it. Tucking it into the pocket of his baggy, mud-colored pants, the clerk turned and took the last remaining key off the pegboard to his left. He slapped it on the counter, then took a step back as if he was afraid of getting hit. "Yes, sir. Room 10. Dead center. Can't miss it."

She didn't appreciate the word *dead.* C.J. tugged on Warrick's arm. "Let's just go, Warrick. I'm dying to take a hot shower."

The clerk cleared his throat, still eyeing Warrick warily. "Oh, sorry, can't accommodate you there. The shower's not working. But the sink's got water," he added brightly, then a wicked smirk came over his lips. "You could always sponge each other off."

The glare Warrick gave the man had him backing farther away from his desk, his hands raised in mute surrender, his eyes fearful.

"Or not," he added in a mumble.

The shower wasn't working. Somehow that only seemed par for the course. C.J. turned away from the desk.

"Great," she muttered to Warrick. "It'll be like washing up in a birdbath." She didn't appreciate the fact that her partner looked as if he was struggling not to laugh.

Warrick opened the door for her. ''Let's go.''

He didn't have to say it twice.

They fought their way outside and down the cracked walkway. The red clay roof that jutted out overhead offered next to no shelter. The rain was lashing at them from all directions, swirling around almost like a whirlpool.

Water was lapping over the edges of the thin sidewalk, but most of the walkway wasn't submerged. Warrick looked over his shoulder to make sure that C.J. was still behind him. ''Doing okay?''

His question, served by the wind, seemed to sweep over her like a physical entity. ''Just peachy. Keep walking.''

He couldn't hear her. The wind was stealing her words. He cupped his hand over his ear. ''What?''

In reply, C.J. planted her hands against his back and pushed him forward. ''Keep walking!''

''Good idea.''

When they reached number 10's door, Warrick put the key the desk clerk had given them into the lock. Turning it took a bit of finesse. He jiggled it slightly and felt rather than heard a click.

''Maybe he gave us the wrong key,'' C.J. guessed, raising her voice. In which case she was going to go back and strangle the man.

''No, I think it's giving.'' Jiggling the key again did nothing. Warrick finally wound up pushing the door open with his shoulder. ''Flimsy.''

''Well, that makes me feel secure,'' C.J. commented, rushing into the room. She shook off as much of the rain as she could once she was inside.

Flipping on the light switch next to the entrance, Warrick shut the door behind them and looked around the room. "All the comforts of home."

"Yeah, if home's a brothel." Scarlet seemed to be the color of choice for the decor. There were dusty, sagging scarlet drapes, a scarlet bedspread that was worn in several places and scarlet lamp shades perched on small, erotic-looking lamps. "Who the hell did the decorating for this place, Hookers R Us?"

Warrick laughed. The room did go a long way in negating any kind of a romantic mood that might have been created by the rain. He only wished he could maintain that frame of mind. Soaking wet, C.J. still looked better than she should.

He stripped off his jacket and his shirt and walked into the adjacent bathroom to hang them up on the curtain rod. With any luck, they'd be dry by morning.

"Look on the bright side," he told her. "At least it's dry and the power's still on."

The wind was rattling the windows, which looked none too secure in their casings. "For now," C.J. qualified.

She wished he'd kept his shirt on. Or that his chest was flat and pasty like so many other men's were. But he was a walking testament to the hours he spent in the gym working out. She walked by an oval mirror hung over a broken-down bureau. One of its handles was gone. The silver all along the bottom of the mirror had begun to peel away.

But she saw enough to make her cringe. ''God, is that mud in my hair?''

Warrick came up behind her and began examining the top of her head. When she tried to bat away his hands, he batted back. ''I'm only trying to help. No, no mud, it looks like twigs.'' He laughed. ''Thinking of starting a nest?''

''Very funny.'' C.J. shook her head, brushing the twigs out with her fingers. She made a point of moving away from Warrick and his bare chest. She looked toward the bathroom. ''My kingdom for a shower.''

''There's always the sink. The clerk said it was working.'' Walking back into the bathroom, he turned the faucet on. After making one sputtering noise, water began to flow. ''At least he didn't lie about that.'' Rain was lashing at the small bathroom window. ''Or you could always stand outside with a bar of soap.''

Now there was an idea, she thought cynically. ''The clerk would probably charge admission.'' Moving past Warrick, careful not to brush against him, she turned on the shower taps. Nothing happened.

With a sigh she looked at the sink. Better than nothing. ''At least I could wash my hair—if I had some shampoo.'' This was not going down as one of her better days. ''I didn't exactly pack for an overnighter.'' When she turned from the shower, she saw Warrick squatting down in front of the sink, rummaging through the faded yellow cabinet. "What are you doing?"

"Finding you some shampoo." He held his trophy up for her to see. It was a half-empty bottle of pink liquid.

She looked closer. "That's dishwashing liquid."

Rising, Warrick looked at the bottle, then shrugged. "Soap's soap." He arched an amused brow. "Beggars can't be choosers."

She took the bottle from him, resigned. "I hate it when you're right."

His mouth curved. "You must spend a lot of time being upset."

"In your dreams."

The deep-scarlet towel on the rack beside the sink was surprisingly fluffy. She placed it within easy reach. C.J. turned in the collar of her shirt so it wouldn't get in the way and then turned on the water. Testing it with her fingers, she waited until the water temperature was fairly decent, then lowered her head. She angled it under the faucet to wet her hair with clean water.

"Might have gone faster for you if you stuck your head out the door," Warrick observed. Her only answer was to sigh. Crossing his arms before his chest, he leaned against the doorjamb and watched her begin to lather her hair.

The tawdry surroundings began to fade into the background. There was something almost sensual about what she was doing, her fingers working up a lather, working it through her hair.

He could feel that same stirring again within him. The nameless one he didn't want to dwell on.

"This whole trip's been a bust," she told him, raising her voice in case he couldn't hear her above the running water. "I hope there's a signal in here. I've got to call home. Otherwise, my mother's going to have the state troopers looking for both of us. Kind of funny, really. Here we are, two special agents with the FBI, trained to the hilt in self-defense and there's my mother, probably worrying about us getting lost in the rain."

Suddenly she felt another set of hands beginning to massage her scalp. She started. "What the—"

Gently, Warrick pressed her back down. She was as skittish as a cat, he thought. He could see the tension all through her shoulders. Not that he was supposed to be noticing that about her.

"Relax," he soothed. "It's just me."

Just him, right. Just as it was "just raining" outside. A more apt description was monsooning. And there was no "just" about Warrick.

Drawing on anger, she worked to steady her pulse. "What the hell do you think you're doing?"

"Testing your theory," he answered. Definitely sensual, he thought as he continued massaging her hair. "I thought you said women liked having a man do this sort of thing."

"They do. We do," she corrected before he could make a comment about her excluding herself from the gender. "But what do you know about washing hair?"

"I wash my own. How much different can this

be?'' He smiled at her back. ''Okay, now relax and let me do this. You've been through a lot lately. I thought I'd do something nice for you.''

She didn't want him doing something nice for her. She was having a hard enough time thinking of him as her partner and nothing more. Especially since he'd taken off his shirt.

C.J. tried to twist away, but he held her body fast against the sink. ''But—''

He laughed. ''Just shut up, Jones, and enjoy it, okay? I am.''

She froze. It had to be the acoustics here in the sink. She could have sworn he said he was enjoying this, too. ''What did you say?''

That had just slipped out. His mind scrambled for a plausible explanation. ''There's something therapeutic about immersing your hands in hot water and suds.''

He's your partner, your partner. She chanted the line in her mind like a mantra. ''Remind me to have you around when I wash dishes.''

''You still wash dishes?'' He couldn't picture her doing anything domestic. Trouble was, he was picturing her a whole different way, which had nothing to do with dishes and everything to do with suds. He ran a tongue along dry lips. ''What about the dishwasher?''

C.J. clung to the mundane topic. ''Wasteful. There's never enough dishes to put in.''

He'd never noticed how inviting the slope of her neck was, gently curving just enough for a man's hand to hold while he was kissing her. "Maybe you should entertain more."

His voice was low, sultry and wreaking havoc on her nervous system.

"Maybe."

Why did it feel as if every word was sticking to the roof of her mouth? And why was she so aware of the heat coming from his body? The rest of the room wasn't warm. Or hadn't been when she'd entered.

He finally stopped just as she felt herself melting. The warm water caressed her scalp, washing away the lather. She dug her nails into her palms. It didn't help divert her attention.

She swallowed, trying her hardest not give herself away. "You're very good at this."

He worked a stubborn tangle out of her hair, then moved his fingers through the strands, making sure the soap was all out of it. "Thanks."

"You've done this before." Nobody was this good without practice. Had he done this for his ex-wife? A lover, maybe?

Jealousy flickered through her. Appalled, she shut it away.

"No. Just a natural, I guess. There." He shook off his hands. "Done."

She raised her head, looking at him oddly as she wrung out the remaining water from her hair with her hands. Taking the towel, she blotted her face and neck before lowering her head again in order to wrap the towel around it like a turban.

She raised her head. The light in the room wasn't

bright. It didn't matter. She could see the look in his eyes. It called to something within her.

Every pulse point within her body began to hammer.

Chapter 9

C.J. remained very still, not daring to take a breath, to blink an eye. Everything within her felt as if it had suddenly frozen.

''Warrick?''

''Yes?'' He stood less than two feet away from her, his eyes never leaving her face.

His eyes were holding her captive. ''What are you thinking?''

His voice was soft, low, each word carefully measured out, as if spilling it too soon was unthinkable.

''That this rain is never going to stop. That we should have gotten more take-out food when we had a chance.'' He moved forward. The two feet between them began to disappear until it was almost all gone. ''And that I want to kiss you. Very much.''

''Why don't you?'' she whispered.

Very slowly Warrick ran his hand along her cheek, then cupped the back of her head and brought her lips halfway to his.

He met her the rest of the way.

His lips were hard, firm.

Gentle.

And they drew the very life out of her, creating something wild and uncontainable in its place. Heat surged all around her. Through her. She might as well have been standing in a sauna.

Abandoning any pretense that this wasn't affecting her, C.J. rose up high on her toes, as far as she could reach, falling deep into the kiss. Not wanting to miss a single nuance.

The towel slipped from her head onto the floor, completely unnoticed. All she was aware of was this fire burning within her.

Fire and craving.

His arms were around her, pulling her closer to him. She could feel the heat radiating from his bare chest.

At least she wasn't the only one in overdrive, she thought. A lot of good that did her.

This was bad, Warrick thought, really bad. Kissing C.J. hadn't satisfied anything. It just opened up the floodgates. Made him want her all the more.

For a man who liked to maintain control of every waking moment of his life, he found himself a hopeless captive of what was happening right now.

What was more, he didn't care.

Didn't care that things were twisting around him, didn't care that what he felt was so out of character it might as well have been happening to someone else. All he cared about was kissing her.

Having her.

The realization came like a crashing blow to his brain. He wanted to make love with her. With C.J. His partner.

This was getting way out of hand.

Drawing a deep breath, Warrick managed to separate himself from her. It almost surprised him to discover that there was an end to him and a beginning to her. For a moment he'd felt they had formed one continuous whole. One endless circle.

He struggled to pull himself together, to cover up what he was feeling. She looked dazed. That made two of them, he thought.

He took another step back and noticed the towel. ''Um,'' he pointed to the floor behind her, ''I think your turban fell.''

Numbly C.J. turned to look where he was pointing. She stared down at the damp towel as if she didn't recognize what it was.

''Oh, right. It did.''

How long had the room been spinning around like this? Though it was secretly humiliating, she held on to his arms a second longer. Trying to regain the use of her mind as well as her legs. Both became available to her in small increments. She took what she could get.

C.J. drew another deep breath, realizing that there was no air in her lungs. ''I'd...I'd better call my mother.'' She dropped her hands to her sides.

‘‘She’ll be worried. And I need to check on the baby.’’ Her throat had never felt this dry.

All the moisture seemed to have gone to other parts of her body.

Warrick stepped aside. After retrieving the towel, he handed it to her. Rather than wrap her hair again, she just toweled it dry as she walked into the other room on wobbly legs.

The room felt terribly cramped suddenly. It was dominated by the bed, and the scarlet walls began to close in on her.

She wished it wasn’t raining so she could go out for a walk. But if it hadn’t been raining, she wouldn’t be here. They wouldn’t be here.

Her head hurt.

Her body ached.

Taking out her cell phone, C.J. found the ever-annoying message written across her screen. The phone couldn’t find a network. It wasn’t receiving a signal. She looked around for Warrick. He was still standing in the bathroom doorway. Watching her.

She tossed her cell phone on the bed. ‘‘Give me your cell phone.’’

Crossing to her as he took the small silver phone out of his back pocket, he held it out to her. ‘‘Why don’t you just use the motel phone?’’

She took the phone from his hand. ‘‘It’s probably just programmed for phone sex.’’

C.J. glanced down at the cell phone’s LCD screen. Warrick had a different service provider, but the message was the same. The storm was playing havoc with all manner of signals.

Hers included.

With a sigh C.J. handed him back his cell. ''You're not receiving signals, either.''

''Oh,'' he tossed the phone on the nightstand, a smile slipping across his lips, ''I wouldn't exactly say that.'' And he had absolutely no idea what to make of them, or where to go from here.

Ignoring his comment, C.J. sat on the edge of the bed facing the regular phone. Gingerly she picked up the receiver and held it to her ear. The motel phone still had a rotary dial. Maybe whoever ran this place thought it was sexier. Or nostalgic. Or maybe they'd just been too cheap to replace the phones. Whatever the reason, it was inconvenient to use.

Deliberately blocking out Warrick, she dialed her mother's number.

The phone was picked up on the first ring. ''Where are you?''

She was right. Her mother was worried. ''That's not how you answer the phone, Mom,'' she chided, struggling to keep her voice level, grateful that she had this minor distraction to cling to. ''What if this was an obscene phone call?''

''I'd hand it to your father,'' Diane said matter-of-factly. ''And don't talk to me about phone etiquette. You should have been home by now, or called earlier. Where are you?''

C.J. ran her hands along her forehead where the ache was forming. *In Limbo, Mom. Halfway between heaven and hell.* ''We're still in the Santa Barbara area. The storm's really bad up here.''

As if to punctuate her statement, the wind picked up and rattled the windows and the door. It felt as if the breeze went right through the room. Mercifully, the rain didn't.

"It's no picnic here, either," her mother told her. "It's been coming down all afternoon and evening. So are you at a hotel?"

"Motel," C.J. corrected.

"Not a sleazy one I hope."

C.J. looked around at the scarlet furnishings. "No, not sleazy." This place was way beyond sleazy. On a scale of one to ten, it had fallen off the charts.

She heard her mother sigh with relief. "Good, I won't have to worry about you driving back in this. Wait until the rain lets up," Diane advised. "And don't worry about the baby. She's being a little fussy, but your father's having a ball with her. He thinks Joy's middle name should be Cynthia. What do you think?"

The only Cynthia she knew had stolen her boyfriend in college. The name did not hold pleasant memories. "We'll pick names when I get back, Mom."

Her mother sighed again, this time like a long-suffering saint. "Like I believe that. All right, she's your daughter. Tell Byron I said hello."

C.J. ran her tongue along her lips. It didn't help. They were as dry as dust. "If I see him," she murmured. "'Night mother. Kiss the baby for me."

"Already have. Bye."

She held the receiver a moment more, even though her mother was no longer on the other end.

When she finally hung up, Warrick was standing in front of her.

Tiny nerve endings all along her body came to life. Every single one of them was desperately telegraphing ''Mayday'' to her.

''Everything all right?'' he asked. She had a strange look on her face. Maybe there was something wrong with the baby.

Nodding in slow motion, C.J. rose to her feet. She pushed the telephone back on the nightstand. She couldn't think, couldn't piece two thoughts together. She'd had one of the sharpest minds in her class at the Academy, and it was now the consistency of warm mutton.

''My mother says to say hi.'' She took a deep breath and looked up at him. ''Hi.''

''Hi,'' he answered softly.

Warrick slipped his hands around her waist.

She cleared her throat nervously. ''I don't suppose there's anything on TV.'' C.J. glanced over at the ancient console against the wall.

''Cable's out,'' he told her. ''I checked.''

''Oh.'' She couldn't draw her eyes away from his face, from his mouth. ''So now what do we do?'' Each word found its way out slowly.

Her hair was curling around her head. He kind of liked that. ''I thought maybe we could explore that kiss again.''

He hadn't moved. How was it that he was closer to her than he'd been just a heartbeat ago? Or was she the one who was moving? ‘‘Do you think that’s wise?’’

‘‘No.’’ The admission was honest, skimming along her skin like a seduction. He brushed a wet curl aside, his lips lingering a moment on the curve of her neck. Sending shivers down her spine. ‘‘I’m not feeling very wise tonight.’’

‘‘Me, neither,’’ she murmured as she encircled her arms around his neck.

His lips found hers.

It was like an explosion. The instant his mouth made contact with hers, she felt as if all the stops had suddenly been pulled out. As if her entire body had launched into fourth gear without ever bothering to go through the other three.

As the storm continued to release its fury outside, another raged within the small room. Within her. All the safeguards, all the warnings she had so strictly issued to herself had been completely incinerated.

None of it mattered.

His mouth made all her thoughts, all her former protests null and void. Vaporizing them as if they’d never existed. The way he kissed her, tenderly, possessively, made her want to give herself to him without qualms, without reservations.

She just wanted him to make love with her.

To her.

They tumbled backward onto the bed, their lips still sealed to each other’s. The urgency inside of her scrambled wildly in her chest, not for higher ground but for fulfillment.

Warrick could feel his heart slamming against his ribs like a jackhammer gone out of control. His mind was a jumble of thoughts, of fragments, very few of which made any sense at all.

Thoughts gave way to a higher order. Sensations were traveling through him, memories of sweet things, erotic things, all brought on by the taste of her lips, the promise of her body.

He ran his hands over her, striving not to be rough, succeeding only marginally.

As he pressed his lips against the hollow of her throat and heard her breath quicken, he worked away at the buttons on her blouse. Reining himself in to keep from ripping them off.

Undone, the material parted. Very lightly he ran his fingers along her skin. It quivered beneath his touch. Something quickened in his belly, the sensation echoing in his loins.

Over and over again he caressed the soft contours of her body, finding, exploring. Claiming. Feasting. He couldn't get enough. More just bred a desire for more. There was no end.

Warrick freed her from her blouse, tossing it aside. He pushed her back down against the lurid scarlet comforter, his mouth exploring the contours of her face, his fingers tugging away the straps of her bra.

One movement of his fingers and the barrier was gone. He covered her breasts with his hand, first one, then the other. The hairs along his arm gliding along her skin, making her twist and strain against him.

Her breasts were soft, tempting. Desire surged through him, hardening him further.

His hand was replaced by his mouth. It encircled each peak, his tongue lightly flicked against the small, hardening flesh.

C.J. moaned, arching, wanting. Her breath grew shorter. She undid his belt buckle, then the zipper on his pants, tugging the immediate material aside. She cupped him. He kissed her harder, making the flame grow.

She wiggled into him, pressing her body against his as he tugged away her skirt, leaving her in her underwear. Her heart was beating so hard she was having trouble breathing.

His hands were everywhere, caressing her, taking her. Heating her. Making her damp.

She tugged urgently on his pants, wanting to tear away the final barrier. ''Damn it, get rid of them,'' she cried in frustration when they wouldn't go down any farther.

Rolling away from her, Warrick laughed softly, teasingly, his eyes devouring her body. She was nude except for the lacy next-to-nothing she still had on.

She was magnificent, he thought. Somehow, he'd always known she would be.

He kicked off his pants. ''Your wish is my command.''

''Not hardly,'' she countered as his mouth came down again on hers.

She tangled her fingers in the underwear he'd left on. It was small, covering just enough. Conservatively black. Somehow she'd known he wouldn't wear boxers. It excited her.

Everything about him excited her.

She kicked the last of her own underwear away after he'd teased them slowly down her legs.

With a cry that was half victory, half surrender, she turned into him.

He kissed her lips, her chin, her throat, his hands massaging her body as he slowly worked his way downward, covering her belly, her navel, until he found the very core of her.

Her eyes flew open as the first shock wave hit, undulating all through her with a force that sucked away her ability to breathe.

She dug her fingers into his shoulders, trying to anchor herself to something before she was swept away. This was something new, something she'd never experienced before.

Her body continued to hum as he drew himself up along her, his skin rubbing over hers.

When he rolled his body onto hers, she summoned every last stitch of strength she had and moved quickly. Catching him off guard, she reversed their positions. He was looking up at her. There was surprise in his eyes. Good. She grinned at him.

''My turn,'' she announced and proceeded to emulate the path he had taken on her body.

She succeeded royally in heightening both his arousal as well as her own. With each pass of her lips, each nip of her teeth, each teasing flick of her tongue, she could feel her excitement rising up to a fever pitch. Could feel him wanting her.

She felt triumphant.

She felt eager.

And then his hands were on her shoulders. Gently he dragged her up along his body until his eyes were level with hers.

"No more turns," he told her, his voice low, deep. The promise in it penetrated her very being.

With a movement that was every bit as swift as her own had been, Warrick was suddenly over her, his body less than a breath away from hers. Tantalizing them both.

He laced his fingers with hers and entered.

Warrick felt her tightening around him instantly. He drove himself further into her. Her sharp intake of breath echoed in his mouth as he kissed her hard and with all the passion that had flowered within him.

The dance began, going ever faster with each second that passed. They were both master and prisoner of the other, all at the same time.

The dance brought them to a plane that was miles above anything either of them had ever imagined. Ever experienced.

With a cry C.J. arched against him, silently imploring him to bring the final climax before she died from wanting.

They moved faster and faster, each following the other, each inspiring the other.

The last crescendo came, sweeping them up and

over the plateau they had discovered together. He thought she cried out his name; he wasn't sure.

And when it was over, when the afterglow descended, embracing them with misty arms that held fast, he rolled off C.J. and then gathered her to him with his last ounce of energy.

He'd never felt so drained and so good before in his life.

Warrick had no idea what that meant, or what to make of it. Maybe he was feeling this way because it had been a while since he'd been with a woman.

He didn't know.

All he knew was that he liked being here with this one. For now.

His arm tightened around her as he waited for the world to stop spinning around.

Chapter 10

He was watching her.

She looked so pretty, the way her long, blond hair swayed along her back when she walked. He'd heard someone call her Jackie, but they were wrong.

She was Claire. Claire had come back to him.

She had the same hair, the same eyes. The same smile. She was Claire no matter what they called her.

His Claire.

And he had to make her his again. Just like the last time. His so that that she couldn't tell him to leave her alone, couldn't call him a frog.

No, not a frog, a toad. That was it, a toad. She'd called him a toad, but he knew she didn't mean it.

She was too pretty to be mean.

And she would smile at him when he gave her

her present, he knew she would. A secret smile only he could see.

He put his hand into his pocket. The little pearls felt smooth and shiny beneath his fingers. He couldn't wait to give it to her.

And when she wore it, she'd be his again.

Forever.

Just like the last time.

C.J. stirred. There was something heavy on her chest, something keeping her from drawing in a deep breath. Eyes still closed, she tried to push it away and realized that it was an arm. A man's arm.

She pried her eyes open. Warrick.

C.J. sat bolt upright. "Oh, God."

Warrick's eyes flew open, instantly alert, scanning the immediate vicinity to see what had caused the exclamation that was echoing even now in his head.

And then he saw C.J. sitting up next to him, completely devoid of makeup, her hair rumpled. C.J. looking like the best thing he'd ever seen. The sheet she held against her exposed more than it hid.

The fight-or-flight tension left his body. Another tension, far more pleasant, entered, taking its place. He felt something stirring within him. Hunger for food took a back seat to a different, even more basic kind of hunger.

Last night returned to him in vivid shades that made the room's decor pale in comparison.

"'Morning." Propping himself up on his elbows, he lightly swept his fingers along her cheek, brushing back the hair that had fallen into her eyes.

Her heart again on double time, C.J. jerked her head away. Every single disastrous story about doomed relationships in the workplace filed by her in a snaking conga line that jolted her system. At the end of the line was her own dismal experience with Tom Thorndyke.

He'd been an FBI special agent, too.

What the hell had she been thinking last night?

That was just it, she hadn't been thinking. Not for one second. What she'd been doing was feeling, always a bad move on her part.

"Yes," she acknowledge testily, "it is."

His rock-hard chest seemed to be mocking her. In an effort to save herself, she glanced toward the window. The sun was pushing its way through the clouds like a merchant, late opening up his store, pushing his way through the gathered throng.

"The rain stopped," she announced needlessly. "We can get going now."

Warrick glanced at the wristwatch he never removed. It was almost seven. Seven on a Sunday morning. Even God rested on Sunday. He was in no mood to hit the road just yet. Far more enjoyable scenarios presented themselves to him than a three-hour road trip.

Maybe it was because he felt that once they left this room, this site of their unexpected aberration, they would go back to being partners. Partners and nothing more.

He wanted more.

Just within the confines of this gaudy room, he

wanted more. He wanted to hold on to last night for just a little longer.

Was that too much to ask?

He slid light exploring fingers along C.J.'s bare back and saw her shiver in response. Saw her eyes flutter closed before springing open again.

"What's your hurry?" His question sounded incredibly seductive.

Even as she stiffened, tiny sensations had begun marching through her body, picketing for a return to last night. There was no denying that it had been leagues beyond wonderful. But that was last night. In the light of day, things had to be different. *Were* different.

"Stop touching me," she told him.

Slowly, seductively he withdrew his fingers. "Why?" He watched her face. "Because you don't like it?"

She wanted to lie. It was easier that way. Easier for her, maybe even for him. But she couldn't. Not even to save herself. Not to Warrick.

"Because I do like it."

The smile that curved his lips was nothing short of sensual and worked its way instantly beneath her skin, heating it.

"I'm beginning to understand why your parents called you Christmas." Warrick sat up, then pressed a single, soft kiss to her shoulder. Sending skyrockets launching through her. "Open the package and there's something entirely different under the wrappings." Lifting the hair away from her neck, he pressed another kiss there. C.J. felt herself losing ground. Rapidly. "You were quite a revelation last night."

It was getting hard for her to think again. What *was* this effect he had on her?

"I wasn't myself last night."

She felt his lips curving against her skin. He was smiling. She could feel warmth flowing to every part of her.

"Any chance of your secret identity making a reappearance this morning?" he asked.

He was dissolving her will faster than a gale traveling through soap suds. It was a struggle just to keep her eyes from shutting, her body from sinking back down. Her protest barely carried conviction. "Warrick, we're on a case—"

"We're on a bed," he countered, working his way to the other side of her neck. Causing miniquakes in her stomach. "And once we go out of this room, it's going to be business as usual. I want to stay here with you like this a little longer, maybe make a few more memories to sustain me." She felt his breath along her back. Everything inside of her tightened in anticipation. Suddenly she was looking up into his eyes as he cupped her cheek. It took everything she had not to curl into his palm. "Is that so bad?"

"No," she breathed. From some dark region, a little voice urged her to remember the fiasco that resulted when she had been with Thorndyke. She snapped to attention. "Yes. Look, we can't do this."

He knew that she was probably right, knew all the arguments against this. Knew only one argument for it. Because he wanted her. Again. ''Newsflash, we already *did* do this.''

''Okay.'' She told herself to get up out of bed. That's all she needed to do. After all, this was Warrick. She knew him. He wouldn't force her to do anything she didn't want to do. Wherein lay her problem. Because she *did* want to. ''We can't do this again.''

''Why?'' Straightening, he looked at her. Maybe they needed to say this aloud. ''We're both adults, both know the rules of the game.''

Right now, with Warrick touching her like that, looking at her like that, she wasn't sure she even knew her own name.

C.J. cleared her throat. It was impossibly dry. Where was saliva when you needed it? ''And those are?''

''No strings. No promises. Just two consenting adults…'' He smiled warmly into her eyes, touching her again. ''Consenting.''

She wondered what the melting point for people was. The way she felt, she was very nearly there. ''No strings?'' she echoed. That sounded good. In theory.

He nodded slowly, his eyes never leaving hers. ''No strings. We both know that strings only tangle you up, make you trip.''

''Right.'' He was absolutely right. So why did she suddenly want to start a string collection? Why this desire to gather together the world's biggest ball of twine? No, no, Warrick was right. They were two sane adults—hungering for a few insane moments.

Her heart was hammering too hard, surrendering the battle without a decent shot being fired. The next minute he had pulled her down until she was flat on her back and under him.

''Right,'' he echoed just before he brought his mouth down on hers.

The fire ignited a beat before his lips even touched hers. Anticipation had primed her response to him.

Primed her.

God help her, but she wanted this with every fiber of her being, even though she knew she shouldn't. In the light of day, with reason returning, she really shouldn't.

But she did.

The sound of bells began to peal in her soul, in her brain. Bells. Ringing.

The urgent sound took a moment before it penetrated. It took her a moment longer before she could identify it. Not bells, a cell phone. One of their cell phones was ringing.

Warrick had heard it, too. He lifted his head, drawing back. Impatience creased his forehead. They knew it could be important. He rose away from her, sitting back on his knees. ''Yours or mine?''

''I don't know.'' They both rang the same. Sitting up, still more than a little dazed, she looked where both cell phones lay on the nightstand where they'd been left last night. Obviously, the signal problem had cleared itself up. Talk about bad timing.

She picked up his first, then hers. Hers had the lit screen.

"Mine," she told him. Taking a deep breath, she hoped that she didn't sound breathless as she felt. "This is Jones."

"Chris, it's Mom."

Responses programmed before the beginning of time made C.J. pull the sheet up around her more tightly, covering her breasts. "Hi, Mom, what's up?"

"The baby's temperature."

"What?" Alert, concerned, C.J. sat up, swinging her legs over the side of the bed. Behind her, she felt Warrick tap her on the shoulder, silently asking to be enlightened. She waved him back, her attention riveted to the voice on the other end of the line. Something was wrong with her baby. "How high is it?"

Her mother didn't answer immediately, as if debating whether or not to tell her. "A hundred and two."

"Omigod."

The bed moved behind her. Warrick came around it to face her. "What is it?"

Shaking, she covered the receiver. "The baby has a 102-degree temperature." C.J. removed her hand, her attention back to her mother. How was this possible? She'd left the baby in perfect health just yesterday morning. "But she was all right when I called you last night."

"Baby's temperatures can suddenly go up and just as suddenly go down again. I didn't call to panic you, Chris. I knew you'd want to know. I've got a call in to her pediatrician."

Dr. DuCane had come with excellent references and she hadn't been disappointed when she'd met the woman. But this was her baby they were talking about. C.J. struggled to get ahold of herself.

"Maybe you should go to the emergency room with her, have the doctor meet you there." C.J. ran her hand over her forehead and tried to think. Why couldn't she think? Why was everything such a jumble in her head? She'd always been able to think on her feet before, that was her greatest strength. Up until now. "I'll be there as fast as I can."

"There's nothing you can do, honey," her mother told her. "Everything's being taken care of. I don't want you breaking any speed limits. Ethan had a fever of 106 once, and he's still with us." She recited chapter and verse from a book that had guided her through all five of her children's childhoods. "'Babies temperatures fluctuate all over the place until they're seven.'"

She didn't care about other babies, she cared about hers. And she needed to be there with her.

"I'll be there as soon as possible," C.J. reiterated. "Call me after you talk to the doctor."

Slapping the cover down on the phone as she ended the conversation, she realized that her hands were shaking. This having a baby was so much harder than she thought. Labor was only the beginning.

"Here."

C.J. looked up and saw that Warrick had gathered her clothes together and had placed them on the bed next to her. He was stepping into his underwear.

Even in the midst of a crisis, she couldn't help thinking that he had to have one of the most magnificent bodies she had ever seen. The next moment she upbraided herself. What kind of a mother *was* she, having the hots for someone while her baby was burning up?

"We can be on the road in fifteen minutes," he told her. She nodded in response. Something on her face must have caught his attention because he stopped after he pulled up his pants and buttoned them. "She's going to be all right, C.J." She didn't remember ever hearing him sound so comforting. "Babies get sick all the time."

She snapped out of her stupor and began hurrying into her clothes. "That's what my mother said."

"She ought to know." He pushed his arms through his sleeves and quickly buttoned his shirt. "She raised five of you."

C.J. nodded, knowing she should have felt comforted. Knowing that all she felt was scared.

After one quick ten-minute stop at a drive-through for something that vaguely passed as breakfast, plus four containers of black coffee, they were on the road for home.

The tension inside the vehicle was almost tangible. There was tension because they hadn't had the opportunity to either redefine or renew the boundaries that they had crossed over last night, nor would they. Not until the reason for the preponderance of tension was resolved.

When they'd left the motel, C.J. had gone to the driver's side. Warrick blocked her and claimed the wheel. "I don't think you're in any condition to drive right now, and I don't have a death wish." He'd expected an argument. Instead she'd merely nodded her head and gone to the passenger side.

That was when he knew the extent of her concern.

The silence was making him uneasy. Warrick turned on the radio, selecting a station he knew she liked over one for himself. They had extremely different taste in music. Hers was modern, his leaned toward the oldies. Anything after 1970 was far too modern for him.

He glanced at her profile. If she was any more rigid, she would have qualified as granite. He pressed down on the accelerator. The speedometer climbed over the legal limit.

"She's going to be all right," he finally said, breaking the silence for the second time. He wasn't even sure she'd heard him the first time around.

I have to believe that, C.J. thought desperately. Anything else was unthinkable. Two months into the relationship and she couldn't imagine her life without her daughter. But she was so little....

C.J. clenched her hands in her lap as she tore her mind away from going through that door. She refused to allow herself to think of anything bad happening.

She slanted a look in his direction. There was something comforting about his smile. "Thanks," she whispered.

He glanced at the rearview mirror to make sure there were no police cars in the vicinity. The road had opened up and there were no other cars in either direction. ‘‘For what?’’

Her nails were sinking into her palms. She unclenched her hands. ‘‘For not saying ‘I told you so.’ ’’

Where the hell had that come from? ‘‘Why would I say that?’’

Didn’t he remember? ‘‘You were the one who told me to stay home. Twice.’’

Warrick carefully negotiated a curve, then resumed his former speed. ‘‘And what…if you were home, the fever wouldn’t have happened?’’

He made the basis of her guilt and self-reproach sound foolish. ‘‘No, but—’’

He didn’t give her a chance to come up with an argument. The whole thing was ridiculous.

‘‘And don’t tell me that if you were home, you would have handled it any better than your mother’s handling it right now. You probably would have called her for advice.’’ When she said nothing, Warrick spared her a look. ‘‘Am I wrong?’’

C.J. dragged her hand through her hair. ‘‘No, you’re right.’’ A hint of a smile slipped over her lips. ‘‘Damn it, I really do hate saying that.’’

Warrick grinned. ‘‘That’s just your natural competitiveness coming to the fore.’’ The road stretched unobstructed for the next two miles. He spared her a look. ‘‘You know, C.J., just because you grew up in a house full of competitive boys who you were constantly pitting yourself against doesn’t mean that everyone is interested in competing with you.’’

As if they hadn’t been in constant competition

from the first moment they were partnered up. ''Are you turning over a new leaf?''

''I was never in competition with you.'' Warrick paused for a moment, then couldn't resist adding, ''I was your mentor.''

She shifted in her seat to look at him. ''I beg your pardon, who was whose mentor?'' She was the one with seniority, albeit only by six weeks. In actuality they had grown up together at the Bureau.

''There you go again, competing.'' A motorcycle policeman was approaching from the opposite direction. Warrick eased back on the accelerator. He glanced in her direction and smiled. It was nice to have her bounce back.

They didn't bother going first to the federal building but instead went directly to her parents' house. Warrick barely had time to stop the car before she was jumping out and hurrying up the walk.

''Remember to open the door, not tear it off its hinges,'' he called after her.

C.J. ignored him as she fumbled with her keys, then opened the door. Her mother was in the living room. Her father sat in his recliner, holding a fussing baby in his arms.

She crossed to him immediately and took the baby in her arms, breathlessly asking, ''How is she? Did she see the doctor? What did the doctor say?''

Behind her, she heard Warrick come in and close the door.

''Dr. DuCane came to her office and saw her,''

her father told her. "She said it would be less costly that way."

"I don't care about the cost. How *is* she?" In time-honored tradition C.J. pressed a kiss to her daughter's forehead to check for a fever. The baby was warm but not burning up the way she'd feared.

"Dr. DuCane prescribed an antibiotic. Your father's already picked it up at the drugstore." Her mother's voice, for once, was calm, soothing. "She has otitis media." C.J. looked at her mother blankly. "Middle ear infection," Diane explained. "You and Wayne were both prone to that when you were little."

C.J. frowned, kissing the baby's forehead again. "She still feels warm."

Diane leaned over and performed her own test. "Her fever's down considerably from late last night. But don't get alarmed if it shoots up again." She spoke from experience. "Children can be sick in the morning, perfectly fine in the afternoon and sick again in the evening."

C.J. sighed. This was a great deal more than she'd thought she'd signed on for initially. Her stomach felt as if it was tied up in knots. "God, when does it stop, Mom?"

"I don't know." Diane laughed softly. "How old are you now?"

C.J. cradled the baby against her. The fussing had lessened a degree. "Point taken."

"You can stay here tonight if you'd like," her mother invited. "I can get your old room ready."

C.J. was sorely tempted by the offer. It would be

easy just to let her mother take over. She was clearly the expert here. But she didn't want to grow dependent on her mother's help. She had to do this on her own.

"Thanks." She addressed both her mother and her father, knowing that he had probably been right there, taking his turn at pacing the floor with the baby. "But I just want to get her home and into her own bed."

"Fine." Diane accepted her daughter's choice. "Then I'll come along with you."

C.J. was torn. There was pride and then there was stupidity. She'd already done one stupid thing in the past twenty-four hours. She wasn't about to go for two. Her protest lacked conviction. "You don't have to do that, Mom."

Diane read between the lines. She'd been a young mother once, too. "Don't worry, I'm not crowding you. I'll just stay long enough to give you an opportunity to shower and change your clothes. You want to get the feel of the road off you, don't you?"

C.J. looked at Warrick significantly. "Yes, I guess that's for the best."

Chapter 11

"You gave me quite a scare there, kidlet."

Finished feeding the baby, C.J. got up from the kitchen table and put the empty bottle on the counter with one hand while she held her daughter close to her with the other. It had been a tough few hours, but, as her mother had promised, things were settling down again. The baby's fever was gone. Thank God.

Walking to the living room, she kissed the top of her baby's head. The soft, fine blond hair brushed against her lips. Not quite ready to put her down for the night, C.J. took her into living room and sat down on the sofa. She needed to give the baby her medicine, anyway.

She looked down at the small face that seemed to watch her with rapt attention. "Of course, I'm new at this, you realize, but I think I might have this panic thing under control.''

C.J. knew better, actually. She had a feeling there would always be an element of underlying panic involved. It was only a matter of how well she hid it when it occurred and how well she performed under its influence.

''Until the next time, probably.'' The baby nestled against her, C.J. unscrewed the top and measured out the prescribed dose on a curved baby teaspoon. ''Now take your medicine like a good girl. The pharmacist told Grandpa it tastes like bubblegum.'' She laughed at that. ''Yeah, right, like you know what bubblegum tastes like. Time enough for that later, when I'm not afraid you're going to swallow it.'' She smiled as the baby's lips parted and she swallowed the medicine without complaint. ''That's a good girl, Joy.''

Then, putting the teaspoon down on the coffee table beside the bottle, C.J. looked at her daughter again and shook her head. She'd been so worried, so scared returning home. How had her mother done it? How had she survived five of them?

''Your grandmother's incredible, cupcake, I hope you know that.'' She rose again, patting the baby on the back. As she started for the stairs, someone rang her doorbell. Perfect timing.

''You expecting anyone?'' she asked the baby. ''It's too late for the Avon lady.'' Setting the baby down in the portacrib she had set up beside the sofa, C.J. made her way to the front door. ''Who is it?''

''Ice-cream man.''

Even through the door, she recognized the voice. C.J. swung open the door. ''Warrick? Was there a break in the case?''

''No, no break.'' He held up the paper bag he was holding. ''I just thought you might need one, so I brought you some ice cream.''

She looked at him incredulously. ''At ten o'clock at night?''

''I stayed late at the office, thought I'd tackle some paperwork for a change.'' He always put it off as long as he could. It was his least favorite part of the job. Warrick nodded at the car in the driveway. ''I see Rodriguez dropped off your car like I asked.''

''Yes, he got here about six. Thanks.''

''No problem. Are you planning on letting me in anytime soon, or would you rather just lick melted mint chip ice cream straight off your doorstep?''

''Sorry about that.'' C.J. stepped to the side, letting him pass. ''Mint chip, huh?'' Grinning, she looked down at the bag and recognized the emblem on the side. He'd bought the ice cream at a place where she and the other Mom Squad members used to congregate after Lamaze classes. C.J. raised her eyes to his. ''You stopped at the Ice Cream Parlor?''

''You were always raving about their ice cream, I figured why not.'' She closed the door behind him. ''It was on the way.''

The hell it was. ''To the opposite side of town.''

He frowned, thrusting the bag at her. ''Just take it, will you, and stop talking.'' Warrick crossed to the portacrib and looked down at his special delivery. The baby's eyes had drifted closed. He lowered his voice as he asked, ''So how's she doing?''

C.J. was in the kitchen, getting a couple of bowls from the cabinet. ''Her fever's down, thank goodness. She's still fussing, but I think the worst is over.''

He could hear the relieved smile in her voice. Warrick lingered a moment longer by the portacrib. Funny how something so little could hold on to your heart so tightly, he mused.

He crossed into the kitchen. ''I figured I'd see your mother here.''

''I sent her home a few hours ago.'' C.J. scooped out two servings. It hadn't been easy, finally getting her mother to leave. ''She left under protest, but I've got to get a handle on this mothering thing on my own.'' She handed Warrick his bowl, then picked up her own and walked over to the kitchen table. Pulling out a chair, she sat down. ''I can't keep depending on her.''

''One time doesn't make you hopelessly dependent, C.J.'' Sampling his portion, he raised his eyebrows in surprise. ''Hey, this is good.''

She smiled as she slid in another spoonful. ''Told you.''

Damn but she looked sensual, slipping the spoon between her lips like that. Warrick forced his mind back onto the subject and took another heaping spoonful for good measure.

''You know, accepting help doesn't make you a bad mother—it makes you a rested mother,'' he pointed out. ''Speaking of which, why don't I stick around for a while after we finish our ice cream, maybe let you catch a catnap."

She knew he probably meant well, but it was still an affront to her capabilities. "I don't need a catnap, or any other animal nap."

"Sure you do." His grin was wicked as it came into his eyes. "You didn't exactly get much sleep last night."

Was he gloating? She couldn't tell. "Neither did you."

He inclined his head in agreement. "Which is why I'm only going to spell you for a few hours." He indicated the bowl before her. "Now eat your ice cream like a good girl and do what I tell you."

She laughed shortly. "In your dreams. Since when did you become in charge?"

"The captain is relieved of duty when showing signs of undue stress and/or insanity," he recited. "Sleep deprivation has been known to cause both." He polished off his own bowl and debated getting a second serving. "Now eat, sleep, and I'll take care of the merry."

"That's eat, *drink* and be merry," she corrected. Maybe she should relent a little. Nobody could do everything. "You're nuts, you know that?" Her laugh was affectionate.

"I know." He pulled the carton over to him and scooped out half a serving more. The serious look in his eyes was at odds with his light tone. "My partner made me that way."

Why was it that she could almost feel his words dancing along her skin?

''Okay,'' she lowered her eyes to her bowl. Communing with green ice cream was a great deal safer right now than looking into Warrick's eyes. ''I'll let you stay—but just for a little while.''

C.J. looked up from her cluttered desk. Every pile on it represented another possible lead that had to be checked out. Hopefully somewhere was the legitimate tip that would lead them to the killer.

But right now, she was frowning at Warrick. She hadn't seen him when she'd first walked in this morning. He'd pulled phone duty and she'd thought it was best to stay away before someone asked her to do the same.

''You shouldn't have let me sleep that long.''

He downed the last of his less than mediocre coffee, then put his mug down on the corner of his desk. ''You needed it. Besides, the baby slept right along with you.'' He was honest about his limitations. ''If I'd had to face a dirty diaper, maybe I would have woken you up sooner.'' He'd left her house at two in the morning to get a few hours of sleep himself before going in to the office. ''Feel any better today?''

''Yes. Thanks.''

He grinned, digging in again. ''Don't mention it.''

''I'm also probably five pounds heavier, thanks to the ice cream.''

He laughed. ''Hey, nobody told you to finish it.'' His eyes swept over her. ''Besides, the five pounds look as if they found a good home. You always were a little too thin.''

She arched a brow. "I beg your pardon?"

The assistant director, Edward Alberdeen, picked that moment to walk in, curtailing any further exchange.

"Heads up, people." His booming voice brought everything within the noisy room to a standstill. "Our boy's struck again."

Warrick was the first to reach the A.D. It was a grim fact of life that every new strike meant that much more of a chance that there might be a slip-up, a clue that would finally lead them to their quarry. But the grim reality was that it also meant someone else had died.

"Are we sure it's him this time?" They all knew he was referring to the wild-goose chase he and C.J. had gone on on Saturday. "Lots of people are getting edgy, seeing things that aren't there."

In reply, Alberdeen placed the photograph he'd just received via a colored fax and turned it around so that Warrick, C.J. and the others could all see. The woman in the photograph looked like all the others: blond, a rose clutched in her hands, a cheap pearl choker on her neck to hide the bruising.

"We're sure," he replied grimly. "The M.E. thinks death was within the last twelve hours." He looked down at the photograph, shaking his head. "She's dressed as if she was going to a party."

"Maybe she was. Maybe our killer picked her up and decided to add her to his collection," C.J. suggested. She looked at Alberdeen. "We have a name?"

"Jackie Meyers. Purse wasn't touched, same as

the others. Mother made a positive ID. Here's the address.'' The A.D. handed it to Warrick. ''Go canvass the area, see if we can get lucky this time.'' He said what they'd been saying since the very beginning. ''He's got to slip up sometime.''

''You'd think,'' C.J. muttered under her breath. She looked at the photograph again. It was the face of pure innocence. Just like the other victims had appeared. ''Damn, it's a shame.''

''It's always a shame when someone's murdered,'' Alberdeen interjected. ''You getting anywhere with that theory of yours, Jones?''

She looked back at the piles on her desk. She was going to have to apply good old-fashioned legwork to them soon. With no other strong leads to follow, she'd gone back to her theory that perhaps their killer had been away either in prison or a mental facility somewhere in the county for the past three years and had taken up where he'd left off as soon as he was released. Another possibility was that he might have enlisted. But no other murders matching the killer's MO had turned up anywhere else, so she was less inclined to go that route.

''Not yet. Checking out former inmates is slow work, A.D. Orange County has its fair share of loonies and felons.''

The expression on the A.D.'s long, thin face said that no one had to tell him that. ''Well, keep at it. We don't have much else to go on—yet.''

She nodded, then glanced at the address in Warrick's hand. It wasn't far from where she lived. Had she known the girl, passed her in the mall, perhaps in the supermarket?

The thought of the Sleeping Beauty Killer lurking somewhere close by made C.J.'s blood run cold. Suddenly, she felt too restless to just sit behind a desk. "Okay let's go, boys, and see if we can't catch ourselves a killer."

Warrick gestured toward the door. "You heard the lady, let's roll."

Warrick looked at her as they drove back to the field office. They'd put in a long day, interviewing all the people Jackie Meyers might have interacted with on her last day. A few names had been provided by the girl's mother, and they had gone from there.

The silence got to him. "You're being awfully quiet—again."

She shook her head, as if unaware of her lapse. "I was just thinking how much I hate having to talk to the parents of a victim."

The girl had lived with her widowed mother. The woman broke down twice while talking to them. C.J.'s heart went out to her, but there was nothing she could do. Except catch the killer.

She only hoped that she could.

Warrick slowed down as a late-model Thunderbird merged into his lane in front of them. "Not exactly on my top five list of favorite things, either, C.J." He blew out a breath. The case was getting to all of them. "I wish we'd catch a break."

"Yeah, me, too." She stared out the window, trying desperately to keep her mind focused only on the case and nothing more. Or, if it drifted in any direction, that it only settle on thoughts about her daughter. Anything but on the man sitting beside her.

She'd made up her mind this morning on the way to work after she'd dropped off the baby with her mother that what had happened between her and Warrick that night outside of Santa Barbara was a mixture of opportunity, curiosity and, just possibly, stress. Why else would she have been so vulnerable? So willing to do something she knew damn well was a mistake?

Okay, so somewhere in her mind she'd always wondered what it would be like to be kissed by Warrick, to make love with him.

Now she knew.

Now she could move on.

The hell she could, she thought.

Didn't matter what she felt, what she wanted—again. She just wasn't going to go there. He was a box of chocolates and she was on a diet and that's all there was to that.

Maybe.

Stopping at a light, Warrick glanced at her. "I never thought I'd say this, but I do miss the sound of your voice. Talk to me, C.J. Bounce theories off me. Something. Anything."

She mentally grabbed on to the lifeline he threw her. That's what this was all about, what it *should* be about: catching the killer, not about an itch she couldn't allow herself to scratch again. The last time she scratched, she was left pregnant and her pride was devastated. She wasn't going to go through that again.

Warrick might not be another Thorndyke, but he wasn't her Prince Charming, either.

She forced her mind back on the case.

C.J. watched the early evening traffic as it went by in both directions. Was the killer in one of these cars? Or was he safely hiding inside his house, waiting for the cover of night before he ventured out to make a move? When would he make a move?

''We're going to be hearing from the crazies again,'' she finally said. The crazies, well-meaning callers and nut jobs who came out of the woodwork to point fingers in a quest for the limelight, give tips that led nowhere and periodically made confessions that ninety-nine times out of a hundred weren't true. Every crime brought them out in droves.

She and the others had all put in their time on the phones, hoping against hope that the next call would be the one that would lead them somewhere.

''Maybe we'll get lucky,'' Warrick said, ''and Alberdeen'll bring in more people to handle the phones.''

She laughed, turning toward him. ''You're kidding, right? Alberdeen's a company man. Cost conscious to the ultimate degree. He'll just make everyone work harder until this guy's caught.''

''If this guy is caught,'' he amended.

C.J. frowned. ''Damn your pessimism, Warrick. *When,*'' she repeated, daring him to contradict her.

Warrick shrugged carelessly. "When," he echoed just to appease her.

He certainly hoped she was right, but odds were not in their favor. They never were. For every crime that was solved, a great many more weren't.

He wished he could stop thinking about C.J. Whenever he wasn't around her, she dominated his thoughts and had ever since they'd slept together last Saturday. The harder he tried to eradicate her from his mind, the less he succeeded.

Sleeping with her hadn't satisfied anything, just as kissing hadn't. It only made him want more. Working alongside of her didn't help matters any, either, but he couldn't very well ask for another partner. If nothing else, it would have been cowardly.

Besides, she was a damn good partner and what she lacked in self-discipline, she more than made up for in tenacity and enthusiasm. He didn't want to work with anyone else. He just didn't want to keep thinking about her *that* way. It was frustrating the hell out of him.

Warrick stopped by her desk. She'd been at it all morning, calling the various people on her lists, narrowing them down as best she could. No one on the outside realized how tedious the work that went into apprehending a killer could be.

He was behind her. She could feel it. It wasn't exactly the way it used to be, when she had almost a sixth sense about her partner. Now it was more.

Now it was driving her crazy.

He flipped a page. ''Come up with any good suspects yet?''

Several. None. It all depended on how you looked at it. ''I'm winnowing it down to a manageable crowd.'' She pointed to a clipboard on her desk. ''Those I plan to interview face-to-face.'' She glanced up at him and smiled. ''Yeah, I know what you're thinking. Glutton for punishment, that's me.''

Especially, she added silently, where he was concerned. They were alone in the office, something that didn't happen very often. She decided to screw up her courage and confront him with what had been nagging at her ever since Sunday. ''Why haven't you called me?''

He stared at her. Was she turning all female on him, wanting to know ''where this is going'' and throw a noose around his neck? ''What?''

''You don't drop by to hang out anymore.'' She didn't want him getting the wrong idea. She just wanted her partner back. If she wanted anything else, that was her problem, not theirs. ''My brothers want to know what I did to you.''

The word *nothing* was right there, waiting to be set free. But it was a lie. She'd done something to him, all right, he just didn't know exactly what to call it. ''Do people still use the word *bedeviled?*''

C.J. cocked her head, determined to keep this light, determined to get back on even keel. ''Only if they have long lacy cuffs and wear powdered wigs.'' She looked at him. ''So what do I tell them? My brothers,'' she prompted when he didn't say anything.

"Tell them the truth. That I've been burning the midnight oil on this case." The case had just taken on major proportions. "It seems the last victim was also the niece of a congressman from Nevada. There's pressure to bring this guy in as soon as possible."

C.J. leaned back in her chair, looking at the screen on her monitor but not really seeing it. She had been toying with a thought for the past two days. Maybe it was time to say it out loud and see how it fared in the light of day.

"Maybe it's not a guy." She could see the skepticism on Warrick's face. "Maybe it's a jealous woman. There *are* female serial killers."

"Not many," he pointed out. He couldn't think of more than a handful. "And she'd have to be strong. All the bodies were moved."

"Not so strong," C.J. countered. She looked at the bulletin board with its photographs of the victims. "Most of the women were small." That fed her theory. "Maybe that's one of the things she has against them. In this image-conscious world, maybe they typify everything she isn't." C.J. shrugged. It was thin, but there was a possibility she could be right. "It might explain the nail polish."

"What, that she's playing house with them? Or beauty parlor?" Warrick shook his head. "I think you're reaching."

She blew out a breath and pushed herself away from the desk. C.J. rose to her feet. Maybe it was time for a break. There was a candy bar in the vending machine with her name on it. "Damn straight

I'm reaching. Reaching for anything I can latch on to, hoping to catch a break."

As she was about to go out the door, Rodriguez stuck his head in. "Guess what?"

"Your fiancée came to her senses and called off the engagement?" Warrick deadpanned behind her.

"Very funny. We think we might have caught a break. Someone just called in saying they remember seeing a car parked in the vicinity where the last body was found. He puts it there around the time the M.E. guessed the victim was killed."

C.J. wasn't biting just yet. "And why would this 'witness' remember that?"

"Because he said he came damn near close to hitting the car. It was half-hidden in the shadows. As a matter of fact, he thinks that maybe he might have scraped a fender."

This was too much to hope for. C.J. tried not to let her enthusiasm go just yet. "This so-called witness wouldn't have by any chance taken down the license plate number, would he?"

Rodriguez grinned. "He did better than that, he took a picture."

C.J. and Warrick exchanged looks. Maybe this *was* too good to be true.

"What?" C.J. cried.

"Why?" Warrick wanted to know.

Rodriguez couldn't wait to tell them. "Listen to this. He said he was burned badly in a minor fender bender once. Hardly tapped the car and the other guy sued him for a hundred grand one day short of a year to the date of the accident. The other guy's car was a wreck and his insurance company wound up dropping him.''

''The point, Rodriguez, the point,'' Warrick prodded impatiently.

''I'm getting to it,'' the other man told him. ''Since then, our witness has been driving around with one of these disposable cameras in his car.''

''Thank God for paranoid people,'' C.J. commented. Taking her purse out, she kicked the drawer shut again. ''Let's go see that witness and get that picture.''

''You don't really think there's anything to this, do you?'' Culpepper had walked in just in time to get the general gist of the story. He looked dubious now.

''Hey, Son of Sam was caught because of unpaid traffic tickets,'' C.J. reminded him. ''Stranger things have happened. Solving a case requires hundreds of hours of dedicated work—and one lucky, totally unrelated break. I hope this is ours.'' She looked at Warrick. ''Wanna join me?''

''As if you could stop me,'' he rejoined, heading out the door right behind her.

''Hey, it was my phone call,'' Rodriguez called after them.

''And we'll see that you get full credit,'' C.J. promised. ''All I want,'' she told Warrick as he pressed for the elevator, ''is this guy's head on a platter.''

''You'll get no argument from me.''

''First time for everything,'' she quipped as she got into the elevator.

Chapter 12

Harry Maxwell was a quiet, soft-spoken man in his midthirties. He lived in a one-bedroom apartment in a run-down building that was situated in the heart of Santa Ana. A trace through the DMV using the photograph of the rear of the vehicle with its license plate supplied by their paranoid witness had led them to Maxwell's door.

After they had identified themselves, Maxwell had hesitantly let them come in. It was clear that the mild-mannered man was not at his best with people. He told them that he liked dogs best. There were three of no particular breed in the apartment that C.J. could see. Possibly more in another room.

He'd led them to his postage-size living room and offered them a seat on his sagging corduroy sofa. Harry perched on the coffee table, the only other furniture in the room besides an old TV mounted on a shipping barrel older than he was.

Small brown eyes bounded back and forth from C.J.'s face to Warrick's as he patiently answered their questions about his vehicle.

He nodded twice at the last question. "Yes, my car was parked by William Mason Park three nights ago. I'm not sure about the time." The admission was made fearfully. "Was that illegal?" His voice was hurried, breathless as he made his apology. "I'm sorry, I stop there all the time. Mostly at night. To think. There's nobody there then. I like it better that way. I won't do it again if it's wrong."

He made C.J. think of someone who had the word *victim* painted in neon colors on his forehead. The kind of man who, when he was a boy, everyone ridiculed. Even the geeks.

Was it an act? Or the truth?

Warrick was incredibly patient as he calmed the man down. "We just want to find out if you saw anyone there that night."

After taking a moment to think, Harry shook his head vigorously. "No. Some ducks, but that's all. Should I stop going there?" he pressed. It was clear that he hoped the answer was no.

C.J. smiled at him kindly. "It might be a good idea to go when the park's open. There's no attendant at night."

At night the gate was closed, but it didn't really offer much of a deterrent. Except for a small three-foot wooden fence around the perimeter, the park was wide-open, easily accessible from the road on foot. Bedford had a low crime rate. People tended to feel safer there.

Until they were killed, C.J. thought.

A shy smile twisted the man's lips as he looked at C.J.. "Thank you. I'll remember that."

C.J. exchanged glances with Warrick, then took out her card. "If you happen to think of anything unusual you might have seen that night after we leave, please give me a call."

He read the card intently. "Yes, ma'am, um, Special Agent..." Harry's voice trailed off as he looked at her hesitantly again, obviously at a loss as to what to call her.

"Agent Jones will do," C.J. told him. She rose to her feet. Warrick followed suit. She nodded at Harry. "Thank you for your time."

C.J. waited until she and Warrick were back inside their own vehicle before turning to him and asking, "What do you think?"

"Could be an act," he allowed. "But right off the top of my head, I'd say he's genuine, which means he's not our guy."

She buckled up as he started up the car. "He looks about as harmless as an anesthetized flea."

There was a break in traffic and Warrick darted in. Someone honked impatiently behind him. He glanced at C.J. "I'm trying to picture that."

If he wasn't their man, then they were back to where they started, wading through the endless phone tips that came in with nothing else to go on. "Never mind, let's just drive back."

The streets in that part of Santa Ana were narrow,

barely allowing enough room for the flow of single-lane traffic and parked cars by the curb. Warrick waited until they were stopped at a light. There seemed to be one every few hundred yards. ''So, any news about the christening?''

Father Gannon was still in Ireland. It seemed, miracle of miracles, that his eighty-three-year-old mother had rallied and was on the mend. C.J. had spoken with the secretary, who seemed very hopeful about the priest's pending return. C.J. was keeping her fingers crossed. Father Gannon had been the one to marry her parents and had officiated at all five of their christenings. She was determined that he would baptize her daughter, as well. No one else would do.

''Tentatively it's set for two weeks from Saturday.''

Warrick took his foot off the brake. They began inching their way to the next light. ''Your daughter's going to be applying to college before she ever gets baptized. Or a middle name.'' He slanted a quick look at her profile. ''You haven't by any chance—''

''No,'' C.J. snapped, knowing exactly what he was going to ask. ''I haven't.''

Warrick grinned as he shook his head. ''Touchy.''

She wasn't touchy, she was desperate. And it wasn't as if she had a clear head and could concentrate on nothing else. There was the added complication of the serial killer they were trying to catch, not to mention that her personal life had been set on its ear because of one fatal slip in a motel room. She was as afraid as ever of getting hurt, but now not quite so sure that she was swearing off all men for life.

C.J. concentrated on the dilemma under discussion. ''Look, this is getting worse, not better. Every time I think I have a name, I use it a couple of times and it just doesn't feel right calling her that.'' She shrugged. He was a man, he wouldn't understand. Men understood very little.

Warrick blew out a breath. ''You're making this way more complicated than it is. Names don't have to feel, C.J., they just have to be.''

She frowned deeply. Why did she ever think she'd get any support from him? ''You're beginning to sound like my mother.''

Warrick laughed at the comparison. ''I'm not insulted. I like your mother.''

''A little support wouldn't hurt, you know.''

''I gave you support,'' he reminded her. ''I came over with not one names-for-the-baby book, but two. Any normal person...'' His voice trailed off. ''Sorry, forgot who I was talking to.''

''Very funny. I'll come up with a name and it'll be perfect.'' She sighed as she looked out the window. They were still going nowhere. In so many ways. ''Back to canvassing,'' she murmured, sliding down a little in her seat. She hated going around in circles, ending up where she'd started.

His sigh was an echo of her own. ''Yeah.''

C.J. rubbed her temples. Everything was getting blurry.

She'd been at it for the past four hours straight,

staring at screen after screen of inmate names. It felt as if she was going cross-eyed. This was probably going to lead nowhere, just like everything else. She began to doubt the validity of her initial premise, that the killer had been locked away for three years, unable to continue his gruesome spree.

Maybe she should just knock it off for the time being, do something more useful. C.J. started to close the program when a name caught her eye.

She blinked and looked at it again, then blinked one more time, almost convinced that she was imagining it. It certainly wouldn't have been the first time she'd misread a name.

The name remained where it was. In the center of the list of inmates released from the county jail in the last six months.

She was afraid to raise her eyes, afraid the name would disappear. This was too good to be true. Too good to be a coincidence. "Hey, Warrick?"

"What?"

He realized that he'd snapped the word at her. The combination of sifting through endless "tips," all of which had to be investigated before being disregarded, and the tension that had all but become a permanent part of his day had momentarily gotten the better of him.

He had help with the sifting, everyone on the task force was taking turns at that. But the tension, well, that was a whole different matter entirely. That was his own damn fault.

His and C.J.'s.

He should never have followed through on his

curiosity that night. If you don't know, you don't miss. And he did. Missed the feel of her. Missed making love with her. Missed it a great deal.

Could that kind of thing happen after just one night together?

He didn't think it could, but then, if it couldn't, why did he feel this way? As if he'd been turned inside out and every part of him was aching to have her again. He hadn't even felt this way when he'd slept with his ex-wife the first time.

The memory of his ex-wife threw cold water on his thoughts. Now there was one hell of a mistake, marrying her. His ego wasn't inflated, but he knew he was sharp when it came to working his cases, sharp when it came to picking through clues. But he was hopelessly inept when it came to relationships that didn't involve a Bureau-issued vehicle or weapon.

''Sorry,'' he apologized, running his hand over his forehead. ''Just tired. What have you got?''

She knew she shouldn't allow herself to get carried away, but there had been so many dead ends that the slightest glimmer of something turned into a veritable rainbow of multicolored lights.

She put her finger on the screen, marking her place and looked over toward Warrick. ''Guess who was released five months ago from the county jail?''

''The Easter Bunny, I don't know, C.J. It's a little late to be playing games.'' Despite his less-than-cheerful mood, he got up and came up behind her to see what her sudden burst of excitement was all about.

''Harry Maxwell.'' She read what was on the screen despite the fact that Warrick was standing behind her and could see for himself. ''He was convicted of driving around in a stolen vehicle. Claimed he thought it was his. First-time offense, extenuating circumstances and a little creative lawyering got him a reduced sentence.''

''What is it about Maxwell and cars?'' Warrick commented. Unlike C.J. he reserved his excitement until they could come up with something more tangible.

''I don't know.'' She was beaming at him. ''But guess how long he was in prison?''

Warrick skimmed down the screen, reading. ''Three years.''

''Bingo.'' She swung her chair around to face him. ''Give the man a prize.''

Because the change in position placed her practically against him, C.J. moved her chair back again. Spears of heat went through her. Stupid time for a carnal reaction, she upbraided herself. She was getting paid to work on the case, not foster the hots for Warrick.

''So, what do we have here?'' Warrick reviewed the situation out loud. ''A man who's been out of circulation for three years—''

C.J. held up a finger. This was not to be shrugged off. ''The length of time that the killings stopped,'' she emphasized.

''And his car is seen near the vicinity where the body of the last victim was found.'' He looked at C.J. She knew better. ''Circumstantial evidence, nothing more. The grand jury would never indict on this.''

She sighed, deflated. ''I know, I know, we need something else.''

He turned her around to look at him. She had good hunches and he'd learned to listen to them, no matter what he said to the contrary. ''Do you really think that guy's our killer?''

C.J. could tell by his tone that Warrick was highly skeptical. She could see his point, even agree with his point after meeting Maxwell, but something didn't allow her to rule the man out.

''Ted Bundy was gregarious,'' she reminded him. ''Nobody thought he did it, either. And he never fit any profile they came up with for the killer.''

A noise in the doorway had them both looking in that direction. Rodriguez and Culpepper walked in, one more tired looking than the other. They sank down in their respective chairs, both sighing almost simultaneously.

''Where've you been?'' C.J. looked from one man to the other. ''You both look as if someone wiped the floor with you.''

Culpepper grumbled, digging into his pocket for another stick of nicotine gum. ''Alberdeen's got us talking to the families of the victims again, trying to find some kind of link between them other than their looks.''

Warrick moved closer. ''And?''

Rodriguez looked disgusted. ''Still zilch.'' He nodded at C.J. ''He's got us asking questions you should be handling.''

She knew he didn't mean that as an insult, but Rodriguez, like Culpepper, had some very definite ideas about male and female territory. "Like?"

He pulled the top off the soda can he'd brought in with him and drank deeply before answering. "Like where they shopped, what beauty parlor they went to, you know, girl stuff."

C.J. laughed. She could just hear what the two men had to say about the assignment when the A.D. had given it to them. "Consider it an education for when you get married."

"I don't need an education." He drank again, obviously totally parched. "Jane goes to a place called Nina's. I don't like her going because it's not in the best neighborhood, but she raves about it. Wants me to go get my hair styled there, too," he laughed incredulously, running a hand through his mop of curling black hair. "Can you just picture that, me in a place like that? I told her real men don't get their hair styled." He thumped his chest. "Just cut."

"Nina's?" Culpepper echoed, chewing on the name. "Hey, wasn't that the name of the beauty parlor the last victim went to the day she died?" His dull eyes brightened as he looked at his partner. "Her mother said something about her wanting to look her best for that party." He glanced at the bulletin board where the young woman's photograph had been added to the others. "Poor kid."

Warrick suddenly started riffling through his notes. Pads and loose pages began sliding down right and left, some falling on the floor. Culpepper stared at him, puzzled. ''What's the matter with you?''

''I've heard that name before.'' Finding the right set of notes seemed almost impossible. His desk had taken on the appearance of the aftermath of a particularly devastating tornado.

''How?'' C.J. pressed, getting up and crossing to his side. Offhand, she didn't remember hearing the name. ''One of the people we interviewed?''

''No, one of the victims.'' He was digging through things with both hands, stopping to read, then discard. ''I think she was working there before she was killed.'' He suddenly remembered the name and went to a different pile. Warrick scanned a couple of notes, then held the spiral pad aloft. ''Yeah, here it is. Victim number one. Claire Farrel.'' He read further. ''No, I was wrong, she wasn't working there, she'd quit the week before.''

More coincidences? C.J. wondered. But something in her gut told her that they were more than just that. She stood on her toes, trying to read over Warrick's shoulder. The man's handwriting made chicken scratch look like perfect penmanship.

''I give up,'' she declared, then looked at him for the answer. ''Do we know why she quit?''

That wasn't in there. Warrick flipped the pad closed. ''Anybody's guess.''

Guessing right was the name of the game. For the second time that day, her enthusiasm began to build. She looked at the three men in the room. ''How did we miss this before?''

Rodriquez shrugged. ''I dunno, it fell through the

cracks, I guess. Probably didn't seem important at the time. Hey, we're only human.''

She nodded. That they were. She tried to think positively. ''What matters is that we found it now.'' She looked at the three men. ''Okay, we've got two victims who went to Nina's. Let's find out if the others went there, too.''

''So what have we got here?'' Culpepper grumbled. His tone indicated that he thought it was all a tempest in a teapot, one of his favorite expressions. ''They were stalked by an irate beautician?''

''We might have a connection,'' C.J. emphasized. ''Who knows where that'll lead us?'' She stopped and looked at the older man. ''You have a better idea?''

''Yeah,'' Warrick cut in, ''instead of pawing through illegible notes, why don't we just go to Nina's and get a client list?''

''Brilliant.'' C.J. already had her purse out of her drawer. She kicked it shut. Culpepper groaned. ''Warrick and I'll go. You two get your beauty rest.'' She turned to her partner. ''Last one to the car's a rotten egg.''

It occurred to him, as he hurried to catch up, that he liked the way her face lit up when she was being enthusiastic about something.

The woman who owned and ran Nina's was a still semi-attractive woman in her midsixties. She gave the impression of having been a knockout when she was younger and behaved as if she still believed that to be true. She'd all but devoured Warrick with her eyes as she listened to him.

C.J. felt as if she might as well not be there, for all the attention the woman was paying to what she had to say.

The owner balked at the idea of producing her client list until Warrick reiterated C.J.'s request. With a surrendering sigh and something about never being able to say no to a good-looking man, the woman pulled up her client list on the antiquated computer.

Warrick sent a less-than-subtle grin toward C.J. before scrolling through the list.

Unwilling to be ignored, Nina sighed loudly. "This is too much, just too much." She rang her hands, careful not to ruin the polish on her long, bloodred nails. "I can't handle any more. First my son, now this."

"Your son?" C.J. echoed.

Warrick raised his eyes from the client list. Every one of the murdered women had come here, at least once, if not repeatedly. They had their connection. Now what did they do with it?

"What about your son?"

C.J. had asked the question, but Nina gave her answer to Warrick. "I just finished paying off the lawyer's fees. Stupid lawyer couldn't even get him free."

Warrick exchanged glances with C.J. "What was he charged with?"

"Some crazy, trumped-up deal. The police claimed he stole a car. My son's not a thief, he's a dear, sweet boy.'' She fluttered her lashes. C.J. struggled to keep from laughing. ''A little slow, maybe, but that doesn't mean someone gets the right to just throw him in jail like that. He used to work here for me, did the shampooing. Sometimes helped with the manicures. The clients all liked him.''

Warrick exchanged looks with C.J. ''What's your son's name?''

Suspicion suddenly entered the carefully made-up eyes. Slim brows gathered over the bridge of her nose. Suddenly she transformed into the protective lioness, fighting for her cub. ''Why, so you can do something to the records and throw him back in? I know how this system works, honey. Always against the little man—''

Exasperated, C.J. looked at the hairstylist closest to her. The woman made no attempt to look as if she wasn't listening to every word of the conversation in the back room. ''You know her son's name?''

''Henry, Herbie, Harry, something like that,'' the woman replied.

C.J.'s eyes darted to the name on the business license. The woman's full name was Nina Maxwell Claymore. Maxwell. *Bingo.* Tapping Warrick, C.J. pointed to the framed sign.

''We'd like a copy of your client list to take with us, please,'' C.J. told the woman.

''And then we'll be out of your hair,'' Warrick added for good measure.

The woman looked uncertainly at them, then with

a huff hit the print button. In the recesses of the back room, a dot matrix printer wheezed to life.

''Still circumstantial, you know,'' Warrick pointed out as they left the beauty salon.

C.J. finished folding the list and stuck it into her purse. ''If you keep tripping over arrows pointing in the same direction, eventually you have to think that maybe that's the direction you should be taking.'' Opening the door on the passenger side, she got in.

Warrick slid in behind the steering wheel. ''You want to try to sell that to a D.A.?''

This was a lot more than they had yesterday. Impatience mingled with a sense of urgency. ''So what, we wait until he kills another girl?''

''No,'' starting the car, he backed out of the small parking lot that Nina's shared with a fortune teller called Madam Alexis, ''we catch him in the act and stop him. You have to admit if we get him with a dime-store choker and a rose in his possession, that'll make a stronger case for arresting him.''

She crossed her arms before her as he picked up speed. ''Don't you ever get tired of being right?''

Warrick grinned. ''Hasn't happened yet.''

She wished he wouldn't grin like that. It went straight to her gut. The last thing she wanted. C.J. looked out the window. ''So what do you want our next move to be? Questioning Harry again? He might break.''

''And he might surprise us and not be the guy after all.'' He turned right at the corner, heading toward the southbound 405 Freeway. "Don't forget, we didn't think it was him after we talked to him."

"*You* didn't think it was him," C.J. emphasized. "I had my doubts."

"Yeah, right."

She didn't particularly care for his smirk. "I did the whole Ted Bundy analogy, remember?"

"Right." It was easier to agree than to argue with her. "Let's see if we can get some surveillance time authorized."

Surveillance, he reflected. That meant the two of them together in cramped quarters for hours at a time. The thought was at once exciting and unsettling. He was just asking for trouble, he realized.

"By the way—" he deliberately tried to keep his tone light "—if Alberdeen authorizes the time, you can't wear your perfume."

"My perfume?" She looked at him in confusion. "Why? What's wrong with my perfume?"

Hands on the wheel, Warrick looked straight ahead. "It's sexy."

"You think it's sexy?"

He could hear the smile in her voice. That probably made her think it gave her some kind of power over him. He shouldn't have said anything.

Too late now.

"Just don't wear it, okay?" he said shortly, switching lanes and speeding up as he made his way onto the freeway.

Chapter 13

Warrick shifted restlessly. His legs were beginning to feel cramped. After three days of fruitless surveillance, all of him was beginning to feel cramped.

C.J. was sitting less than six inches away from him, looking at a bank of monitors. He scowled in her direction. You'd think she'd have a little consideration.

"I thought I specifically asked you not to wear your perfume."

They'd been sitting inside the U-Haul truck parked across the street from Maxwell's apartment building for the past six hours, and the air felt as if it was getting rather scarce. Yesterday it had been a cable truck, the day before, to avoid any undue attention, the truck had borne the insignia of the local electric company.

Maybe it was his imagination, but her perfume seemed to be filling up every available space. It was certainly doing a number on his nervous system.

C.J. didn't bother turning around. "I know."

Maybe this surveillance thing wasn't such a good idea. "Then why did you?"

This time she did turn her stool to face him. What the hell was he talking about? "For your information, I'm not wearing any perfume."

Yeah, right. Did she think he'd lost his sense of smell? "Then what's that scent hovering all through the truck?"

To underscore his point, Warrick leaned over and sniffed her hair. Wildflowers came instantly to mind. A field of wildflowers. With C.J. lying in them, nude, her arms raised toward him.

He backed off, shaking his head. Hopefully shaking out the thought.

C.J. paused, thinking. "That's my shampoo. Or maybe my soap, I don't know." She looked at him. He'd been getting progressively antsier with each hour that went by. "What's the matter with you?"

He looked at her pointedly. Lately, he felt as if his grasp on things was slipping. "I'm not sure."

C.J. put her hand on his forehead, checking for a fever. "Are you coming down with something?"

"I think I'm already down with it." Warrick jerked back his head. It was best if they kept contact down to a minimum. "You don't have to mother me."

"Sorry. Once I'm in the mode, it's hard to stop." Because of the erratic hours she was keeping, the baby was at her mother's. C.J. anticipated coming into an empty house and missed her daughter already. ''Maybe you should see a doctor.''

He shrugged off her words, turning away from her. He found himself facing a wall of control panels. ''A doctor can't help with this.''

There was no place to move.

It felt as if the very sides of the truck were closing in, pushing him closer to her. Ever since that night, she'd been on his mind more and more. Like a drug addict who couldn't think of anything else but the source of his addiction and getting just one more hit, he couldn't move his mind far from thoughts of her.

Especially when she was only a reach away.

Warrick moved closer to her almost against his will. Certainly against his common sense. ''C.J.?''

There was something in his voice that had her looking away from the monitor that was trained on the building's front entrance.

''What?'' The word caught in her throat.

His mind took a coffee break. There was no other way to explain it. Warrick brushed the back of his hand along her cheek, watched as her eyes grew larger. His desire mushroomed.

He lowered his mouth to hers.

The knock on the truck's side panel had them both springing back, startled, two tightly wound coils being released.

C.J. looked at the monitor trained at the rear of the truck and let out a relieved breath. They hadn't been made. She nodded at the sliding door. ''It's the B team.''

Warrick pulled open the door. Rodriguez and Culpepper climbed in.

''We prefer thinking of ourselves as the A team,'' Rodriguez informed them. Any available space was all but eaten up. There wasn't enough room left over for a complicated idea.

C.J. looked at the two men who had come to relieve them and deadpanned, ''So which one's Mr. T.?''

''Very funny,'' Culpepper grumbled. He changed places with C.J. and took the stool in front of the monitors. ''It's bad enough I've got to trade a warm bed for this.'' The world outside the van looked fairly dead. ''Anything?''

She shook her head. She and Warrick had taken over from yet another team. The two men in the Mustang had followed Maxwell to and from his job as a busboy at a nearby family-style restaurant. ''He hasn't left the apartment all night.''

''Three days and nothing. I'm beginning to think we're barking up the wrong tree,'' Rodriguez complained.

He moved past Warrick as best he could, taking his place. Other than a small table, littered with chips, sandwich wrappers and empty containers of mediocre coffee, the inside was dominated by the bank of four monitors, focused on different parts of the building.

There'd been one instance where they thought they'd gotten lucky. Maxwell had left his apartment the first night of the surveillance and driven to Mason Park, the place where the last victim had been found. Unable to follow him without attracting his attention, Warrick had alerted an alternate unit to drive by the area. But when Maxwell got out of his car, his hands were in his pockets, not around a body he was looking to dispose of.

Sneaking past the guard rail, he had made his way to the lake. He walked along its perimeter for almost an hour before returning to his car and driving home again. It appeared that he'd been seeking solitude, just as he'd told them in his statement.

''Give it time.'' Getting out, Warrick waited for C.J. to join him. ''He just satisfied his blood lust. He needs time to work it up again.''

''Now there's a comforting thought.'' With a dramatic sigh, Culpepper closed the van door on them.

The cool air failed to have any effect on him. He still felt warm. Warrick shoved his hands into his pockets, feeling at loose ends. He glanced at C.J. as they headed to the Bureau's car. ''You want to go somewhere for a drink or a cup of nonstale coffee?''

She was tempted, but she shook her head. ''It's nearly midnight, Warrick. I'd better not.''

Both hands on the wheel, he pulled away from the curb. ''Right.''

Don't say it, don't say it. She might as well have been talking Greek to herself. ''But you're welcome to come over if you want a good cup of coffee.''

Warrick looked at her, struggling with nobler instincts, instincts that told him this wasn't going to go anywhere so he shouldn't pursue it. He thought of his parents, of his all-but-stillborn marriage. He felt he was a man who didn't know how to love, not by example, not by experience. The best thing he could do for himself, and for C.J., was to call it a night and go home.

He turned the car in the direction of her house. Away from the field office. "Okay."

They both knew it wasn't about coffee.

The house was still when she opened the front door. Just as she'd expected it to be. But the all-pervading loneliness didn't come.

Except for the lamp on in the living room, there was no illumination. Warrick closed the door behind them. "Where's your mother?"

"Home. Her home," she clarified. "With the baby." She tossed her purse on the sofa and led the way to the kitchen. "I thought it would be easier on everyone like that." She smiled ruefully. "Except on me." Reaching in the overhead cabinet for the coffee filters, she laughed softly at herself. "I'm still grappling with separation anxiety, I guess." She flipped open the top and took out a single filter. "I hate being away from her."

He leaned against the counter, watching her. Wanting her. "Then why don't you quit?"

She moved past him, to the refrigerator. The coffee can was on a shelf mounted on the door. "In case you haven't noticed, I'm not exactly independently wealthy. There're bills to pay."

"You've got a law degree," he reminded her. "Your father would be happy to take you into the firm." The man had told him so more than once.

Moving Warrick aside, she opened the drawer he'd been blocking and took out a tablespoon.

''My father would be overjoyed to take me into the firm.'' She measured out two cups worth of crystals. ''It's what he's wanted all along.''

He watched her eyes as she spoke. He knew how much her family meant to her. But so did her own self-esteem. ''But you wouldn't be happy,'' he guessed.

''No, I wouldn't.'' C.J. snapped the plastic lid back on the can. ''I'd make a fair lawyer,'' she judged. ''I make a great FBI agent. And I love my work.'' She returned the can to its rightful place and closed the refrigerator door. ''I like catching the bad guys.'' She turned away from him, measuring out two cups of water and pouring them into the coffeemaker. ''Not finding loopholes for them.''

He was behind her, so close that all she had to do was take a breath and she would find herself against him. Pinpricks of excitement raced up and down a conveyor belt along her spine.

''What else do you like?''

She could feel his breath on her neck. Everything within her tightened with anticipation. C.J. placed the coffeepot back on the counter and turned around. Her body brushed against his, sending electrical charges between them. She looked up into his face. ''Long, slow kisses that go on forever.''

He framed her face with his hands and lowered his mouth to hers.

She felt as if he was making love to her just by kissing her lips. Slowly, deeply, until she felt as if she was completely anesthetized. Completely mesmerized. She stood up on her toes trying to draw in ever nuance, every taste, savor every delicious second that their lips were together.

Warrick drew his mouth away and looked at her. Tension tightened around his body, squeezing. Begging for release. "Like that?"

"Just like that," she breathed.

The next moment he swept C.J. into his arms and kissed her again, not so slowly, not so gently. The flame was lit and it traveled through both of them with lightning speed.

C.J.'s arms went around his neck almost of their own volition, her heart pounding. It had been forever since he had made love with her. They had been dancing around each other as if that night in the motel wasn't between them, as if they didn't want this.

They'd both been living a lie.

They both wanted it.

Breathing hard, C.J. moved back, creating just enough space to begin pulling off his clothes.

His movements mimicked hers.

She was making his head spin, his blood pump wildly through his veins. Drawing his head back a fraction, he grinned at her. "I guess this means I have to wait for the coffee."

Damn, if he hadn't started this tonight, she would have. "Shut up and kiss me, Warrick," she ordered.

"Yes, ma'am."

And then the smile faded from his lips as something hot and strong took over. His mind and common sense faded somewhere behind a curtain. All that remained were the needs he'd been grappling with.

He yanked off her bra, her skirt, her blouse was already a casualty. His belly quickened as he felt her hands moving his zipper down the length of him, then stripping away his pants. Her hands felt cool against his flesh, hardening him even further.

Warrick kicked his pants aside, separating their bodies just long enough to throw his shirt off his arms. The next heartbeat he was holding her against him again, his hands traveling along the length of her, making her his, everywhere he touched. Everywhere he promised to touch.

Now. She wanted him now…inside of her, filling her. Making her think of nothing else, no serial killers, no responsibilities, no fears.

Just Warrick.

Just him.

C.J. felt almost feral in his arms. She wanted him to feel as wild as she did at this very moment.

Her mouth traveled along his mouth, his neck, his ear. Branding him. Driving him out of his head.

It took everything he had not to throw her on the floor, to take her here, this moment. But that would be too soon, too quick. That would be placing his own pleasure above hers, and he wanted to pleasure her. Because seeing her twist and turn beneath his lips, wanting him, wanting more, heightened his own excitement beyond measure.

Locked in a heated embrace, C.J. wound her legs around his torso. Desire surged. She could feel herself moistening, wanting him. The next moment she felt herself being lowered onto the kitchen table.

C.J. could barely swallow. The throbbing pulse in her throat wouldn't let her.

Trying to draw air into her lungs, she moved her head away from him. "It's too late for dinner," she whispered.

His eyes were dark with longing as he looked at her. There was only a hint of a teasing smile on his lips. "But not for a feast."

Before she could ask him what he meant, Warrick showed her.

His mouth worked along her body, tempting, teasing, leaving his mark damply on every inch he passed. C.J. arched her body against his lips, tiny explosions beginning to take hold along her skin, within the very center of her.

Her need for him grew to astronomical proportions. She reached for him, but he gently, firmly, moved her hands away, all the while continuing the long, sensual journey along her body.

His tongue trailed along her belly, making it quiver in anticipation. She felt herself ripening for him to the point that she didn't think she could stand it a moment longer.

And then, after anointing each thigh in slow, moist strokes, he found the very core of her.

C.J. moaned something almost unintelligible, her body separating from her mind as an avalanche of sensations thundered all through her.

First one wave hit and then another. She felt like

a wild animal, glorying in the pleasure, but wanting him to be with her.

Summoning strength from some nether region, C.J. drew herself up, pushing him away just far enough to be able to slide her legs back around his torso.

She pulled him to her, teasing him with her body, her invitation clear. Her mouth sealed to his.

The next moment she was flat against the table again with Warrick looming over her, like a lord over a slave.

But this wasn't about control, about power. It was only about pleasure. About giving.

''Now.''

It was half an order, half a plea, the single word dragged along her raw throat.

She thought she heard him murmur, ''Yes, ma'am.'' Thought she felt his smile against her skin, but she wasn't sure. All she knew was that she wanted him. Despite the climaxes he had given her, shc wanted him, wanted to join with him the way it was always meant to be.

Wanted Warrick to feel the jarring power the way she had.

This time, when he entered her, she was the one who initiated the rhythm. At least the first step. The rest of the dance he led, taking her with him every step of the way.

Her breathing became erratic, or maybe she stopped breathing altogether. She wasn't sure.

Nothing mattered except climbing up to the summit together.

And then the explosion reached her, shaking her body. She dug her nails into his back, glorying in the feel of him, in the moment they shared, her heart hammering so hard she was certain it would take a team of cardiac surgeons to return it to its rightful place.

She didn't care.

C.J. kept her eyes closed, lost in the swirls of sensations that were settling all over her. Lost in the feel of him, of the length of his body covering hers.

How was he managing that without crushing her?

She opened her eyes and realized that he was raised on his elbows, balancing his weight, looking down into her face.

He kissed her lips softly.

She almost felt shy. How was that possible? What was he doing to her? She felt as if she'd been turned inside out and then back again.

And wanted more.

"Definitely more stimulating than coffee," he whispered against her ear.

The next moment he was rising up, then getting off the table. He took her hand, helping her up.

C.J. felt a little woozy as she sat up. She must have swayed, because she felt his arms closing around her protectively. She loved the feel of his hard chest against her.

"You okay?"

She nodded, or thought she did. C.J. put her hand to her head, as if that would still the room and put the world back into focus.

"Just a little adrenaline rush. I think the blood

totally drained out of my head.'' Taking a deep breath, she hopped off the table. He drew her to him, closing his arms around her. C.J. leaned her cheek against him. She felt safe, protected. Happy. She looked at the table. ''You realize, of course, that I'm going to have to burn that now.''

He tilted her head back a little, smiling into her eyes. ''Funny, I was thinking of having it bronzed, myself.''

''A trophy?''

That sounded much too harsh, much too cold. Neither had any place here. ''A keepsake,'' he corrected.

It was a silly word. But it still managed to warm her heart.

The next moment she felt herself being swept off the floor and up into his arms. ''I'd like to see your bedroom now.''

She'd half expected him to say something about the hour and needing to get home. C.J. smiled as she laced her arms around his neck. ''First door to your right.''

''And straight out to morning.''

''What?''

''Nothing, just paraphrasing Peter Pan's flight plan to Neverland.''

Never. The word she'd used when thinking of falling in love. Never. The word that didn't work anymore. Nerves moved through her, cautioning her not to say anything. Not to ruin the moment. Not to expect what couldn't be.

"Are you planning on flying tonight?" she asked as he took the stairs.

Warrick brushed a kiss against her hair. "I already have. But the plane isn't grounded yet."

"Big words," she teased.

He came to the landing. "I never say anything I don't mean."

He stared at the house.

They were inside. Claire and that man. He'd seen them walk in. He'd sneaked out of his apartment, using his secret route through the old basement that linked to the next house.

No one saw him.

But he saw them. Saw them watching him.

Tag, they were it.

But he didn't have time to play. Not now, not when everything inside him hurt so bad.

She was doing it again, just like the last time. She was giving herself to someone else when she should have been his. Would have been his.

He had to claim her again, just as he had the last time. And the time before that.

He needed to save her. Before she became any more spoiled.

He settled into the shadows of the greenbelt, watching the house. His fingers rubbed the pearls on the necklace in his pocket.

Chapter 14

As the mists of contentment began to fade away, Warrick slowly became aware of something else hovering in the recesses of his mind. A small, nagging sensation that had been steadily nibbling away at him, taking tiny bites out of the fabric of his resolve with sharp, steely teeth.

He recognized it for what it was. Fear.

Not the kind of energizing fear that accompanied him into darkened alleys, stood beside him in confrontations with thieves and killers who could end life as he knew it in the blink of an eye if he so much as let a fraction of his guard down. That fear helped keep him alive.

This fear ate away at the lining of his stomach.

This fear had to do with C.J. And what she was doing to his world.

It was as if, no matter how alert he was, he had no control, no say over what was happening to him. He didn't like it. It made him uneasy. At any moment his life could go completely out of kilter.

How had he let that happen?

She could sense the change in him.

C.J. turned her head, her cheek brushing along his bare chest, sending delicious little shock waves through her body. There was a pensive look in his eyes. ''What are you thinking about?''

Warrick couldn't tell her. Couldn't give voice to his thoughts. Maybe he should have, maybe saying his fears out loud would dissolve them like ghosts in the night, but that wasn't his way. He'd learned early on to work things out for himself. Now was no different.

Besides, she was the problem, so how could he tell her what was on his mind? Simple, he couldn't. Since she was waiting for him to say something, he lied. There was nothing else he could do.

''Just that the christening's this Saturday—'' He lowered his glance to her face. ''It is this Saturday, isn't it?''

After all the postponements, she didn't blame him for being sarcastic. ''Yes, it's this Saturday. Father Gannon's back, his calendar's clear, and there don't appear to be any emergencies in the making, so I feel pretty safe in saying that there's nothing to get in the way.''

He played with a strand of her hair, sifting it through his fingers, wondering how he could go back to life as it had been. Feeling that he couldn't. "Have you come up with a middle name yet?"

She sighed mightily, staring off at the ceiling. Feeling his eyes on her. "No."

"That's okay, she doesn't need a middle name."

In her present vulnerable state, defensiveness seemed second nature to her. "Yes, she does."

"Then come up with one." It sounded almost like an order. He knew his patience was short, not because of her inability to come up with some name no one would ever use, but because of the turmoil going on inside him.

Why was he snapping at her? "Don't you think I would if I could? I told you, this is important to me. To her." C.J. sighed. She'd fallen asleep twice this week with the baby book opened to one page or another. "I have to find just the right name."

He'd never seen anyone have so much trouble with a name. "You're not thinking of postponing the christening, are you?"

"No." C.J. ran her hand over her forehead. She could feel a headache in the making. "I don't know what I'm going to do."

"Just pick a name, any name." It shouldn't be so hard. He locked his fingers together, holding her to him. "If you find one you like better, you can always have it legally changed."

She sat up and looked at him. "I can't do that. That'll mess with her mind."

He blew out a breath, thinking for a moment. "Tell you what, I'll put the five top contenders in a hat and just pick one."

Because she was more than a little afraid that she had emotionally abdicated control over her life to him, she was immediately on her guard, taking offense. "Why do you get to do it?"

She was nitpicking. "Fine, you do it." Made no difference to him, he thought. "Have your mother do it. Have the bag boy at the grocery store do it. It doesn't matter who does it, C.J. It doesn't even matter if she *has* a middle name, except to you. Stop obsessing and just pick one. It shouldn't be this hard."

There was no point in bristling. "You're right, it shouldn't be," C.J. relented. "I guess it's this case, it has me completely preoccupied."

As if to prove her wrong, Warrick ran his hand along the swell of her body. She could feel a small wave of heat following the path he'd created.

"Okay, maybe not completely," she allowed. "But it's on my mind almost every waking minute." With a frustrated sigh, she curled into him, resting her head on his chest. The wheels in her brain began to turn. "This investigation's not going anywhere. It could be weeks before Maxwell zeroes in on anyone. Just because we think he killed two women in a short time frame doesn't mean he'll do it again."

He'd worked with her long enough to know she was going somewhere with this. Warrick stopped stroking her hair. "So what are you saying?"

She hesitated for a second, looking for the right words. "Why don't we set a trap for him? We know where he works. I can show up there, really get into his line of vision. Find a way to talk to him, get him to fixate on me.'' She raised her head to look at him, becoming enthusiastic. ''After all, I more than fit the general description of women he seeks out.''

Was she out of her mind? ''No.''

He'd all but fired the word at her point-blank. She stared at him, dumbfounded. ''What do you mean, 'No'?''

Why did she have to challenge everything? ''It's a two-letter word, what's so hard about it? No. As in no, it's a dumb idea. And I want you to drop it.''

She didn't like being dismissed out of hand like this. ''You have any better ones?''

''Yes,'' he answered evenly, ''we continue the surveillance.''

C.J. frowned. This wasn't like him. He knew as well as she did why this wouldn't work. ''We can't continue it indefinitely, and it could be weeks or months before Maxwell does anything, we don't know. He doesn't have a pattern—we've already established that. Besides, we're on a day-to-day basis as it is. Alberdeen can pull the plug on surveillance anytime.''

''Then Alberdeen'll come up with another idea,'' he snapped at her. ''You're not going to dangle yourself in front of a serial killer like so much bait on a damn hook, C.J., and that's that.''

Her eyes widened. He'd never treated her like this before. ''Since when did you get the right to make decisions for me?''

''Since now,'' he said tersely. Since she'd messed with his mind and turned his world inside out. Since he'd started thinking of her as something other than his partner.

He was acting territorial, and if he thought she was going to put up with it, he was sorely mistaken. ''Just because we're sleeping together doesn't give you the right to interfere in my life.''

''Interfere?'' She made him sound like some kind of doorstop. ''Is that what it is?''

She'd wounded him and she knew it. That hadn't been her intent. She just wanted him to see reason. It *had* to be this way. ''It is when you start telling me what I can or can't do, yes.''

''Well then, maybe we shouldn't be sleeping together.'' He threw off the covers and got up. Warrick kept his back to her as he started to put on the clothes they'd brought upstairs earlier. ''Maybe this whole thing was a mistake.'' He could feel his anger flaring out of control. Just as his emotions had. It had something to do with reflexes and self preservation. ''You know, that's what it was. A mistake. And I made it—'' he pulled on his pants ''—thinking that this would work.''

''A mistake?'' she echoed, staring at his back. The word couldn't have cut into her more than if it had been placed on the edge of an arrow and fired directly into her heart.

In a huff she pulled on her sweater and her jeans, foregoing any underclothing. She wasn't about to be naked when he was dressed to the teeth. It made her feel much too vulnerable and she'd exposed herself far too much already.

Warrick left his shirt unbuttoned as he tucked it

into the waistband of his pants. He was furious with her for the foolish risks she wanted to take, furious with himself for caring so much that he felt his emotions going out of control.

This was what he got for letting his guard down. He'd given her this power over him. What had he been thinking?

Damn it, hadn't he known this wasn't going to work? He knew he was no good at male-female relationships. How had he let this go so far, allowed it to affect him so deeply?

"Yeah, a mistake," he snapped back. "Neither one of us has a great track record when it comes to relationships. That should have given us a clue that this was all wrong." He blamed himself most of all. "I, at least, should have seen it coming."

What was he saying? That she was too stupid to learn from her mistakes? The headache grew, tangling her thoughts with her emotions, making everything murky, everything painful. "And you don't think I should have?"

Jamming his feet into his shoes, he got up and headed for the hall. "You've got your head up in the clouds so many times, I'm surprised you don't periodically fall off the sidewalk."

She followed him out, stifling the urge to pummel his back with her fists. Not knowing how they got to this point. "If I did, it would be because I was tripping over you. You always see the dark side of everything, always refuse to even entertain the idea of letting a little sunlight in."

He swung around to look at her. ''What the hell are you talking about?''

''I don't know.'' And she didn't. Everything felt confused. But he'd hurt her and she wanted to lash out. ''Just get out.''

He turned away from her and crossed to the stairs. ''That's what I'm doing. As fast as I can.''

''Not fast enough to satisfy me.''

But even as he headed down the stairs, she went after him, stunned, appalled. Watching everything unfold before her like some kind of disaster she was unable to stop. Something was making her egg him on, grasping at the excuse, at straws.

Anything to make him leave.

Because to have him stay was too frightening.

She'd seen the vulnerable side of herself and she didn't like it, didn't want it. He made her weak because he made her want.

He had to go.

''And you can forget about this Saturday,'' she shouted at him. Warrick glared at her over his shoulder as he yanked open the door. ''I'll get one of my brothers to be the baby's godfather. I don't want to have someone like you in her life.''

''Fine with me.'' He slammed the door.

She jerked it open. ''You don't get to slam the door in my house,'' she shouted at Warrick's retreating back. ''I do!''

And she did. She slammed it as hard as she could. Then sank down against the door and started to cry huge, body-shaking, soul-racking sobs.

She wasn't sure just how long she sat there on

the floor, her arms wrapped around her knees, her face buried against them.

Long enough to cry herself out.

She felt exhausted. Numb. Rising to her feet, C.J. tried to think, to pull her thoughts together out of the quagmire they'd descended into.

She dragged her hand through her hair. She felt shell-shocked. What the hell had just happened here?

Putting one foot in front of the other, she made it to the small powder room just off the foyer.

This is what she got for letting herself fall in love again. No, not again, this had been something different from what she'd felt for Tom. When she'd loved him, she hadn't lost a part of herself. She had this time. Warrick had taken out a piece of her soul. And then he'd twisted her inside out until she didn't know which way was up.

Who the hell did he think he was, telling her what to do?

He was the man she was in love with, that's who. And that had been *her* big mistake.

Damn it, what was wrong with her? How could she have let something like this happen?

But that was just it, she hadn't "let" it happen, it just had.

The feelings for Warrick had been there all along. All they had needed was the right catalyst to be set free. He'd kissed her, and suddenly all those feelings made a run for the border, a break for freedom.

And look where that had gotten her. Miserable in

a semidark house, carrying on futile arguments in the recesses of her mind.

"You would have thought you'd have learned after Tom," she said to the tear-stained face staring back at her in the mirror. "What would it take for you to realize that you aren't going to find the kind of thing your parents have...that relationships like theirs are the exception, not the rule?"

C.J. realized she was shouting at herself. "Oh, great, now I'm going crazy. Perfect, just perfect."

Trying to pull herself together, she splashed cold water on her face, hoping that would somehow wash away all the unwanted emotions that were running rampant through her.

She was not about to allow Byron Warrick to have control over her, to affect her this way. They had made love, so what? Not even love, she amended silently, they'd had sex. That was it, pure and simple. Nothing more, just sex.

A sad smile curved her lips.

Who was she kidding? Maybe it had been "just sex" to him but not to her, she thought miserably. To her it had been something more, something special.

Too bad. It hadn't been to him, and it took two to make a decent relationship. She'd learned that much from Tom. Time to pick up the pieces and move on.

She realized that she'd wandered into the kitchen. The coffee was still in the filter inside the coffeemaker, where they'd left it. Untouched.

She debated for a minute, then shrugged. What

the hell, she wasn't going to get any sleep tonight, anyway. Maybe she'd have a cup of coffee and call Culpepper to see if there'd been any new developments.

C.J. placed the glass coffeepot under the spout and hit the on button. Grumbling noises slowly filled the stillness around her.

She could feel tears forming again. She needed noise, music, something to fill the awful void she felt inside of her. C.J. switched on the radio on the counter.

A mournful tune greeted her. Swallowing choice words, C.J. switched the radio off again rather than hunt for another station. With her luck, every station would be playing a sad song about love that had gone wrong.

She didn't need music, she told herself. What she needed to do was concentrate on the case.

The hell with what Warrick thought. As far as she was concerned, she'd come up with a damn good plan. It was a whole lot better than waiting for the Sleeping Beauty Killer to try to do away with another innocent, unsuspecting woman. Even with the task force waiting in the wings to protect her, the next would-be victim would undoubtedly be traumatized by her contact with the serial killer.

But not her.

Her nerves were stronger than that. This was what she was paid to do. The only thing that traumatized her were special agents who didn't turn out to be so special after all.

She picked up the phone and punched the buttons

on the keyboard with the number to Culpepper's cell phone. He answered after two rings.

"Hi, it's Jones. Anything?"

"What's the matter, C.J., you can't sleep?" Culpepper guessed. "Try coming back here. Watching the monitors'll put you right out. It's dead as a doornail outside. It looks like Maxwell's tucked in for the night. Sure wish I was."

She nodded. No escape for her there. "Call me if anything changes."

"Other than a cat wandering down the street?"

She laughed shortly. "Other than that."

"You got it. Now go to bed, Jones, or come here and spell me because I could use the sleep."

"G'night, Culpepper." She replaced the receiver and turned to the coffeemaker.

Clearing off the counter, she opened the cabinet below the sink to throw the crumpled napkin away. The garbage pail was full to overflowing. She thought of just leaving it, but this time of year it was an open invitation to ants. With a sigh she tied up the white garbage bag and pulled it out of the pail.

She went out to the side of the house where the garbage containers were kept. She threw the bag into the largest one, then turned to go back inside.

Her head jerked up. She thought she'd heard something.

Listening, she couldn't make anything out. Probably just the neighbor's cat, running through the bushes. With a shrug she went to her door. Opening it, she was almost across the threshold when someone came up behind her and bumped into her.

Caught off guard, C.J. stumbled into her living room. She swung around, arms raised defensively in front of her.

Harry Maxwell was standing inside her house.

Chapter 15

Warrick glared into the night, struggling to rein in his anger as he drove down the quiet streets. The windows of his car were down. The air fought a duel as it rushed in on both sides of him, pushing his hair into his eyes. He hardly noticed.

He flew past a light that was about to turn red, barely squeaking through.

Damn it, he'd let her get to him. He'd known better, and yet he'd let her get to him.

His knuckles tightened on the steering wheel as he beat another light before it turned red.

He should never have let any of this happen. Should have stopped it before it ever started. He wasn't a novice at this sort of thing. That first kiss should have warned him that he was on dangerous ground and that it would only get worse.

But that first kiss had stirred him just enough to make him want more.

Well, he'd gotten more, a hell of a lot more than he bargained for, and the whole thing had just blown up in his face.

Warrick shook his head. Half an hour ago he'd been in bed with C.J., feeling utterly invulnerable, and now he was driving home, angry and at a complete loss as to what had happened back there, other than the fact that C.J. had gone off like a Roman candle at a Fourth of July display.

His timing off, Warrick was five feet away from the crosswalk as the light began to turn red. He thought of racing through it. There was no traffic in either direction. At this hour the streets of Bedford were deserted. Shrugging, he eased back on the gas pedal and came to a stop just over the line.

Any way he sliced it, C.J. had a hell of a lot of explaining to do.

He let out a long, measured breath, waging a silent battle in his head. He'd always moved on when things turned sour. No reason to change his mode of operation this late in the game. He was just going to go straight home and forget about everything, put all of this behind him.

When the light turned green, he made a U-turn.

C.J.'s heart started to race as she stared at the stooped man before her. There were smudges of soot or something black on his beige shirt and across one cheek.

What was he doing here? How had he gotten past

Culpepper and Rodriguez and the surveillance cameras? Wouldn't they have seen him? But Culpepper had just told her everything was quiet.

Were there two of Maxwell, a twin they didn't know about?

C.J. told herself to remain calm. ''Hello.'' She smiled warmly at him.

Harry was fidgeting with the edge of his sweater with one hand. He was holding a single long-stemmed red rose in the other.

C.J.'s breath hitched in her throat.

''Is it too late?'' Harry asked hesitantly, his eyes fastened on the tips of his run-down loafers. ''Because I can come back if it's too late.''

Adrenaline was rushing through her veins. She forced herself to tear her eyes away from the rose. She wasn't going to catch this man by being afraid.

''No, it's not too late.'' Her voice was deliberately soft, coaxing. She wanted him off his guard. ''Did you want to tell me something, Harry?''

At the mention of his given name, Maxwell looked up shyly, an almost bashful smile playing on his lips. ''I like it when you call me Harry.''

''That's your name, isn't it? Harry. Harry Maxwell.'' More like Harry Houdini, she thought, if he could elude both the surveillance team and the cameras.

Harry nodded his head like a child eager to answer a question right, eager to please the teacher.

The rose made her uneasy. Had he come to kill her? But he seemed so guileless, so uncertain of himself. Could he really be a serial killer?

She forced herself not to look over her shoulder. Her weapon was on the side table, but she felt fairly confident that she could get to it in time if she needed to. Still, she wished she was wearing her spare, the small pistol she kept strapped to the inside of her thigh.

Well, she'd wanted to play bait. This was her chance. "Would you like to come in, Harry?"

He nodded again, his hair bobbing into his face. He pushed it away nervously. C.J. stepped back, opening the door farther, her smile inviting.

Harry moved across the threshold as if an invisible hand was tugging on his sleeve, leading him inside. He looked around like a tourist at a national shrine, taking it all in reverently.

"This is nice."

"Thank you." She eased the door closed, glancing out into the street. She would have felt a great deal better if she could have spotted a squad car, or one of their own vehicles. But the street was deserted.

"You've changed some things."

The comment caught her off guard. C.J. turned away from the door and tried not to stare at him. Had Maxwell been in here before? When she wasn't at home? She struggled not to shiver at the thought. It gave her the creeps.

"A little," she answered evasively. If he was the killer, maybe he was confusing her with one of the women he'd killed. C.J. was careful to keep some room between them. "Do you like it?"

He nodded, then turned to her. The rose was

pointing toward the floor. "You've been watching me."

Oh damn, she thought. He suspected. Was that why he was here? Was this all just an act?

"You don't think I notice, but I do," he was saying. "I notice you watching me. I've been watching you watching me. That's why I used the old route to get here."

"The old route?" She didn't understand. Was this some ritual he was referring to?

Maxwell nodded. He drifted about the room, smoke looking for somewhere to settle, leaving a trail in its wake. She moved with him, always wary that he could turn suddenly.

"Through the basement. I found a tunnel there. It goes to the other building. The one I used to live in with my mother before I went away."

Was he referring to being sent to prison? Or when his mother had married his stepfather and they'd moved to another city? She never took her eyes off him.

"I use that when I don't want anyone watching me."

They needed something more than circumstantial evidence and gut hunches. She needed to get him to say something incriminating.

C.J. took a step closer to him. Friend, confidante. "Why don't you want anyone watching you?"

"Because it's a secret. The way I feel about you, Claire," he told her breathlessly, then added, "I can't tell anyone."

Claire, he'd called her Claire. Who was Claire?

C.J.'s mind raced, trying to recall the names of all the victims. Wasn't one of them named Claire?

And then she remembered. The first victim's name had been Claire. In his mind was he killing the woman over and over again for some transgression?

"Why can't you tell anyone?" she coaxed.

He began to fidget again, as if to avoid something. "Because they'd laugh at me." Maxwell raised his eyes to her face. They were filled with pain. "Like you did."

Damn, he almost had her going. *He* was coming across like the victim, not the women he killed. "When, Harry, when did I laugh at you?"

"The first time." His eyes were sad as he looked at her. He made her think of a stray puppy. A very dangerous stray puppy, she reminded herself. "When I followed you home from my mother's shop." His face clouded at the memory. "I had to get you to stop laughing."

Okay, we're going for the jackpot here. "How, Harry, how did you get me to stop laughing?"

He looked at her in confusion. "You know how, Claire." He looked down at his hands as if they were a thing apart from him. "I put my hands where the sound was coming from." As he spoke, he seemed to be reliving the moment, his voice getting more agitated. "I could feel it under my fingers. Coming up. Hurting me. So I squeezed it." He looked at her again. "I squeezed until you stopped laughing. And then you were so still." He smiled the same shy smile. But this time it seemed eerie to her. ‘‘You looked like you were sleeping. And then you were mine. Just mine. He couldn’t have you anymore.’’

There was more to this? An accomplice, maybe? ‘‘He?’’

‘‘That guy you were with.’’ Anger contorted his face, looking strangely out of place. ‘‘The one who kept touching you.’’ His eyes darkened as he looked at her accusingly. ‘‘He’s back again, isn’t he? He looks different, but he’s back. Touching you. Don’t deny it. I saw him.’’ He took a step toward her, squaring his shoulders. It was the first time she realized that he was taller than she was. ‘‘He can’t have you. You belong to me.’’ Agitated, Maxwell was yelling now.

She had to placate him until she could reach her gun, C.J. thought. She’d allowed him to lead her away from the weapon.

Her tone was soft, compliant. ‘‘Okay. I belong to you. Just you.’’

He shook his head stubbornly, like a child refusing to be lied to.

‘‘No, you say that now, but I know you. You’ll see him again.’’ He was breathing hard now, struggling with a rage that colored his face. ‘‘I don’t want you to. It hurts to see you with him like that. You never look at me like that.’’

She licked her lips, stalling for time. Trying to play up to him. ‘‘Like what?’’

‘‘Like you love me,’’ he pouted.

Because she was trying to calm him, to lull him

into a false sense of security, she took a step closer to him. "But I do, Harry, I do love you."

He shook his head again. Maxwell was clutching the rose so hard he was bending the stem. She saw it drooping.

"That's what your mouth says, but not your eyes."

"That's not true, Harry," C.J. protested with feeling.

It only seemed to anger him more. "Don't lie to me! You want me to go," he guessed. "But don't you see, I can't go? I love you. I just want to be close to you. To touch you."

He combed his fingers awkwardly through her hair. C.J. held herself perfectly still. He was as dangerous as a bear invading a campsite.

His eyes seemed to bore into her. "You're afraid of me. Why are you afraid of me?" He dropped his hand to his side. "I won't hurt you, Claire. It won't hurt, I promise."

Her heart began to hammer. He *had* come to kill her. "What won't hurt?" she prodded. "What are you going to do to me, Harry?"

"Make you mine again. See, I brought you a present." Digging into his coat pocket, he pulled something out and held it up for her to look at.

It was a cheap, imitation pearl choker. The same kind that the others had on.

Bingo.

He beamed at it proudly. "People say I don't think. My mother says I don't think. But I do. I think of everything.'' He dangled the necklace before her, eager for her approval. ''This is so no one'll see.''

Her mouth was so dry, she thought she was going to choke. But she had to keep him talking, had to get him to say he killed the others.

''See what?''

Her questions seemed to be annoying him. ''How I made you mine.''

''You mean the bruises?''

He frowned. ''No bruises. You'll be perfect.'' And then he looked at her hands. ''You bite your nails.'' He beamed proudly. ''I can fix that. I'll make them pretty. Just like you.''

C.J. took a step back. One more step and she could pivot and lunge for her gun.

Maxwell saw her looking toward the weapon. His breath shortened and was audible as anger came. ''No, you can't have that, Claire. You can't hurt me with that, I won't let you.''

Okay, maybe a little verbal shock treatment would work here. ''I'm not Claire, Harry. I'm Chris. You killed Claire.''

There was horror in his eyes. ''No, no, I didn't. *You're* Claire, my Claire.''

''We can get help for you, Harry. Your mother's very worried about you.'' She saw rage in his eyes at the mention of his mother. So much for thinking that all serial killers hating their mothers was a load of garbage. Maxwell clearly detested his. ''*I'm* very worried about you.'' She put her hand on top of his. ''Won't you let me help you?''

He jerked his hand away. "I don't want help, I want you. Forever. This time it'll be forever."

When she tried to turn away, Maxwell grabbed her by the wrist, his fingers closing around it like a vise. He was a great deal stronger than he appeared.

The sound of breaking glass coming from the back of the house made him jump. It was all the distraction she needed. C.J. yanked her hand out of his grasp and ran for her weapon.

The next second, searing pain shot through her scalp. Maxwell had grabbed her by her hair. He pulled her to him roughly. "No!"

He looked crazy, she thought. Was this the face the victims saw before they died? "Harry—"

"No, you can't scream." He shook his head from side to side, adamant. "You can't. They'll hear you. Everyone'll hear you."

He released her hair only to grab her by the throat. And then both hands were around it, squeezing, stealing her air. C.J. clawed at his fingers, trying to pull them away, but he wouldn't release his hold.

"Let her go, Maxwell!" Warrick roared. His weapon was trained on the other man.

Warrick. C.J. couldn't even cry out his name. Her windpipe was closing.

Harry looked at him as if Warrick had just told him to do something that was beyond his scope.

"I can't. She won't be mine if I let go. She'll be yours." He squeezed harder. "You can't love her like I do."

Panic seized Warrick. Maxwell wasn't going to let her go. He was going to kill her. Warrick cocked his weapon. "Yes, I can, Maxwell. I do. I love her more than you. Now let her go or I'll shoot!"

But Harry shook his head again, squeezing harder.

The air was gone from her lungs, from her body. There was nothing left to draw on. Her head was spinning, the room was darkening.

She thought she heard an explosion just before she hit the floor.

She blacked out for one terrible second. And then there was air, sweet air and she was gasping, coughing, trying to suck it all into her lungs.

She thought she heard Warrick's voice yelling, saying something about "agent down" and needing "immediate assistance." There were more words. Garbled, they floated through her head, mixing with shooting lights. She heard him say "ambulance."

Still gasping, her chest heaving, C.J. realized that her eyes were shut.

Prying the lids opened, she saw Warrick looking down at her. She was on the floor and he was cradling her against him.

She'd never seen him look so worried before, not even the night she gave birth to her baby.

He saw her eyes flutter. His heart echoed the movement. He'd just been to hell and back in the space of an eternal minute.

He hugged her to him. "Oh, God, C.J., are you all right?"

C.J. struggled to sit up. She ran her fingers tentatively over her throat. It ached something awful. She could still feel Harry's fingers, pressing the life out of her.

Trying to swallow, she coughed, then nodded. "Yes." The word came out in a gasp. She tried again after a beat. "But I think my concert-singing career is over."

He rocked back on his heels. "Damn it, C.J., you scared the hell out of me." Shouting at her, Warrick offered up a silent prayer of thanksgiving. "I thought you were dead."

"That makes two of us."

Shakily she tried to gain her feet and almost fell. Warrick rose quickly and helped her up. It was then she saw Harry on the floor, blood pooling beneath him. Her breath caught.

"Is he—"

"No, just knocked out." He'd already checked for a pulse. "I hit him in the shoulder." When he'd doubled back, he recognized Maxwell's car parked several houses down. Approaching her house, he'd heard the man's raised voice. He'd circled around to the back. Not wanting to waste time, he'd broken a window to get in. "What the hell was going on here?"

"Harry was about to make me 'permanently his.'" She took in another deep breath. It hurt her lungs. "He thought I was Claire."

Warrick looked at her blankly. "Claire?"

She nodded. Pain shot up to the top of her head. This was going to take a while, she thought. "Claire Farrel. The first victim. Apparently, that was an accident."

"How the hell do you accidentally strangle someone?" He laughed shortly. "And all the others?"

She put it together as she went along. ''I guess he thought they were Claire coming back to him. I think he probably followed each one around and when he saw someone moving in on what he thought was his 'territory,' he made sure that he wouldn't lose the girl.''

Warrick looked down at the unconscious killer. ''By choking her to death.''

''Worked for him,'' she said grimly. Maxwell looked like a harmless rag doll. Just went to show how deceiving appearances could be.

It still didn't make sense to him. ''But how did he get here?'' They had cameras at all the exits. Were there more kills under this lunatic's belt? ''Did you call Culpepper and Rodriguez?''

''I talked to Culpepper before Maxwell's little visit.'' Her voice was beginning to return to normal. ''He has a secret tunnel.''

Warrick stared at her, dumbfound. ''You're kidding me.''

She smiled. God, but he looked good to her. If he hadn't come when he had, right now nothing would be looking good to her. ''Hey, these old buildings in the county have lots of secrets. He said he used the connection that ran through the basement. Apparently he knew he was being watched.''

Warrick blew out a breath in wonder. ''He's not as dumb as he looks.''

She shrugged. ''Survival instincts. Even the lowest creatures have them.'' She took a step and her legs almost gave out from beneath her. Warrick was quick to grab her before she could fall.

"Why don't you sit down?" He nodded toward the sofa behind her.

But she shook her head. Standing up made her feel more in control, and she was still somewhat spooked over what had almost happened.

And then she looked at Warrick. He'd left in a huff and she'd thought she'd never see him again outside of the job. "What are you doing here?"

He grinned. "Rescuing you."

Was he just being cute, or was there something more? "You anticipated this?"

"No." He blew out a breath. The excitement had knocked his original purpose out of his head. Time to get back to business. "I came back to apologize." Something he didn't do very often. Warrick shook his head, mystified. "I don't know what the hell we're arguing about."

"I do," she said. He looked at her in surprise. "We're both scared."

"Scared—" About to protest that that was absurd, he thought better of it and dropped his defensive tone. After all, he'd admitted as much to himself. "Yeah, maybe you're on to something there."

Before she could say anything in response, someone was banging on the door. She heard Rodriguez on the other side calling to her

She smiled, relieved. It was over. "Must be the rest of the cavalry. I'd better get that."

He nodded. "Good idea." He watched her as she went to the door. What the hell would he have done if he hadn't decided to come back tonight? If Maxwell had succeeded in killing C.J.?

He wasn't allowed to be with the thought long. The next moment her living room was filled with special agents all talking at once. Culpepper and Rodriguez had arrived at the same time as the backup team Warrick had called.

Storming in, Culpepper stopped short, looking at the floor as Maxwell began to stir and moan. "What the hell do we have here?" He turned to Rodriguez, confused. "I thought we were watching this clown."

"He outsmarted you," Warrick told him. "Maxwell knew he was being watched. C.J. said he used a tunnel that ran from the basement of his building to another one.

Rodriguez was closest to C.J. He took a closer look at her. "You look shaken up. You okay?" His eyes skimmed over her. "He didn't hurt you, did he?"

"No." She smiled as she nodded at Warrick. "Superhero here arrived just in the nick of time."

"Just in the nick of time, huh?" Culpepper peered at her throat. "Then what are those marks I see on your throat?"

Her hand went to her throat. Warrick pushed it aside, examining the damage himself. He scowled, banking down an urge to strangle Maxwell himself. "Those look pretty nasty, C.J."

She tried to sound cavalier. "I guess I'll be wearing turtleneck sweaters for a while. Good thing the weather's still cool."

They heard the sound of an ambulance approaching in the distance. "One of you ride in with him,"

Warrick said to Culpepper and Rodriguez. And then he glanced at C.J. "Wouldn't hurt for you to go to the hospital, either."

"I think Culpepper can handle—"

Warrick cut in. "As a patient."

She shook her head, raising her face up to his. Whether he liked it or not, he was her hero. And always would be, no matter what. "I'm fine just where I am."

Chapter 16

Warrick pulled his car up into C.J.'s driveway. Setting the parking brake, he turned off the engine and looked at her. They'd just spent the past two hours at the field office, filling in a groggy Alberdeen on the major salient points of recent events and explaining why their prime suspect had been wounded.

Then they had stopped at her parents' house to get the baby. Shaken, C.J. needed to hold her child in her arms, needed to feel that everything was still normal and good. She had forbidden him to say anything to her parents about this evening, only that she had a sudden urge to be with her daughter. Warrick gave her no argument.

She was still pale, Warrick thought, even when

he took the poor lighting into account. He resisted the temptation to take her into his arms and just hold her. Besides, it wasn't too prudent with the parking brake in the way. ''You sure you're all right?''

''No,'' she admitted. It still hurt every time she took a breath. She slanted a look in his direction and smiled. It was official. He was her hero. ''But I'll get there.''

If she admitted that she wasn't all right, it had to be bad. The woman never listened to reason. ''Damn it, why won't you let me take you to the hospital?''

She sighed before answering. It was her head that was the real problem, not her body. It was going to take her a while before she could forget how close she'd come to being victim number fifteen.

''Because nothing's broken and I don't want any sedatives. Besides, I have the best medicine in the world right there.'' Turning her body rather than just her head, she looked at her sleeping daughter in the car seat.

He frowned. ''You don't have to tough out everything, you know.''

''I know.'' C.J. paused, her hand on the door handle. ''Would you like to come in?''

Warrick felt the ground suddenly turn to quicksand beneath his feet. ''Do you want me to?''

C.J. rolled her eyes. She wasn't about to get pulled into this nebulous, gray area. ''Don't start that. I don't want to play a theme and variation of the Saturday night scene in *Marty*.''

Warrick stared at her, shaking his head. "You know, Jones, half the time I don't know what you're talking about."

She grinned for the first time since the blowup in her bedroom.

"Keeps the mystery alive, Warrick." And then she looked at him for a long moment. "As I recall, you said something about coming back to apologize."

It seemed like a century ago that he'd said those words. "Oh, you remember that, huh?"

"Yes." Opening the door, she got out of the car. He followed suit, rounding the hood and taking the sleeping baby out, car seat and all. C.J. fished her keys out of her pocket. "I also think I heard you tell Maxwell you loved me. Was that just to distract him?"

He watched her unlock the door. "Yes and no."

She walked inside ahead of him. Everything looked different to her. She wondered how long it would be before things got back to normal. "Which is it? You can't have it both ways."

"That's just the problem—" he shut the door behind them "—I want it both ways."

She took the baby from him. Joy stirred just a little, then went on sleeping. She resisted the temptation of taking her out of the seat and just holding her. Instead, giving in to the need to have the baby close by, she set the seat down beside the sofa and then looked at Warrick. "And you said I'm the one you don't understand? What are you talking about?"

He felt like a man on a tightrope, crossing the Grand Canyon. One misstep and it was all over. "I want you as my partner. I don't want to give that up."

She tried to read his expression and got nowhere. The man always was a hell of a poker player. "But?"

His eyes held hers as he tried to gauge how she would take this. "But I don't want to give up something else, either."

She threw up her hands. "It's like pulling teeth." C.J. planted herself directly in front of him, her hands on her hips. "What, Warrick, what don't you want to give up? Beer? Fish on Fridays? What?" she demanded. If he cared, if he loved her, why couldn't he just come out and say it? Or had it really been just a ruse? Had everything they'd just shared been an interlude?

Bit by bit, she was forcing him to shed his protective armor. To leave himself exposed. It took more courage than he'd thought. "I don't want to give you up. I don't want to give this up."

"'This'?" She shook her head. "You're going to have to get more specific than that, Warrick. I'm feeling a little dense tonight." She ran her hand along her throat. "Must have been the lack of oxygen to my brain earlier. Spell it out for me."

He didn't want to be the only one out on this limb. "You've got to give me something to work with, too, you know."

"Well..." C.J. blew out a breath, thinking. Stalling. He still hadn't said anything, committed himself to anything, not really. She didn't want to go first. "The next time a serial killer wants to kill you, I'll tell them they can't, because I love you."

That wasn't good enough. "And if a serial killer didn't want to kill me?" he pressed. "If he just wanted to wound me, would you still say you loved me?"

She turned on her heel and headed to the kitchen. In all the excitement she'd left the light on. "You ask a lot of questions."

"Answer the question, Jones." He was right behind her. "Would you still say you loved me?"

She raised her shoulders in what she hoped was a careless shrug. "Maybe."

He turned her around to face him. "C.J.—"

She caved. She knew she would. It would just have been nicer to have had him cave first. "Okay, yes, I'd still say I loved you, even if a serial killer was only threatening to wound you."

Warrick grinned at her, triumphant. "Okay, next question—"

C.J. covered her face with her hands. "Oh, God," she groaned.

He pulled her hands away from her face. A bit of sunshine was opening up within his chest around the vicinity of his heart. "*Do* you love me?"

She tried to pull away. When he wouldn't release her hands, she nodded toward the counter. "I left the coffeemaker on. I could have burned down the house."

Warrick looked at her intently. They were beyond petty distractions. ''They're programmed to shut off automatically, and don't change the subject. Do you love me?''

She closed her eyes. When she opened them again, he was still looking at her. C.J. surrendered. ''Yes. Yes, I love you. I'm crazy and I love you. Are you satisfied?'' she demanded.

He moved his head slowly from side to side, his eyes never leaving her face, his smile never leaving his lips. ''Not yet.''

She groaned again. She yanked her hands away from him and turned away, afraid that he would start gloating any minute. ''What is it you want, blood?''

''No, I want you to marry me.''

C.J. turned around slowly. She was too young for her hearing to be going. ''What?''

He saw the disbelief in her eyes and tried to interpret it.

''I know, I know,'' he said quickly before she could turn him down. ''I've got a lousy track record, but, hey, that just means I'm due for a run of good luck. I figure it can start with you. And Joy.''

She was still staring at him. ''You're serious.''

The quicksand was back beneath his feet. ''I never joke after wrapping up a serial killer case.''

''You want to marry me.'' She enunciated each word as if she was testing it out first with her tongue.

''Yes.'' He was still watching her eyes for some

kind of sign, wondering if he'd just made a first-class jackass out of himself.

She didn't believe him. He was having fun at her expense. "Why?"

What did she want from him? "Why does anyone want to get married?" He began to turn from her.

She stopped him before he could turn away. He'd started this and they were damn well going to finish it together. "I'm not asking about anyone, I'm asking about you."

"Because I love you," he shouted at her. "Because you've turned my whole world upside down and I can't seem to think unless you're somehow involved." Realizing he was shouting, he lowered his voice. The confession was painful, but maybe if it was out in the open, she'd understand. She wouldn't say no. "I always felt, because of what I saw as a kid and my own botched attempt at marriage, that I didn't have a clue how to make a relationship work. But driving home tonight, I realized that the answer isn't out there somewhere. It's in here." He tapped his chest. "And here." He touched her chest where he deemed her heart to be. Warrick looked into her eyes. "And no matter what direction my heart takes, it just keeps coming back to you."

C.J. stood looking at him for a long time, then finally uttered one word, more like a sound, actually. "Huh."

Warrick stared at her incredulously. "I've just

crawled out on a limb and spilled my guts here. I was kind of hoping for something a little more substantial than 'huh.''' Was that a smile flirting with her lips? Or just his imagination? ''You still haven't answered me, you know.''

She looked at him innocently. ''I know.''

Well, at least she hadn't turned him down. ''You want time to think it over?''

C.J. inclined her head. ''That would be nice.''

This was going to be torture, he thought. ''You going to take as long as you're taking coming up with the baby's middle name?''

And then she allowed herself a smile. A wide one. She glanced back at her daughter. Her small mouth was moving in her sleep. The baby would be waking soon. ''Funny you should mention that. I've come up with one.''

He looked at her uncertainly. She hadn't said anything about finding a name. ''When?''

''Just now.'' She turned her face up to his. ''And it's perfect.''

''What is it?''

''Hope.'' The name floated between them. Her eyes crinkled. ''Because that's what I'm feeling right now. Because that's what's going to be part of my life from now on.''

He nodded his head. ''I like it.'' He eyed her. With C.J. nothing was ever certain until she said it was. ''So your answer's yes? I'm not taking anything for granted here.''

''You'd better not. Especially not me. And, yes—'' she threaded her arms around his neck and leaned her body into his ''—my answer's yes.''

''Good,'' he said just before he brought his mouth down on hers, ''because I wasn't about to take no.'' The kiss was long and languid, melting any bones she had left. ''Now let's put our daughter to bed.'' He grinned, stooping to pick up the car seat. ''And then we'll see about putting you to bed, too.''

She looked at Warrick holding Joy. Her heart had never felt this full. ''Sounds like a plan to me.''

* * * * *

Her Baby Secret

VICTORIA PADE

VICTORIA PADE

is a bestselling author of both historical and contemporary romantic fiction, and mother of two energetic daughters, Cori and Erin. Although she enjoys her chosen career as a novelist, she occasionally laments that she has never travelled further from her Colorado home than Disneyland, instead spending all her spare time plugging away at her computer. She takes breaks from writing by indulging in her favourite hobby – eating chocolate.

Chapter One

Paris Hanley recognized the voice the minute she heard it. A baritone as deep and rich as Dutch cocoa.

It was coming from the family room of the house she shared with her mother and her daughter, Hannah, and it made Paris forget all about shucking the shoes she'd been dying to get off her aching feet the minute she walked in the door. It made her follow the sound of that distinctive voice in a rush.

"There she is!" her mother exclaimed when Paris burst through the archway of the family room. Then, to Paris, she said, "Look who's here."

Paris had been right. There, with Janine Hanley, sat Ethan Tarlington.

But his presence didn't please her as much as it seemed to please her mother.

"Hi," he greeted.

''Hello,'' Paris responded without a bit of warmth.

The coolness was uncalled for. He hadn't done anything wrong. In fact, he'd done everything as right as he possibly could have. It was just that she wasn't proud of what she'd let happen between them the one and only other time they'd been together. And the fact that it had served her purposes only complicated things.

So she amended her tone to one of curiosity even as she put herself between Ethan Tarlington and the playpen where her five-month-old daughter was peacefully napping.

''This is a surprise,'' she said then.

''I knew it would be,'' her mother said, even though Paris hadn't intended the comment for her. ''Imagine the man from the picture showing up on our doorstep. Of course, I wouldn't have let him in if I hadn't recognized him from the snapshot, but since I did I thought you'd be glad to see him again.''

The snapshot.

The instant snapshot that Paris had taken when she was supposed to be taking pictures of the tables for the caterer's portfolio and Ethan Tarlington had somehow found his way into the viewfinder instead.

The snapshot she'd pocketed for no reason she'd understood and kept in her sweater drawer ever since. In her sweater drawer where her mother had happened upon it and come to her own false conclusions about Paris having some kind of crush on him.

''Well, I have things to do, so I'll leave you two to talk,'' Janine said then, getting up from the wicker chair that faced the identical one Ethan Tarlington was sitting in.

Paris wanted to tell her mother to take Hannah with her but she was afraid of drawing too much attention to the baby. In fact, it occurred to her that standing where she was, nearly hovering over the playpen, might do the same thing, so she moved to sit in the seat her mother had vacated.

''Ick, you smell like sausage,'' Janine said with a laugh as their paths crossed.

''That's what I've been demo-ing all day.''

''At the grocery store,'' Ethan Tarlington contributed. ''Your mother told me you're still doing odd jobs so you can paint.''

''Yes, I am.''

Janine bid them a general goodbye and left, and for the first time since Paris had come into the room she let her gaze settle directly on Ethan Tarlington.

Either he'd gotten even better-looking or the snapshot and her memory of him hadn't done him justice because it struck Paris all over again how devastatingly handsome he was.

Hair the color of espresso, which he wore devil-may-care longer on top than on the sides or back and finger-combed to perfection. Cerulean-blue eyes so striking, so piercing, they hardly seemed real. A nose that was just hawkish enough to give him character and distinction. Chiseled cheekbones and a jawline so sharp it could slice bread. Lips that managed to be thin and sensuous at once. Broad shoulders and the body to go with them on legs that she knew would elevate him to a full six-four if he were standing.

The perfect specimen.

But that was the last thing she should be thinking about.

So she tried not to, put a businesslike tone into her voice and said, ''This really is a surprise.''

''Not one you sound too happy about,'' he said with an arch of well-shaped eyebrows.

No, she *wasn't* happy about seeing him again. But she couldn't say that so she didn't say anything at all.

''Cinderella is supposed to be thrilled to see the prince, isn't she?'' he added into the brief silence she left. ''Or don't I fit that bill?''

Oh, he fit it, all right. At least, he would have under different circumstances.

''I don't think that I'm a likely Cinderella.''

''We met at the ball, spent the evening together and you disappeared into thin air. Isn't that Cinderella?''

Except the *ball* had been a Denver-area charity dinner in his honor and she hadn't been there as a guest all dolled up in a fairy godmother's gift of gown and slippers. She'd been hired by the caterer as a cocktail waitress and she'd been wearing black trousers and a tuxedo shirt.

And she hadn't disappeared at the respectable stroke of midnight…

''I tried to find you before this,'' Ethan Tarlington continued. ''For that whole next week afterward. But you aren't listed in the phone book and you didn't leave me even an e-mail address. The caterer wouldn't give me any information about you—in case I was a stalker, I guess. Plus you didn't really tell me anything about yourself except that you were a struggling artist. When I called several galleries and finally found someone who had heard of you, she wouldn't tell me anything, either, because she was angling to be the middleman if I was interested in buying some of your work. Then I ran out of time and—''

''Left the country—you told me you were going to. And that you didn't know when you'd be back. That made it seem unlikely that there would be a second...date.''

''Still, I thought we hit it off.''

''It was a nice enough night,'' was all Paris would concede. Then she said, ''How did you find me now?''

''It was fate. I was flying home last week, reading magazines on the plane, and I hit an article about up-and-coming young artists in the Denver area. Since I'd met one of those—namely you—I read the article and there you were. So I thought, why not give it another try? I called the magazine, talked to the writer, and here I am—looking you up.''

''Ah.''

Maybe fate was paying her back.

''What snapshot was your mother talking about?'' Ethan Tarlington asked then.

''It was one of several I took for the caterer that night. The kind that develop within a few minutes. I caught you by mistake and it wasn't a very good shot of the table setting so I stuck it in my pocket and just happened to bring it home with me.''

Okay, so that was partially untrue. She could easily have altered her view before she took the picture, but she wasn't really sure why she hadn't, and she wasn't going to tell him that any more than she was going to let him know she'd hung on to it all this time.

Besides, she didn't want to talk about that night so she changed the subject. ''Did everything go the way you'd planned overseas?''

''It took longer than I thought it would, but, yes, I did what I set out to do. I opened offices in London, Paris, Amsterdam, Geneva, Hong Kong and Brisbane for Tarlington Integrated Business and Government Software.''

''So you're worldwide. Congratulations.''

''Thanks,'' he said without conceit. But then, that was one of the things she'd liked about him when she'd met him—his ego was not proportional to his reputation, status or megamillion-dollar net worth as one of the stars in the computer software industry.

It seemed to be his turn to change the subject. ''Looks like you've been pretty busy yourself,'' he said with a nod in the direction of the playpen. ''A baby by artificial insemination, according to your mother.''

Paris couldn't keep from grimacing at that. ''She told you?''

''She said you had some female problems and couldn't wait around for Mr. Right.''

The details were even worse. How could her mother have blabbed about her health problems, too?

"My mother talks too much."

"Hannah is a beautiful baby, though."

"You saw her? I mean, was she awake when you got here?"

"Awake and cooing and smiling at me like an angel."

That was not good news to Paris.

But what was done was done and there wasn't anything she could do about it now, so instead she decided to try for a little damage control by cutting this visit short.

"I'm afraid that angel has a doctor's appointment I need to get her to," she lied. "I don't mean to be rude but—"

"Is she sick?"

"No, it's just a well-baby checkup."

"I see."

But he didn't get up to go. Instead he turned his head to look at the playpen again for a long moment.

Then he focused on Paris again and said, "Your mom is a nice lady. Talkative."

"I suppose she is." Paris wondered why he'd started that rather than taking her invitation to leave.

"She told me some things about what's going on with you now."

A wave of panic washed through Paris until she remembered that her mother couldn't tell what she didn't know. But still, she was curious about what he meant so she said, "And what exactly did my talkative mother have to say about me?"

"That it was harder for you to make ends meet with the baby and that you really need money for a new car—which was why you were handing out food samples at the grocery store."

"And she probably made me sound like a martyr or something when she said it, too," Paris said with a small laugh to downplay her mother's report. "My being a single parent by choice is something she's had a hard time grasping."

"Maybe. But she's proud of you. And she's crazy about Hannah."

"Hannah is the light of her life."

"What she said got me to thinking while I've been here, though, and there might be a job you could do for me."

"Do you have sausages that need demonstrating?"

She had absolutely not intended that to sound suggestive in any way. But somehow that's how it had come out.

And it hadn't escaped Ethan Tarlington because his sensuous mouth stretched into a slow smile. A slow smile she remembered all too well.

"No, no sausage demonstrations," he said with a hint of innuendo in his tone, too. "But you do temporary work and that's what this is. Every year I throw a formal dinner party for the people who live in the town where my brothers and I grew up. Dunbar—it's out on the eastern plains, just before Limon. A small town. Not many people this close to Denver have heard of it."

"I haven't."

"Well, anyway, the party takes a lot of preparation

and organization, and since I like to relax and catch up with old friends while I'm there I need someone else to oversee everything. It's a week from tomorrow—next Saturday night—and it's the last-minute things that can bog me down. So what if you came along to Dunbar to do it for me? There's no hotel or motel, but I'll put you up in my house, and for that single week's work I'll pay you enough to buy a new car outright."

"You're kidding."

"I'm not. It isn't the reason I looked you up, but since things seem to have changed and we're both in need, we'd both come out ahead."

Her need was clearly greater than his. Which made for quite a dilemma suddenly.

Her mother had been right about the fact that since she'd had Hannah it had been more and more difficult to make ends meet selling the occasional painting and doing odd jobs. And just since Hannah's birth her old clunker of a car had broken down three times, one of them stranding the two of them on a miserably cold, rainy night just two weeks before. The incident had left Paris worried every time she took Hannah out in it now.

The mechanic had left no question that the car had to be replaced, but without steady employment she hadn't been able to qualify for either a loan or a lease on anything else. And she honestly didn't know what to do about it.

Except that now, sitting only a few feet away from her, was a solution.

It was just that that solution was Ethan Tarlington. The man she'd counted on never seeing again.

"I don't have anyone to leave Hannah with," she said suddenly. "My mother is the only person I feel comfortable leaving her with for a whole week, and she's going to Florida tomorrow to visit her sister."

"I know, she told me."

What *hadn't* she told him?

"But that's not a problem," Ethan assured her. "The house in Dunbar is big enough to get lost in so there's plenty of room for Hannah, too. Most of what you'll do can be done with her right by your side, but if it can't, there'll be someone to stay with her because there's a live-in staff of three, plus both of my brothers will be there."

He leaned slightly forward and added in a confidential tone, "That also means five chaperones, in case that makes you feel any better."

It didn't.

But Paris found herself considering his offer in spite of that.

The thought just kept going through her mind that he was only talking about one week. A single week's work that would net her enough money to replace her car.

How much time would Ethan really be spending with her or Hannah, anyway? she reasoned. He was hiring her to free himself to see his friends. Didn't that mean that she would merely be part of the staff and that he wouldn't be giving her or her daughter a second glance?

It seemed likely. More than likely.

And then she could buy a new, safe car...

"If I do this I want it clear that what happened between us before is not going to happen again. I'll be working for you and that's all. Strictly business."

"Strictly business," he agreed without hesitation.

Something about the speed of that concession stung her, though. She didn't understand it, and while she was examining her reaction he seemed to consider the matter settled and stood.

But rather than heading for the front of the house to leave, he surprised her yet again by going to the playpen.

That stopped Paris's examination of her feelings instantly as she nearly jumped to her feet to follow him like a protective mother bear.

"Still snoozing," he said softly, peering into the playpen.

"She's a sound sleeper. She probably won't wake up until I get her to the doctor's office," Paris said to restate her earlier claim of an appointment so that he really might leave.

"Guess I won't be able to say goodbye to her, then."

"No, I guess not."

But he still stood there for another long moment, watching the baby sleep. And giving Paris second thoughts about accepting his job offer.

But it was for Hannah's sake, she reminded herself. The new car she would get out of it was for Hannah's safety.

Then Ethan Tarlington finally broke off his scrutiny of her daughter and headed out of the family room.

"So you'll take the job in Dunbar?" he said along the way.

Again Paris had doubts.

But again she also had to consider the benefits, and choose those over the risks.

"Yes, I'll take the job."

"Strictly business," he reminded, as if he could tell she'd wanted him to.

"Strictly business," she confirmed.

"Okay, then, I'll pick you up at nine Monday morning."

"Maybe it would be better if Hannah and I got there on our own. Is there a bus or train or something?"

"There's a bus that runs from Denver and back but I don't know what the schedule is. And if you drive in with me you'll get there in time to go right to work."

And he was the boss, so what was she going to say to that?

"Nine o'clock Monday morning it is, then, I guess."

They'd reached the door and Paris opened it for him, hoping he wouldn't linger any longer than he already had.

But her hopes were for naught because that's just what he did. Lingering to take a slow, concentrated look at her, his azure eyes going from the top of her short spiky brown hair to her still-aching toes and back again.

"You don't look like a woman who was pregnant

only five months ago. You look great. Even better than I remembered.''

Paris hated how much that pleased her. "I was careful during the pregnancy. I ate a lot of fruits and vegetables so I didn't gain too much more than baby weight. It went away not long after Hannah was born.''

And why was she telling him that, when she should have been telling him the whole subject was not something an employer and an employee had any reason to be discussing?

''Will there be a uniform I'll need to wear?'' she asked then, as if that were the only reason she could think of for him to say anything about her appearance. And to cover her own unwelcome response to his compliment.

''No, no uniform. You can wear your regular clothes. I was just appreciating the postnatal you is all,'' he said with another of those smiles that were one of thc reasons she'd let him sweep her off her feet that other time they'd met.

But she had a lot at stake now and she was determined not to lose sight of that. So she raised a prudish chin to him and said, ''Strictly business.''

''Strictly business,'' he agreed again, just as quickly as the first time.

And like the first time, it stung once more.

Then he said, ''Have a nice weekend,'' and stepped out onto the porch.

''Thanks,'' she responded just before she closed the door behind him and deflated against it.

And that was when it occurred to her why Ethan Tarlington had been so eager to keep things between them strictly business.

It was because of Hannah.

After all, hadn't he said that first night that he wasn't ready for marriage and kids? That they weren't on his near horizon?

He had. And she hadn't doubted for a minute that he'd meant it.

Plus he'd originally "looked her up" because he'd thought they had "hit it off" and he wanted to see her again, yet somewhere along the way he'd obviously gone from wanting to see her again to just wanting her to work for him.

Hannah. It had to be Hannah who had changed things.

But that was okay. It was better than okay, it was for the best.

Because if Ethan Tarlington didn't want to date someone with a child he would keep his distance. He would relegate her completely to the role of employee while he went on about his business.

And that was a good thing. It was just what she wanted.

Except that if it was just what she wanted, why did it sting the same way his eager agreements to keep things strictly business between them had?

She hated to admit it, but this time when she explored her own feelings she realized that it was disappointing that he didn't want her. Child or no child.

But it *was* for the best, she told herself firmly. Because as long as Ethan Tarlington didn't want her, as long as he saw her as nothing more than an employee, as long as he stayed away from her and away from Hannah, he could remain oblivious to the fact that Hannah was his daughter.

And that was just how Paris wanted it.

Chapter Two

Saturday and Sunday had passed more slowly for Ethan than any weekend he could remember. He hadn't been able to concentrate on work. He hadn't been interested in play. He'd had trouble sleeping. And nothing he'd eaten had tasted good.

It wasn't hard to figure out why, when the same thoughts had been going through his mind since the minute he'd left Paris Hanley's house on Friday. The same thoughts that were still going through his mind Monday morning as he had his coffee.

The thoughts all started the same way. At the beginning. The night he'd met Paris.

He'd liked her almost immediately. It hadn't mattered that she was a waitress in a room full of attorneys, executives, financial and computer wizards. It had only mattered that she hadn't fallen all over herself trying to impress him, suck up to him or seduce him. That she hadn't put on any pretenses, any airs.

Plus the way she looked certainly hadn't hurt.

She was a compact little thing. Only about five feet four inches of tight rear end and flat stomach. Of legs that were long despite her height. Of breasts that were just big enough to make a man look twice.

He'd liked the way her short, chestnut-colored hair had a slightly wild air about it in the flipped ends in back and the wisps here and there at the sides and top. It was carefree and cute.

But it framed a face that was more than that.

She had incredible bone structure and skin that was nothing less than luminous. Her mouth was sultry with full lips that old movie magazines would have called kissable. Her nose was an artwork all its own. And then there were her eyes. Eyes with long, thick lashes.

They were actually a pale silver. Not blue. Not gray. But a remarkable, radiant combination of the two that had left him mesmerized the moment he'd looked into them that night.

Mesmerized.

It was still hard for him to believe. Being that awestruck by anyone was an experience he'd never had before, and he'd found himself not caring anymore about the award he'd been receiving. Not caring about any of the other people he was with. Not caring about anything but getting the woman alone so he could have her all to himself.

But that hadn't been easy. She wasn't supposed to

fraternize with the guests, she'd told him. And she'd seemed determined to abide by the rules.

But he'd been more determined to break them. Driven almost.

So he'd kept at her and kept at her.

It had taken him all evening to get her to warm up to him and long after the number of partygoers had dwindled to convince her to have a late dinner with him.

A late dinner at a chic bistro he'd persuaded to stay open just for them. Followed by a walk through the gardens around his house. Then a nightcap in the formal living room so she could see his original Matisse. And then, when one thing led to another…

Wow.

Ethan had relived that encounter in his mind so many times he'd lost count. And it still had the power to rock him even as he sat at his kitchen table on a Monday morning.

Okay, so, no, they hadn't gotten to know much about each other outside the bedroom. A few surface facts mingled with all the flirting and teasing and the palpable sexual attraction. But he hadn't thought that would matter because even though he'd been on the verge of leaving the country, he'd felt as if there would be time after that night to get into the nuts and bolts of things.

But then she'd disappeared.

She was gone when he'd awakened the next morning. Without having said goodbye. Without so much as scrawling her phone number in lipstick on the bathroom mirror. She was just gone. Like Cinderella.

Except she hadn't lost her glass slipper on the way, and he hadn't had only a small kingdom to search for her.

And then he'd had to leave, too, before he'd been able to find her.

Over the months away he'd tried to tell himself to chalk it up to a one-night stand and forget about her.

But that had been easier said than done.

Even when he was so swamped with work that he could hardly see straight, even with no shortage of women willing to keep him company when he wasn't, Paris Hanley had still popped into his thoughts again and again and again.

But the longer he'd been out of the country, the less likely it had seemed that they'd ever reconnect. And he *had* been out of the country for a long time.

The trip he'd initially intended to last six months had stretched to eight. Then ten. Then a full year. Then two months more. And even though Paris Hanley had still been on his mind he'd come to think that too much time had passed, that he'd never see her again. That that single mind-boggling night they'd had together was destined to be the only one and that he would just have to savor the memory that he knew would still be putting a secret smile on his face when he was old and infirm.

And then he'd seen that magazine article on the plane. Complete with a picture that had captured those eyes of hers. Reminding him just how beautiful she was. Reigniting the urge to see her again. Nudging him to try once more to find her.

Fate. When he'd actually managed to persuade the

article's author to give him enough information to track her down—on top of the happenstance of seeing the article in the first place—he'd figured it was fate telling him something.

It was just that now, as he poured his second cup of coffee, he couldn't help wondering exactly *what* fate might have been telling him.

Because now there was Hannah, too.

And that fact was what he'd been going over and over in his mind all weekend as much as thoughts of Paris.

Janine Hanley had been carrying the baby on her hip when she'd answered the door on Friday afternoon. Once the older woman had recognized him from some photograph she'd said her daughter had of him and decided to let him in to wait for Paris's return from work, it hadn't been a big jump for Janine to introduce Hannah to him.

And from there the doting grandmother had been more than willing to tell him all about the baby.

Hannah was five months old.

"I didn't know Paris was involved with anyone," he'd said to Janine as the wheels in his head had begun to turn.

That was when Janine had told him about Paris having some kind of female problem that had thrust her into a now-or-never situation if she wanted to have a child.

"And since she wasn't married or in a relationship, she had artificial insemination," Janine had said.

Artificial insemination.

Ethan hadn't doubted for a minute that Janine Hanley believed that.

But he hadn't found it quite so easy to buy.

Not when Hannah just happened to have been born almost nine months to the day after the night he and Paris had spent together.

Janine Hanley hadn't seemed to know anything about that night, but as she went on talking Ethan had taken a closer look at the baby.

Maybe he was wrong. But Hannah's eyes were remarkable, too. Only not in the same way her mother's were.

In fact, they weren't anything like her mother's eyes.

They were a vibrant aquamarine blue.

Like *his* mother's eyes.

Ethan caught himself staring at the tile floor, picturing Paris in his mind. Picturing Hannah…

Curiosity was eating him up inside.

Was it possible that Hannah was his child?

It certainly seemed possible.

The timing was right. The artificial insemination story could be bogus even if the female problems weren't. And there was the unusual eye color.

But if Hannah was his child, why hadn't Paris said something?

Even though he'd left the country, she could still have tracked him down through his company when she'd found out she was pregnant. And barring that, she could have told him on Friday.

But not only hadn't she, he'd had the sense that she was sorry he'd been anywhere near Hannah. That she was trying to run interference to keep him away from the baby altogether.

But if Hannah was his child why *wouldn't* Paris want him to know? That was the part that most made him doubt his paternity.

Too many other women he knew would have been beating a path to his door for child support. And Paris needed the money more than anyone.

Of course, nothing else about her was like other women, so why should that be? But still he'd had women—okay, one woman in particular—who had gone to great lengths to get all she could out of him for far less reason, and she hadn't been handing out sausages at a supermarket to make ends meet or driving an old junk heap of a car.

So maybe Hannah really was the product of artificial insemination, and the similarity between her aquamarine eyes and his mother's aquamarine eyes was purely a coincidence.

Or maybe one of his brothers had donated sperm to a sperm bank at some point and he just didn't know about it.

"I wouldn't give very good odds on that one," he muttered to himself as he took his coffee cup to the sink.

But his brothers *did* play a role in his reason for that job offer he'd made Paris.

He wanted them to get a look at Hannah, too. To see if they saw in her what he saw in her. To know what they thought.

And maybe in the process he'd be able to figure out what could possibly be going on with Paris to make her keep the fact of his own child from him if Hannah *was* his.

But either way, one thing was certain: he was going to get to the bottom of this.

He clasped the edge of the countertop with both hands and leaned forward, hanging his head as he shook it from side to side.

What a mess this could all be, he thought.

He just hoped that whatever it was that was going on with Paris wasn't what it looked like.

Because what it looked like was that she'd had his baby and kept the news from him.

And that deceit—*any* deceit—was a very big deal to him. Deceitful women were women he didn't want anything to do with. Women he'd vowed to be on the lookout for. And if Paris Hanley was one of those women they had a problem.

If Paris Hanley was one of those women *and* she was the mother of his child they had an even bigger problem.

But he was reserving judgment until he knew the facts.

And keeping his fingers crossed that the facts wouldn't prove the worst.

Because baby or no baby, there was some inexplicable something about Paris Hanley that flipped a switch in him.

And when that switch was flipped it was as if he came alive in a way he never had with any other woman. In a way he never had in his whole life.

And he wasn't sure what that would mean to him

if he discovered she was keeping a secret as enormous as a child of his own making.

Paris hoped none of her neighbors were around to see the limousine that pulled up in front of her house at exactly nine o'clock in the morning. It would cause no end of talk and she didn't relish being the subject of it. At least, she didn't relish being the subject of neighborhood gossip any more than she already had been as the resident unwed mother who everyone believed had been artificially inseminated.

Luckily she had everything packed and ready to go. Including Hannah, who was soundly napping in her car seat. A baby blanket draped over it to keep out the August sunshine and Ethan Tarlington's prying eyes.

He did look wonderful as he got out of the car and came up to her open front door, though—casual and comfortable in khaki slacks and a garnet-colored polo shirt that hugged his broad shoulders and sculpted chest.

Not that the way he looked mattered to her. She was just glad to see that she wasn't underdressed by comparison since she hadn't been sure what to wear. She'd opted for a pair of navy-blue linen drawstring pants and a white split-V-necked T-shirt tucked into them, and it helped that the outfit had been the right choice.

Or at least she told herself that was the only reason watching Ethan approach the house brought her pleasure.

The limousine driver followed him to her door as

Paris slid her suitcase and the smaller one for Hannah out onto the porch.

"Morning," she said perfunctorily.

"Hi," Ethan greeted, much as he had on Friday afternoon.

"I'm all set," she added, turning back inside to sling her purse and diaper bag over her shoulder and pick up the car seat by its handle.

But Ethan didn't let her hang on to the car seat for long. He took it from her with a simple "Let me get this."

As his driver took the suitcases to the limo's trunk, Ethan peeked under the baby blanket canopy. "Is she sleeping again?"

"Morning nap time," Paris confirmed, repositioning the blanket to block his view.

Once she'd locked the front door, she and Ethan followed the driver to the car. The rear door had been left open, and inside Paris could see two rows of seats facing each other. Ethan set the carrier on the backward-facing seat.

"Is there a special trick to this thing?" he asked as he did.

"I need to do it," Paris answered, glad to take over.

Ethan ducked out of the car and freed the way for her to climb in.

She deposited her purse and diaper bag on the roomy floor while she used the seat belts to secure the carrier. It was a whole lot easier job in the limousine than it was in her car. Her car only had two doors, and getting the carrier and herself into the back seat required contortions.

But she was extremely aware that while doing it in the expansive limo might be more convenient, it also had her bending over and giving Ethan a bull's-eye view of her derriere. Which she didn't appreciate.

There was nothing to be done about it, however, so she just buckled the baby carrier in as quickly as she could and then sat beside it, leaving the opposite seat free for Ethan.

"All set?" he asked from the sidewalk.

"All set."

He joined them, then, closing the door behind him rather than waiting for the driver to do it. When he'd settled in he pointed to his left, pushed a button and out came a fully equipped bar. "Would you like something to drink? Coffee? Tea? Soda?"

"I'm fine, thanks."

Another push of the button and the bar disappeared, just as the engine purred to life and the limo moved away from the curb.

The car seemed to glide into motion so quietly, so smoothly, it was as if they were floating. Paris was thrilled with that. It meant Hannah would likely sleep all the way to their destination, and that was exactly what Paris wanted.

"How far is it to Dunbar?" she asked then.

"About 150 miles. It'll take a while."

Too long a while, Paris thought as she realized she was going to spend that entire time one-on-one with

Ethan Tarlington and those blue eyes of his that seemed to be studying her.

She was wondering what to talk about to distract him, when he said, "The drive will give us a chance to get to know a little about each other."

"Like a job interview?"

"I think we're beyond that, don't you?"

Paris wasn't happy about any reference to the intimacy they'd shared fourteen months before but she tried not to show it.

"I'd really like to know about your health problems," Ethan said. "They must have been pretty severe to push you into doing something as extreme as artificial insemination."

The last thing she wanted to talk about with Ethan Tarlington was her health problems. But it occurred to her that telling him what he wanted to know might reinforce her claim that Hannah was the product of artificial insemination, and for the sake of that she decided to allow the conversation.

"I guess any artificial means of having a baby does seem extreme from the outside looking in. But for me it was just a solution. I was diagnosed with endometriosis and cystic ovaries so bad that the first doctor I saw wanted to do a hysterectomy."

"I'm not sure what endometriosis and cystic ovaries are, but they sound serious."

"Female problems," she repeated to simplify, leaving it at that because she didn't want to go into a lecture about uterine lining traveling through her abdominal cavity to attach itself and cause miserable pain and cramping, or about the monthly development of cysts from which ovulation occurred and the problems that developed when those cysts didn't spontaneously dissolve every month the way they were supposed to.

But apparently he was satisfied with her simplification because rather than asking for details, he said, "The *first* doctor—I assume that means you saw others?"

"I wanted kids, not a hysterectomy at twenty-eight. So yes, I got a second opinion."

"And how did that stack up against the first?"

"It was pretty much the same. But the second doctor understood that I wanted to try to have at least one baby before I did anything as final as surgery."

The truth was that having kids had been something Paris had wanted for as long as she could remember and the thought of being denied that was a devastating blow to her. She'd ended up sobbing in the second doctor's office.

"Anyway," she continued, "the second doctor made it clear that having a baby was a now-or-never proposition. If it wasn't already too late. And since I'd just come out of a relationship and there weren't any immediate candidates for husband or father, I looked into artificial insemination."

That was true, too. She *had* looked into it and discovered that it was expensive. So expensive that she'd been terrified that what little window of opportunity she might have would be closed by the time she could save enough money to do it.

Which was when Ethan Tarlington had come along.

That night was vivid in Paris's memory.

Yes, she'd noticed the incredible-looking guest of honor when he'd entered the banquet room, but the last thing she'd been thinking about was having him father her child. Doing a good job and being able to put the evening's pay into her artificial insemination fund was more what was on her mind.

Then he'd started to flirt with her. To tease her. To go all-out in persuading her to see him later on.

He'd been so persistent. So amazingly handsome. So charming and funny. He'd just worn down her defenses until she'd finally given in to having dinner with him. *Just* to having dinner with him.

Certainly making babies with him had not been a consideration. The furthest thing from it, in fact. After all, she'd only slept with one man before that, and it certainly hadn't been on her first date with him. She rarely even kissed on a first date.

But what a date that night with Ethan had turned out to be!

It was like no other date she'd ever been on. Not even with Jason.

Hours had gone by like mere moments. Ethan had made her laugh. He'd been able to talk about art with her more comprehensively than most art professors. He'd paid attention to everything she'd had to say. He'd made her feel as if she were the only woman in the world. And he'd been a perfect gentleman.

Even when he'd finally kissed her it had felt long overdue, and she'd been dying for him to.

Of course it hadn't hurt that by then they'd finished an entire bottle of champagne. But still, the man could kiss. Plus he had a way of holding her, a way no one had ever held her before, that was arousing all on its own. It was as if she could feel the power in his arms, in his muscular body. A primitive, masculine power, leashed into a gentleness that made her feel safe, protected, cherished.

And very turned on.

So turned on that she had wanted to stay kissing him forever. She'd wanted to stay held in his arms forever.

But more than that, she'd wanted to feel his touch, too. His hands on her body...

"I didn't know you were having health problems that night."

"I wasn't," she said. "I mean, I was, but I felt fine that night." And this was where she had to begin the lies. "The appointment with the first doctor was on that Monday after we were together. That was when I got the bad news. I saw the second doctor on that Thursday and everything went fast from there."

She hated lying. To him or to anyone else. But she'd decided that if she was going to be with him for the next week, if Hannah was going to be around him, she would say anything she had to, to throw him off the track.

"You must have had artificial insemination right away."

"Right away. Within two weeks of when we met," she confirmed. "And then Hannah was born early." Only four days early, but Paris didn't offer that little detail.

"So that night we were together—"

"Was just a moment out of time before I got the worst news of my life and had to find a way to deal with it."

A moment during which she'd discovered in herself such a strong urge to have him make love to her that she hadn't been able to resist it.

She'd wanted it as badly as if they'd been together for months. As if there had been a prolonged mounting of sexual tension that had culminated on that night in a need so demanding it had to be satisfied.

Then—and only then—had baby making come to mind for her.

Not as a driving force, by any means. Not as the reason she was with Ethan. Not as the reason she wanted him. Not as a calculated act. Just as a little whisper in the back of her mind that told her she was likely ovulating. That here was a handsome, successful, intelligent, creative, personable man who was a better candidate for fathering her child than anyone she would ever find in a sperm bank's catalog.

And so she'd done what she'd never done before. She'd thrown caution to the wind and spent the remainder of the night in bed with Ethan Tarlington.

"It *was* a moment out of time, wasn't it?" he repeated as if she'd struck a chord with that phrase, smiling as if he were remembering just how good that moment had been.

That moment that had culminated not only in the most incredible lovemaking she'd ever experienced, but as a moment out of time that had given her her heart's desire when she'd needed it most. Because astonishingly, she'd gotten pregnant from that single night with him.

She thought her lies about the timing must have appeased whatever it was that had been going through his mind, because Ethan returned to the earlier part of the conversation. ''Didn't artificial insemination seem...I don't know, impersonal? Clinical?''

''Of course there's that element to it. But there are advantages, too.''

''For instance?''

''For instance, a baby by artificial insemination belongs only to that baby's mother. And that mother is free to raise that baby as she sees fit, without any interference.'' And without anyone being able to demand custody of the child and take the child away from that mother.

''You don't think it's a problem that Hannah doesn't have a dad?''

''There are a lot of kids raised in single-parent homes. I was. I think what's important is that the parent she has is devoted to her. That I'm determined to be the best parent I can be. And that I love her as much as any two parents possibly could.''

Ethan nodded as if he understood, but was still not convinced that was preferable to a traditional family.

He let it drop, though, and said, ''And you don't have any idea who the father is?''

Again she answered in general rather than specifically. ''In artificial insemination there's complete anonymity. The woman is given the donor's physical description but no picture. She knows his occupation, his educational background, his health history and the health history of his family. But that's all. The man himself is known only by number.''

''And basically rendered obsolete.''

''I don't think anything is ever going to make men obsolete,'' she assured. ''I'm actually grateful to the man who gave me Hannah. I feel as if he did something wonderful and extremely generous for me when I needed it most.''

Ethan raised his chin in what looked like acknowledgment of that.

''What will you tell her when she asks about her father?'' he asked then.

''Now *that* one I haven't come up with an answer for yet.''

''No, I don't suppose that would be an easy one to come up with,'' he agreed. ''How about your health now? Did you have to have the surgery once Hannah was born?''

''Actually the pregnancy helped things. It was like a nine-month reprieve from thc damage that was being compounded monthly and there's been an improvement. The doctor says it's likely only a temporary moratorium and I'll still end up having to have the hysterectomy before too long. But for now things are being managed with medication. Which is why Hannah has to be bottle fed. But still, I'm grateful for the improvement, too.''

A muted ringing startled Paris. An indication of how tense this conversation was making her.

''I'm sorry, but I need to take this call,'' Ethan said as he took a tiny cellular phone out of his pants pocket. "There's a situation at the Hong Kong office."

Then he answered the phone with a clipped "Tarlington."

Paris didn't want to appear to be listening in, even though it was impossible not to, so she raised the blanket from over the car seat to look in at Hannah.

The baby was still sleeping soundly, her chubby cheeks like two red rosebuds, one fist pressed to her tiny nub of a nose, her milk-chocolate-colored wisps of hair curled around her head.

The sight of it all made Paris smile.

But for some reason it also caused her to think again about the chat she'd just had with Ethan, and she realized that was the source of her stress.

Had her fibs about when her health problems had been diagnosed and the timetable of Hannah's birth convinced him he had no reason to suspect that he'd been involved in any way in Hannah's conception?

It had seemed like it.

But even so the very fact that he'd asked questions in the first place made her all the more uneasy about having taken this job.

It was too late now, though. So she reminded herself why she'd agreed to it in the first place and that she was going with him to Dunbar to work, not to while away the time with him.

Besides, Paris reasoned, it wasn't as if Hannah had *Tarlington* tattooed across her forehead. There wasn't any reason—beyond the math—for Ethan to think Hannah might be his, and it was Ethan himself who had made the assumption that Paris had gone ahead and had the artificial insemination after their night together.

So maybe it would be all right.

Except that she was going to have to be on guard for the next week.

But that was okay. It was only for a short time, and then she'd have the money for a new car. One short week, in and out, and Ethan Tarlington would never be the wiser.

At least, that was what she was gambling on.

Because no matter how drop-dead gorgeous he was, no matter how many things had been set alive inside her by being with him again and thinking about that night they'd had together, no matter how difficult it had been to keep from thinking about him in the past fourteen months, Paris was not going to let him get too close. To her or to Hannah.

She knew about rich, powerful men, and as Ethan made his demands of whoever he was talking to on the phone at that moment and Paris heard in his voice the unshakable confidence that he could have whatever he wanted and have it his way, she knew she was right.

Rich and powerful men were conquerors. They became accustomed to owning things. And people. To getting what they wanted and to not letting anything stand in the way of that.

And children fit into all of those categories.

Paris knew it from her own experience. From what she'd seen with her own eyes. And she wasn't going to let herself or her baby fall victim to that.

Not under any circumstances.

Not for any man.

Not even for one who looked like Ethan Tarlington and made everything female in her stand up and take notice.

Chapter Three

Ethan's house was on the west side of Dunbar, which meant that they reached it without going through the small town.

There were no signs and not even a mailbox to claim the property as his when the limousine turned off the main road onto a private driveway. The driveway was lined on both sides by red oak trees, the branches reaching out to each other to form an arc overhead that blocked most of the sun's scorching rays.

Paris wasn't sure exactly how far it was to the house, but it had to have been at least a mile before the place even came into view.

And when it did she could hardy believe her eyes.

She'd thought Ethan's house in Denver was impressive. It was three stories of Tudor mansion encompassing twenty-six rooms and an English garden in back.

But the house in Dunbar was even more incredible. It could have been a sprawling, luxury resort.

Granted it was two levels rather than three and it was built of rustic logs. But somehow those rustic logs managed to look refined, and the U-shaped home stretched a full city block around a fountain made to look like a natural rock formation complete with a rippling waterfall.

''Software has been very good to you,'' she said in awe as the car came to a stop in front of the walkway that led to the oversize, carved double-door entrance.

''I don't have any complaints, that's for sure,'' he said, again without a drop of swelled-headedness in his attitude.

Ethan leaned to the side to open the door, then straightened up again and motioned with his chiseled chin for Paris to precede him.

''Go ahead and stretch your legs. I'll get the car seat and Hannah,'' he said.

Paris was quick to decline the offer. ''That's okay. I can manage.''

But he wasn't having any of that. ''I'll be right behind you and I promise not to jiggle her enough to wake her up.''

There wasn't much Paris could say to that without sounding rude or making him wonder why she put herself between him and her baby every chance she got. So she had to concede.

"Okay. Thanks," she said as she got out of the car.

It did feel good to stand after the long ride. As good as it was to breathe the fresh, clean, country air perfumed with the scent of wildflowers planted around the rock fountain. And although it had been nice that the interior of the limousine was climate controlled, it was also good to feel the naturally cooling shade of the red oak trees that surrounded the house, too.

"There we go."

Paris heard Ethan's uttering from inside the car and glanced in that direction just as he got out with the baby carrier.

But as Paris reached to take it from him, he said, "Oh-oh. I hear something," and rather than handing over the baby seat, he set it on the roof and looked under the blanket.

At six-four and standing directly in front of the carrier, Ethan had the advantage. When he removed the blanket Paris could see her daughter and that Hannah's big bright aquamarine eyes were open, but she couldn't get to her.

"Yep. Wide-awake. Am I in trouble?" Ethan asked.

"No. She was about due to wake up, anyway." Paris answered with the truth, omitting the fact that she'd been hoping to get Hannah out of sight before it happened, though.

"Can I take her out of this thing?" was Ethan's next question.

"Oh, I don't know about that. You're a stranger and—"

''I don't think she cares. She's smiling at me,'' he informed Paris. Then, in a softer voice to her daughter, he said, ''Hello there, little Hannah. Did you have a nice nap?''

''She's probably wet,'' Paris said, figuring that could ward off anything.

But not Ethan, who said, ''I don't mind.''

He didn't wait for any more go-ahead. Instead he unbuckled the carrier's restraints and held out his big hands to the baby.

And what did her ordinarily shy, slightly wary daughter do?

Hannah gave him her biggest grin—the one that put a tiny dimple just over the right side of her mouth—and held her arms out to him, too.

''See, she wants me to hold her,'' he said as he scooped the baby out of her seat.

He was surprisingly adept at it. He actually set her on his hip like an old pro.

''Can she hold her own head up?'' he asked, supporting it until he knew whether or not she needed it.

''Yes, she holds her head up just fine on her own,'' Paris assured him.

She was itching to snatch Hannah away from him. But she was also struck by how touching—and appealing—was the sight of the big man holding the tiny child so carefully.

''Hi, Hannah,'' he repeated then. ''Remember me?''

Hannah went on grinning at him and, in the process of flailing her arms around in apparent glee, accidentally grabbed his nose.

Ethan laughed. "I think she likes me."

And he seemed to like her.

It was very alarming to Paris.

"I can take her now," she said, reaching for the baby.

"You don't have to. Let me hold her for a minute."

His denial to turn Hannah over when Paris was angling for it raised more red flags in her. Even though she knew it wasn't as if he were actually usurping her child, that was the button it pushed in her.

"Really," she insisted more forcefully. "She has very fair skin and if she's left in a wet diaper for too long she gets a rash."

This time Paris didn't give him the opportunity to refuse her. She took Hannah out of his arms before he could do anything to stop her.

"Maybe we can play later, when your mom's not so nervous," he said to Hannah without seeming to take offense.

Paris doubted that she would spend any of the coming week not being nervous, but she didn't tell him that. Instead, as the limousine driver unloaded suitcases from the trunk, she draped her purse and diaper bag over her shoulder and said, "If you'll point me in the direction of our room I'll just take her inside. Is there a staff wing or something?"

"There's a section of the house where the live-in

staff have rooms of their own, but you and Hannah will be right across the hall from me. I called ahead and made arrangements. My housekeeper should have outfitted Hannah's room with some baby necessities—a crib and whatnot. But you won't be able to find your way without the nickel tour. I was planning to do that this afternoon but now I'll be on the phone to Hong Kong again, so we'll have to save that for tonight after dinner and I'll just have someone else take you to your rooms now.''

''Wait a minute,'' Paris said as she sorted through all the things he'd said. ''We're having dinner together, and you bought furniture, and you're putting us in the room just across the hall from you? I know you said we'd be staying in your house, but you also said it was so big you'd hardly know we were here. There was nothing about having meals together or you buying furniture or my staying across the hall from you.''

''I don't recall saying anything about hardly knowing you'd be here.''

Okay, so maybe that had just been what she'd thought. And planned. But it would be impossible to pull off if she and Hannah were within a few feet of his room the whole time.

''I'm just staff,'' she reminded. ''I shouldn't be staying in a guest room.''

''You're only technically staff. I'm also considering you and Hannah guests.''

''I don't think that's a good idea.''

''Sure it is. I'm looking forward to the pleasure of your company.''

"There's no pleasure in my company," Paris said, too flustered to realize before the words came out how they sounded. But she didn't pause to amend it. Instead she went on to say, "I agreed to this whole arrangement only on a strictly business basis."

"Right. Strictly business. So let's look at it that way. Let's say you were a business consultant who had come to Dunbar at my request to advise me about something. Where would you be staying? Dunbar doesn't have a hotel so you'd be staying here. In the same room you'll be in. Which would make you my guest as well as my business associate. And as my guest, where would you be having your meals? In the kitchen? No. You'd be eating meals with me. And what would you be doing in the evenings or when you had a free afternoon? Would I leave you to twiddle your thumbs? No, I'd be entertaining you. But would it be anything personal? Of course not. It would just be common courtesy and management having its privileges. No big deal."

It was a big deal. This whole thing was turning into a much bigger deal than Paris had anticipated.

But she was beginning to think that it was her own fault for not asking more questions about accommodations and how her nonwork hours might be spent.

"Maybe this wasn't a good idea after all. Maybe Hannah and I should take the next bus back to the city."

"Now why would you want to do that?" Ethan asked, his tone cajoling.

"I meant it when I said what happened between

us before is not going to happen again. I'm here to do a job and that's it. I'm not here to spend a week with you at your country house.''

''Would that be so bad?'' he asked quietly.

It would probably be too good.

''Other people doing jobs around here aren't in guest rooms, they haven't had furniture bought especially for them, and they aren't being wined and dined with members of the family.''

He leaned in closer and said in a warm gust of confidentiality, ''But you aren't *other people.* You are my party coordinator, here at my special request.''

There was just no arguing with him.

And then, too, the man could get to her. He really could. Standing there so tall and handsome, so sexy, and so mischievously sweet on top of everything else…

''Come on,'' he coaxed. ''Let's just call it a middle ground and agree that we can mix business with pleasure as long as the pleasure is just good, clean fun. The same kind of good, clean fun I might have with any business associate I brought out here.''

Again, that was a perspective that was hard to dispute. Especially when she thought once more about the money she needed for a new car and the fact that this simple week's worth of work was going to get that for her.

And if there was the tiniest part of her—deep, deep down—that wanted to stay in this beautiful home for a week, that wanted to spend a little time with Ethan? It was a part she didn't want to acknowledge.

Even as it made her waver. "Good, clean fun and no 'hanky-panky,'" she warned.

"Strictly business when business needs to be attended to. Good, clean fun the rest of the time. And no 'hanky-panky,'" he agreed with a crooked smile when he said hanky-panky.

Paris wondered if she could trust him.

She wasn't too sure she could.

But that tiny part of her that wanted to stay suddenly asserted itself with a surprising strength, and she couldn't force herself to go through with catching the bus back to Denver.

Instead she again reminded herself that Hannah did not have *Tarlington* stamped on her to give away her secret, so they should be relatively safe regardless.

And if Paris saw more of Ethan than she'd originally thought she would?

It wasn't as if she couldn't control herself. Just because he was great-looking and charming, just because she'd succumbed to his appeal once, didn't mean she would do it again. Especially not with his brothers and his house staff around as chaperones and deterrents.

But still she didn't concede gracefully. "Why do I feel as if I was brought here under false pretenses?"

Ethan seemed to know that he'd won because he smiled a wickedly victorious smile and said, "I can't imagine."

His eyes held hers for a moment then. Warm blue eyes that set off something much too titillating in the pit of her stomach and made her wonder if she was doing the right thing.

But the matter seemed to have been resolved and forgotten about when a plump older woman with extremely short gray hair, very red cheeks and a nose with a bulb on the end came out of the house, and Ethan spun toward her to hug her as if he were greeting his mother or his favorite aunt.

"Lolly, Lolly, Lolly, you're looking younger and more beautiful every day," he exclaimed.

"You better believe it," she countered as Paris looked on.

They both had a laugh at that as their hug ended and Ethan turned back to Paris.

"Paris, this is Lolly McGinty. She runs things around here. Lolly, this is Paris Hanley and Hannah."

Paris held out her hand. "It's nice to meet you."

"Likewise."

"Paris is all yours for the afternoon, Lolly," Ethan said when the amenities were concluded. Then, to Paris again, he added, "Lolly will get you set up and fill you in on what's going on with the party while I reconnect with the Hong Kong office and try to sort things out there. Then I'll see you again at dinner."

In other words, she was dismissed. Like any other employee might have been.

And for some reason that chafed a bit.

But she refused to fuel the feeling and instead focused on the housekeeper.

"Lead the way," she said, turning her back on Ethan without another word.

She could feel his gaze on her as she followed Lolly into the house, though.

She did her best to ignore it. To ignore it and the swell of satisfaction she felt at the thought that he might be admiring what he saw.

It was more important to remember that she'd ventured onto thin ice by coming here with him in the first place.

And that anyone on thin ice should tread very carefully.

"So, big A, is it just me or do you feel like old Ethan here has brought us into his den to make some kind of announcement?"

"Could be, Dev, I hear he all of a sudden brought a woman along this year. Could be it has something to do with her."

Ethan let his brothers play their game while he poured the three glasses of twenty-year-old Scotch that was their kickoff to this week in Dunbar.

When he turned from the bar to bring the drinks with him to the high-backed leather chairs where they sat, he said, "Don't take that act out on the road or you'll starve trying to make a living with it."

His brothers just smiled.

"What's the big thing you wanted to talk to us about that couldn't wait until we unpacked and had dinner?" Aiden asked as he accepted his Scotch and sampled it.

"I need your opinion on something."

"Okay, shoot," Devon ordered, savoring a sip from his glass, too.

"The week before I left the country last year I met this woman," Ethan began.

"The woman you brought with you here?"

"Right. Paris Hanley. Anyway, we spent the night together—"

"And you wanted to make sure we knew that you aren't all work and no play?" Aiden goaded.

"Will you cut the jokes? This is serious."

Ethan went on to explain what had led to his discovery that Paris had a baby.

"And you think she's yours?" Devon said when his brother had finished.

"That's the thing—I don't know. Paris claims she had artificial insemination right after our night together and that Hannah was born early. But that could just be a story she's feeding me."

"Oh, I doubt that," Aiden said as if he thought it was far-fetched.

"You can't say Hannah isn't mine until you see her," Ethan insisted. "Until you see if you see the same thing in her that I do." Although, Ethan hadn't told his brothers what it was he thought he recognized in Hannah because he didn't want to influence them.

"Look around you, Ethan," Aiden said, continuing to support his position. "You're a big-bucks guy. If this woman—or any woman—ended up having your baby, she would want child support from you. She'd be crazy not to come after you with both barrels."

"That's what makes the whole thing so damn weird. But I'm telling you, I think Hannah is mine."

"But you didn't ask point-blank," Devon said.

"No, I didn't and I don't want to. Not until I know I'm not imagining what I see in Hannah. And if you guys see what I see and I'm *not* imagining it, then I still don't want to ask outright until I get some sort of handle on what possible reason Paris could have for keeping the truth from me."

"It's not really ethical but I could do a blood test on the baby behind Mom's back," Aiden offered. "It wouldn't be as conclusive as testing you both for a DNA match but it would be a start. Maybe rule you out from the get-go."

Ethan shook his head. "I couldn't do that. It's too sneaky and deceitful."

"And what do you call it if the baby is yours and the mother is pretending she isn't?" Devon asked.

"I call it sneaky and deceitful. And something I want to know, if that's what Paris is."

"Ah," Aiden muttered, setting his half-empty glass on the end table. "So what we have here is also a test for the mom. To see if she's like Bettina."

"Which means you must like Paris—a minor detail you left out," Devon concluded.

"I just want to know the truth," Ethan said. "And why she isn't telling me I'm Hannah's father if I *am* Hannah's father."

"Do you *want* the baby to be yours?" Aiden asked then.

"I don't know," he answered honestly. "The whole thing has blindsided me. I guess for the moment I just want you two to take a close look at Hannah and tell me what you think."

"And if what we think is that she's yours?" Devon asked.

Ethan took the last drink of his Scotch and then stared into the empty glass. "I don't know the answer to that, either. I'm just flyin' by the seat of my pants on this."

And wishing along the way that he could stop noticing that Paris had a laugh like wind chimes and eyes that sparkled like stars and lips so pink and soft they put rose petals to shame....

Paris spent the afternoon with Lolly. The older woman brought her up to speed on all the party preparations and helped her and Hannah settle in.

They finished just as Hannah was ready for her dinner, and by the time Paris had fed her daughter and put her down for the night, Paris was smeared with strained pears and needed to change for her own dinner.

Her clothes were all hung in an opulent walk-in closet, so that was where she went in search of something to wear, trying not to think about Ethan as she did.

Why should it matter what he might like or what might make her waist look smallest or her rear end look firmest or her breasts look a little larger than they were?

It shouldn't.

But as she stood surveying her choices, she suddenly regretted that her limited budget had left her wardrobe on the practical side. And since she'd expected this to be a working trip, she'd only brought the most practical, at that.

Well, since she'd expected this to be a working trip and because she'd steadfastly held to the determination that she would not be fraternizing with Ethan, she had no need to be overly concerned with what she looked like.

Except, now that she actually was going to fraternize with him, she *did* care.

Luckily Lolly had said casual attire was the norm, so even though Paris didn't have anything she considered impressive, she wouldn't be underdressed.

She assumed jeans were too casual, though, and opted for a pair of gray twill slacks and a plain white blouse with a banded collar.

The closet was actually more like a dressing room, allowing her to change right there before going back into the bedroom to freshen her mascara and blush and put a comb through her hair.

As she did she couldn't help marveling yet again at the room itself and the bathroom connected to it.

The bathroom was a study in luxury, with a navy-blue marble floor, countertops, shower stall and wainscoting halfway up the walls. It also had a sunken tub with a whirlpool she could switch on at the touch of a button, and an octagonal stained-glass window on the wall behind it.

The bedroom had a king-size brass bed with an ornate scroll design in the headboard and the footboard, as well as four tall posts that reached up to hold a fringed canopy. The mattress was covered in a hand-stitched country quilt and stacked with half a dozen fluffy pillows covered in shams that matched different patterns in the quilt.

There were two bureaus—one tall and strictly for clothing and linens, the other long and low. The lower of the two contained a fully stocked bar in one section and an equally well-equipped refrigerated drawer in another. Plus the push of a button here, too, raised the top of the bureau and out came a complete entertainment center.

In addition to the bureaus, there was an armoire and the matching dressing table Paris was using at that moment, plus a fainting couch and two overstuffed chairs positioned around a fireplace with a carved mantel. And still there was enough floor space left over for aerobic exercise or ballroom dancing.

And this was only a guest room. She couldn't imagine what the master suite was like.

Although that was something she *shouldn't* be imagining, she reminded herself. Ethan's bedroom was so off-limits it shouldn't even be a passing thought.

Yet there she was, wondering about it, anyway. And worse than that, picturing Ethan in it. With maybe just a towel around his waist, his chest and shoulders bare and muscular, his stomach flat, and that line of hair from his navel downward…

''Oh, that's not good,'' she informed herself, closing her eyes as if that would block the mental picture.

Then she opened them again and forced her focus onto herself to make sure she was at least presentable.

Presentable. As in: he was caviar and she was

mashed potatoes. And that was something she had to remember. Despite the fact that she secretly wished she was so stunning it would take his breath away.

Which was also something she shouldn't be thinking, let alone wishing for.

"Strictly business," she told her reflection, much more sternly than she'd ever said it to Ethan.

Then she turned away from the mirror and moved on silent steps across carpeting that was so thick it was almost like walking through unmowed lawn.

Wanting to check on Hannah before she left for dinner, Paris went through the connecting door into Hannah's room.

Hannah's room was every bit as incredible as Paris's. The regular bed had been removed to accommodate an array of Jenny Lind furniture—crib, dresser, changing table, playpen and a matching rocking chair that was not only beautiful but more comfortable than the one Paris had at home.

It was all slightly mind-boggling. Especially to someone who clipped coupons not only for groceries but for haircuts, too.

Hannah was sleeping soundly, and since the air-conditioned room was slightly cool, Paris pulled the blanket over her and allowed herself a few minutes of unbridled joy at the sight.

There had never been anything or anyone Paris loved the way she loved Hannah.

And that, coupled with the splendor of their accommodations, only reinforced her determination to keep her secret about Hannah.

She had seen what the wealth and power of a

prominent surgeon could do to a woman of lesser means. She'd seen how ruthless that wealth and power could make a man and how helpless those lesser means could leave a woman. And Jason's wealth and power had obviously been nothing compared to Ethan's.

It was definitely better that Ethan not know Hannah was his daughter.

Paris bent over the crib railing and kissed the baby's head, wishing just a kiss could somehow brand Hannah as hers and chase away the feeling that something—or someone—could take her baby away from her.

Then she took the portable portion of a state-of-the-art baby monitor from Hannah's dresser, clipped it to her belt and left the room.

Paris hadn't seen much of the rest of the house yet, but Lolly had told her she need only retrace her path to the front entrance where Ethan and his brothers would be through the doors to the left waiting for her in the den.

Paris thought retracing her steps might be easier said than done but she didn't do too badly in finding her way.

When she reached the foyer she checked the baby monitor to make sure she could hear Hannah, smiling at the sucking noise her daughter sometimes made in her sleep and feeling reassured that she would be alerted if the baby woke up. Then she turned to the den's doors and knocked a split second before it opened.

"There you are! I was just going to see if you

were lost,'' Ethan said from the opposite side of the doorway.

''I was feeding Hannah and getting her to sleep. You didn't need to wait for me.''

Ethan grinned. ''Yes, I did.'' Then he gave her the once-over and added, ''Besides, it was worth the wait.''

The compliment and the appreciative, slightly insinuative smile that went with it thrilled Paris more than she wanted to admit. But how could it not when she was a mere five months away from maternity tops and elastic panels in her pants, and there he was, tall and handsome and making every fiber of her being stand up and take notice?

He hadn't changed clothes. He was still wearing the khaki slacks and garnet-colored polo shirt he'd had on when he'd picked her up that morning. But they didn't look any the worse for wear. And neither did he.

He was freshly shaved, and the scent of a woodsy cologne wafted out to her.

She tried not to think about how much she liked it. Or how much she liked that first glimpse of him after not having seen him since that morning.

But it was all there, anyway, just below the surface as he stepped back and said, ''Come on in and meet my brothers. They got in about an hour ago.''

Paris went into the room, taking one long whiff of him as she passed by but promising herself that would be her only indulgence.

The den was paneled in dark oak, furnished in

tufted leather and antique wood and lit by library lamps so it was very cozy and restful.

The other two men stood when she entered the room, and Paris's first thought was that the Tarlingtons were a big lot. When they got to their feet, both of Ethan's brothers rose to more than six feet. And they were as handsome as they were tall and well built.

"Hello," she greeted.

They returned her hello as Ethan came up beside her to perform the introductions.

"This is Aiden, in from Alaska. He's a doctor up there, family medicine. And this is Devon, our wild-man wildlife photographer. He globe-trots but calls Denver home base."

Aiden had lighter-blue eyes than Ethan or Devon, and Devon had sort of a bad-boy air about him, but the three of them together looked so much alike that no one would ever doubt they were brothers.

"And this is Paris," Ethan concluded, "who is probably as starved as we are, so shall we go in to eat?"

There was general agreement and then the three men escorted her out of the den, down the hallway and to a dining room that Ethan referred to as the small dining room.

It was larger than the kitchen, dining room and living room combined in Paris's house, but she had the impression that it was probably the everyday dining room because it was more warm and homey than fancy, with a sideboard taking up one wall, a curio cabinet on another and an oblong walnut table in the center.

Ethan seated her at the place setting at the head of the table as if she were the guest of honor and only then did he and his brothers sit down.

"Paris the party planner, huh?" Devon said as the first course—lobster parfait—was served.

"I'm not ordinarily a party planner, no," Paris answered. "It's just that I've avoided taking a nine-to-five job since I graduated from art school so that I can paint."

That seemed to spark Devon's curiosity particularly. "Have you had any gallery showings?"

"A few."

"Successful?"

"Enough so that I'm slowly gaining a following. But I'm still not earning enough from the sale of my work to make a comfortable living. So, to supplement my income, I take whatever temporary job I can that doesn't interfere too much with my artwork or with the time I spend with my daughter."

That led to questions about what kind of odd jobs she might have had and the conversation flowed from there as Paris found Ethan's brothers to be as easy to talk to as he was, and as intelligent and funny and charming, too.

But as the meal progressed, even though she was enjoying herself, Paris also began to be aware of something in her that she didn't want to be aware of.

She was itching to be alone with Ethan.

She knew it would be a mistake. She knew it was

unwise. She knew she shouldn't even allow it if something were to happen and they were left alone.

But more than itching for it, she actually began to will his brothers to excuse themselves. In fact, that was so much on her mind that, at one point, she lost track of the conversation and had to admit her mind had wandered.

And then, just as she was mentally taking herself to task for it, Ethan himself turned to her and said, ''How about that tour of the house now? I'm sure these guys will survive if we duck out on them.''

His brothers encouraged them to go and all thoughts of not allowing herself to be alone with Ethan fled from her mind like horses from a lightning strike.

She told herself she was only doing it so she could get her bearings in the house. That it was pure necessity.

But the fact that something inside her took wing the moment they left the table made a lie out of it.

There were more than twenty rooms in the house and, as Ethan explained the basic floor plan, all Paris could think was, Good, then it will be a long tour.

But even though her every sense seemed filled by his presence along the way, she still found herself in awe of his home.

Each room was larger and more amazing than the next. Restaurant-size kitchen. Formal dining room. Breakfast room. Den. Formal living room. Family room. Ethan's office. A library. A movie theater. A bowling alley. A full basketball court. And that was only on the first floor.

Upstairs there were eight bedrooms—all of them with private bathrooms. There were also two sitting rooms and a sound-proof music room where, Ethan confided, both he and his brothers had been known to blast their music and play a little air guitar when no one was supposed to be looking.

''And that's it,'' he said as they reached the door to Paris's room an hour later.

Well, that wasn't *completely* it since he hadn't shown her his rooms across the hall, but it seemed obvious that he didn't intend to, and she knew that was for the best, so she didn't point it out.

''Think you'll be able to find your way around all right?'' he asked then.

''I think so. The layout isn't too complicated.''

''And there are intercoms in all the rooms so if you get stuck you can just call for help.''

''I'm sure I'll be fine.''

And that really did seem to be that—the natural conclusion to the evening.

Paris waited for him to say good-night, knowing it was for the best and yet feeling her own spirits sink slightly.

But Ethan didn't say good-night. He leaned one shoulder against the wall next to her door, crossed his arms over his chest, one ankle over the other and said, ''So how did this afternoon go? Did Lolly tell you all you needed to know?''

''She told me enough to make it clear that there isn't much for me to do for your party. I'll make a few phone calls to suppliers who are late with deliveries and inventory things as they come in, but for the most part everything is under control.''

''I told you it was. But those phone calls and inventories are things I'd have to do and now I won't. That's worth a lot to me.''

She thought it was worth a lot more to her but she didn't say that.

''How about if tomorrow I show you around Dunbar?'' Ethan said then. ''You should have the lay of the land, and I'll introduce you to the people you'll be dealing with when they bring things in for the party or come in to set up or serve or cook. We'll make a day of it.''

Together. Just what she knew she should be avoiding. But they'd already had the discussion about her spending nonwork time with him, and Paris had lost that battle. She knew it was useless to argue about spending work time with him.

And if the prospect had suddenly raised her deflated spirits again? She didn't want to consider why that was.

''Will Lolly watch Hannah, do you think?''

''I'm sure she will. Or we could take Hannah along if you'd rather. I don't mind.''

''That's not a good idea. She needs naps and feedings, and I don't like her to be out in the sun too long.''

''Okay, then we'll have Lolly baby-sit.''

With that settled, Paris again expected him to say good-night.

But again he didn't. He just stayed leaning against the wall, studying her.

"I'm really glad you're here," he said then, as if it were a confession. "I've thought about you a lot since the night we met."

She definitely didn't want to talk about that night. Or how much she'd thought about him since then, too.

Especially not when the air around them seemed to have already taken a shift to intimacy.

So instead she said, "I should probably go in and check on Hannah."

But Ethan ignored the exit line and just went on looking into her eyes. "It's almost like I've been carrying around a part of you since then."

And certainly she'd been carrying around a part of—him…

But again, not something she wanted to say. Any more than she wanted to feel the warm rush his words were sending through her.

"Things are different now," she reminded him. "I'm working for you."

His smile was crooked and devilish. "You're working for me, all right."

In spite of herself, Paris smiled at his innuendo-laced turn of the phrase.

Then in a quiet voice she said, "Don't do this to me, okay?"

"Don't do what to you? I'm just standing here, enjoying the view."

"That—don't flirt and compliment me and be nice and—"

Did he have to have eyes so blue they made it hard for her to maintain her train of thought? Did he have to look at her that way? Did he have to smile that secret smile that seemed to say he hadn't forgotten a single thing about that night they'd shared?

"What do you want me to do? Insult you?" he asked.

It would make things a lot easier on her.

"You know what I want." At least what she'd *told* him she wanted. But every minute that he stood there made her want something entirely different.

Still she said, "I want a business relationship and that's all."

"Are you sure that's all?" he asked in a soft, husky voice.

And as he did, he leaned forward. Just slightly.

Was he testing her resolve? Wondering what she would do?

Or was he actually going to kiss her?

"Yes, I'm sure," Paris said before she'd decided which it was.

But her own tone was almost a whisper because her resolve really was weak. So weak that at that same moment her chin tilted upward just a bit all on its own and her gaze attached itself to his lips. Sensual lips that she'd once felt all over her body. That, deep down, she was screaming to feel again....

But just as she thought he really was going to close the last of that distance between them and press his mouth to hers, he took her at her word and drew back.

"Maybe you're right," he said.

There was actually a part of Paris that told her to say, *No, never mind, I wasn't right. I was so not right.* A part of her that craved that almost-kiss so much that there wasn't a single thing more important than that.

But of course there was.

So Paris drew back, too, standing a little taller, a little straighter, a little stronger than she felt.

And now it seemed as if the ball was in her court.

So, in a stronger voice which concealed the fact that she still felt like mush inside, she said, "I'll see you tomorrow."

"Sleep well," he answered.

Paris raised her chin again, this time only in acknowledgment, and slipped into her room, closing the door behind her.

But quite a few minutes passed before she heard Ethan push off the wall outside her door. Before she heard the door across the hall open and close. Before she moved from just inside hers.

And as she did she wondered if it was possible that she was even more attracted to him now than she had been fourteen months ago.

Because that was almost how it seemed.

Of course, it didn't help matters that he was simply the sexiest man she'd ever encountered. Or that something about him drew her to him.

Not that it made any difference, though. Because she wasn't going to act on it.

But the way things were shaping up, it was going to be a long week.

A very long week.

A very long and uncomfortable week if she didn't nip in the bud things like wanting him to kiss her.

Wanting him to kiss her so badly that it was still a living, breathing thing inside her.

But it wasn't going to happen. She swore to herself that it wasn't.

She had too much at stake.

But she also knew that it was no wonder she'd succumbed to Ethan that night fourteen months ago.

Because falling into his arms, giving herself over to him with wanton abandon, was a fierce urge that was running through her all over again.

Chapter Four

Although Ethan spent as much time in Dunbar as he could, the week of his annual party was usually the only week out of the year that he planned on total rest and relaxation. But that still didn't mean he could make himself sleep late in the mornings, and so, even without an alarm clock, he was awake to watch the sun rise the next day.

He wasn't thinking about the beauty of it, though. His mind was wandering. Just the way it had been wandering so much since Friday. So much since he'd met Paris, really. But more since Friday.

He felt as if he should be angry with her. He knew he should be leery of her. Certainly he should be totally turned off by her and the idea that she could be hiding something as monumental as the fact that Hannah might be his child.

But he wasn't any of those things. He couldn't even make himself be when he tried.

And he *did* try. He told himself over and over again that Paris could be lying to him. Lying to him on a bigger scale than Bettina ever had.

But it didn't work.

Yes, he knew intellectually that he should be barely able to tolerate someone who could even potentially be doing such a thing.

But on an emotional level?

That was a different story altogether.

There was just something about her.

Something more than a great body. More than silken hair and luminous skin. More than shining silver eyes. Something more, even, than the pure, raw sexual attraction to her that made him want to feel her compact body against him, that made him want to wrap his arms around her, kiss her, touch her, do more than just kiss her and touch her.

There was also something about her that reached out and drew him in. Something about her that, whenever she walked into a room, caused everything else to pale and fade into the background for him.

He was intrigued by Paris Hanley, and there was nothing he could do about it. As intrigued as he'd been the night they'd met. Maybe more intrigued.

Actually, maybe the whole baby thing was adding to her intrigue, he thought. Because he still hadn't come up with any idea why she would keep it from him if it were true, and the mystery of that was an intrigue all its own.

And if Hannah *was* his child, Paris was most definitely keeping it a mystery.

But for the life of him he couldn't understand why.

He just didn't have an answer for it, and it was driving him crazy.

Unless the answer was the only obvious one and Hannah really *wasn't* his.

He hadn't thought as much about that as he'd thought about her being his baby.

But now he considered it more seriously.

What if he was just imagining what he thought he saw in Hannah? What if it was some kind of trick his brain was playing on him? Or just a coincidence?

Was that possible?

Anything was possible.

And what if Hannah really wasn't his? he asked himself. What if Paris really had had artificial insemination and wasn't keeping anything from him after all? What then?

Free sailing.

That was the first thing that came into Ethan's head. He could have free sailing with Paris because it would mean she wasn't like Bettina. That Paris was on the up and up.

And maybe that was the truth and that was why, deep down, he couldn't be angry with her or leery of her or turned off by her.

It made a certain amount of sense to him.

It made more sense, he reasoned, than that Hannah was his and Paris was keeping it a secret from him rather than asking him for the help she so obviously needed.

It made a whole lot more sense. And it was definitely a scenario he liked better, so he worked to embrace it.

Because if Paris was being honest with him, then this week didn't have to have a cloud hanging over it. And he could genuinely relax and let go and enjoy himself. Enjoy Paris.

Oh, yeah, he liked that scenario a whole lot better.

So why not? Why not give her the benefit of the doubt? She wasn't Bettina, and as far as he knew for sure, Paris hadn't earned his distrust.

So figure that you're wrong and Paris isn't hiding anything.

Or at least give it a try.

He could do that, couldn't he?

He thought he could. He knew he wanted to.

So, with a renewed eagerness to face the day—a day he was spending with Paris—Ethan pushed off the French doors he'd been leaning against to watch the sunrise and decided he needed a cup of coffee.

He grabbed his robe from the foot of his bed and put it on, cinching it around his waist before he left his rooms, even though he was relatively sure he was the only one in the house who was up yet.

But he got just a few feet out the door when he heard something that told him he *wasn't* the only early riser.

Something high-pitched and lilting and sweet.

It was coming from Hannah's room.

He moved closer to her door and nearly pressed his ear to the panel to listen.

Cooing. The baby was cooing.

It made him smile.

It also made him want to see her.

So he ventured a light tap on the door with just one knuckle.

There was no response from inside. All he heard were more baby sounds.

It occurred to him then that Paris might not be up yet. That maybe only Hannah was awake.

He knocked again, but when there still wasn't any response he eased the door open and stuck his head inside.

Paris was nowhere in sight and so Ethan went into the room.

Early daylight came through the curtains to lend a rosy glow as he crossed to the crib.

Hannah was wide-awake, lying on her back, holding one foot in each hand.

She turned her head to him when he came up to the side of the crib and instantly gave him a huge grin.

''Good morning, little lady,'' he whispered to her.

She gurgled at him as if in answer and that made him laugh quietly.

''Whatcha got there?'' he asked, rubbing the very tips of her chubby toes with a single index finger.

Hannah let go of her feet and grabbed his finger with one of her free hands, cooing this time the way he'd heard her from out in the hall.

Ethan wiggled his finger for her, delighting her. And him, too.

And in that moment all the reasoning he'd just done, all the benefit of the doubt he'd thought to give

Paris, flew out the window. Because he saw all over again in Hannah what he'd seen on Friday.

He saw his mother.

He saw her in Hannah's aquamarine eyes. And he also saw something he hadn't seen before—he saw a dimple that appeared over the corner of the baby's mouth when she smiled. The same dimple that his mother had had in the same spot.

And he knew he wasn't imagining it—not what he was seeing and not what he was feeling, either. Because as he stood there with Hannah's tiny hand clinging to his finger, something welled up in his chest and told him she was his.

No, it wasn't conclusive proof. Not the eyes. Not the dimple. Not the swell of his heart. But he believed Hannah was his, anyway.

And that put him right back to square one—if she was his, why didn't Paris admit it?

It was enough to drive him crazy.

So maybe he should just force the issue, he thought. Maybe he should confront her. Demand to know the truth. Maybe insist on DNA testing to give himself some peace.

But a split second after considering that he knew he wasn't going to do any of it. It was a hard line he just wasn't ready to take. Not yet, anyway.

Yes, he hated thinking that Hannah might be his child and Paris wasn't telling him. He hated thinking Paris was lying to him.

But he hated more the mental picture he got when he thought about calling her on it. He hated more the picture of the two of them on opposite sides.

So maybe if he couldn't give her the benefit of the doubt about Hannah, he could at least try to keep an open mind about *why* Paris wasn't telling him the truth. He could trust that she had a good reason and that if he gave her some time, if he let her know she could trust him, she might let him know what was going on in that pretty head of hers.

Because after fourteen months of thinking about her, of wanting to see her again, after finally getting her here where he could be with her every day, he couldn't make himself give that up. And even if it was only for a week, it was still a week he wouldn't have if he forced the issue of what he believed about Hannah.

The baby let go of his finger then and made a sound that almost seemed like a giggle as she kicked her legs up in the air and grabbed her toes once more.

And that was another thing, Ethan thought. He wanted a little time with Hannah, too. A little time to sort out how he felt about the possibility of fatherhood.

The door that connected Hannah's room to Paris's opened and there was Paris.

Ethan saw the surprise in her face just before she jumped behind the door so he wouldn't see her in the big Tweety Bird T-shirt she apparently wore as pajamas.

''I was just going to the kitchen for coffee and I heard Hannah in here,'' Ethan explained from the distance. ''I thought I'd look in on her.''

''I'll take care of her,'' Paris called back, still out of sight.

Ethan glanced at the baby again, rubbing the top of her head with only two fingertips. ''She's pretty cute in the morning.''

''I better get her changed and fed or she won't be for long.''

Ethan got the hint. ''Okay, I'm going.''

But he didn't go immediately. He allowed himself one more look at Hannah, at his mother in Hannah, before he finally retraced his steps to the hall door.

''The coast is clear. See you later,'' he called to Paris, and then he closed the door behind him.

But as he paused in the hallway, picturing Paris with her hair sleep-tousled, padding to the crib in her Tweety Bird T-shirt and picking up her daughter to hold her for the first time that day, he knew for sure that he was going to temporarily let lie whatever was going on with Paris, that he was going to give her the chance to be open and honest with him.

And if Paris still hadn't told him what he believed was the truth by the end of the week, he'd have to push it.

But he hoped it didn't come to that.

And if it didn't, then maybe they could go from there.

Because just that momentary glimpse of her was enough to churn things up inside him. Enough to make that one night they'd spent together an even more vivid memory than it had been.

Just that momentary glimpse of her was enough to make him want to take her hand and lead her back into her room, leaving Hannah to entertain herself a little longer while he entertained Hannah's mom....

* * *

Despite the plans for Ethan to show Paris around Dunbar, most of that day passed without her seeing him again after her morning's surprise.

According to Lolly, his brothers had talked him into a horseback ride, and so the trip to Dunbar was postponed until late in the afternoon.

"That's okay," Paris told the older woman, thinking that maybe keeping her distance from Ethan might be possible after all. "I wanted to get right to work on those delinquent suppliers, anyway. In fact, this is much better."

And she'd meant it, too. It was good to get busy and earn the exorbitant fee Ethan was paying her. It was good to have a calm day with Hannah, especially when they were both in new and unfamiliar surroundings with a lot of strangers around them. It was good that Paris could put Hannah down for her naps and be there when she woke up. It was good that Paris didn't have to be with Ethan.

But did it *feel* good?

It didn't.

In fact, it spoiled Paris's mood altogether. And no matter how hard she tried not to analyze why that was, she still knew that what was running rampant through her was plain old disappointment.

Because as much as she'd told herself otherwise, she'd been looking forward to having all day with Ethan.

It's a warning sign, she told herself.

A warning sign she needed to pay attention to.

She knew she was particularly susceptible to the

man. How could she deny that when she'd already spent the night with him? Being disappointed at not seeing as much of him as she'd thought she was going to was an indication that she was every bit as susceptible to him now as she had been then.

And that was something she had to watch out for. Something she had to fight.

So she went through the day tending to business and her baby and tamping down every thought of Ethan the minute one popped into her head.

But then three o'clock came and Lolly arrived at the door to the den where Paris was going over party preparations, announcing that Ethan was back from his ride and ready to go into Dunbar whenever she was.

And the sun suddenly seemed to shine a little brighter, and nothing Paris did, nothing she told herself, made it dim again.

Just watch yourself, she cautioned.

And she had every intention of doing just that.

Even as she changed out of the looser-fitting pants and top she had on and replaced them with a pair of pencil-thin black spandex capri slacks and a body-hugging funnel-neck sleeveless T-shirt.

Both of which were a long way from her very unsexy Tweety Bird nightshirt.

But the clothes notwithstanding, she swore she wasn't going to give in to her weakness for Ethan Tarlington.

She would merely accept his tour of the town and maintain an attitude of professionalism the whole time.... If it was the last thing she ever did.

And if her tighter outfit made him regret keeping her waiting for him?

It served him right.

Dunbar was hardly the sleepy small town Paris had expected. It wasn't a bustling metropolis, either, but it was a medium-size community with a half-dozen streets lined with shops—and businesses at its heart and a widespread residential area sprouting out in all directions around it.

The first thing that struck Paris about it was how clean and well kept everything was. Granted, she was viewing it from a distance as Ethan drove the SUV that had replaced the limousine that had brought them from Denver, but still she didn't see a single spot of peeling paint or a missing shutter or even a lopsided sign on the mostly post-World War II era buildings.

There were some newer structures, too, that had crept in among the mom-and-pop diner and the old-fashioned, counter-service ice-cream parlor and the family-owned-and-operated hardware store. Two rivaling grocery chains had built markets that had a more contemporary look to them, the major fast-food establishments had set up shop in their own distinctive styles, and there was the requisite Starbucks, as well as a gas station complete with minimart.

But for the most part it seemed as if the best use was made of the spaces already available from years gone by so that the small-town flavor hadn't been lost.

And that small-town flavor was particularly evident when Ethan parked the car so they could walk.

It seemed as if nearly every person they passed on the street either greeted Ethan by name or stopped to talk to him as if he were the prodigal son returning home.

After a while Paris began to wonder about it. But with so many people wanting to say hello to Ethan, there wasn't an opportunity to ask why he was so popular.

It was nearly six before Paris had met the retailers and service providers she would be working with, and by then it was too late for Ethan to finish the tour with the headquarters of Tarlington Software.

He did drive her past it, though.

It was an enormous, old, red stone factory that had been renovated with an eye toward retaining the original design.

Paris was curious about the fact that Dunbar Steel Foundry was carved into a granite arch above the main entrance, but just as she was on the verge of asking about it, Ethan had to answer his cell phone.

They were all the way back home again before that call ended and by then he'd moved on to a different topic.

"I asked Lolly if we could eat earlier tonight so Hannah could join us," he informed Paris once he'd rounded the SUV and opened her door for her. "Is that okay?"

"She's not much of a conversationalist. I don't know why you'd want her to have dinner with everyone."

"I just thought it would be fun. And nicer for you than hiding away somewhere with her. Let's do it this once and see how it goes. And if you'd rather go back to the way it was last night after this, we will."

So again he was making sure he got his way. Just as Jason always had.

Paris bristled slightly at that.

Of course, by then she was bristling slightly over the fact that he hadn't shown any signs of noticing her tighter clothes—or being affected by them—so she might have been nitpicking a little. Especially since *she* had noticed right off the bat that he'd shaved and showered after his horseback ride and that he looked fresh and smelled wonderful. And that seeing him in blue jeans and the navy T-shirt that managed to be casual and yet dressy, too, was a treat worth waiting for because no jeans and T-shirt had ever fit anyone as well. Or as sexily.

But under the circumstances what could she say?

"I guess it'll be all right if I feed Hannah in the dining room while everyone else eats. For tonight. But I really don't think you want to make a habit of it."

"We'll see you both in a little bit, then," Ethan said as they went into the house.

"Okay, but expect an I-told-you-so if you end up with baby food all over that nice carpeting in the dining room. Out of the blue she can spit it everywhere."

That idea seemed to amuse him. "Shall I wear a raincoat?"

"Just be prepared."

But Paris didn't end up getting to say "I told you so" because Hannah couldn't have been a better dinner companion.

With the infant seat strapped into the high chair, Hannah could see all three Tarlington men and it was clearly a view she liked. She smiled for them. She cooed for them. She waved her arms and kicked her legs in delight for them. And she ate without so much as dribbling a drop down her chin.

For their part, Ethan and his brothers seemed to enjoy Hannah just as much. They showed a surprising interest in her and in what she could and couldn't do, in what her routine was and how many hours of sleep she needed and how she made her wants and needs known.

It occurred to Paris that they might just be being polite but if that was the case they hid it well because by the time the meal was over and Hannah's bedtime had arrived, they all seemed as sorry to lose her as kids having their new toy put away.

Although Ethan didn't merely accept that. He asked if he could tag along and watch Paris put Hannah to bed.

"There isn't a whole lot to it," Paris told him. "I change her diaper, put on her pajamas, give her a bottle, and she's usually out like a light by the time I put her in her crib."

But he insisted he wanted to watch, and so that was what he did.

It was only when it was all done and Hannah was tucked in that Paris wondered if maybe Ethan had

had an ulterior motive. Because that was when he said, ''Let's go into the den and have a nightcap—I have a new bottle of cream sherry from Napa Valley that's so smooth you hardly know it's going down. I think you'll like it.''

He was pretty smooth himself with the way he'd slipped that in as if it were a given that they would be spending the rest of the evening together, she thought.

Still, smooth or not, she knew she should say thanks, but no thanks.

Except that what she knew and what she was inclined toward were two different things.

After all, it *was* only eight o'clock. And her sole other option was watching television in her room.

Hmm. Close the day with a glass of sherry and the company of a man who could fill out a pair of jeans like nobody's business? Or sit alone in her room and watch reruns?

The scales were tipped heavily in his favor.

Heavily enough to outweigh her better judgment.

It was only a harmless nightcap, she reasoned. It didn't have to mean anything and it didn't have to go any further than that.

''Maybe just a quick one,'' she finally agreed.

Then she grabbed the baby monitor and followed Ethan.

And if following him caused her eyes to stray to his backside? If it left her admiring the way the denim rode his tight buns?

It was purely accidental.

But it also made her stomach flutter in a way that it shouldn't have.

"Maybe your brothers would like to try the sherry, too," Paris said when they reached the den, thinking that there was safety in numbers.

"Are you nervous about being alone with me?" he asked as he went to the bar built into the paneling of one wall.

"I wouldn't say I was nervous, no. Why would I be nervous?" she said nervously.

"I don't know, why would you be?"

"I wouldn't be. I'm not."

"Then we don't need my brothers."

Ethan turned from the bar with a glass of sherry in each hand and motioned with one of them to the section of the room where a leather sofa and two matching chairs were positioned around a low coffee table.

It took Paris a moment for the meaning of that motion to sink in, though, because her gaze had gone to his hands and she got lost in an instant flash of what it had felt like to have those same big, strong, adept hands on her body.

Then she yanked herself out of that memory and the unwanted tingling her flesh had answered it with and went to one of the chairs.

Ethan handed her a sherry when she was seated and then took the chair across from her. All the way across the very large, square box coffee table.

She'd purposely avoided the couch so there was no chance of their sitting close together there. But still, the fact that he added to the distance rather than taking a spot on the sofa to at least be slightly nearer to her raised the same disappointment she'd felt when he'd postponed their trip into Dunbar today.

It was crazy and she knew it. But there it was.

She reminded herself that she really did want to keep things on an impersonal basis with him. And sitting far apart definitely accomplished that.

Yet there was also a small, totally illogical part of her that would have liked him to pursue her anyway. The way he had the night they'd met. Even in the face of her rejection of him.

But that part of her that would have liked to be pursued no matter what was probably just ego, she told herself. And it didn't need to be paid attention to.

So she tried not to.

Instead she attempted to distract herself by finally asking the question she would have asked on the way home had he not been on the cell phone.

"Why does it say Dunbar Steel Foundry over the entrance to Tarlington Software?"

"Because that's what it was for nearly a hundred years before. Dunbar was the name of the town's founding family. They built the town around the steel foundry and until about ten years ago that's what kept almost everybody here going, in one way or another."

"What happened ten years ago?"

"The last of the Dunbars died off and the foundation that inherited everything closed down the foundry without a thought about what it would do to the whole economy of Dunbar."

"And you stepped in?"

"It was the least I could do. I bought the foundry, remodeled it to meet the needs of manufacturing and distributing our line of mass-market software and games, and then retrained everybody so they could do that instead of steelwork."

"You turned steelworkers into computer geeks?"

"Don't sound so amazed. It wasn't that hard for a lot of people, and the ones who couldn't grasp the technical stuff were put in other areas they *could* handle. It worked out all the way around, if I do say so myself."

No wonder he was so popular. He was the town's savior.

"You said it was the least you could do—what does that mean?"

He didn't answer that right away. He pointed toward her glass with the chin she suddenly remembered kissing in the process of kissing her way from the hollow below one of his ears, along his jaw to the hollow of the other…

"How's the sherry?" he asked.

"Good," she said with a quiet catch in her voice.

But, quiet or not, he heard it anyway.

"If you don't like it I can get you something else."

She took a sip to prove she did like it. And also in hopes that the firy alcohol would cauterize her unruly thoughts.

Then she said, "No, I really do like it," in a more controlled tone.

Apparently satisfied, Ethan finally answered her question.

"Bringing Tarlington Software here was the least I could do because this town raised my brothers and me."

"The whole town?"

"A big part of it. The population was considerably less then—a lot of people have moved in since I brought the software business here. But still there was a joining of forces to keep Aiden, Devon and me in Dunbar after our parents were killed in a car accident just outside of town."

"When was this?"

"I was ten. Aiden was nine. Devon, eight. We didn't have any other family so we were orphaned, and if it hadn't been for the efforts of a whole lot of our neighbors we would have been separated and put in foster care. We'd have probably lost each other."

"And the town didn't let that happen?"

Ethan nodded and took a sip of his sherry.

Paris fought not to be so aware of a lot of the little things he did. Like the way he tilted his head back slightly to drink from the sherry glass, letting her see his Adam's apple—another spot she'd taken a turn kissing. Or his mouth on the glass's edge the way it had been on her mouth once upon a time....

Then he said, "No, the town didn't let anything happen to separate us. But the foundry didn't pay all that well, so folks around here were just making ends meet. Nobody could afford to take on three growing boys alone. So a fair share of the townsfolk formed a sort of coalition to raise us. Everybody pitched in.

There was a fund set up at the bank, and every payday people donated a little to provide for us financially so the costs of raising three extra kids wasn't a hardship on any one family.''

''And where did you all live?''

''Our house was mortgaged so it had to be sold and after that we lived pretty much nomadically. I know that sounds not much better than being shuffled between foster homes, but it really wasn't bad. We knew everybody and everybody knew us so we weren't going into strangers' homes. Plus we were never treated like burdens by anyone. One family would take us in for a while and then another would come along and say they'd like to have us and we'd go. I imagine it was prearranged, but as far as we knew, we were like the trophy that folks were vying to have a turn at keeping at their place. And wherever we were, we were treated like part of the family.''

''So you paid the town back by moving Tarlington Software here when they needed it and singlehandedly brought new life to the place. Apparently, they made a good investment when they raised you,'' Paris said, admiring not only the people of Dunbar who had gone to such trouble to keep the brothers together, but also admiring Ethan for coming back to take care of them when he could.

''Or maybe they just raised us right. Either way, I think it worked out for everybody,'' he said, only impressing Paris all the more because he wouldn't take his part of the credit.

''Does this party have anything to do with paying them back for what they did for you and your brothers?'' she asked to soothe her own curiosity about what was being celebrated so elaborately.

''The party serves a couple of purposes. We hold it every year on the week of our parents' joint birthdays and their wedding anniversary—they always got a big kick out of sharing the same birthday so that was also the day they chose to be married. We do the party in remembrance of them, but it's also like a gift we give to the people who put a lot of time and energy and money into raising us. I guess you could say it's a thank-you to all of our parents collectively.''

''It's a pretty spectacular affair,'' Paris said, unable to hide the awe that was mounting in her with every new thing she learned about what the event would entail. ''I can't quite believe the scale it's on.''

''Spectacular—that's a good word for it,'' he said as if it really did please him. ''That's what I aim for every year. I want it to be a spectacular reward for all that was done for us.''

''Mountains of caviar. Beef, veal, pheasant, lobster, soft-shell crabs, shrimp, salmon aspic. The finest champagne. Gold-dusted fondant frosted cake filled with French custard. Truffles—the mushroom kind and the chocolate kind. A full greenhouse worth of flowers. Five hundred strings of lights. A violin quintet coming in from Vienna to play during the meal. An orchestra for dancing afterward. An hour-long fireworks display—just to name a few of the things you have planned? I think spectacular might be an understatement.''

Ethan just smiled.

And Paris was struck all over again by how great-looking he was.

Only, now that she knew something of his history, now that she knew he was the kind of man who paid his debts and looked after people who had looked after him, it was as if there was a new depth to his handsomeness that she hadn't seen before. A level of maturity and responsibility that was very sexy.

And then, too, they'd both finished their sherry and the liquor had gone straight to her head, strengthening her responses to him, which could also have been a contributing factor.

But either way she thought that she should put an end to the evening before something as simple as the blink of his eyes drove her to jump into his lap.

Ethan seemed to realize their glasses were empty just then, too. He held up his and said, ''Another?''

Paris shook her head. ''No, thanks. In fact I was just thinking that I should call it a night. As you discovered this morning, Hannah is not a late sleeper.''

''Neither am I.''

''I gathered as much,'' she countered pointedly.

''Was I out of bounds to go in there this morning?''

''No. But you don't need to worry that she isn't being taken care of. I always hear her and I know just about how long I can snooze before she gets irate and wants some attention.''

''I didn't think you neglected her,'' he said as if he meant it.

''Good, because I don't.''

"How about if I got her up a morning or two and let you sleep in?" he offered then, out of the blue and surprising her.

"Oh, I don't think that would be a good idea."

"Why not?"

"She's usually drenched and hungry and—"

"So I'd change her and feed her."

"Thanks, anyway, but I enjoy our mornings." And she wouldn't enjoy having them taken over by the man she was most worried about taking over more than that.

She didn't even want to talk about it any longer. So she stood and returned her glass to the wet bar, saying along the way, "But if I don't get some sleep now I might be less likely to hear her when she does wake up."

Then Paris turned around again to say good-night, expecting to find Ethan where she'd left him.

But instead he was halfway to the door.

"If I can't talk you into staying up I guess I'll just have to walk you to your room then."

"I can find my way now. You don't have to."

"I do if I want five more minutes with you. And since you look the way you do in those pants and that shirt, I definitely want five more minutes with you."

He *had* noticed.

In fact, he was noticing right then as his eyes did a slow crawl from her bare ankles up to her face. And from his expression, Paris had no doubt he liked what he saw.

She only wished she didn't like that he liked what

he saw quite as much as she did. And that she wasn't so tempted to stay in that den with him to languish in the warmth of his gaze. And maybe in his arms, too...

"I really need to get to bed," she said before she gave in to her own temptations.

He smiled again, this time with a wickedness to it, as if she were inviting him along.

"Alone," she said before she realized he hadn't actually given her any overt reason to say that.

His smile widened to a grin, and she just knew he wasn't going to let that slide.

"Did I say anything about joining you?"

"No, but you were thinking it," she accused, deciding that since she'd gotten herself into this, she might as well bluff her way through it.

"Was I?"

"It looked like it."

"I looked like I was thinking about going to bed with you?"

How had she gotten into this? And how was she going to get out of it?

"Yes, you did," she said with more bravado than she felt at that moment.

"Maybe you just *thought* that was what I was thinking because that's what *you* were thinking."

"I was only thinking that your sherry made me sleepy."

"Uh-huh," he said as if he didn't believe it for a minute.

Intent on playing this hand right to the end, Paris sighed and shook her head as if she were merely exasperated with him. ''I think I'll just say good-night.''

''Not until I have my last five minutes,'' he reminded. ''But just in the hallway,'' he added pointedly.

He opened the door for her then, and Paris decided that keeping her mouth shut was the best thing she could do for herself as she led the way out.

Ethan followed and fell into step with her.

But thankfully he let the previous subject drop and said, ''So I think I have some making up to do.''

''You've lost me.''

''Well, I spent half the drive in from Denver on the cell phone. I stood you up most of today and then spent the ride home on the phone again. I want to make up for that.''

''There's nothing to make up for. Employees have no expectation of undivided attention.''

''Okay, let's say I'm making it up to me, then, for missing out on your company. Here's what I was thinking—I need to do some things with my brothers tomorrow in the daytime—''

''Which is good because I have work to do.''

''So how about a picnic supper in the evening? You, me, Hannah and a dinner I'll have Lolly pack for us? It stays light late and it'll actually be cooler than trying to do it in the middle of the day, I think it's the perfect time for it.''

''That doesn't sound very businesslike.''

''No, it doesn't, does it? But let's do it anyway.''

They'd reached her bedroom door by then, and when Paris glanced up at him she found a smile on his sensual lips, this one full of devilry as those luscious blue eyes stared down at her, searching her face, her own eyes.

And before she had time to think about it, she heard herself say, ‘‘All right,’’ in a voice that was barely more than a whisper, as if then her better judgment wouldn’t hear.

That made Ethan’s smile even broader, and Paris seemed to get lost in it. In that smile and those eyes and in the scent of his aftershave all around her and just in his presence—big and tall and muscular and all man…

He was going to kiss her.

She didn’t know how she knew it but she did.

And she was going to let him. Even though she knew without a doubt that she shouldn’t.

He came closer.

He leaned in.

She tilted her chin ever so slightly.

And then he did it. He kissed her.

On the cheek.

‘‘I’ll let Lolly know about our picnic,’’ he said as he stepped back afterward. ‘‘Have a good night’s sleep.’’

It took Paris a moment to realize what had happened. A moment in which she just stood there, stunned and a little embarrassed that that tilt of her chin might have let him know she’d expected more. That she’d wanted more. That she would have accepted more.

Then she got hold of herself, straightened her shoulders like a soldier standing for inspection and said a brisk, "Good night," before slipping into her room and leaving him unceremoniously behind.

But the truth was, more than embarrassed that he might have known she was anticipating a real kiss, Paris felt her third wave of disappointment for the day.

And that was when it occurred to her that of the two of them, *she* was behaving a whole lot more *un*businesslike than he was.

He was spending time with his brothers. He was sitting a respectable distance away from her. Even that kiss on the cheek was something he might have given any acquaintance.

While she had been pining for his company all day and offended that he hadn't sat nearer to her in the den and waiting for a kiss on the lips at her door.

Which meant that she needed to practice what she preached. Beginning immediately, by putting a stop to that latest disappointment that was running rampant through her.

But getting rid of that disappointment was easier said than done. Because no matter how hard she tried, she couldn't seem to stop wishing he would have pulled her into his arms and kissed her smack-dab on the mouth.

And kept on kissing her until her toes curled and she couldn't remember what day it was.

Chapter Five

It was the Tarlington brothers' tradition to visit their parents' graves on the actual date of their common birthday and anniversary. That date fell on the following day.

Ethan had a blanket of flowers made for the occasion, and he and his brothers picked it up at the florist before they went to the Dunbar cemetery far on the outskirts of town.

After so long a time the visits each year weren't really sad so much as they were poignant. They followed no particular pattern. Sometimes one or two or all three of the brothers had something to say, as if the headstone were an intercom connecting them to their lost parents. Sometimes no one spoke. Sometimes Ethan, Aiden and Devon reminisced about something they remembered from when their folks were alive.

But always they decorated the graves. They wished their parents a happy birthday and a happy anniversary. And when they all felt ready to go, they each touched the marble headstone and then spent several miles of the drive back into town in silence, dealing in their own ways with the feelings that rose to the surface.

It was when that silent time had naturally passed and they'd begun to talk again that Ethan finally broached the question he'd wanted to ask his brothers since dinner the night before.

"So you've seen Hannah. What do you think about her?"

"I think we should have brought her out here with us today so Mom and Dad could see their first grandchild," Devon said without hesitation from where he sat in the back seat of Ethan's SUV.

"Her eyes are Mom's eyes and she has that same dimple when she smiles really big," Aiden added from the passenger seat.

"That's what I thought," Ethan said quietly, not sure where the confirmation of his suspicions left him now that he had it.

"Neither of you guys have ever donated to a sperm bank, have you?" he asked with a lame chuckle.

"Not me."

"Not me, either. You're not off the hook that easily," Devon joked just as lamely.

"The thing is, though," Aiden said more seriously, "I really like Paris. She seems like a genuinely nice person."

"Yeah," Devon agreed. "And she's great-looking and has a sense of humor, and she's easy to talk to. I can't figure out why she wouldn't tell you if Hannah *is* yours. Did you scare her off with talk about hating kids or something?"

"I don't hate kids," Ethan said. "But we did talk about having them the night we met." He shook his head. "I don't mean that the way it sounded. What I mean is that when she asked if I was married I said I wasn't and that I had too much on my plate to even think about a wife or kids, that I was building my business and devoting myself to that, and that there was no way I was even close to wanting a family anytime in the near future."

"Let me get this straight," Aiden said with a laugh. "She asked you if you were married—a simple question—and instead of a plain no, you told her about why you didn't want a wife and kids right now?"

"I didn't tell her all about it, no. I just wanted to be clear from the get-go. I'd only come off the Bettina mess a few months before that and I was a little raw about the whole subject."

"Still, Paris couldn't have known that you went overboard because of some other woman," Aiden pointed out. "She had to have believed you meant what you said—no wife and no kids, no way."

"And after that diatribe it's a wonder she let you anywhere near her."

"So maybe," Aiden said, "she's keeping the fact

of your fatherhood to herself because she believes—rightly so after what you told her—that there's no way in hell you'd *want* to know or want anything to do with being a parent even if you did.''

It was a theory Ethan had thought about himself.

But even hearing it from someone else didn't make it ring true to him.

''I don't think that's it. I just have this feeling that there's more to it. It's really like she doesn't want me to know.''

''Could it be that she's just waiting for the right time?'' Aiden asked.

''And what would be the right time? After I've fallen for her? Are you saying that maybe she's setting some kind of trap because she thinks I'd bow out of the picture if I knew Hannah was mine now? That Paris is pretending Hannah isn't mine and then when I'm in deep enough she'll tell me she is? That Paris is as conniving as Bettina, only with a different angle?''

''Talk about taking the ball and running with it in the wrong direction! No, that's not what I was saying. I was saying that maybe Paris is just waiting for a time that feels right. I didn't know you were so paranoid.''

''Maybe that was a little overboard,'' Ethan admitted. ''It's just that this whole thing is so damn frustrating. And aggravating. And confusing.''

''So, okay,'' Devon said then. ''When we talked about this before, you didn't want to ask Paris straight-out if Hannah is yours because you wanted to wait until you knew if we saw the same thing in

Hannah that you did. But now that we have, why not just confront Paris?''

''Because remember there was a second part to it,'' Aiden answered before Ethan could. ''He wants to understand the reason behind Paris not telling him Hannah is his. If that's the case.''

''Besides,'' Ethan added now, ''what if she just denies it, takes the baby and goes as far away from me as she can get? And then the only way I'll ever know for sure is to go to court and force paternity tests, and the whole thing will end up ugly and hurtful.''

''And you'll lose Paris,'' Aiden finished.

''I don't *have* Paris,'' Ethan said more under his breath than not.

''But you must be thinking along the lines of *wanting* her or you wouldn't care why she isn't telling you the truth or if you ticked her off by pushing the issue,'' Aiden persisted.

''Which means we were right from the start—you do like her,'' Devon concluded.

''That was always a given. I don't sleep with women I don't like.''

''I think there's more to it than that,'' Aiden said. ''I've been watching how you are around her. I don't think you just like Paris. I think she's gotten pretty far under your skin.''

''I'm glad to know I've been scrutinized,'' Ethan commented without conceding anything.

''Does liking the lady change your mind about doing the whole family bit?'' Devon asked.

''I don't know if I'd go that far,'' Ethan hedged.

"How far would you go?" This from Aiden.

Ethan took a deep breath and blew it out as if he were aiming for candles on a cake. "Don't ask me hard questions."

"Since you don't seem to have any answers maybe you should be grateful that Paris is giving you some time to get used to the idea and figure things out," Aiden suggested.

"Except that it's hard to be putting the moves on her the way he wants to with that hanging over his head."

Ethan laughed wryly at that. And the element of the truth it had to it.

"So what're you going to do?" Aiden asked.

"Wait and see," Ethan answered.

"And take a lot of cold showers in the meantime," Devon goaded.

But it was true.

Because no matter what was going on with Hannah, Ethan was as hot for Paris as he'd been the night they'd met. Hotter, actually. Hotter with each minute he spent with her.

And it was taking every ounce of willpower he could muster not to go after her with all he had.

It was just that he kept asking himself what would happen if he gave in to all the urges that were driving him to distraction and then found out later that Paris was just working some scam on him the way Bettina had.

There couldn't have been a better evening than that one for a picnic.

By six o'clock the sun was no longer beating down

with the intensity of midday. The sky was still a bright, cloudless blue, and even though it was over eighty degrees, it was a pleasant heat.

The wicker basket beside Hannah in the back seat of the SUV Ethan was driving was filled with fried chicken, potato salad, deviled eggs, fresh fruit and brownies, and in a cooler on the floor was a bottle of chilled wine.

They didn't have far to go from the house to be out in the country, but when Ethan pulled off the road and headed for the location he'd picked out, Paris could see that it was the perfect spot.

There was a huge, ancient oak tree near a quietly babbling brook. Lush green grass grew as far as the eye could see, and several guernsey cows grazed only a few yards in the distance.

"We're having dinner with the cattle tonight, huh?" Paris joked when Ethan parked the SUV near the tree.

"We were invited and I just couldn't refuse," he joked in return. "But they must be good company because my brothers wanted to tag along and I had to put my foot down to get them to stay home."

"They could have come," Paris was quick to say. Actually she'd been warring with herself all day, knowing it would be safer if Ethan ended up asking Aiden and Devon to join them, hoping he didn't and knowing she shouldn't be hoping any such thing.

"You could call them on your cell phone right now and tell them to come if you want," she said, continuing the war by hoping he wouldn't and knowing she shouldn't have that hope.

Ethan had turned off the engine by then and he leaned over to say confidentially, "I didn't want them. I wanted to be alone with you. And Hannah."

A ripple of delight rolled all through Paris at that but she tried not to acknowledge it.

Not that it was easy not acknowledging anything that the man did to her. Especially when she'd been so exquisitely aware of every detail about him since the moment she'd laid eyes on him tonight.

He was wearing a pair of age-faded jeans that fitted him like a familiar lover's caress. A yellow short-sleeved mock-turtleneck T-shirt that hugged his broad shoulders, his hard chest and his bountiful biceps. His hair fell in finger-combed disarray that made her own hands want to run through it. He was freshly shaved and smelled of that intoxicating after-shave he wore. And it was definitely difficult not to acknowledge just how much she liked the whole package. Just how much it made her feel all feminine inside.

Of course, it didn't hurt that after changing her clothes three times in anticipation of this simple picnic she'd settled on about the most feminine thing she owned to wear—a wispy white, ankle-length sundress and strappy sandals.

"They liked you, though," Ethan was saying, the sound of his voice reminding her to pay attention to something more than the way he looked and smelled and made her feel.

"My brothers. Aiden and Devon liked you," he

clarified as if her expression had led him to believe she didn't know who he was talking about.

''I liked them, too,'' she answered, still sounding a little dim.

But Ethan let it pass and got out of the SUV.

''I brought rope,'' he said as he opened her door for her. ''I thought I'd hang Hannah's car seat from the tree so she'll have a swing.''

''She ought to like that,'' Paris said as she got out, appreciating that he'd thought of it and was willing to go to the trouble.

But nothing about setting up their picnic site seemed to be trouble for Ethan. Which surprised Paris a little.

It almost seemed strange that a man of his means, who even had his car driven for him when he chose and certainly didn't have to bother with any of the mundane day-to-day chores of life, was willing to spread a blanket on the ground for her and leave her to fish out Hannah's dinner from the diaper bag while he unloaded the rest of the car. Certainly Jason—who had considered laying out his own clothes to be beneath him—would not have done it, let alone volunteered to rig a swing for Hannah.

''I thought we could have some wine while you feed Hannah, play with her awhile, and then eat our own supper later on. Does that sound all right?'' Ethan asked as he uncorked the bottle.

''Sounds fine,'' Paris said when, in fact, it sounded great.

''Can we prop her up against something so I can

work with the car seat?'' he asked as he handed Paris one of the two glasses of wine he'd poured.

''Sure.''

She positioned the diaper bag so that it braced Hannah at approximately the same angle she would have been in the carrier.

Then, as Ethan went to work with that and the rope, she opened the jars of Hannah's food and began to spoon the strained carrots and peaches alternately into her daughter's mouth.

But as she did, her focus was actually less on the baby than on Ethan.

She told herself she just wanted to make sure he was securing the seat in a way that it would be safe. But the truth was she couldn't unglue her eyes from the sight of Ethan himself as he tossed the rope over a high branch and then worked with it until it cradled the seat.

He really did have a body to die for. He was tall and tight and lean and muscular. And without warning, watching him now gave her a sudden flash of the way it had felt to lie naked against him; her bare flesh pressed to his; those long, powerful legs entwined with hers; his strong arms holding her; the satiny heat of him all around her....

Hannah protested just then and Paris realized belatedly that she'd let too much time lapse between bites. Feeling guilty for that, she readjusted her focus.

But apparently the baby's complaint had drawn Ethan's attention, too.

''Everything okay?''

''Fine,'' Paris answered in a voice that had a

squeak to it as she forced her gaze to remain on Hannah so she wouldn't be distracted again.

"I think we're all set," Ethan said then. "See? I think it would even bear my weight."

Paris had no choice but to glance at him again as he demonstrated how sturdy the swing was by pushing down on it with all his might.

"Looks like it," she responded, making sure her voice didn't give her away a second time.

Then Ethan joined her on the blanket, sitting beside both her and Hannah.

"So how was your day?" he asked then, picking up his glass and tasting the wine Paris had forgotten about.

"Fine, dear. How was yours?" she said as if she were reciting a line from a 1950s sitcom, because that's what his question had sounded like.

Ethan laughed and played along. "Oh, you know, just a day at the office."

But Paris switched gears then and gave him a real answer to let him know that she was doing what little she'd been hired to do. "I had it out with your New York chocolatier. He was dragging his feet about sending the truffles in the heat. He wanted to charge more for sending them overnight delivery in an insulated container that would keep them from melting. But I brought it to his attention that there was already a provision for both the fast delivery and the dry ice containers in the contract, at the contracted price. So the truffles should be here tomorrow."

"Great."

"I also finally convinced the liquor distributor that

they did, indeed, short the champagne order by six cases. Those will be here tomorrow, too. And other than that, everything is under control and, so far, right on schedule.''

''That's what I like to hear.''

Paris was curious about how he'd spent his day since there had been quiet mutterings throughout the house staff about whatever it was he and his brothers were doing. But she didn't feel free to just ask outright, so without taking her eyes off Hannah, she said, ''Did you and your brothers do something fun?''

''Not fun, no,'' he said before drinking more of his wine.

For a moment Paris thought that might be all he was going to say.

But then he went on. ''Today is the real day of our parents' birthdays and anniversary. We always visit their graves.''

''Oh,'' she said, unsure what else to say and sorry she'd brought it up.

But Ethan didn't seem to be. ''When you lose your folks as young as we were, it's easy to...I don't know, not forget them exactly, but the memory fades. And with so many other people taking their place, we like to do this one thing every year to keep them a part of us, I guess. Or to let them know we *haven't* forgotten them, maybe.''

''That's really nice,'' Paris said quietly, touched by the fact that the brothers took pains to honor the parents they'd lost.

''What about you?'' Ethan said then, lightening

the tone somewhat. "I met your mom, but is your dad still living?"

Paris shrugged. "I don't know. He came home from work one day when I was five, announced that he wanted a new life, and that was the last Mom or I ever saw or heard from him again."

"Wow. I'm sorry."

"It definitely wasn't a nice thing to do. It also wasn't nice that he didn't pay child support. That made it really hard on my mom and that's why she's a little freaked out that I chose to have and raise a baby on my own. But in a way I think Mom and I are closer because my father was out of the picture, and I've always seen that as the up side."

"So you have a precedent in your family for single mothers."

"I've never thought of it that way, but I suppose we do."

"Is that how you envision your relationship with Hannah—closer than it would be with a dad in the picture?"

For some reason that question felt as if it held more weight than anything else they'd been talking about and Paris wasn't sure why.

She glanced up from feeding Hannah to look at Ethan and found a very serious expression on his face, but she still didn't understand the reason for it.

She answered him anyway. "I didn't have Hannah on my own just for that purpose. But yes, I hope she and I are as close as my mom and I are."

"Didn't you miss having a father in your life?"

"Here and there. But not so much that it was a

huge thing to me that there wouldn't be a father around when I made the decision to have Hannah. For me, fathers are like dessert—nice to have. But I survived without one and I think I turned out pretty well. I know I'm none the worse for wear because my father wasn't around. I have to believe that Hannah won't be, either."

Of course the whole time Paris was saying that, Hannah was grinning a toothless grin at Ethan as if he were the most wonderful thing she'd ever seen.

He noticed it at about the same time Paris did and grinned back at her the same way, letting her hang on to one of his index fingers.

"I don't know," he said pointedly, "I think fathers are pretty important."

"All I'm saying is that I did okay without one. And apparently so did you."

"I may not have had my own father, but I had a lot of male role models."

Paris laughed. "Do you think Hannah is going to need to learn how to be a man?"

"She might need to know how to relate to one."

Paris glanced from him to her daughter, who was trying to get his finger into her mouth while still grinning at him. "She seems to know how to do that naturally. Besides," Paris added, "it isn't as if she'll be sheltered from all men. I have male cousins and friends and neighbors. The world is full of your kind," she ended with another joke.

"My kind?" he repeated with a laugh.

Paris just smiled.

"Are we done eating strained stuff here?" he asked then, nodding toward Hannah.

Paris offered the baby another spoonful of fruit but Hannah wasn't interested.

"Looks like it."

"Then *my kind* wants to introduce her to the cows."

"Now that *is* a *your kind* kind of thing. Are you sure they won't bite or charge or something?"

"I'm sure. And it's something *my kind* knows."

"Ah, cows are a man thing. I was wondering," Paris said, going along with the joke he didn't seem to want to let die.

She wiped Hannah's face, and before she could say more, Ethan stood and picked up the baby.

"You're welcome to come, too," he invited, holding out his free hand to help her up.

Paris had every intention of going, and it seemed rude not to accept his help. It was just that of all the things she was trying not to acknowledge, the sparks his touch set off in her were harder to ignore than the rest all put together.

And the fact that once she was on her feet she didn't want him to let go? That she wanted him to go on holding her hand?

Not a good thing.

But he did let go, and that, too, was a problem for Paris, because when he did she felt that same disappointment rampant in her the day and evening before.

It just wasn't easy being with him, she decided. And she might as well accept that and ride it out.

Of course it wasn't easy *not* being with him, either, because then all she did was think about him and *want* to be with him.

But it's only this week, she told herself as they headed across the meadow in the direction of one of the guernseys. Just this week, and then they'd go their separate ways.

Yet somehow that thought wasn't altogether good, either.

But this wasn't the time to analyze it, she thought, letting herself off the hook. She was on a picnic. It was a beautiful evening. And there was nothing she could do about any of it, anyway, except try not to think about it.

''This is Betsy,'' Ethan said as they drew near the big brown-and-white animal.

Betsy had a mouthful of grass she was working on with a back-and-forth motion of her lower jaw, and she eyed them without much interest.

Hannah was thrilled, though. She was waving her arms as if she might take wing, and making sounds Paris had never heard her make before.

''Want to pet her?'' Ethan asked the baby as if Hannah could answer.

He held her close enough so that one of her hands came into contact with the side of the cow's neck.

Betsy flicked an ear as if to shoo away a fly, and Hannah let out a squeal of delight.

''I think you might have to bring one of these home with you,'' Ethan said to Paris over Hannah's head as Hannah leaned forward to let him know she wanted to feel the cow again.

"I could be wrong but I think there are ordinances against keeping cows in the backyard."

Ethan set Hannah on the animal's back, keeping hold of her.

Hannah liked that, too, and kicked her legs as enthusiastically as she was flailing her arms.

Betsy turned her head in slow motion to eye the activities and then exhibited her displeasure by doing a leisurely stroll away from them.

And that seemed to be it for Hannah's introduction to cows.

They took a walk through the meadow from there, with Ethan carrying Hannah and regaling Paris with stories of adolescent antics he and his brothers and friends had pulled in this same countryside.

Then they wound up sitting beside the brook so Ethan could dip Hannah's feet in it—but only after clearing it with Paris and assuring her the water had been tested and it was free of unsavory organisms or bacteria.

He taught Paris how to skip rocks and teased her with threats to throw her in. And as the evening passed Paris began to remember one of the reasons she'd liked him so much that first night they'd met. Without the cell phone interruptions, without other people vying for his attention, Ethan was extremely good company. He was calm and intelligent. He was interesting and knowledgeable. He was interested in anything she had to say. He could be very funny. And it was just nice to be with him.

Something she almost wished she hadn't been reminded of.

The lower the sun got in the sky, the heavier Hannah's eyelids seemed to get. Paris had come prepared for that and laid her daughter on the blanket to change her diaper and put on her pajamas.

As she did, Ethan tickled Hannah's chubby cheek with a blade of grass, and when Paris was finished he asked if he could give Hannah her bedtime bottle.

Paris hesitated. That last cuddle of every day was one of her favorite times, and she didn't like relinquishing it to anyone. But seeing Ethan with Hannah since they'd arrived at their picnic site had done something strange to her and she discovered in herself the slight inkling to let him do it. To see him hold his child that way.

So, even though a part of her was against it, she let that other part rule just this once and agreed.

And it was something to see. Ethan leaned back against the tree trunk, and Hannah looked so safe there against his massive chest, so protected, so right.

And as the tiny baby gazed up into his face with fascination and accepted the bottle he offered her, the image of the two of them together gave Paris such a twinge that for the first time in fourteen months she felt a tiny, tiny urge to tell him he was Hannah's father.

But she shied away from it in a hurry.

"How did you get so good at handling babies?" she asked to distract herself from her own thoughts, her own unwanted inclinations.

"One of the families my brothers and I stayed with when we were kids had a baby Hannah's age. A boy.

I was about fourteen—old enough to baby-sit—so that became my job.''

''Did you like that?''

He laughed. ''No, I wasn't thrilled with it. But it wasn't as if we went into these homes as guests. Everybody thought it was important to teach us things along the way the same as they taught their own kids—life skills, table manners, right from wrong. And we had chores everywhere we went, like taking out the trash or cleaning the garage or helping out around the house.''

''And in this particular house you were the baby-sitter?''

''It wasn't as if anyone took advantage of us. But, yes, I did some baby-sitting there. Anyway, once I got over balking at what I considered a *girl's* job, it wasn't so bad. Well, the diaper changing was—I never liked that. But I had some fun with the rest of it and, like a lot of what my surrogate parents taught me, you never know when it might come in handy.''

Hannah had finished her bottle and was still staring up at Ethan as if she were mesmerized by him.

He stood and set her in the baby carrier, strapping her in. Then he nudged it gently, putting the make-shift swing into motion and staying there to keep it going as she fought sleep to keep watching him.

But she could only fight it for so long, and she finally dozed off, freeing Ethan to join Paris on the blanket so they could eat.

''It seems like you've had an amazing number of good people in your life,'' Paris said.

''I have. All but one, actually.''

"That sounds very ominous." Not to mention intriguing. "Man or woman?"

"Woman."

"Someone who took you guys in as kids?"

"No, she came into my life three years ago."

"Ah. A romantic interest?"

"A romantic interest," he confirmed just as he was taking a bite of potato salad. But rather than soothing Paris's growing curiosity, when he could go on he said, "But that's not a picnic story. I don't want to ruin this with that."

Another bite of the creamy, spicy dish interrupted their conversation and when he'd finished it he said, "Besides, that's enough about my past for one day. Let's talk about your future."

"Are you going to make me a job offer?" Paris joked because of the way he'd worded that.

"I wasn't, no. But I could. Want to design my packaging or my advertising copy or my brochures? Or you could do something else. You could write your own ticket."

She wasn't sure if he was joking in return or not. "Are you playing fairy godfather?" she asked with a laugh.

"Is that what you want?"

Why did that sound like a test?

Paris just laughed again. "What I want is to paint. And raise my daughter."

"Alone."

"I don't know that I *want* to raise her alone. It's just the way things are."

"Does that mean if the right guy came along you'd marry him?"

Was she mistaken, or was there a note of jealousy in his tone?

"Yes," she answered honestly. "If the right guy came along—"

"What would make him the right guy?"

She thought about it. And tried to block the image of Ethan from her mind's eye. "He'd have to be down-to-earth, kind, considerate, levelheaded, fun to be with, ethical, honest, compassionate, unselfish—"

"So if you found Mr. Perfect you'd marry him?"

"I'd consider letting him into Hannah's and my life, yes. I'm not antimarriage. That was your deal, as I recall, not mine."

Ethan's brow beetled as if she'd struck a note with that. "I had a conversation about that with my brothers today as a matter of fact. Did I give you the impression that I was antimarriage?"

"No, you didn't give me that *impression.* You told me straight out—no marriage, no family for you. You were too busy and more interested in work."

He flinched slightly. "I was just coming off that bad experience we were talking about tonight—"

"With the bad woman."

"With the bad woman. So I may have been a little...overly negative."

"I don't know, you seem pretty busy to me. And pretty work oriented. I can't see where you have time for a wife or kids."

They'd finished eating by then and he glanced around them, obviously taking in the setting sun and the cattle in the distance, and the brook nearby. And Hannah.

"I'm not busy now. I'm not working now," he pointed out.

Paris just laughed again. "Tonight. And for all of one week out of the year that so far hasn't been without work phone calls."

"That doesn't mean I couldn't make time for marriage and a family if I wanted them. I could always delegate."

"And become a laid-back mogul?" she teased.

"Maybe. Anything's possible."

"Are you telling me that now you've decided you want marriage and a family in *your* future?"

He arched his eyebrows and shrugged his shoulders, too. "Never know."

"And what you want, you make sure you get," she said somewhat under her breath.

"What does that mean?"

"Just what it sounds like. You're used to getting whatever it is you decide you want. So I guess if you decide you want a wife and kids nothing will stop you from going out and getting them."

"Don't most people go after what they want? You did, didn't you? You wanted a baby and so you went for artificial insemination to get one."

Okay, now they were venturing into territory Paris didn't want to be in.

Luckily the mosquitoes were coming out in force right about then, and Ethan slapping one away from his arm gave her an out.

"We'd better get going before the bugs decide to have baby for brunch."

Ethan didn't jump into action. He just went on studying her as if he thought if he looked closely enough he might see something he might not see otherwise.

But when Paris began to reload the picnic basket with the remnants of their meal, he finally stood, untied the car seat and put Hannah in the SUV, out of harm's way.

Then he came back to help Paris clean up, and as he did he said, "So how is it different for me to go after what I want than for anyone else to?"

Keeping her eyes on what she was doing rather than letting them meet Ethan's, she said, "It's different because you have so much money. People with a lot of money lose the concept that they *can't* have whatever they want, and they also have the means to go after what they want at all costs. Even if it hurts other people."

"Are you thinking that I'm going to buy a wife and kids?"

"I think this is something *I* don't want to talk about tonight."

She regretted that she'd let it be known just how raw a nerve this was to her. But since he respected her wishes not to continue discussing it and went on to small talk, she just let it lie.

In fact, he stuck to small talk for the entire drive home, so Paris thought the subject was completely dead and she relaxed again.

Back at his house Ethan carried Hannah and the

seat inside. Then he stood by, watching Paris carefully put her daughter in the crib, and followed her out of the room into the hall when she had.

''I wanted to call my mom tonight and see how she's doing,'' Paris said then. ''So I should say good-night and do that before it gets too late.''

But again Ethan didn't seem inclined to move from that spot just outside Hannah's closed door any more than he'd been in a hurry to leave their picnic blanket earlier. He remained standing there, looking down at Paris, searching her face yet again just the way he had then.

''I'm really not all work and no play, you know,'' he said with a crooked smile. ''And I can't imagine ever using money to gain a wife or kids—if that was even possible.''

''Whatever you say,'' she said, not thrilled to have the sore subject brought up again.

''If I was all work and no play I wouldn't have enjoyed tonight as much as I did.''

''It was nice,'' she admitted.

He still didn't budge, though. He went on studying her with those blue eyes that were so intense Paris knew no color on her palette could do them justice.

And as much as she didn't want them to, those eyes drew her to him as if they were casting a spell over her.

''There's a dinner and dance tomorrow night at the church in town,'' he said then. ''It's sort of in honor of me and Aiden and Devon. Will you go with me? As my date?''

''Oh, I don't know if that's such a good idea,''

she said in reaction to the word *date,* even as a little voice in the back of her mind said, *And what was tonight if not a date?*

''I think it's a great idea,'' Ethan persisted.

Paris shook her head, but before she could say anything, he said, ''Come on. I want to be there with you. I want you to be there with me. No games.''

All the reasons why she shouldn't do that were like a chorus in her head. But it was just background noise as Ethan's eyes held hers, as the power, the potency of the man himself seemed to engulf her.

''I shouldn't,'' she whispered, a denial that made it clear she was going to, anyway.

''Yes, you should.''

''Hannah—''

''Can come along. There'll be a lot of kids there.''

And then he did the one thing that put her completely over the edge. He touched her. He reached a big, capable hand to the side of her neck and rubbed it with the most tender brush of his fingertips as he said, ''Say you'll come.''

Paris thought she might have the weakest will of anyone in the whole world because that was all it took for her to say, ''Okay.''

It made him smile. A slow, pleased smile without a trace of self-satisfaction. Purely a smile that said she'd made him a happy man.

And then, as if it were perfectly natural, he bent over enough to kiss her.

Not merely a peck on the cheek like the night before, but a kiss in which his warm, sensual lips captured hers, parted over hers, lingered over hers and erupted memories in Paris that she'd been trying not to entertain. A kiss that reminded her how good he was at it. How much she liked it.

Then he ended it almost as unexpectedly as he'd started it and smiled down at her again. A smile that seemed to wash away the last fourteen months along with all the distance, all the formalities, all the barriers she'd tried to erect between them. A smile that took her back to a moment after they'd made love all that time ago, when they were both stripped bare literally and emotionally before each other.

''Good night,'' Ethan said then, sliding his hand away from her neck and leaving that spot feeling naked for the loss.

Paris didn't say anything at all. She just opened Hannah's door and slipped back into her daughter's room rather than move down to her own and risk that even another second of being without a physical barrier between herself and Ethan might make her completely incapable of leaving him at all.

But even once she was in the seclusion of Hannah's room, Paris knew she still hadn't really escaped.

Because what she wanted was to just go back out into the hall and throw herself into Ethan's arms.

So he could remind her of more than just how much she liked the way he kissed.

Chapter Six

"Let me hold her while you finish your lunch," Lolly offered.

Paris and Hannah were alone with the older woman in the kitchen the next day, and Hannah was fussy. Paris had hoped feeding her daughter would help, but it hadn't. Hannah didn't want to stay in her high chair and she kept wiggling around in Paris's lap, making it difficult for Paris to eat the egg salad sandwich Lolly had made her. So she didn't argue, she just handed Hannah over.

"Thanks. I don't know why she's so out of sorts today."

As the other woman bounced Hannah gently on her knee to occupy her, Paris finally gave in to curiosity and ventured the question she'd been trying not to ask since she'd come from working in the den and discovered she, Hannah and Lolly were dining alone in the kitchen.

"Did the Tarlington men jump ship?"

"They did. After breakfast the boys took off for town. Ethan has his work cut out for him with Dr. B."

Lolly said that as if Paris knew what she was talking about. Since she didn't, she said, "Dr. B.?"

"Bob Briscoe. He was the doctor around here until he retired about five years ago."

"Why does Ethan have his work cut out for him with Dr. B.?"

"The old dear is going blind and he just can't be living alone anymore. The trouble is he won't admit he needs help."

"He doesn't have any family?"

"His wife died about ten years ago and his daughter was killed in an accident last year, so, no, he doesn't have any family left. Except Ethan, Aiden and Devon—they consider themselves his family."

"Surrogate family? I know how they were raised, Ethan told me."

"We all like to think of ourselves as extended family. It sounds so much better," Lolly corrected. "Anyway, yes, Dr. B. and his wife took their turn having the boys live with them. In fact, I think it was because of Dr. B.'s influence that Aiden became a doctor."

Which still didn't explain why Ethan had his work cut out for him in regards to the man.

"Is Ethan hoping to convince him that he needs

help?'' Paris asked to remind Lolly of what they were talking about.

''I think he'll be doing a little more than convincing him. When Ethan heard about what was going on with Dr. B. he sent word from overseas to hire someone to live with him to take care of the house and look after him. Of course Ethan will pay for it—a country doctor doesn't get rich, and Ethan does things like that whenever a need arises around here. But poor Devon has been coming into town almost every week since then, trying to persuade Dr. B. to accept the help, and Dr. B. just keeps saying he doesn't want anybody in his house with him. No matter what Devon does, Dr. B. won't agree. He's a stubborn old cuss. Actually, he was a stubborn young cuss, too.''

''So what is Ethan going to do about it?''

Lolly slid Hannah down to straddle her shin, holding the baby's hands and giving her a horsy ride. ''He'll make sure it happens.''

''How will he do that if Dr. B. is so stubborn?''

''Ethan is more stubborn,'' Lolly said with a laugh.

Paris had taken a bite of her sandwich and she had to swallow before she said, ''You say that as if you know it for a fact.''

''I do. I had a hand in raising him, too, you know.''

Paris hadn't known that for sure but she'd assumed as much since Lolly acted more like a mother helping out around her son's home than like a housekeeper.

"And Ethan is even more stubborn than a stubborn old cuss?" Paris concluded.

"Maybe stubborn isn't the right word for Ethan," Lolly amended. "Determined might be better. Dr. B. is stubborn, but Ethan is determined, and Ethan is more determined than Dr. B. is stubborn."

"In other words, Ethan gets what Ethan wants."

Lolly laughed again and lifted Hannah back to her lap to bounce her there once more. "Ethan definitely gets what he wants. He'll steamroll Dr. B. if he has to. In fact, I believe the plan is to tell Dr. B. that Social Services has decided he's unable to live on his own and either accepts live-in help or he has to go to a nursing home."

"Is that true?"

"Not technically, no. But Ethan said that Dr. B. will have a live-in helper before he leaves there today, and I know *that's* true. Like I told you, Ethan is going to steamroll him."

Steamroll. Paris had never thought of what Jason did as steamrolling. Somehow that sounded a little friendlier than Jason's hiring a private investigator and a battery of lawyers and psychiatric experts who could slant their opinion whichever way he told them to.

But wasn't the end result the same? One person imposing his will on another?

Paris could feel her stomach tighten at just the thought.

"Does Ethan do a lot of steamrolling?" she asked.

"He does a lot of getting the job done."

"By steamrolling."

''By whatever means are necessary. Like I said, he's determined. But since old Dr. B. won't do what's good for him, what other choice is there? And it isn't as if Ethan won't keep Dr. B.'s wishes in mind. By the time Ethan is through, Dr. B. will end up with someone living with him, and the old stinker will think it was his idea all along.''

For Dr. B.'s sake, Paris hoped Lolly was right. But whether or not she was, clearly she knew Ethan well enough to feel sure he would come out on top no matter what. And that served as a reminder to Paris that she shouldn't forget just how powerful a man he was. Which was certainly not what she'd been thinking about when she'd let him kiss her the night before.

''Poor Dr. B,'' Paris said more to herself than to Lolly.

''I know. We all feel bad for him,'' Lolly agreed, misinterpreting Paris's sentiments.

But Paris didn't correct the other woman's impression. She merely renewed her vow to herself to keep in mind who she was dealing with when she was dealing with Ethan Tarlington, that he was a man who always got what he wanted.

At any cost.

But by six o'clock that evening, when Paris was getting dressed to be Ethan's date at the dinner and dance in his and his brothers' honor, the last thing she was thinking about was that Ethan was a rich and powerful man she should be wary of.

She was just thinking about what to wear.

And how eager she was to see him again and the fact that a mere ten hours without seeing him felt like an eternity.

"I wish it was as easy to dress me as it is to dress you," she told Hannah, who was in the baby carrier on the floor of the closet dressing room.

Hannah had awakened from her afternoon nap in better spirits and was happily playing with her own feet in the tiny white shoes that went with her pink overalls and white T-shirt with pink rosebuds embroidered all over it. She looked adorable. But Paris was having more difficulty choosing something for herself.

She'd packed mainly work clothes, not date clothes, and even though she had a few dresses with her, they were the kind of dresses she'd have worn to a temp job in an office. The only exception was a slightly fancier, ankle-length, black jersey, mock-turtleneck dress that she'd included just in case she was invited to attend the party she was working on for Saturday night. But if she wore it tonight, she wouldn't have anything for Saturday.

Still, with no other options, she finally decided on the black dress for tonight. She would talk to Lolly about where in Dunbar she might buy something else if she did end up going to Saturday's affair.

The dress fitted her well, falling around her curves with just enough of a hug to accentuate them, and she wasn't sorry once she got it on. Then she slipped her feet into the black two-inch heels she'd brought to wear with it and grasped the handle on the baby carrier as if it were a basket of flowers to carry from the closet to the bathroom with her.

"You know I shouldn't be doing this," she told her daughter as she took special pains with her mascara and added a little eyeliner to her upper and lower lids. "I should never have accepted this being a date. This man has the potential to be a complication in our lives that neither one of us needs. A huge complication. A huge, huge complication. And if I had any sense at all, you and I would be staying right here in this room tonight, by ourselves. We wouldn't be going on a *date* with him."

Hannah made a cooing sound as if in answer, and even though Paris knew it was absolutely ridiculous, it was as if that sound soothed and reassured her that what she was doing, what she was looking forward to so much, was okay.

"I really am still trying to keep things cool with him," she continued as if justifying Hannah's imagined support. "And even though he said this was a date, it isn't as if it will be an intimate private date. We'll be in a public place, with probably the whole town there, too. It's completely innocent."

Her conscience called her a liar for that as she brushed a light clay-colored blush on each high cheekbone.

"Okay, so kissing him last night doesn't qualify as completely innocent. I know I shouldn't have done that. But there can't be any kissing going on at this dinner tonight. Not with him being one of the guests of honor and a lot of people around. So even if I did let things go further than they should have, this is still all right tonight because it's safe.''

Hannah giggled.

''Really,'' Paris said as if the giggle had conveyed the baby's doubts. ''From here on I'll be more careful. I'm absolutely *not* going to let this get out of hand. I know what's at stake. Believe me, I know.''

Hannah made the soothing sound again, and again Paris felt better about what she was doing as she spun around to face her daughter.

''Well, what do you think? Not too bad?'' she asked, referring to the finished product of her change of clothes, application of makeup and combing of her hair.

Hannah went into a paroxysm of excitedly flailing arms and kicking legs to accompany her toothless grin.

''I'll take that as a compliment,'' Paris said, hoping Ethan would be as enthusiastic, even as she warned herself that it shouldn't matter.

She picked up the baby carrier by the handle the way she'd done before and left the bathroom, pausing to give herself one last look in the full-length cheval mirror in the corner of the bedroom.

Satisfied with what she saw and knowing she was already five minutes late, she crossed to the door to leave.

''So, okay, here we go. Just a simple evening with a bunch of other people. No harm in that,'' she muttered as she stepped into the hall and headed for the formal living room where she was to meet Ethan.

All three Tarlington brothers were waiting for her

when she got there, but it was only Ethan she actually took note of.

He had on a pair of charcoal-colored slacks and a dove-gray dress shirt. He was freshly shaved, his hair was neatly combed back, and although there wasn't anything out of the ordinary about him, that one glimpse of him was enough for something purely sensual to skitter along the surface of Paris's skin and leave her with goose bumps.

"She cleans up nice, Ethan," Devon said loudly enough for Paris to hear, jabbing a teasing elbow in his brother's rib cage.

"I know," Ethan said with a rumble of appreciation in his voice and his eyes glued to her.

"You do look great," Aiden assured her without the note of machismo his brothers were batting back and forth. "And so do you, little Hannah," he added, bending over slightly to talk to the baby.

"Here, let me carry her," Ethan said, reaching to take the baby seat from Paris.

When he did, his hand brushed hers and set off a whole new wave of gooseflesh she was worried he might notice.

But if he did, he didn't comment on it.

Instead he said, "Are we ready to go?"

"If the diaper bag I packed earlier is still by the door, we are," she answered.

"Actually I already had it put in my car."

"Then I guess Hannah and I are ready."

Ethan nodded at his brothers and said, "See you guys there."

"I thought we might all be riding together," Paris

said, thinking that it would be better if that were the case and wondering if making the suggestion might inspire him to invite them along, after all.

But Ethan merely smiled a sly smile and said, "I haven't taken my brothers on my dates for a long time."

"Besides, he wants you all to himself," Devon confided.

"That, too," Ethan agreed, ushering Paris out of the house before anyone could say anything else.

His SUV was parked out front, and he secured Hannah's carrier to the back seat, flirting shamelessly with the baby the whole time.

And Hannah, as usual, flirted right back as if he were the greatest thing since strained plums.

Then Ethan opened the front passenger door for Paris.

She got in quickly, not giving him the opportunity to offer her help because she was afraid of what further contact with him might do to her.

But she couldn't help feasting on the sight of him as he rounded the front of the SUV, and that was all it took for a fresh outbreak of goose bumps.

She didn't know why she was having an even stronger reaction to him than normal. Her normal reaction to him was strong enough; she certainly didn't need it to get worse.

Then he got in behind the steering wheel and she caught a whiff of his aftershave and that only compounded it, leaving her almost desperate to find something about him to turn herself off.

Which was when she remembered her lunchtime conversation with Lolly.

''Did you persuade Dr. B. to have someone move in with him?'' Paris asked as Ethan started the engine and pulled away from the curb.

He took his eyes off the road just long enough to cast her a curious gaze. ''How did you know about Dr. B.?''

''Lolly told me what you were doing today.''

Ethan drew his head back slightly on his shoulders and shot her another glance. ''Why does that sound so accusatory? Did I do something wrong?''

''I don't know, did you?''

''I don't think so.''

''Did you force him to have someone come in and live with him against his will?''

Ethan chuckled. ''I persuaded him that that was what he needed or Social Services—called in by the hospital when he burned himself a few months ago because he couldn't see what he was doing at the stove—was going to make him go into a nursing home.''

''But Lolly said that wasn't true.''

''Well, not entirely. But Social Services assigned him a case worker who's been checking on him, and she's on the verge of passing down that mandate. I think the only reason she hasn't is that she lives here in Dunbar and has known Dr. B. her whole life. So I just fudged a little.''

Like Lolly's steamrolling comment that made it sound so much better than what it actually was—a lie Ethan had used to accomplish what he'd set out to do.

"So you led him to believe he didn't have a choice."

"He thought he had the choice of going to a nursing home or having someone move in to help out."

"When he really still had the choice of living there alone the way he wants to."

This time when Ethan looked over at her he was frowning. "I introduced Dr. B. to Shirley McGillis. Shirley is a healthy, active seventy-five-year-old retired nurse who shares Dr. B.'s interests. And Dr. B. ended up more than happy to open his home to her by the end of today. Now, this not only serves Dr. B. It also works out for Shirley since her late husband gambled away all their retirement money and left her with so much debt she had to sell her house and was not only in need of a place to stay, but was going to have to go out and try to find a job again. So, if the truth be known, what I did today was solve two problems with what came out more as matchmaking than as forcing anyone to do anything, thank you very much."

That did put a better spin on it.

But then Paris couldn't help recalling that Jason talking about what *he* was doing had made him sound like a great guy, too.

Before she had a chance to say anything Ethan continued.

"Shirley and Dr. B. will be at this dinner tonight—something Dr. B. wasn't going to attend before because he was too proud to ask for a ride and he can't drive anymore. But Shirley can still drive and so now he has the advantage of mobility, again, too. And you can see for yourself if I did something bad today."

"You manipulated two people's lives," Paris persisted, but it was getting more difficult to put any conviction behind it.

"I put two people together to the benefit of them both."

"And if, down the road, Dr. B. decides he doesn't like Shirley or having her in his house? Is he going to believe his only other option is a nursing home?"

"I've known Shirley for a long time. She came in and took care of me just before she retired when I broke my leg in three places skiing. I've kept up with her over the years and I'm here to tell you Dr. B. will love her."

"And if he doesn't?"

"I'll take care of it."

They'd reached the Dunbar church by then—a white frame country chapel with a tall steeple—and once Ethan had parked in the lot beside it and turned off the engine, he draped his left forearm over the steering wheel and pivoted just enough to look Paris square in the eye.

"Are you mad at me for something?" he asked, confusion echoing in his tone.

If only she were. It would have made things so much easier.

"No, I'm not mad at you. I just didn't like thinking that you were out forcing someone to do something against their will."

"Not my style."

He held her eyes with his for a moment longer but then his brothers pulled up beside them and several other people also arrived, getting out of their vehicles to call to the brothers and approach them. It was clear Ethan and Paris couldn't stay sitting in the SUV.

But before Ethan let his attention stray, he reached over and took her hand, sending more goose bumps rippling up her arms.

"Can we just go in and have a nice time?" he asked with a smile so sweet, so charming, it felt like the sun's rays at the end of a cold winter.

And because of that and those goose bumps, Paris was afraid if she answered him, her voice would betray her, so she merely nodded.

Ethan squeezed her hand and then let go. "Good. Because that's what I was looking forward to tonight."

She melted a little more to know that she hadn't been the only one eager for their date and tried to recoup some of her determination to resist her attraction to him.

But it didn't help a whole lot, and as Paris let herself out of the car while Ethan opened the rear door and released Hannah's seat, she decided it was a good thing they wouldn't be alone tonight.

A very good thing.

The dinner was in the church basement. There was a long buffet table and several more tables set up around the perimeters of the big, open room, leaving one corner for the live band and the center of the floor free for dancing afterward.

It was surprising to Paris how many faces she already recognized even after being in town such a short time. And not only was she recognized in return, but she and Hannah were both treated as warmly as the Tarlingtons were.

Which was no small thing because Ethan, Aiden and Devon seemed to be the darlings of Dunbar.

Lolly and the rest of the house staff were there with their respective spouses and children so Paris got to meet them all. The florist, the grocer, the butcher, the baker and everyone else she was working with on the party couldn't wait to introduce her to their families. The town's mayor was there, letting her hair down as if she didn't have a political thought in the world. Four of the five members of the police force had come. The church minister, his wife and six kids were there, and that was just who Paris talked to the first hour.

By the second hour the room was brimming with adults and kids and food and drink galore.

Lolly confiscated Hannah like a doting grandmother who wanted to show her off, leaving Paris unencumbered as Ethan mingled and took her along with him.

Not that she had any complaints. Ethan made sure no one he spoke to went without meeting her and learning a little about her. He included her in every conversation and told her a little something about each new person she met that made most of them easy to remember.

All in all Paris was having a very pleasant time until they were approached by a woman named Honey Willis.

Ethan introduced Honey Willis as an old friend.

Honey amended the introduction to let Paris know she and Ethan had been a couple the entire way through high school—the *cutest* couple. That she'd been instrumental in getting him voted best kisser in their senior class, because, after all, who would know better than she. And that she'd been sure they would end up married to each other. Which could still happen since she was newly divorced and free to take up where she and Ethan had left off when Ethan had gone away to college.

Ethan treated the open come-on as if he didn't take her seriously, as if she were only teasing, but Paris knew she wasn't and she was reasonably sure Ethan did, too.

And although Ethan's touch did unsettling things to Paris's insides, she was glad when he draped an arm around her waist, excused them and took Paris to the buffet table to get something to eat.

Paris wasn't so glad, though, when, after dinner, Honey charged Ethan, grabbed his free hand and literally dragged him onto the dance floor for the first dance.

Lolly was nearby at the time and provided the distraction of pointing out to Paris that she'd changed Hannah into her pajamas and put the baby to sleep in the carrier on the chair beside her. But even that only kept Paris's eyes off the former high school sweethearts for so long.

Before she knew it she was watching them even as she tried to pretend she wasn't. And she saw it all. All five feet eight inches of slender, curvaceous blonde in Ethan's arms, smiling coyly at him, sensually massaging his biceps and shoulder, arching her back so her voluptuous breasts made themselves known at his chest.

And Paris was being eaten alive by jealousy, plain and simple. Jealousy that no amount of reasonable, rational thought could temper.

It seemed like the longest dance in the history of mankind. Paris didn't think it would ever end, and she wondered if, when it did, Honey Willis would have won Ethan over. If, when that dance ended, he might look at Honey with the warmth in his eyes that he'd reserved for Paris of late. If this date might take a turn for the worse in a way she hadn't anticipated.

And no amount of telling herself that it shouldn't make any difference to her if he rekindled his old romance or not calmed down the turmoil she was feeling as she watched them. No amount of telling herself that it would actually be great if Ethan rediscovered an interest in the other woman convinced her it was so. No amount of reminding herself that she didn't want him in her and Hannah's life made her not want to rush that dance floor and yank Honey Willis away by the hair.

The dance finally did end, but Honey didn't let go of Ethan immediately. Instead she kept hold of him and stood on her tiptoes to whisper something in his ear. Something that caused him to laugh that deep, rich, whiskey laugh that sent a fresh wave of jealousy through Paris.

But then he shook his head, reared back slightly and held up both hands—palms out as if he were warding off something.

Whatever Honey Willis had said—or suggested, or offered—he was apparently declining.

And some of Paris's jealousy ebbed at the sight.

Then Ethan pointed in Paris's direction as if he'd said he had to get back to her, and that was just what he did.

He came off the dance floor, straight to where Paris was sitting and stood behind her chair with both hands on her shoulders. Both big, strong hands taking her firmly in his grip and shooting a shock wave of electricity from there all the way through her. And even though she didn't mean to, she leaned into it.

"I just told Honey that I promised the rest of my dances to you," he said, bending to speak into her ear where the warmth of his breath only intensified her reaction to him. "Don't make a liar out of me."

Paris's spirits took quite a leap and she had to put some conscious effort into not letting her actions follow suit by jumping to her feet to dance with him.

Instead she gazed up at him and gave him a coy smile of her own. "What am I? Your protection?" she joked.

"Oh, yeah," he said with a laugh as he straightened up, abandoned her shoulders to reach for her hand and pulled her to her feet to take her to the dance floor.

''Keep the slow ones coming for a while, will you, Pete?'' he said to one of the members of the band.

Then he swung Paris into his arms, holding her just a little closer, she thought, than he'd held Honey.

But still, a small wedge of jealousy jabbed at Paris and before she even knew she was going to say it, she said, ''She was your first, wasn't she?''

Ethan didn't answer that for a moment. He just looked down into Paris's eyes.

Then he smiled a small smile and, in a voice for her alone, he said, ''You were my last.''

She knew she shouldn't have been so glad to hear that but she couldn't keep another smile from tugging at the corners of her mouth.

''Oh, you're good. You're very good,'' she said as if she thought he were only feeding her a line, not wanting him to know how pleased she'd been by his answer.

But he opted for misinterpreting her comment and putting a lascivious spin on it. ''I'm happy to hear you thought so.''

Paris suddenly lost all jealousy and with it a large portion of the reticence she'd been trying so hard to hold on to, and she just laughed.

''Did she proposition you?'' she asked as if she had the right to, amazed at the boldness that was coming from nowhere to spur her on.

''She did. But I turned her down. For some reason I haven't been interested in other women for the past fourteen months.''

''So I'm pretty good, too,'' Paris said, shocking

herself even more and making Ethan laugh again, this time heartily.

"Good enough to keep you on my mind ever since."

"Guess I should have been voted best kisser, too, then."

"You get my vote, that's for sure. Best kisser. Best everything. I'm just not sure what makes you so touchy about some things," he added as if he were confiding a secret.

"Who me? Touchy?" Paris responded as if she couldn't imagine what he was talking about.

Ethan pointed his well-defined chin toward where the old town doctor was dancing with his new companion.

"Dr. B. and Shirley McGillis," he said as if she needed reminding who they were even though he'd made a point of introducing her to them. "They look like they're enjoying themselves, wouldn't you say?"

"Mmm," Paris said noncommittally.

"So why were you so touchy about them earlier?"

"I wasn't touchy about them. I just wasn't sure about you," she said, couching the truth in a tone that made it sound as if she were teasing.

"About me," he said, seeing through her.

Paris shrugged. "I know you're used to having things your own way and—"

"I wasn't getting my 'own way' here. I was trying to do what was in the best interest of Dr. B. and Shirley."

Paris had heard that before. She raised her chin in

silent affront despite the fact that the entire conversation was amiable.

"Why do I feel like this has roots in something else?" he asked then.

"Take my word for it, you don't want to talk about that now," she advised.

"I want to talk about anything that lets me know what makes you tick."

"It isn't something that makes me tick. It's just something I've seen before," she said, as if her past experience hadn't affected her almost as much as it had the people who had been in the middle of it.

"What have you seen before? Someone telling a little white lie to accomplish what was best for someone else?"

In the best interest of Dr. B. Telling a little white lie to accomplish what was best for someone else— Paris nearly flinched at all the phrases that were so much the same as what Jason had said to her about his own actions when those actions and what those actions revealed about the kind of person he was caused her to end it with him.

"I've seen someone misuse his power and position and money for what he said was in the best interest of others when the truth was, it was just to hurt another person and get his own way. To control things and people."

"Nice," Ethan said facetiously. "And who was this Machiavellian gem?"

"A man I was engaged to."

That made Ethan frown. "Was it you he hurt?"

"Not directly. But when I learned what he was

doing, what he was capable of, and saw how he could justify it to himself without any remorse whatsoever, I ended the engagement, which was painful for me, too. Just not as painful as what he was doing to someone else.''

''Which was what?''

It was so nice dancing with Ethan, being in his arms, basking in the heat of his eyes that Paris seriously considered not getting into this subject.

But then it occurred to her that maybe she should get into it exactly *because* she liked dancing with him so much, to keep herself in check.

So she said, ''Jason—that's his name, Jason Hervay—had been married before and he had two kids with his ex-wife. He hadn't left her, she'd left him because—or so he said—she couldn't take his long, erratic work hours.''

''What did he do?''

''He's one of the most prominent thoracic surgeons in Denver.''

''I thought surgeons kept pretty regular hours.''

''They aren't on call as much as other types of doctors, but there were more days than not when surgeries ran long or emergencies had to be dealt with, so there were still a lot of unpredictable hours. In the end I doubt that was really the reason, but before I found out what he was really like, I bought it.''

''I see.''

''Anyway, when I met him the marriage was long over, but the divorce proceedings were still dragging on. I found out later that that was all Jason's doing. Since he could afford to pay his lawyers indefinitely and he knew it was a terrible strain on his ex-wife—that was how he got what he wanted on every issue—she'd eventually be forced to give in because she needed the whole thing to get over with more than he did. Then it came down to the custody of the kids.''

''By then you were engaged to this guy?''

''I was. It was sort of a whirlwind romance. But I had no idea what was really going on with the divorce. He blamed his ex-wife for prolonging things and I believed him. I wasn't involved in any of it, the divorce wranglings were all handled by his lawyers. I only knew that Jason was charming and charismatic and suave. That he was hard to resist. It was only when he started to do what he did over the children that his ex-wife reached the breaking point. She came to the house one day to see him. To beg him to stop. Only Jason wasn't there. I was. And she ended up telling me what he'd been doing.''

''Which was what?''

''Just about every awful, underhanded, unethical thing you can imagine. For instance, the fact that she had to work two jobs to make a dent in her legal fees translated into her neglecting the kids or abusing them because she had to pick them up late from the baby-sitter a night or two. The stress he was causing her led to a doctor putting her on antidepressants—that turned into her being an unstable drug user. Bringing a male friend from her church in for coffee one evening was twisted into lewd and inappropriate behavior in front of the kids. The list just went on and on. Jason had private eyes harassing her, following her, following the kids, openly investigating everyone she or the kids came into contact with—the baby-sitter, his former in-laws, even one of her bosses—and Jason managed to find stones to throw at her in one form or another at every turn.''

''Wow.''

''I did some investigating of my own, after talking to her. According to Jason, of course, she was a horrible person, but she just seemed distraught to me. And I kept remembering a time or two when Jason had gloated over something that had happened with her and it hadn't sat well with me even before meeting her. So I talked to the kids, to the house staff members who had been there during the marriage, even to the wife of Jason's best friend. And what I discovered was that his ex-wife had been telling the truth—she wasn't an unfit mother. In fact, she was a good mother and Jason was really just manufacturing—or paying other people to manufacture—most things against her.''

''So did you help her keep her kids?''

''I tried. I even testified in court that Jason had lied about her. But it just didn't do any good. Jason claimed that he'd broken our engagement—which wasn't true, either, I'm the one who did that—and that I was just trying to get even with him by siding with his ex-wife. The judge apparently believed that, too. Prestige goes a long way, after all. Jason was granted custody.''

''Well, at least you did what you could. There aren't a lot of people who would sacrifice their own relationship to help someone else.''

"It wasn't a sacrifice. Yes, I loved Jason—or thought I did before I found out what kind of person he really was. But not only did I not want a man who could do what he'd done, I looked at this ex-wife and I saw myself. I saw what could happen to me if things between us didn't work out. And it was terrifying."

"Did he take your leaving him in stride?"

"No. But luckily I didn't have the connections with him that his ex-wife did. He had introduced me to a gallery owner who was going to give me a career-launching showing of my work and that, of course, got canceled first thing. And for a while that gallery owner bad-mouthed me and I had some problems, but eventually it died down and there was nothing else he could do to me."

"How long ago was this?"

"I'd broken up with him about six months before I met you."

Ethan nodded, searching her expression for a moment before he said, "And how does this all compare to me arranging for Shirley to take care of Dr. B.?"

"You manipulated the facts, didn't you? You pressured Dr. B. You made up your mind how things should be for him and—"

"It was all out of necessity, which made it a *justifiable* manipulation of the facts," Ethan said, defending himself.

"Jason said what he was doing was justifiable, too. When I had it out with him, he said he could give the kids more, give them a better life than their mother, so it was all right that he'd exaggerated a few things or made things look worse than they actually were. The ends justified the means—that's what he said. But he was just getting even with his ex-wife for the audacity of leaving him, plain and simple.''

''I wasn't getting even with anybody today, Paris. You can see for yourself that what I did was not a bad thing.''

''It was still the strong overpowering the weak,'' she said softly.

''But it wasn't out of vindictiveness. There's a big difference there.''

Okay, maybe there was a difference. But still Paris knew she had to be leery. ''I'm just saying that a person with money and power behind them can do damage to other people's lives.''

''And you were just looking out for the underdog today in case I was running amok.''

Paris shrugged again. ''It's a sore spot with me.''

Ethan stared at her for a moment before he said, ''You know, money and power notwithstanding, some people can take it on the chin. Not everyone has the need to destroy the person who hurt them.''

There was something in his voice when he said that that caused Paris to look more closely at him. ''Are you speaking from experience now?''

He smiled down at her again. ''Maybe. But that really *is* a story for another time. In fact, I'm thinking I should have taken your word for it about this one and left it out of tonight. What do you say we call an end to the debate and just dance, like the old cuss who got me into trouble today?''

This time it was Paris who nodded in the direction of Dr. B. and Shirley McGillis who had returned to one of the tables surrounding the dance floor.

"They aren't dancing anymore," Paris said, just to be contrary.

"But we are. So let's just enjoy it." He leaned to speak into her ear again. "We are supposed to be on a date here, remember?"

She couldn't argue that. Especially not when, despite what they'd been talking about, she was enjoying dancing with him.

"Okay," she agreed.

That was all Ethan needed to pull her even closer. So close she had to rest her head against his shoulder.

And that was how they stayed through two more dances, just swaying together, holding each other, oblivious to anyone else in the room.

Until Devon called from the sidelines to the band, "Enough of this slow stuff. Can't we shake it up a little?"

The band leader Ethan had told to keep playing slow songs looked to Ethan. "What do you say?"

"I guess if you have to," Ethan agreed reluctantly.

And with that go-ahead, the band broke into some hard core rock and roll.

"Think Hannah will sleep through this?" Ethan asked as he and Paris stopped dancing, his voice raised to be heard over the din.

"Not for long," Paris shouted back.

"Then let's get her out of here."

It seemed perfectly normal for Ethan to take her hand and lead her off the dance floor. Not so perfectly normal to keep hold of it as he picked up the baby carrier with his other hand and they said their goodbyes, but nice all the same.

So nice that Paris hated it when he had to let it go once they reached the SUV and he needed both hands to strap in Hannah's seat.

On the short drive back to the house they talked about the dinner and the people there, and then paused to put Hannah to bed so their voices didn't disturb the silence of her room.

But once the baby was tucked in, Ethan surprised Paris by taking her hand again to pull her out of the room into the hallway.

"I don't suppose you'd have a nightcap with me even if I asked, so I won't," he said when he had her there with Hannah's door closed behind them.

Actually, tonight Paris thought she might have accepted. But since he wasn't asking, and spending the evening in his arms had already pushed her willpower to the limits, she didn't tell him that. She merely let him believe he was right.

He went on holding her hand, though, raising it to study her fingers as he said, "But I want to talk to you about tomorrow. We need to go into town about four o'clock tomorrow afternoon. Just you and me."

"Oh?"

"I can't tell you why. But I've set it up with Lolly to baby-sit Hannah. I thought we'd stay and have dinner there, too. Just you and me. Will you do it?"

"Is this for work?"

"Nope."

His complete lack of subterfuge made her laugh. ''Is this another date?''

''In between.''

''In between,'' she repeated, having no idea what that could mean. ''And you can't tell me what the trip into town is for?''

''Well, I *could* tell you. I just don't want to. I want you to see when you get there. So what do you say?''

Her curiosity was intense. Almost as intense as his charm and her desire to spend the next evening with him. Alone. ''I suppose it would be all right,'' she finally agreed, fully aware that she was giving in to temptation when she shouldn't be.

''I hope it'll be better than all right,'' Ethan countered. ''Like tonight. I had a great time tonight. Even if you do think I might be as big a jerk as that other guy,'' he joked.

''Did I say that?'' Paris joked in return.

''What about you? Did you have a good time?'' he asked, running his thumb over her knuckles in a slow, barely-there sweep, back and forth.

''You mean did I have a good time even if you did have your old high school sweetheart hanging all over you?''

He chuckled at that one. ''Yeah, even though we both had some history intervening, did you have a good time tonight?''

''I did. How could I not have when I was with Dunbar's best kisser?''

He used his grip on her hand to pull her nearer, looking into her eyes. ''Well, that's true,'' he said with a devilish smile and a low, intimate voice.

"And now that you have me alone you should probably avail yourself of my talents."

Paris laughed but somehow it came out a more breathy, sensual laugh than she'd intended. "I don't know about that."

"I do," he responded with confidence just before he leaned in enough to press his lips to hers.

At first it seemed as if it would be a quick kiss, and Paris was all ready to tease him about it not being up to best-kisser standards. But then, rather than ending it after only a few moments the way he had the kiss the night before and giving her the opening, he deepened it.

His lips parted over hers and hers parted in purely unconscious response as he released her hand and wrapped his arms around her in a way that made holding her on the dance floor nothing at all.

One hand cradled the back of her head, the other supported her back against a kiss that could have won him the world title for best kisser as his tongue traced the tips of her teeth and came to say a sexy *hello* to her tongue.

All on their own Paris's hands slipped under his arms and around to his back where she could feel the hard strength of muscle and tendon honed to perfection.

She knew she shouldn't be doing this. But she just couldn't deny herself that moment of pleasure.

And pleasure it was. Pleasure that sent a raging river rushing through her, tightening her nipples into solid nubs against his chest, bringing every nerve ending to the surface of her skin, heightening her awareness of everything about him—his wonderful scent, the heat of his breath on her face, the perfect pressure and enticement of a kiss to wash away all thought, the way his body cupped around hers protectively and seductively all at once, the feel of his solid back beneath her hands…

But for some reason she didn't understand, she suddenly started to think about what they'd talked about on the dance floor. About Jason. And the intrusion of the past into that kiss reminded her why she really shouldn't be doing what she was doing. Why she really did have to stop it.

She pulled her arms back and pressed her hands to a chest so glorious her palms ached to stay pressed to it, to explore it.

But that wasn't what she did. She forced herself to push slightly against him even as she drew away from his kiss.

"Okay, okay, you get my vote, too," she said, trying to make light of what had turned into much more, and giving herself away with the huskiness of her voice.

Ethan searched her face with his azure eyes and he seemed to know why she'd stopped, because in a very quiet voice, he said, "Do me a favor. Take a good, long look at who *I* am without coloring it with who he is."

She just lifted her chin at that. She couldn't comment because she was too lost in the warm depths of his eyes.

But he must have taken her silence as agreement

because he smiled again and said, "Tomorrow at four."

Paris nodded. "I'll be ready."

Then Ethan leaned over and kissed her again. Softly. Sweetly. Gently. As if to leave her with that memory rather than the one that had brought Jason with it.

And it worked.

Because as Ethan said good-night and left her to go to her room, it wasn't her former fiancé Paris was thinking about.

It was Ethan. Only Ethan.

And how much she was craving more of that kiss she'd ended.

More of that kiss and more than kissing....

Chapter Seven

"What do we have here?"

Ethan had been out skeet shooting with his brothers for a good portion of the day and had returned home to clean up before taking Paris into Dunbar. But he altered his course when he passed by the entrance to the living room and spotted Lolly sitting on a blanket on the floor playing with Hannah.

"We have the cutest baby in the world, is all," Lolly answered, dangling a toy octopus over Hannah so Hannah could try grabbing the legs.

"Where's Paris?" Ethan asked.

"She's overseeing the tent being set up out back and working with your chef, who arrived a couple of hours ago to officially take over the kitchen, to make sure he has everything he ordered. Then she said she was going upstairs to get ready for her trip into town with you.''

''That's why I came home—to shower. But I think I can spare a few minutes,'' he said, joining them on the blanket.

''Hello, little Miss Hannah,'' he greeted the infant.

''Would you look at that smile! Does she love you!'' Lolly exclaimed with a laugh.

Lolly took the octopus out of his way, and Ethan held out both index fingers for Hannah to grab on to instead. Then he pulled her to her tiptoes.

''I think she wants to walk,'' Ethan said, feeling a rush of pride he still didn't know if he was entitled to. Or even *wanted* to feel.

Lolly must have heard something in his voice that opened a door for her because she said, ''She's yours, isn't she?''

''Why do you say that?'' Ethan hedged, letting Hannah bounce slightly and delighting himself and the baby.

''I was your mother's best friend, remember? We were closer than sisters from the time we were in diapers ourselves. I still have her photograph on my dresser. And every time I look at Hannah, I see her.''

Ethan had wondered about that. In fact, he'd wanted Lolly's opinion more than his brothers'. After all, his brothers had been even younger than he was the last time they'd seen their mother in person. But Lolly—Lolly had known their mother better than anyone.

''I didn't want to be the one to bring it up,'' Ethan

said by way of explaining why he hadn't said anything to her.

''Is it a secret?''

''From me. If it's true,'' he said with a wry laugh and then some baby talk to answer the chattering Hannah seemed to be directing at him.

''I don't understand,'' Lolly said.

''Join the club. I didn't even know there *was* a Hannah until I paid Paris an impromptu visit last Friday and discovered her. Paris says she had Hannah by artificial insemination.''

''And you called me and had me put away all the pictures of your mother before you got here so Paris wouldn't see that anyone who took one look at Hannah would notice she's the spitting image of your mom. I wondered why you wanted that done. This is very strange, Ethan.''

Ethan smiled at that. The comment itself and the fact that the tone Lolly delivered it in sounded very motherly, almost like one of the reprimands he remembered her giving when he was a kid.

''Hey, don't look at me,'' he answered, much the way he would have years ago. ''I'm supposed to be in the dark, too.''

He transferred his hands to Hannah's rib cage so he could toss her gently in the air and catch her again, making her giggle.

''Why?'' Lolly asked.

''Paris couldn't very well explain why she's keeping a secret when she's still keeping it, could she? So your guess is as good as mine.''

''Do you think she has an angle? Like Bettina?''

"I don't know. I've wondered about that. I guess there's a part of me that's still wondering about it. But after last night I'm beginning to get another idea of what might be behind Paris pretending Hannah isn't mine. I'm thinking she might be afraid of me."

"Afraid of you? That's crazy."

"I don't think it's crazy to her." In fact, it explained why she seemed so protective of Hannah when he'd first seen the baby. "I'm just hoping she'll get over it."

"Do you want me to talk to her? We've gotten pretty friendly since she's been here."

"No, don't do that. Don't even hint about Hannah looking like Mom. I don't want Paris scared away, and that might do it."

"So you do like her—baby or no baby."

"You could say that," he said as if it were no big deal when the truth was it was a very big deal. The biggest deal, and it was getting bigger all the time, no matter how hard he fought it. It was getting to be such a big deal that he couldn't spend five minutes not thinking about her, not wanting to be with her, not wanting to hold her and kiss her, to have his hands all over her, to pull her off to a private spot somewhere, anywhere, to make love to her before he exploded...

Lolly laughed as if she knew exactly how much he liked Paris. "I like her, too, if that counts for anything."

"It's always good to have your approval since you're a pretty good judge of character. Unless I'm mistaken, you didn't like Bettina, did you?"

''No, I didn't. But I think Paris might be a keeper. And if this baby is yours, well...''

''You're not going to give me a do-the-right-thing lecture, are you?'' Ethan teased.

''I haven't had to do that since you swiped Old Man Nichols's boxer shorts off the line and ran them up the flagpole in front of the courthouse.''

''Those were some *big* shorts.''

''A 450-pound man couldn't get into small ones.''

They both laughed at the memory, and Hannah joined in as if she shared the joke.

But Ethan didn't want to talk about doing the right thing. He didn't even know what the right thing was at this point. And he definitely didn't want to be thinking about the complications of this whole situation or how he felt about it all when he was headed for an evening alone with Paris.

So, before Lolly could go on with the conversation, he rubbed noses with Hannah and said, ''I'd better hit the shower.''

Lolly took the hint and reached for the baby. ''Come on, little love, your daddy has to go.''

''Shh! What if Paris heard *that?*'' Ethan said, surprised by the note of panic in his own voice. The note that went with the slight ripple of panic that ran through him all of a sudden.

He handed Hannah over to Lolly and headed for the stairs, wondering as he did why Lolly's calling him daddy had rocked him so much.

Was it genuinely the idea of Paris overhearing it?

Or was it hearing it himself for the first time?

As if it were a reality....

* * *

"You know, there are a gazillion things I'm supposed to be checking on before the party tomorrow night. I really shouldn't be doing this instead—whatever this is we're doing," Paris said as Ethan drove into Dunbar at a little after five that afternoon.

"You'll have all day tomorrow. For now it's Friday night and you're off duty," Ethan insisted.

He pulled into a parking spot about halfway down the town's main street, and Paris glanced out her window to see where they were stopping.

They were in front of an old-fashioned storefront with Women's Apparel stenciled on both of the two huge cantilevered display windows on either side of a door that looked like the entrance to an English cottage.

That was when he said, "You have to have something special to wear to the party."

"Is that an invitation?" Paris asked, since Ethan hadn't yet extended one.

"I didn't know you needed an invitation. I thought it was assumed that you'd be going."

"Why would that be assumed? I'm here to be the preparations supervisor, remember? Not one of the guests."

"You're one of the guests, too," he confided with a warm whisper in her ear just before he got out of the SUV.

He'd come around to open her door for her before she could gather up her purse and do it herself. As she joined him on the sidewalk he said, "Lolly told me that when she unpacked for you she didn't see party clothes among your things. So we're here to get you some.''

''Ah. And you don't have a doubt that I'm going to accept the invitation,'' she said, just to give him a hard time.

But he didn't take the bait.

''I wouldn't have it any other way,'' he said with confidence. Then he nodded toward the shop. ''Marti Brock owns the store. She always orders in some fancy stuff especially for this. You should be able to find something you like.''

''Is that her looking out the window?'' Paris asked, referring to a very attractive redhead peeking over the pantsuit display with wide-set, exotic eyes that seemed to devour Ethan.

''That's her,'' he confirmed. And if he noticed the way the other woman was looking at him, he didn't show it.

But Paris couldn't help noticing. And thinking, Oh, no, not another one....

''Did you date her, too?'' she asked as if she was joking when she didn't actually find any humor in once again being faced with someone who was attracted to him.

''No, I didn't date her, too. What do you think? That I cut a wide swath through the whole town?''

''Maybe,'' Paris admitted as she followed Ethan to the shop's entrance where he held that door open for her.

Through the introductions and Marti Brock showing her party clothes, Paris was grateful that the other woman wasn't as openly in pursuit of Ethan as

Honey Willis had been at the church dance. But despite the store owner's professional demeanor toward Paris, she still subtly flirted with Ethan. And when it came time for Paris to try on her selections, the store's proprietress left her to her own devices in the dressing room so she could hurry back out to Ethan.

It was better that way, Paris tried to convince herself. After all, she had to be very cost conscious and she didn't particularly want Marti Brock to know that the first thing she did before even putting something on was check the price tag.

But still she heard every one of Marti's lilting laughs from outside the dressing room. Every one of the other woman's coquettish comments. Every one of her veiled hints that she and Ethan should see more of each other while he was in Dunbar.

And because of that, Paris made quick work of choosing a dress.

Then she hurriedly slipped back into her black capri pants, shrugged on her white wrap blouse, crossing the two sides of it so she could tie the long ends into a bow at her left hip, and pulled on her sandals.

''That was fast,'' Marti said, not sounding pleased to see her again so soon when Paris came out of the dressing room.

''I found what I want,'' she answered simply and decisively, thinking that Marti Brock had found what she wanted, too, if the possessive hand she had on Ethan's arm was any indication.

''Don't we get to see a fashion show?'' Ethan asked.

"You'll see what I picked tomorrow night."

"And it's not the pink? I thought Ethan would really like the pink," Marti said with a combination of disappointment and disapproval.

"Not the pink." Definitely not the pink, which was an overly ruffled nightmare of a prom dress. Something she thought the other woman was very well aware of.

Paris stepped up to the counter to pay, and as Marti went behind to write up the receipt Ethan joined Paris.

"It's my treat," he informed her.

"No way," Paris answered without a moment's hesitation.

"Think of it as your bonus for a job well done," he insisted as Marti soaked in the exchange with open interest.

"No. You're overpaying me for this job as it is, and I won't accept more. Either I pay for this or I don't take it."

"If she doesn't want you to pay for it, you shouldn't pay for it, Ethan," Marti said with enough double entendre to make Paris's blood boil.

Ethan ignored her and focused only on Paris. "It's what I want to do. That's why I arranged for this today."

"I was planning to get something new if I was invited to the party. So put your credit card away."

"Paris—"

Paris cut him off with a shake of her head and handed her own credit card to the saleswoman.

Marti cast Ethan a sympathetic glance and reached

across the card he was still holding out to her, to take Paris's card instead.

"I think she has a mind of her own," the shop owner said to Ethan, making it sound like a negative.

But Paris didn't care at that point. She was too busy holding her breath in hopes that the sale didn't suck up what was left of her limit. If it did she thought she might have to commit hara-kiri right there.

But luckily the charge went through without a glitch as Ethan replaced his wallet in his back pocket.

"I didn't want you to have an expense over this," he said.

"It was a splurge," she assured him.

Marti chattered about how much she was looking forward to the party as she unceremoniously put Paris's purchase in a bag and handed it to her without actually looking at her.

Then Marti walked them to the door, saying to Ethan as she did, "I hope you'll save a few dances for me tomorrow night."

Ethan managed to laugh that off without promising anything as he held the door open for Paris.

And Paris was only too happy to step out of that shop.

"So, is there any single woman under fifty in this whole town who doesn't fall all over you?" she asked when she and Ethan were finally in the SUV again.

He laughed slightly, answering Marti Brock's wave goodbye with one of his own before pulling away from the curb.

"It's the money," he said bluntly then.

"What's the money?"

"The main source of my appeal. Marti Block wouldn't give me the time of day when we were growing up. It's only since I made a few bucks that she's discovered what a catch I am."

Paris glanced over at him. His hair was combed carelessly but neatly. His face was clean shaven, and each stark angle, each perfect feature, was in relief against the sun coming in through his window. He had on a black silk shirt with a band collar and a pair of black slacks that couldn't have fit him any better if they'd been made especially to his muscular specifications. And he smelled like heaven.

Somehow Paris doubted that his bank account had as much to do with his appeal to the single women of Dunbar as he might think.

"Maybe you just aged well," she suggested.

"Aged?" he repeated with a sideways glance of those blue eyes that could melt steel at a hundred paces. "You mean like cheese?"

"I mean like grew up. Maybe you were a gawky kid who grew up to be a more attractive man."

"I was a gawky kid," he agreed. Then, with a wickedly teasing smile, he said, "And now you think I'm an attractive man, huh?"

"I said maybe," she countered, rather than give him the satisfaction of a full-out compliment. "Or you could be right and it's just the money."

That made him laugh and change the subject. "Don't you want to know where we're going for dinner?"

"I didn't think there were too many options in Dunbar."

"We're not staying in Dunbar."

"Oh. Where are we going?"

"I'm not telling," he said like an ornery little boy. "I just wondered if you were curious."

"I am now."

"Too bad," he said, enjoying his joke. "Just sit back and enjoy the ride."

Then he slipped on a pair of very sexy sunglasses as if he were preparing himself for a speedway race, pushed a button on the CD player that surrounded them with Chris Isaak's music and hit the open road outside of Dunbar with a lead foot pressed to the gas pedal.

They drove for quite a while in the flat, open countryside of eastern Colorado. Paris kept watch for a restaurant, wondering if it was in the middle of nowhere or in another town.

Then Ethan turned off the main highway onto a two-lane road that ended several miles farther north. But not at a town or at a restaurant in the middle of nowhere. The road stopped at a lake where, at the end of a wooden dock that reached out into the water, was a very large boat.

"We're taking a boat to the restaurant?" Paris asked when he pulled to a halt, turned off the CD player and then the engine.

"Uh-uh. We're eating on the boat," he said as if he'd been bursting to tell her that all along.

Then he got out of the SUV and so did Paris, not

waiting for him to come around to open her door for her.

"Is this yours, too?" she asked over the hollow sound of their steps on the wood as they headed down the dock to where the *Great Escape* was anchored.

"It is," he answered, his affection for the boat ringing in his voice.

Someone had been there ahead of them because as they drew near Paris could see a table already set on the lower deck, complete with a white linen tablecloth, gold-rimmed china, polished silver and crystal goblets for the wine that was chilling in an ice bucket on a stand beside it all.

"Is this a yacht?" was Paris's next question as she took in the considerable size of the two-tiered craft.

"That sounds so pretentious," Ethan said with a proud smile. "You don't get seasick, do you?"

"I don't know. I've never been on a boat. Or a yacht."

"We won't go out too far. And if you start feeling queasy we'll come back and eat on shore instead."

"Okay. I'm game."

Ethan helped her board and left her to sit on the padded bench seat that ran in front of the railing that surrounded the lower deck. Then he climbed to the upper deck where a console full of buttons, levers and a steering wheel waited.

"Do you know what you're doing?" Paris called up to him.

"I've done it a million times before," he shouted over the loud roar of the engine as he started it.

He seemed intent on what he was doing so Paris didn't want to interrupt him and instead fell to just watching him.

He really did seem to be master of the vessel, but it wasn't his skill as captain of his ship that held her interest. It was the way his tight derriere looked in those black pants. And the narrowness of his waist just before it widened into the vee of his back. And shoulders so broad they looked as if they could belong to a swarthy, hard-bodied pirate manning an entirely different kind of ship....

''How're you doing?'' Ethan asked, pulling her out of her study of him once he'd gone about half a mile from the dock and cut the engine so the peacefulness of the water could reign once more.

''I'm fine,'' she said, but her voice came out slightly weak because although she wasn't feeling any seasickness, she was in the throes of some internal rough waters caused by just the sight of him.

''Are you sure?'' he persisted as he came down to the lower deck again.

Paris silently cleared her throat and, in a stronger tone, said, ''I'm sure. It's nice out here.''

''Isn't it?'' he agreed with a satisfied glance around.

''Tell me about this boat,'' she urged him as he opened the wine and poured two glasses of the rosy liquor.

''It was the first thing I splurged on when I found myself in a position to splurge on anything,'' he began, warming to his subject as he came to hand her a glass and sit near her at the railing.

He went on to talk about learning to drive the boat and the fishing trips and water-skiing outings he and his brothers liked to take on it, regaling her with anecdotes of their adventures.

But Paris didn't hear much of what he was saying because as she sipped her wine she was lost in the moment itself and just being there with him.

The sun was beginning to set on the water. A gentle breeze cooled the hot summer air and gently rocked the boat. And Ethan's face was gilded in golden light that cast into relief the sharp planes of his cheeks, the chiseled blade of his jaw, the perfect patrician line of his nose.

And although Paris kept up her limited part of the conversation even through the cold supper they shared, she couldn't stop watching Ethan, studying him, being every bit as attracted to what she saw and heard as the other two women they'd encountered in the past twenty-four hours had been.

So attracted that as dusk fell and Ethan turned on the boat lights to cast a soft glow all around them, Paris began to worry that she was rapidly becoming even more susceptible to him than she'd been before. Especially when her thoughts began to turn to the hot kiss they'd shared the previous evening. To the way it had felt to be held in his arms. To wishing that was exactly what he'd do again right then and there.

Which was when she decided to guide the talk to something more serious to distract herself.

So as Ethan slid their dinner table and chairs out of the way while she went to sit again at the railing, she said, ''Will you tell me now about the not-good woman in your life three years ago?''

''I didn't want to ruin our picnic with that. Why would I want to ruin tonight with it?''

''Because I want to know?'' Paris said more flirtatiously than she'd intended. ''And because I told you about my past. Doesn't that warrant you telling me about yours?''

Ethan again came to sit with her against the railing, only this time he sat closer than he had earlier. Close enough for his knee to brush her thigh when he sat sideways to face her. And just that small contact sent a heat wave through her that wasn't aided by the long arm he rested along the railing itself so that his hand was scant inches from touching her hair.

''It's an ugly story,'' he warned.

''All the more reason to hear it. The uglier the story, the greater the impact on you.''

Ethan smiled a small smile. ''Are you psychoanalyzing me?''

''Just curious about what makes you tick,'' she said, borrowing his reasoning of the previous evening.

Ethan didn't jump right into telling his tale, but she sensed that he was going to so she merely waited for him to start.

Her patience paid off a few minutes later.

''I told you Bettina came *into* my life three years ago,'' he finally said, addressing the wording of Paris's original question. ''I was with her until just before I met you.''

"Then it ended about the same time my relationship with Jason did," Paris said, getting the time frame straight in her mind.

"Actually it blew up in my face. But, yes, it must have been around the same time."

"And Bettina was her name?" Paris prompted when he stalled again, frowning out at the water.

"Bettina Gregory," he confirmed in a far-off tone.

"How did you meet her?"

"She worked for the interior designer I hired to furnish the house in Denver. She was a former model. Tall, beautiful, well dressed. Any man would have taken a second look."

He said that defensively and Paris didn't comment.

"We seemed to hit it off, so when the project was finished I asked her out. I fell for her fast and she made me think she was just as head over heels for me. We were engaged within six months."

Ethan looked at Paris again. "You're sure you want to hear the gory details?"

"Positive."

He stared at her for a moment, as if gauging whether or not he was going to go through with it.

Apparently he decided he was, because he said, "The first thing that happened was that her mother needed surgery the medical insurance wouldn't pay for. I only learned about it by overhearing a message on Bettina's answering machine and when I questioned her she reluctantly told me what was going on. She said she didn't want to bother me with it and I assured her that her family was my family and wrote a check to send to her mother."

"That was nice of you."

Ethan merely smiled again. This time wryly.

"Didn't her mother have the surgery?"

"Next up was Bettina's car," he said rather than answering Paris's question. "It was stolen. It was a pretty old car so she only carried liability on it."

"Which means it wasn't covered for theft."

Ethan let her know she was right by pointing a single index finger at her. "So I bought her a new car."

"Also a nice thing to do."

"I didn't do it to be nice. I figured we were getting married, my money was her money, why wouldn't we get her what she needed?"

That was a nice way to look at it, but Paris didn't say it since something about her telling him that seemed to aggravate him.

"Then," he continued, "her grandfather died. In Florida, which was where her mother had also had surgery—too far away for me to make a hospital visit or to get away for the funeral since he just happened to die when I was in the middle of a business mess I couldn't get away from."

"Just a coincidence?"

"Not quite but you're ruining my big climax."

"Never something I'd want to do," she said with a heavy dose of innuendo she surprised herself with.

But it helped lighten the tone slightly because Ethan smiled a genuine smile and said, "Good to know."

"Okay, so the grandfather died," Paris said to remind him where they were in the conversation.

"Uh-huh. Granddad died. Leaving a lot of debt and burial expenses the family couldn't pay."

"So you wrote another check. I'm beginning to see a pattern here."

"You're smarter than I am because I still wasn't."

"What finally opened your eyes?"

"About two months after the big death scene Bettina claimed she was getting squeezed out of her condominium."

"You weren't living together?"

"I wanted her to move in with me but she said it was bad luck, that everyone she knew who lived together before they got married never ended up getting married. What she wanted was for me to give her the money to buy the condo. She said the owner wanted to sell and she couldn't afford to buy the place. Or find another place within her price range to rent because the housing market in Colorado had skyrocketed."

"That's true. It's why my mother and I share a place."

"Yes, but Bettina and I had already been engaged for nearly a year by then. I didn't see why we should buy the condo when it was only a matter of time before we got married and she moved out of it, anyway. So that's what I told her."

"And she said..."

"She said the condo would be a good investment and we could rent it after we were married, that she didn't want to rush our marriage. And believe it or not, I was considering it. I wanted her to be happy. I didn't want her to feel as if we had to have a hurry-up wedding for any reason. But just before I wrote *that* check, I surprised her.''

''Why am I thinking it was you who got the real surprise?''

''Maybe you're psychic,'' he said, ''because it was definitely me who got the real surprise. I came home from a business trip two days early and went from the airport to her condominium without calling first.''

''Calling would have ruined the surprise.''

''Exactly. Well, *my* first surprise was that her stolen car was parked out front. But even then no red flags went up for me. I just figured the police had found it and returned it, and I let myself into the condo.''

''She wasn't alone,'' Paris said in a quiet, sympathetic voice.

''She was in bed. With her brother.''

''Her *brother?*''

''The man she had introduced to me as her brother when she'd talked me into paying his credit card debts so he wouldn't have to go bankrupt. In reality he wasn't her brother.''

Paris grimaced. ''That's awful.''

''To say the least. But thanks for not making any cracks about what a *close* family they were. I've heard more than my share of them.''

''What did she say?''

''She tried to lie her way out of it, but by then I was putting two and two together. It took some digging later on to prove it, but there hadn't been any surgery for her mother, her car had never been stolen, her grandfather had died ten years before I'd even met her, and she already owned the condominium. She was fleecing me, plain and simple. She and the boyfriend-slash-brother.''

''What did you do?''

''I learned more than I ever wanted to know about deceit and betrayal.''

That sounded uncomfortably pointed, and although Paris wasn't exactly sure why it should be, she wanted to get past it as quickly as she could. ''I meant did you get your money back.''

He shook his head. ''I didn't care about the money. I'd loved this woman and she'd just been playing me. That was the worst of it.''

''And it's why you're a little jaded about women wanting you only for your money,'' Paris surmised, referring to his comment after leaving Marti Brock's shop.

''I don't know that I'm 'jaded.' But I suppose I have been more on the lookout for honesty in people since then. And for ulterior motives.''

''And you didn't do anything to get back at this Bettina?''

''I thought about retribution at first. It was tempting, I won't deny it. I could have probably had her arrested. Or I could have sued her to get my money back. But once I'd cooled off and thought about it, I decided to chalk it up to experience and put it behind me.''

''You were embarrassed that you'd been duped,'' Paris guessed.

''No, I wasn't embarrassed. I didn't do anything anyone wouldn't have done for someone they thought they were going to spend the rest of their life with. I had the means and I'd trusted her and wanted to help her and her family. But if I had sunk to the level of prosecuting her or suing her... It just didn't sit well with me. In the first place it would have kept me connected to her—''

''Mmm. I began to wonder about that with Jason—whether part of the reason he kept at his wife and prolonged the divorce and even went after the kids was because it gave him a reason to stay connected to her.''

''Well, kids are a whole different thing. They're a part of you. They're your own flesh and blood. They're something worth fighting for if the need arises. But since money—and my pride—were the only real issues, I opted for swallowing the urge for revenge rather than keep in contact with Bettina even through lawyers or the legal system, and even if it meant getting my money back.''

''So that's what you meant last night when you said some people can take it on the chin and not try to destroy the person who hurt them.''

''That's what I meant,'' he said.

And for some reason her seeing that seemed to please him enough to elevate him from the darker mood that had descended over him as he'd talked about his past.

''Aren't you sorry you asked?'' he said with a charming, one-sided smile.

''No, I'm not. I'm glad to know.''

''But now that you do, can we drop it and go back to having a *good* time?''

It was Paris's turn to smile. "I've been having a good time all along."

"Is that so?" he said as if that, too, pleased him. He took his hand away from the railing and toyed with a strand of her hair, letting it curl around his fingers. "Isn't it against the rules to admit it?" he asked.

"Are there rules?"

"You should know, you made them. I'm just a guy who looked up a girl he liked so he could get to know her."

"Are you sure that's an admission you want to make?" she teased him.

"That I like you? I thought it was pretty obvious."

"Or *you* just have an ulterior motive," she playfully accused.

"Like what?"

"Hmm. Let's see. You pick up a waitress at a business party and she ends up in bed with you, then you look her up again next time you're in town..."

He full-out grinned at her, and the crinkles at the corners of his blue eyes only made him all the more appealing. "You think I'm just angling for another night of wild passion?"

She arched her eyebrows in answer.

"Have I seemed disappointed that that's not where this has gone again?" he asked with a chuckle.

"You could just be hiding it well."

"And if an instant replay of fourteen months ago was what I was after wouldn't the 'strictly business' decree at the get-go have canceled this whole thing?"

''You probably just thought you could win me over.''

Which wasn't too far from what he was doing as he let go of her hair and began a slow, featherlight massage with the backs of his fingers against her cheek.

''Is it working?'' he asked in a confidential tone that made him lean slightly forward.

''I'm not going to sleep with you,'' she said with a smile, enjoying their game and the touch of his hand. Especially the touch of his hand as it traveled down the side of her neck and around so that his fingertips caressed her nape to continue that most tender of massages.

''Did I say anything about sleeping together? I wouldn't even if you asked,'' he joked in a low, intimate voice that only increased the heat wave that had begun when he'd joined her at the railing and his knee had brushed her thigh.

''Good, then we agree.''

''Mmm,'' he muttered in a wry sort of moan.

But his eyes went on holding hers, and his hand at her neck went on doing that oh-so-sexy rub, and Paris knew something was going to happen. It had to. Maybe because she wanted it to so badly....

Then he raised his other hand to her cheek, laying his palm there a moment before that hand slid to cup her jaw and tilt her head as he closed the remaining distance between them to kiss her.

She didn't have any intention of letting him make love to her. But kissing him again? No real harm had come from that the past few nights, had it? In fact, at that moment it seemed as if it might actually help the craving that was coursing through her right then. Like one bite of chocolate cake on a diet to keep from feeling completely deprived.

His lips parted over hers and Paris's lips parted, too, as her hands raised to his chest almost on their own. To the solid wall of his pectorals.

Mouths opened wider and Ethan's tongue came to test the tips of her teeth, to find her tongue to torment, to tease, to tempt.

And it all seemed innocent enough.

It really did.

Until that internal heat wave started to grow in Paris. Until she found herself having to fight not to writhe with the awakening of every nerve in her body. Until her skin came alive with a driving need for his touch on more than her face, her neck. Until her nipples turned to stone and cried out for his attention. Until her craving turned into something more, something stronger, something all too demanding.

Their kiss deepened further still and Ethan wrapped an arm around her, pulling her closer to him. Close enough for her breasts to come into slight contact with him.

His shirt was thin and so was hers, and the little lace nothing of a bra she was wearing wasn't much of a barrier between them even though it felt like a brick wall keeping them apart. But still she wondered if he could feel the granite of her nipples, if he would know what was going on with her and if she should retreat enough to make sure he didn't figure it out so he wouldn't think he was being invited to do more than kiss her.

Except that she wanted so much for him to do more than kiss her....

As if Ethan knew she was contemplating moving away from him and he was determined not to let her, he brought her closer still, even as he abandoned her mouth to kiss a path to the hollow of her throat where the flick of his tongue left a dot of moisture to chill-dry in the cool night air and tighten her nipples even more.

Then he kissed a path that followed the deep vee of her wrap blouse. He kissed her collarbone. Her breast bone. He kissed the hint of cleavage that had somehow emerged from the loose blouse, and even though Paris knew she should push him away, she filled her hands with his broad shoulders, with the honed muscles of his expansive back instead.

His hand at the side of her neck went to tag along on the trail of those kisses, sliding down the slope of the blouse's edge as his mouth returned to hers with new urgency in the wide-open command of lips and tongue that Paris matched with equal vigor.

But he still only let his fingertips trace the edge of her shirt—up and down, up and down again—and regardless of what she knew she should or shouldn't be doing, she thought she might burst if he didn't actually come inside and relieve some of the burgeoning need to feel his touch.

Her back arched in silent message, and that seemed to be all the encouragement Ethan required to use the easy access the blouse allowed to finally reach one engorged orb.

And, oh, what a miraculous hand he had! Kneading with the perfect pressure, with the perfect contained power. Slipping under the bra to fit her bare breast to his palm, to let that striving, straining crest snuggle there as if it had found its home. Tantalizing it a moment later with fingertips that circled and gently pinched, that tugged and rolled and sent shards of glittering delight to rain down through her and ignite another need in that spot between her legs that she'd hoped would stay sleeping.

What had she thought before? That she didn't have any intention of letting him make love to her?

Maybe she'd been wrong….

But for some reason she didn't understand, right alongside the thoughts of how much she wanted him to make love to her came an echo of the things he'd told her earlier about his last relationship. About how he'd been deceived.

And even though she had no designs on his money, a stab of guilt over the deception she *was* perpetrating struck her.

And guilt for that suppressed her appetite enough to break away from his kiss with a renewed—if regrettable—will.

''We should stop,'' she said in a breathless whisper that didn't hold much force.

But even so it was enough for Ethan to heed, and he did as she'd ordered and stopped. Instantly.

He pulled his hand from her breast, out of her blouse, and rested it on her waist instead, closing his eyes and letting his head fall back as if searching for the strength to contain himself.

The water lapping at the boat was the only sound. Paris was still enveloped in the warmth of his body, and a thrumming need inside her made her silently beg him to overrule her veto. But he didn't. He stayed that way a moment longer and then he opened his eyes and dropped his chin enough to look into her face.

"I knew I shouldn't have brought those oysters," he said, making a joke in a deep, raspy voice that let her know he'd been as involved as she'd been.

"It's getting late, anyway," Paris said as if it mattered. "We should get back."

Still Ethan studied her and his eyes were filled with the same lingering hunger that was running rampant through her.

But then he smiled his concession, took his hand from her waist and his arm from around her, showing her both palms in surrender.

"Whatever you say," he said with a resigned sigh before he left to climb to the upper deck and restart the engine.

They didn't say much after Ethan had docked the boat and explained that he'd arranged for someone to come and clean up after them so they didn't have to.

They didn't say much on the drive back to his house or as he walked her inside, either.

But it wasn't as if there was a stony silence between them. For Paris's part, not talking was the only way she could hang on to that resolve that had kept her from actually making love with him. And since she didn't have a sense that there was more to it for Ethan, she assumed he was putting his efforts into the same thing.

But it didn't help when they reached her room and he took hold of her arms in a soft grip, sending all new bolts of lightning shooting through her.

"I really didn't mean to get you out on that boat to—"

"I know," she assured him.

"It's just that—"

Paris nodded because she knew without hearing the words what he was going to say—it was just that every time they were together something seemed to carry them away.

Which was exactly what was going to happen again if she didn't get into her room where she couldn't see his chiseled features and smell the scent of his aftershave and feel the magnetic attraction of his big body.

"We should just say good-night," she managed in a weak voice.

"And if I don't want to?"

"We should just say good-night."

He laughed a little wryly, a laugh that was more a rumble, deep in that chest she still wished she had her hands on.

"Good night," he said then, as if only obeying orders.

"See you tomorrow."

"Oh, yeah," he breathed.

Then he kneaded her arms just the way he'd

kneaded her breast only a short time before and leaned in to kiss her again, his mouth open and familiar over hers and very nearly costing her the tenuous hold she had on her self-control.

But in the end he didn't wait for her to put the brakes on a second time. He stopped the kiss as abruptly as he'd started it and let go of her, too.

"Good night," he repeated on another sigh, this one sounding full of frustration.

Then Paris ducked into her room before she lost all ability to go through with it.

But even long after she had looked in on Hannah, long after she had undressed and gone to bed, she still couldn't stop the burning desire she had for Ethan.

And for finishing what they'd started on that boat.

Or maybe what they'd started fourteen months before.

Chapter Eight

The last-minute preparations for the party made Saturday hectic for Paris. And since everyone in the household was just as busy as she was, there wasn't anyone to baby-sit Hannah, and Paris had to attend to most things with her daughter in tow.

That wouldn't have been too bad if Hannah would have been content in the stroller or the playpen. But the infant was having none of that. She was only happy perched on her mother's hip. Which meant that everything Paris had to do, she had to do one-handed.

By late in the afternoon, as Paris tried to make sure all the place settings were right, Hannah had finished her nap and was back with her. But the pure weight of even the small baby was beginning to wear on Paris and, when she tried for about the tenth time to put Hannah in her stroller, Hannah wailed as if she were being abused.

"Let me take her."

Paris hadn't seen Ethan since he'd left her at her bedroom door the night before, but she didn't need to turn around to know it was his voice coming from behind her.

"It's all right. She just wants to be part of all the activity," Paris said as she once more took Hannah out of the stroller and put her on her hip. Then she turned to face Ethan.

He was a little scruffy-looking, in sweatpants and a plain T-shirt that hugged his torso like a second skin. And for some reason he hadn't shaved, so his beard shadowed the lower portion of his face.

But even like that, one glance at him was enough to make Paris's pulse race almost as much as it had the previous evening on his boat, because his scruffy appearance only made him all the more appealing in a purely primitive, elemental way.

"Lolly says you've been carrying Hannah around all day. Let me give you a break," he said, holding out his hands to the baby.

Of course Hannah was delighted with the attention. She grinned and reached for him.

"See? She wants a change of venue," Ethan said, taking her from Paris to prop her on his hip instead. "How about it, Miss Hannah? I have to talk to our bartender, want to come with me?" he said, nuzzling the baby's tiny button nose as he did.

And that was when, for the first time, Paris saw a resemblance between the two of them.

It was vague, but with Ethan's face right there beside Hannah's, Paris thought she could see him reflected in her daughter.

''No, that's okay,'' she said, feeling a wave of anxiousness as she held out her hands to take Hannah back.

But, as Ethan had said, Hannah was perfectly happy for the change of venue and ignored her mother to take a taste of Ethan's shoulder.

''Sorry, she's made her choice,'' he said with a laugh at what Hannah was doing. ''She's decided to use me as a teething ring. So booze talk it is for this kid.''

And with that he took Hannah to the bar, leaving Paris watching them with a fresh resurgence of uneasiness as she worried that it had suddenly become glaringly obvious that Ethan was Hannah's father.

But as she glanced around at Lolly and Aiden and Devon, at the rest of the staff all milling around, at Ethan talking to the bartender just the way he'd said he was going to, it was as if an earthquake had hit and Paris was the only one who felt it. No one else was so much as glancing at father or daughter. No one else was taking any notice of what Paris had just seen. From what she could tell, everyone was as oblivious to it as they'd been all along.

And that helped calm her. Not entirely. But enough to reason that if anyone else *had* noticed a resemblance between Hannah and Ethan, surely they would have commented on it.

So maybe she and Hannah were still safe, she told herself. For the moment, at any rate.

But one thing suddenly became perfectly clear and that was that she needed to get her daughter away from there as soon as possible. Before someone saw the two of them in just the right light, or at just the right angle the way she had, and *did* notice whatever small similarity there was.

Not that she could do anything at that moment. She had a job to do there, and Hannah couldn't be shut up alone in the bedroom while she did it. But luckily it was only a matter of hours before that job was finished. And when it was, Paris knew that she had to put things into motion to get herself and Hannah home.

Home, where they really would be safe. Where there would be no more reason to see Ethan again. Ever.

The champagne flowed like water, from a crystal fountain at a table in the center of the tent. Two giant pyramids of caviar stood sentry on silver pedestaled trays on either side of the fountain. More trays of hors d'oeuvres formed a circle around the champagne and caviar. And around that table were all the tables where the guests would sit when the time came for dinner to be served, each one clothed in white linen, set with china and silver, and adorned with a centerpiece of white roses.

All in all, it was an inviting sight as Paris entered the enormous, open-sided white tent where the party was being held. It was lit by tiny white lights strung in a glittering web overhead. Besides the centerpieces, there were flowers everywhere, scenting the air with their sweet smell. The violin quartet was playing classical music just loudly enough to be heard without making it difficult for anyone to talk. Guests mingled, full glasses in hand, carrying small plates laden with delectables, and from her vantage point Paris didn't see a single dour expression in the entire gathering.

But then, why would she when it was very much the spectacular affair Ethan had wanted it to be. And even though all the real work had been done before she'd come onto the scene, Paris was still proud of having played a last-minute role in it.

Lolly's niece was baby-sitting Hannah in Hannah's room, but the teenager had arrived late so Paris was making a tardy appearance. In fact, it seemed as if she were the only guest not already in attendance as she surveyed the crowd.

She'd considered not coming. Using the time while Ethan was hosting this party to pack her things and Hannah's, find a way to get to the bus station and leave before anyone had any more opportunity to see what she'd seen in Hannah today.

But Paris hadn't been able to make herself do it.

Not yet.

Hannah wouldn't be at the party, she'd reasoned. So if she swore to get her daughter out of there first thing in the morning, she thought she could allow herself these final few hours to attend the party she'd worked on. The party she'd looked forward to. She could allow herself this one last time with Ethan.

She spotted him then. He was across the tent, in a small group of men Paris didn't recognize. But one glance at him and everyone else seemed to drift into the background for her.

He looked much the way he had the night they'd met at the dinner in his honor fourteen months ago. Tall, straight, strong.

He was dressed in an impeccable black suit that had to have been specially made for him by an Italian hand. His shirt and tie were also black, he'd combed his hair more precisely than usual and shaved the day's scruffy beard. And if there was a more staggeringly gorgeous man there, Paris wasn't aware of him.

Then, as if her study of him had radioed her presence, he raised his chin, and his eyes met hers.

It was the stuff songs are made of.

Paris could almost feel his gaze on her and, without taking it from her, she saw him excuse himself so he could cut a path through his guests to come to her.

"Is this the dress you wouldn't let me buy?" he greeted when he reached her.

"It is."

He took her hand, held her arm in the air and made her twirl around so he could see it from every angle.

It was a fairly simple, silk chemise dress with free-form magenta-colored flowers printed on a background of cerulean blue. The blue of his eyes.

It had thin straps, and it dipped just to the initial hint of her cleavage in front and dropped low in back before it whispered down her body to her ankles where two-inch, high-heeled, open-toed mules were all she wore on her feet.

''Very nice,'' Ethan said when she faced him again.

His smile let her know he meant it.

''I like the curls, too,'' he added as he took in her hair.

Paris had curled it for the occasion, leaving it a springy, joyous mass that went well with the more dramatic evening makeup she'd applied.

''You don't look half-bad yourself,'' she countered.

''So I've been told by my two local predators,'' he confided with a nod over his shoulder at the guests in general.

''Honey Willis and Marti Brock,'' Paris guessed.

''Those are the ones. Which is why you'll have to stay close through this whole thing…to protect me.''

''And here I thought you might just want my company.''

''Oh, I definitely want your company,'' he said with a slow, lascivious smile.

Then he pulled her arm through his, closed his hand over hers to lock her in and said, ''Let's go enjoy some of the fruits of your labors.''

Their first stop was for champagne and caviar before Ethan began to make the rounds, introducing her to everyone she hadn't yet met until Paris gave up trying to remember names and just went with the flow.

As the evening truly got underway, Ethan made sure she never left his side, or at least never got farther than an arm's length away. They sat together at dinner, and when the orchestra began to play afterward, he danced only with her—to the chagrin of his other two admirers.

At midnight the party moved out of the tent onto the lawn for the fireworks.

It put to shame every Fourth of July display Paris had ever experienced as the night sky erupted with bright bursts of light that raised oohs and ahhs all around.

When it was over at one o'clock, about half the guests left while the other half went back to the tent where the orchestra struck up once more.

Ethan and Paris were among that half.

But by then Ethan seemed to have handed over all the hosting duties to his brothers, because his focus was so completely on Paris that no one even approached him any longer and they were left to just dance. Much the way they had at the church dinner.

Except that tonight, when Ethan held her in his arms, there was something different about it.

Their bodies seemed to fit together more seamlessly and there was an air of closeness that hadn't been between them that other night.

"So this is it. You're officially relieved of your duties," he said, his voice quiet, deep, sexy.

"I don't think I've ever been terminated quite like this," she joked.

"Not terminated. Just finished with your job. A job well done."

"You make it sound as if I did more than I did."

"You did enough to let me rest and relax more than I have any other year since we've been doing this party. I would never have been able to spend today playing racquetball with my brothers if not for your being here.''

''I guess that's something,'' she said, accepting his praise on those terms. ''And now it's back to the grindstone for you,'' she added.

''Mmm. I don't want to think about that right now.''

Neither did she, so she didn't say any more on the subject.

But even without any prompting Ethan said, ''I want to think about how great this is.''

''Dancing?''

He shook his head and squeezed her slightly. ''Having you right where you are. I'm glad I tracked you down.''

She had too many mixed feelings about his reappearance in her life to comment on that. Besides, her mixed feelings were what *she* didn't want to think about, so she just let him go unanswered.

If he noticed, he didn't remark on it.

Instead he angled his head so he could look into her face, into her eyes, and changed the subject. ''Can you feel it?''

For a split second Paris thought he might be asking her something inappropriate.

But then he explained. ''Whatever this is between us. It's like nothing I've ever felt before with anyone else.''

She knew what he was talking about but she only wished she *didn't* feel it. And rather than admit that, she said, ''Maybe it's the buzz from all the champagne...''

"Except that I've been feeling it even without the champagne. There's something about us together, Paris. About you..."

He let his voice drift off and merely smiled down at her to let her know that that "something" about her was something he liked. Something that intrigued him. Something special.

And that was how he made her feel—special, intriguing, appealing. It went to her head more than all the champagne had.

"We should just be enjoying the dancing," she advised him, because being in his arms was powerful enough. She didn't need the addition of words that were almost as powerful.

But then his eyes did the talking and they had no less impact on her as they searched hers, held hers and drew her in so completely she almost felt hypnotized by those absorbing blue depths.

Then he inclined his head just enough to kiss her. Lightly. Chastely. But it, too, had a power that left her weak-kneed.

"Behave yourself," she said when he ended the kiss.

But the command was as weak as her knees.

"No," he said simply enough. "I won't. I've been behaving myself all week."

"Do it for one more night," she said, not meaning for it to sound as beseeching as it had.

"No," he repeated, kissing her again. A sweet kiss that also managed to be so, so sexy that it chipped away at her resolve.

"I want tonight," he said then, forcefully.

It was her turn to say, ‘‘No.’’

But that, too, came out without volition.

‘‘You don’t want tonight?’’ he challenged. ‘‘You don’t want just this one night like the one we had before?’’

Before, when she’d given in to an attraction so intense it really had been like nothing she’d ever felt? Before, when she’d let herself get carried away and had a night she hadn’t been able to forget no matter how hard she tried? A night when she really had been taken to another plane in space and time by this man who had given her the greatest gift? By this man who made her blood run faster just by looking at her? Who could elicit a response from her body as if it had a mind of its own? Who hadn’t left her thoughts in the past fourteen months? Or her dreams in all the nights since he’d walked back into her life?

Did she want this one night with him before she had to make sure there would never be another?

She did. Heaven help her, she did.

She wanted this night. And she wanted him.

‘‘We shouldn’t,’’ she said, anyway. But it sounded more like a confirmation than a refusal.

‘‘Yes, we should,’’ he said, kissing her neck, touching the tip of his tongue to her skin to tantalize her.

‘‘Ethan…’’ she said, mentally begging him not to entice her.

But he just raised up to look into her eyes and smile again, that smile full of charm and mischief and a devilish streak he didn’t usually let show.

‘‘I know,’’ he said. ‘‘I can come up with half a

dozen reasons why I shouldn't do this. But tonight is a night like no other, Paris. Let's treat it that way. Let me make love to you before I go out of my mind thinking about it.''

She closed her eyes and reminded herself of all the reasons why she shouldn't. Why she couldn't.

But it didn't make any difference.

He was right—tonight was a night like no other. A night that would never come again. And coursing through every inch of her was the desire to just give in to what she wanted, too.

To give in to wanting him.

To wanting him to make love to her just once more....

She opened her eyes to him, struck anew by how masculinely beautiful he was. ''Not all your guests are gone,'' she said, managing to hedge just a little.

''I don't care.''

''And we're just going to slip out together?''

''And we're just going to slip out together. All you have to do is say yes.''

He kissed her neck again, sending electrical shocks all through her before he nipped at her earlobe and, in a deep whiskey voice for her alone, said, ''So say yes.''

Paris closed her eyes again, and once more tried to resist. To resist him. To resist what she was craving.

But even as she did she heard herself say, ''Yes.''

''Oh, yes,'' he said, holding her tightly enough suddenly for her to feel the hard ridge of desire that was hiding behind his suit coat.

Then he stopped dancing and without another word, he took her hand and led her out of the tent, across the yard and into the rear of the house, not stopping to say anything to anyone as he ushered her straight upstairs.

''Yours or mine?'' he asked when they reached the facing door of their bedrooms.

Paris hesitated. It wasn't that she didn't know which room they should use, she was just suddenly unsure if she should go through with this at all.

It wasn't too late, she told herself. She could put a stop to this before it went any further. She could say she'd changed her mind and leave him right there exactly the way she had so many nights this week.

But in the end she couldn't.

She couldn't take her hand out of the big, warm cocoon of his and walk away from him. She couldn't deny everything that was awake and alive within her. She couldn't keep herself from wanting him more than she wanted to breathe....

So she said, ''Yours,'' knowing the baby monitor was in his breast pocket where he'd put it when the baby-sitter had brought it to them before she'd left at midnight. Knowing that she would still be able to hear Hannah from across the hall.

Ethan didn't question the choice, he just opened the door and took her into the lush inner sanctum of chocolate brown where a bed the size of Texas waited on a platform that was a step higher than the rest of a room the size of her whole house.

Something about that bed gave Paris another pause

as Ethan led her to its side and placed the baby monitor on the carved mahogany night stand.

"I hope I don't regret this," she said to herself.

"Did you regret it fourteen months ago?" he asked as he pulled her into his arms.

"No," she answered honestly. And she hadn't. Not for a single second.

That made him grin as he captured her mouth with his in a kiss that bypassed the sweet, chaste beginnings on the dance floor to seize the moment with a passion that seemed to have been waiting just beneath the surface to sweep her away.

And sweep her away it did.

So much so that she barely noticed that he shrugged out of his suit coat, that he got rid of his tie, that he kicked off his shoes.

So much so that she kicked off her own shoes without more than a passing thought as she wrapped her arms around shoulders she could barely span.

He deepened the kiss, sending his tongue to meet hers, to play, to tease, to torment as his hands did an arousing massage of her back where her dress left it bare.

Of course as they'd danced he'd laid his palm to her exposed back, but there was something far more sensual, far more intimate about his touch now. It made her want that same connection with him, so she pulled his shirttails from his slacks to slip her hands underneath it to the satin-over-steel skin of his bare back.

He aided the cause by unbuttoning his shirt and getting out of it, tossing it aside without ever suspending the kiss that was increasingly more open-mouthed.

Paris let her hands do some traveling then, around to his front, to the massive pectorals where male nubs were almost as hard as her own nipples were.

And her own nipples were definitely hard. Kerneled crests that strained for him, that cried out for the touch they hadn't had enough of the night before.

Ethan abandoned her mouth to kiss his way down the side of her neck to her shoulder as he raised a single index finger to the thin strap of her dress and pulled it down to her arm.

Then he returned to her mouth, not kissing her but sending only his tongue to trace the inner edge of her lips as he dropped the strap from her other shoulder, too.

The dress was loose-fitting enough so that without the straps to hold it up it slipped low on her breasts, low enough to brush the highest curve of nipples that were knotted even tighter now than a moment earlier.

Ethan went on kissing her. Her shoulder. Her collarbone, then the upper swell of each breast.

It took her breath away with desire for more. For his hands, for his mouth, on those engorged mounds of flesh that impatiently awaited their turn for his attention.

And then that was what she got as he covered one breast outside her dress at the same time he eased the dress down far enough over the other to free it to his seeking mouth.

She didn't mean to moan, but she couldn't help it

as desire—pulsating and demanding—washed through her, making her want him all the more.

As he kneaded one breast and worked magic with his mouth on the other, she let her hands descend from his pectorals to his flat stomach, to the waistband of his slacks where she unfastened them to drive him just a little crazy, too.

It must have worked because he groaned and used his free hand to shed what remained of his clothes.

Then with only his hands on her breasts, he reclaimed her mouth with his in a hot, wet, sexy kiss that was more tongue play than anything. Tongue play that was a sneak preview of what was to come, as he thrust into her, pulled out and thrust again.

But apparently there was a hint she missed in that, because a moment later he took one of her hands from where it rested at his waist and pushed it down so that she could close it over the burgeoning proof of how much he wanted her.

Long, thick, sleek proof that lit Paris on fire at that first touch and made him draw in a quick, deep breath of his own.

Oh, he was an amazing man!

And Paris relearned just how amazing.

It didn't take much for him to slip her dress the rest of the way off, leaving her in just the lace garter belt she preferred over the strangulation of pantyhose and the dark stockings it held up.

He didn't know, though, what he'd happened upon until he looked and then his second groan was even throatier than his first.

"Ohhh...that stays on," he nearly growled as he

scooped her up into his arms and swung her onto the mattress.

In the moment before he joined her, she got to see him fully naked and gilded by the soft lights from behind the bed. And if he was amazing to feel, he was more amazing to look at.

His body was even more incredible than she'd recalled in fourteen months of fantasies. Sculpted muscles rippled beneath firm flesh she ached to have pressed against her.

Then he was with her, lying beside her, half of him covering half of her.

He kissed her again—short, gentle kisses as if they hadn't already been plundering each other with abandon.

But that only lasted a moment before he deserted her to draw one finger along her jawbone, following it with his mouth, kissing the spot just below her ear, flicking his tongue there, too, and leaving it to air dry as he kissed his way down the side of her neck to the hollow of her throat. He played there without touching her anywhere else, torturing her with the lack of contact her breasts, her whole body was craving.

Then he came back to kiss her yet again, his mouth open and seeking as his fingertips trailed farther down, following the outer curve of her breast, barely brushing her nipple with his thumb, just enough to make it stand tall before his other fingers teased the tip with strokes so light they wouldn't have disturbed the petals of the most delicate flowers.

Up and around the entire globe of her breast those

fingertips went like the strokes of a sable paintbrush, then down her side, holding her in place as he kissed a similar path that brought his mouth where his hand had been.

Kisses, soft, sensual kisses. He circled her nipple with them, then traced it with the tip of his nose before taking it into his mouth.

The man had a wicked tongue that tormented the hardened crest, tugging at it until he'd set so many things alive in her that her spine arched and thrust more of her into the warm velvet of his mouth.

But he didn't stay there long.

Instead he placed slow, intentional kisses in a line to her navel, then down a bit farther to the waistband of the garter belt where his tongue followed the lacy edge, while his hand went lower still and found that spot between her legs that had come awake with a jolt.

Her back arched a second time as he slipped a finger inside her, then two, nearly driving her to the brink. So nearly that her hips writhed beneath his touch, flexing upward, inviting more.

He finally accepted the invitation, fitting himself between her open thighs, replacing his probing fingers with something so much bigger, so much harder, so much better.

And Paris was ready for it all. She wanted it all.

His mouth found hers again, demanding, his tongue delving in just the way that other part of his body was delving into her.

Deeply into her. Again and again. Striving. Straining.

They worked together on a wild ride that left behind all reason, all rationale, all thought but to reach that climax that awaited them both. That climax that took hold of each of them at once, that swept them into the vortex of pure and utter ecstasy. That held them suspended for breathless moments, frozen together, clinging to each other.

And when passion had spent itself and them, it eased them back—slowly, slowly—to satiated, heart-pounding exhaustion.

Neither of them said anything. Only their bodies spoke as he held her tightly and rolled onto his back, bringing her to lie atop him where he flung the edge of the quilt over her and she settled her head on his chest.

Paris was too exhausted to even think. About the next minute or the next hour or the next day. About anything but how incredibly perfect, how incredibly complete, she felt.

And so she allowed herself to just be carried toward the heaviness of sleep.

With Ethan still a part of her.

Chapter Nine

Ethan woke up at dawn the next morning but not without some help.

He was spooned around Paris, where she slept with her little rear end pushed into his lap, arousing him even in his sleep. And from the baby monitor on the night table there also came the soft, sweet sounds of Hannah.

He stayed right where he was, drifting half in and half out of sleep, absorbing it all.

Paris snuggled up against him.

Hannah cooing and chattering just across the hall.

It was a good way to wake up.

A great way to wake up.

In fact, even though he didn't consider himself to be an intuitive person, as he came fully awake he had the strongest, clearest sense that that was exactly how things were supposed to be.

Him and Paris and Hannah.

He opened his eyes and reached for the monitor, turning down the volume slightly so it wouldn't wake Paris, and then replacing it on the nightstand. But he could still hear Hannah's waking sounds, and it was so damn cute it made him smile a bleary smile as he settled his arm around her mother again.

Was Hannah his? he couldn't help wondering, even then as the wheels of his mind started up.

He thought she was. No, he couldn't be absolutely positive, but he definitely thought she was.

And he suddenly surprised himself by hoping she was.

Was he actually doing that? *Hoping* Hannah was his?

He was. Strange as that seemed.

One thing was for sure, it had sneaked up on him.

If someone had told him two weeks earlier that in only that short time he'd find himself wanting to be a father, he would have laughed in their face. He would have said he wasn't anywhere near ready for that. Maybe someday. But not right now.

But it was as if everything had been turned upside down for him just since walking into Paris's house a week ago, and the more he'd been around the baby, the more he'd watched her and carried her and played with her, the more he'd enjoyed her, the more he'd felt connected to her.

That was weird, but it was there inside him as much as the sense that she was supposed to be a part of his life, as much as the hope that she was his child. An intangible connection to Hannah.

Maybe it didn't prove anything. Maybe it didn't make it any more likely that she was his. But it wasn't something he could ignore, either.

Any more than he could ignore the fact that it wasn't only Hannah he felt connected to. The fact that he felt a connection to Paris, too.

But as he thought about that he began to realize that that wasn't all he felt for Paris. That there was more he felt, too.

In fact, it occurred to him that even if there wasn't a baby, he'd be lying there feeling that this was how things were supposed to be for him. That Paris was the woman he was meant to be with.

It seemed like something he'd known somewhere deep inside since the first time he'd set eyes on her. Something that had just been there, waiting for him to discover it.

And really, now that he had, he wondered how he could ever have overlooked it.

After all, the very thought of Paris turned his blood to molten lava. The simple sight of her was enough to stop him in his tracks, to make him forget about everything else.

How could he have missed the fact that she was the woman for him when he wanted to be with her every minute of every day and night? When he only felt completely himself when they were together? When the world only seemed full and colorful and worth being a part of when he was with her?

How could she not be the woman for him when

making love to her was like nothing he'd ever experienced before? When just the idea of making love to anyone *but* her turned him off? When all he could think about was being able to make love to her for the rest of his life?

For the rest of his life?

That gave him pause.

The last time he'd thought in terms of the rest of his life it had been over Bettina.

Bettina who had lied to him. Who had deceived him. Who had made him swear to himself that he would never get involved with another woman who wasn't totally open and honest with him....

Open and honest.

That was something Paris hadn't been with him. Not if Hannah really *was* his and Paris was keeping it from him.

It was easy to lose sight of that sometimes. It was easy to get caught up in his attraction to her, in these feelings that had somehow grown even though he'd tried to suppress them, in his feelings for Hannah. It was easy to forget that Paris might be keeping an even bigger secret from him than Bettina ever had.

But somehow, as he lay there holding Paris as she slept with her hair curling against the pillow and her long eyelashes resting against her porcelain skin, he discovered himself having a difficult time putting the two women in the same category.

Why was that, if they'd both lied to him?

But he knew why when he compared the two.

There had been something cunning about Bettina. Something calculated. And that wasn't the case with

Paris. He truly didn't believe she was angling for anything by keeping the secret he thought she was keeping.

Certainly she wasn't working some kind of scam on him the way Bettina had. Yes, she'd accepted the job he'd pretty obviously trumped up for her so she could get a new car. But once she was here she actually *had* worked for it—something Bettina would never have done.

And that was the only thing Paris had accepted from him. She hadn't even let him buy her dress for the party.

That in itself was the complete opposite of what Bettina would have done. In Paris's position Bettina would have not only had him buy one dress, she'd have come out with half a dozen, plus everything to go with them. And rather than turn down an offer for him to pay for them so she could pay for them herself, Bettina would have *expected* him to foot the bill.

But then, in Paris's position Bettina would have been cashing in royally. More royally than she had. In fact, now that he thought about it, it was a wonder Bettina hadn't borrowed someone else's baby to pull a child-support scam on him, too.

But Paris didn't even seem to want *that* from him. Which, if Hannah was his, she had coming.

So maybe Hannah *wasn't* his…

It always came back to that. Square one.

Just then Hannah let out a fairly loud squeal, and Ethan glanced at the monitor as if he would be able to see her through it.

Which of course he couldn't. But still the squeal seemed more insistent than her other, sweeter sounds, and he thought it was probably what she did when she was growing bored with entertaining herself and wanted some attention.

But the squeal didn't wake Paris and he hated to be the one to disturb her. Especially since, after a brief nap after their first round of lovemaking, he'd roused her for a second and then a third round that he knew had worn her out.

Besides, in that moment of wondering all over again if Hannah really was his, he wanted to see the baby. To once more judge if he was imagining things.

So he slipped carefully out of bed, pulled on a pair of pajama bottoms he took from a dresser drawer, and silently left the room.

He didn't hear so much as a stirring coming from the rest of the house as he went into Hannah's bedroom. It made Hannah's second squeal seem all the louder as he crossed to her crib side.

"Good morning, Miss Hannah," he said quietly.

Hannah took one look at him and grinned that toothless grin, waving her arms and legs in excited pleasure at seeing him.

It was such a small thing, that innocent delight, but the fact that it came in response to him went a long way in turning him to jelly.

She had to be his, he thought. Why else did she have such an overwhelming effect on him? No other child he'd ever encountered had.

He leaned one forearm on the crib rail and let her

take hold of the index finger of his other hand, searching her adorable face as he did.

And again he could see his mother in Hannah's eyes, in her dimple.

She had to be his....

"So why doesn't your mom want me to know?" he asked, as if Hannah might have the answer. "Is it what I thought that night she told me about that other guy? Is she just afraid?"

He considered that, thinking about the night she'd told him about her former fiancé and how he'd so doggedly gone after custody of his children purely out of spite.

But Ethan had tried to let her know that night—and the next when he'd told her about Bettina and taking what she'd done to him on the chin—that she didn't have anything to be afraid of from him.

Had she not gotten the message? Had he not said it forcefully enough to convince her?

Or was she just so terrified of it that nothing, not even the child support she actually needed, was worth taking the risk?

It seemed possible to him. Paris loved Hannah, there was no question about that. She was devoted to her. She believed Hannah was the only child she would ever have. That made Hannah all the more precious to her. And if Paris thought there was any chance of ever losing Hannah the way that other woman had lost her kids?

He could understand Paris keeping his paternity a secret from him.

But if that was the case, then all he had to do was put her fear to rest, he thought.

It seemed like an easy enough fix.

And if he did that? he asked himself as Hannah played with his finger. If he alleviated Paris's fears and she admitted Hannah was his daughter, what then?

Then they could be together. The three of them.

And that, he realized, brought him back to square one on that count, too.

But no matter how he came to it, he knew as he stood there with Hannah and thought about Paris, that he genuinely did want the three of them to be together.

Hannah let out another squeal then, this one louder and more shrill than the other two, letting him know that what she wanted was to be picked up.

He reached into the crib and obliged her, feeling his heart swell as he settled her into the cradle of his arms.

What had Paris said the day they'd had their picnic? That she would consider marriage if she met the right guy?

When she'd said it he'd hated the image of her being with someone else, the image of someone else parenting Hannah.

And now he understood why.

It was because now he knew without a doubt that *he* was that "right guy."

And not only because he believed Hannah was his child.

More than that, it was because he suddenly knew that he *had* to be that right guy in Paris's life.

Because she was the right woman in his.

"So here's the plan," he told the tiny infant. "We'll change you into a dry diaper and then I'll take you over to my room where we'll get your mom up. And maybe once we do, we can straighten out a few things."

As if she understood exactly what he was saying, Hannah cooed her approval.

And as Ethan took her to the changing table all he could think was that he hoped her mom was as easy to convince.

It was Hannah's high-pitched screech coming through the baby monitor that woke Paris. She considered it the warning bell. It meant "Get in here soon or else."

But Paris was sooo tired....

She couldn't move. She couldn't open her eyes.

Maybe Hannah would go back to sleep....

But she knew better. She knew from many mornings of listening to the soft, happy chatter that preceded the squeal, that when her daughter escalated to that, her patience at being kept waiting was spent. So no matter how tired she was, Paris was sure she was going to have to get up.

She forced her eyes open to mere slits then, struggling against the heavy sleep that still wanted to pull her back into its grasp.

That was when she realized she wasn't in the room that had become familiar to her.

But where was she?

First morning light came through windows covered in sheer curtains. The walls were painted brown and trimmed in cream. And she was in a huge bed that seemed to sit up higher than the rest of the large oak furniture.

Ethan's room.

It came back to her then. The party. Dinner. Dancing. A lot of champagne. Coming here to make love. Three times…

Paris's eyes flew open with that, and she shot a glance to the rest of the bed, the rest of the room, looking for him.

But he wasn't there.

Not physically, anyway. But she could smell the scent that was his alone. On the sheets. In the air. On her. And she could feel the essence of him all around her, as if the room echoed with his presence in the calm, confident color of the walls, the solid strength of the decor.

It was enough to make her almost feel as if his big, warm body was still beside her, as if the imprint he'd left in the mattress held her as surely as his arms had.

Or maybe that was what she was still craving even after those three times.

Then she heard his voice, also coming through the baby monitor.

And in a flash she went from wishing he would walk out of the bathroom door and get back into bed with her, to feeling uneasy.

He was with Hannah again. Hannah, whom Paris

had had every intention of whisking away before Ethan got another look at her. Before he had the chance to see himself reflected in her the way Paris had the day before.

She had to get in there, she thought frantically. She had to put herself between Ethan and Hannah before it was too late.

Paris lunged out of the bed, only aware of her own nakedness when the cool morning air touched her skin and reminded her that even the garter belt and nylons had come off by the third time they'd made love.

But she was less concerned with what to wear than with getting to her daughter as quickly as possible, so she grabbed the first thing she could—the black dress shirt Ethan had worn the previous evening.

She threw it on, trying not to notice the even headier scent of his aftershave wafting from the folds of it as she buttoned it as fast as her fingers could manage.

Then, wearing only that and heedless of the size or the fact that the sleeves fell over her hands, she turned toward the door.

But she'd only taken two steps in that direction when it opened and in came Ethan, carrying Hannah on his hip, against the magnificence of his bare chest above a pair of pajama bottoms.

''There she is,'' he said to her daughter when he caught sight of Paris.

The room seemed suddenly warmer just because he'd come into it, but that wasn't something Paris wanted to think about.

She just wanted to get her hands on Hannah and head for the hills as fast as she could.

"I'm sorry if she woke you up," she said to hide her own alarm. "Here, let me take her and you can go back to bed."

But the step she took toward Ethan and Hannah was canceled out by Ethan moving farther away.

"We're fine. I'm not going back to bed," he said as he went to the bureau across the room.

He opened the top dresser drawer and took what appeared to be a picture frame from it. Then he turned and came to Paris, handing it to her. "I want you to see something."

But Paris didn't care what he wanted her to see. She just wanted her baby.

"She's chewing on your shoulder again."

And what an amazing shoulder it was!

But that, too, was something Paris knew she shouldn't be thinking about.

"You'll be drowning in drool in a minute. Let me take her," she repeated.

Still Ethan didn't give Hannah over, though. He offered only the silver picture frame. "I want you to look at this."

Paris finally accepted it because she didn't have a choice. And once she had, Ethan took Hannah over to the largest window on the outside wall, propping one hip on the window seat there.

To Paris it seemed far, far away, and her alarm at still not having Hannah grew.

But since looking at the picture was apparently the only way to satisfy him and possibly get her daughter back, Paris did as he'd told her twice now and glanced at it.

Inside the silver frame was a wedding picture. A color portrait that was dated by the groom's shaggy, hippielike hair and the clownishly large lapels on his tuxedo, and by the flower-child look of the bride.

But that was only Paris's first impression.

Her second look was closer. Particularly at the bride, who had strikingly familiar aquamarine eyes and a tiny dimple just above the corner of her mouth.

And although Paris was looking at a photograph of people she'd never met, it was like seeing what her daughter would look like all grown-up.

She didn't know what to say so she didn't say anything.

"Those are my parents," Ethan said pointedly then.

In that moment, looking at that picture of his mother, Paris knew that he suspected Hannah was his child. That he'd suspected it from the beginning. That her thinking that she and Hannah were in any way safe around him had been an illusion.

A rush of total panic ran through her and she didn't know what to do.

But she did know that to verify it now was to give up the ghost, and she just couldn't do that.

So, hanging on to the hope that she could still bluff her way out of this, she tried to keep outwardly calm.

"They were very attractive," she said, referring to his parents and fighting to sound normal, to say something anyone might.

But Ethan wasn't going to let her off the hook.

''I know Hannah is mine,'' he said, confirming her worst fears.

''No, she isn't,'' Paris said in a hurry, as if the idea were insane and she couldn't imagine why he'd come up with it. ''I had Hannah through artificial insemination.''

''Don't kid yourself, Paris. There was nothing artificial about that night we spent together fourteen months ago. Any more than there was anything artificial about last night.''

Last night was yet another thing Paris didn't want to think about.

''Hannah is *not* yours,'' she insisted.

''She's the image of my mother.''

''She's the image of *my* grandmother,'' Paris countered.

Ethan stared at her with those penetrating blue eyes, and all Paris could think was that she'd been out of her mind to come here in the first place. Out of her mind to bring Hannah. She'd walked right into a disaster and now she was going to have to do whatever it took to get them out of there.

Then Ethan must have decided to change his tack because after a moment of studying her, he said, ''I think I know what has you so determined not to let me know Hannah is mine.''

Every time he said Hannah was his the possessiveness in his tone sent a fresh wave of terror through Paris.

''She isn't,'' she had to say even though it didn't seem to matter.

''I know that having seen what your former fiancé

did to his ex-wife over their kids had a big impact on you,'' Ethan said, rather than argue the point again. ''I think it had such a big impact on you that now you're scared that if you tell me the truth the same thing might happen to you. But it won't, Paris. It won't.''

''She isn't yours,'' Paris repeated firmly.

Again he didn't acknowledge it. ''I considered that you might not want to tell me because I'd made it so clear the night we met that I wasn't ready for marriage or kids or family ties. Hell, until this morning I wasn't sure myself that that had changed. But I woke up with you next to me, with Hannah making those cute little sounds she makes, and I knew right then that *everything* had changed. That I wanted the three of us to be together. That I had to claim Hannah.''

Paris's heart leaped to her throat. He was *claiming* Hannah?

Very slowly, carefully enunciating each word, Paris said, ''Hannah is not yours to claim.''

''Come on, Paris. I can get a court to order blood and DNA tests if I have to, but you and I both know the truth.''

This was getting worse and worse, and Paris's reaction to it must have been evident because he shook his head and used a more cajoling tone.

''Don't go all pale on me. I'm not that other guy and I'm not looking to hurt anybody—especially not you. I told you, I want the three of us to be together. I'm crazy about you. I'm crazy about Hannah. I want you *both* in my life.''

''So you thought you'd threaten me?''

''I'm not threatening you.''

''Court-ordered blood and DNA tests?'' she repeated. ''What is that but a threat?''

''I just want you to be straight with me.''

Paris took several steps in his direction, holding out her hands to Hannah. ''Give her to me.''

He didn't move much, but he did lean back just slightly. Enough for Paris to get the message that he still wasn't going to let her have Hannah.

''Don't do this, Paris,'' he beseeched. ''I had to work to separate you from Bettina, to figure out that even though I know you've been lying to me about Hannah, it wasn't the same as what Bettina did. Now you have to work to separate me from that other guy. You have to separate what's going on between us and what went on between him and his ex-wife. Please.''

''Please give me my baby.''

''And then what? Are you going to run as fast and far away from me as you can take her? Are you going to do everything you can to keep me from ever having anything to do with her? And in the process ruin what you and I have? What we *could* have? I don't want that. I want you. I want Hannah.''

''You can't always have everything you want.''

''Don't tell me it isn't what you want, too.''

''What I want is my baby.''

''Don't make this into something it isn't.''

Don't, don't, don't…

It seemed to Paris that he was giving a lot of orders, and with each one she could feel herself stiffen more and more.

Maybe he saw that, too, because he pushed off the windowsill then and came to stand in front of her, lowering his voice so it was softer. "Take a deep breath and a good long look at me," he said. "I'm not a bad guy. I'm not mean or evil or vindictive. I'm the guy you trusted enough to make love with last night, remember? I'm the father of your baby. There aren't ugly, hurtful, hateful things between us. There are only good things. Think about that. Separate it from the other situation, the other people."

Paris did take a good long look at him. At that face that was handsome enough to stop traffic. At those bare shoulders where her daughter happily teethed. At the broad, honed pectorals she herself had used as a pillow. At the pure splendor of that tall, lean body her own body still craved.

And she was tempted to let down her guard. To do as he told her and separate him and this situation from what she'd witnessed of Jason.

But as she looked at him she also saw the power of him. The confidence. The sure and certain knowledge that he could get what he wanted. Whatever he wanted. The same kind of power and confidence, the same kind of sure and certain knowledge that Jason had had. That Jason had used when his relationship with his wife had soured.

And there Ethan was, with Hannah, holding on to her rather than handing her over. Keeping her from Paris even after Paris had asked for her.

It was just too glaring an example of what Paris feared most.

"Just give her to me," she said, not understanding where the tears that flooded her eyes had come from.

He hesitated another moment but he finally let her take Hannah. And once Paris had her daughter she clung to her, stepping away from Ethan.

"She isn't yours," she said more forcefully than any of the other times. "It's only a coincidence that her eyes are the same color as your mother's. That she has a dimple. Hannah is not your baby."

She could tell by his expression that he still didn't believe that, but he refrained from refuting it. Instead he said, "Okay. Then let's just talk about you and me."

"There's no you and me to talk about."

"Yes, there is. There's plenty of you and me to talk about. We didn't come together fourteen months ago and again last night because there's nothing between us. There's something incredible between us."

Paris shook her head in denial. "Two nights. They were just two nights. No big deal."

"They were two very big deals and you know it."

"All I know is that this is the end. You hired me to supervise the last-minute details of your party, which I did, and now that the party is over, so is the job and everything else."

He closed his eyes and shook his head. "Paris..." he said in frustration. "Don't do this."

But she had to do this. She had to get away from him any way she could, as fast as she could.

And so, before he had even opened his eyes again,

she slipped out of his room and made a beeline for her own, where she swore to herself that she and Hannah would be on the first bus out of there.

And that nothing and no one would stop them.

Chapter Ten

They were sitting on her front porch on Wednesday afternoon when Paris got home. Aiden and Devon. One as handsome as the other and both resembling Ethan enough to make her heart lurch.

But she tried not to show any reaction to them as she went up the walk.

''Hi,'' Devon said as she drew near and both men stood up from the wicker chairs they were waiting in.

''Hello,'' Paris answered with reserve. She wasn't happy to see them and she wouldn't pretend she was.

Aiden met her at the porch's top step. ''Can I take some of this stuff for you?''

Paris had been commissioned to do a mural at the elementary school, which was where she was coming from. Since it was only a few blocks away she'd walked. But she'd walked carrying an oversize sketch pad, her palette, and her paints and brushes in a large tackle box.

"I'm fine," she told him, but Aiden took the tackle box anyway and Devon helped himself to the sketch book and palette.

"You have a smudge of blue on your nose," he pointed out as he did, smiling in a way that also reminded her of Ethan. As if she needed any more reminders of him.

Paris walked to her front door rather than go on looking at the brothers, leaving the smudge where it was in a show of defiance.

"Why are you guys here?" she asked unceremoniously as she held the door open for them and followed them into her living room. She might not have let them in except she knew that her mother had Hannah safely away at a friend's house.

"We came to take you to buy a new car," Devon answered once they'd both set her things down.

"No, thanks."

"Ethan said that was your agreement for the work you did on the party last week," Aiden said, as if he hadn't heard her.

"I don't care what he said or what our agreement was. I don't want anything from him but to be left alone." Alone to maybe, eventually, stop thinking about him every minute of every day the way she had since leaving Dunbar on Sunday morning.

"You can relax," Devon assured her. "We're not here to plead Ethan's case. He told us not to."

She didn't know why that disappointed her, but it did.

''Ethan doesn't have a case,'' she said.

''We all saw the same thing in Hannah that Ethan did, Paris,'' Aiden said then, quietly negating her denial and letting her know they were aware of what was going on.

Paris had felt like a fool for having believed Ethan had accepted her artificial insemination story. For having let Hannah anywhere near him. Now she felt like twice the fool for not having known what had clearly been common knowledge to everyone else.

It didn't help her mood.

And she had no intention of addressing Aiden's comment about Hannah.

Instead she said, ''I'm not going with you to buy a car, so you can go on about your business.''

They ignored her invitation for them to leave.

And then, as if there had also been a decision to ignore Ethan's request not to plead his case, Aiden said, ''You know, Ethan only wants what's best for you and for Hannah. He'd never hurt either of you.''

Too late, Paris thought.

But she didn't say it.

''It looked like you cared about him,'' Devon interjected, apparently opting for speaking up on his brother's behalf, too. ''Was that just an act?''

Like Bettina—that seemed to be the unspoken finish to his question. And even though Paris didn't want to, she hated the idea of being put in the same class with the other woman.

''No, it wasn't an act,'' she admitted reluctantly.

''We know he cares about you,'' Aiden said. ''Can't you just try to work things out?''

Paris's eyes suddenly filled with tears. Tears she should have run out of by then since she'd shed so many of them in the last few days.

But she fought to keep them from falling, turning her back on the brothers so they wouldn't see and going to stand behind one of the overstuffed chairs that was at some distance from them in a shadow of the room.

''No, we can't just work things out,'' she answered definitively.

''Look,'' Devon reasoned, ''we know that Ethan's money and what it buys can bc daunting. There's no denying that it allows him to make things happen or that it can give him an edge in certain circumstances. But the bottom line is that what he makes happen are only good things. He doesn't use it as a weapon and that's what's really important.''

So he'd told them the whole story.

''That's true,'' Aiden confirmed before she could say anything. ''Even now, he could have lawyers beating down your door and he isn't doing that. He's willing to lose you, to lose Hannah and any rights he has to her, rather than force an issue he knows scares you.''

''But we don't want to see that happen—losing you and Hannah,'' Devon said.

''The thing is, Paris,'' Aiden continued, ''we all have someone from our past who leaves a sore spot we try hard to protect. But if we don't put it in its place and just use it to learn from, if we use it to build a wall around us instead, it isn't a lesson anymore, it's a handicap.''

''Is that what you want?'' Devon said, each of them picking up smoothly where the other left off. ''Do you want to be handicapped by your past? Do you want Hannah to be handicapped by it, too? By not having the father she deserves?''

''Do you want Hannah to grow up seeing a mother who has to keep herself closed off to feel safe?''

''I don't have to keep myself closed off to feel safe,'' Paris said defensively, finally interrupting them.

''What do you call it?'' Aiden challenged.

She only wished she *had* kept herself closed off. Then she wouldn't be as miserable as she'd been since getting back to Denver.

But she didn't say that, either. She didn't say anything.

''You're missing out, Paris,'' Devon said then. ''And you're forcing Hannah to miss out, too. Sure, Ethan is setting up a trust fund for her. Sure, he'll make sure she's well provided for. But she'll never know him. And that's lousy. For all of you. When the three of you could be a family if you'd just give it a chance.''

''Just think about it,'' Aiden urged.

They had apparently come to the end of their not pleading Ethan's case, because silence fell in the room and this time they let it stay for a long while before Aiden took a business card out of his pocket.

''This is the salesman at a car dealership near here. They carry most makes, so you'll have a wide selection. The salesman knows to arrange for you to have whatever you want. If you won't go with us, then at least go on your own."

He set the business card on the coffee table in front of the couch.

Then he and Devon retraced their steps to the door.

But as Devon went out, Aiden paused to look back at her.

"Don't ruin this, Paris. Not for Hannah. Not for Ethan. And not for yourself. You really could have something great with him."

Then Aiden went out, too, finally leaving Paris alone.

And that was when she wilted.

Damn all the Tarlingtons, she thought, hating that they could affect her so strongly.

She rounded the overstuffed chair and collapsed into it, thinking that it was a good thing Aiden and Devon *hadn't* come to plead Ethan's case. What would they have said if they had? As it was, they'd portrayed him as the martyred saint who was forgoing his rights to his daughter just so he wouldn't risk freaking Paris out.

But then, how else would they have portrayed Ethan? she reasoned. He was their brother, after all.

Of course it *was* something that Ethan wasn't pushing his paternity suspicions, Paris conceded. That he hadn't sent lawyers to demand medical tests to prove it. That he was letting her denial go unchallenged.

Maybe he had changed his mind back to what he'd said fourteen months ago and he didn't want a child.

But Paris didn't actually believe that. Not after seeing the way he'd held Hannah Sunday morning. Against his naked chest, letting her suck his bare shoulder.

No, what Ethan was doing—or *not* doing—wasn't because he didn't want Hannah. Paris had no doubt that it really was because of her. Because he knew that if he did anything to prove Hannah was his, Paris *would* freak out.

His brothers were right—that was quite a sacrifice. Quite an act of unselfishness.

And definitely *not* something Jason would ever have done.

But just because for the moment Ethan was doing something that Jason wouldn't ever have done didn't mean Paris could overlook the similarities between the two men. The things that made them dangerous—money and power. And what that money and power allowed them to do to other people's lives. People like Jason's ex-wife and kids, people like Dr. B.

Although, since she'd been home with her mother, Paris had been giving the situation with Dr. B. more thought.

Ethan *had* lied to the old man, and that smacked of Jason's manipulations. But she'd come to acknowledge that unlike what Jason had done, what Ethan had done had been in the doctor's best interest. That if she were facing the same situation with her mother, she wouldn't be above doing the same thing.

Which took some of the steam out of her criticism of Ethan. Not to mention that the scenario had never held the same kind of vindictiveness as Jason's actions against his wife.

But then, that was what Ethan had said when she'd told him about Jason in the first place. That there were vindictive personalities and nonvindictive personalities. That some people could take things on the chin. The way he had with Bettina.

Of course, now that Paris knew that Ethan had suspected Hannah was his child all along, she knew that his point had been that because he hadn't gone after revenge for what the other woman had done to him, Paris didn't need to worry that he would ever try to get custody of Hannah from her just out of spite, either.

And maybe it was true.

Or maybe she just hoped it was true because she was trying to talk herself into something.

But then how could she not be inclined to talk herself into something when she'd spent the past few days missing Ethan so much she ached inside? So much she couldn't eat or sleep? How could she not be inclined to talk herself into something when, now that she'd seen Ethan in Hannah, she couldn't stop seeing him in her every time she looked at her daughter? When she couldn't stop wishing he was there to see it, too?

And all of that could be soothed if only she could talk herself into believing she and Ethan really might have a future together.

But talking herself into something could be very unwise, she thought. Especially when it might mean underestimating Ethan or the impact even a suspicion of parenthood might have on him.

After all, what had happened between Ethan and Bettina was on a whole different level. Bettina had swindled him out of money. Money he had to spare.

But a child was something else entirely. A child was something to fight for—he'd said that himself.

Only he wasn't fighting for her, Paris reminded herself again.

He wasn't dragging Paris through courts. He wasn't trying to force anything…

"And I'm going in circles," she muttered to herself since she was back where she'd started in thinking about this whole thing.

But maybe there was something to just that. Maybe if she was going in circles about it she should give the beginning of that circle more merit.

After all, for the past fourteen months she'd been convinced that the safest route for her and Hannah was to stay away from Ethan because if he knew Hannah was his daughter, and if he and Paris had any involvement and that involvement ended, he could try to take Hannah away from her.

But what was that last week if not an involvement? An involvement that had ended?

Yet Ethan hadn't sent lawyers to beat down her door demanding anything of her.

And maybe that was a bigger deal than she was acknowledging.

Maybe it was proof of just how different Ethan actually was.

Was that possible? she asked herself, again trying

hard not to talk herself into anything, trying to take an objective look at the two men.

But there were differences, she realized when she compared them as people. As men.

Where Jason was selfish, Ethan was anything but. Where Jason was thoughtless and unfeeling, Ethan was thoughtful and compassionate. Where Jason expected to be catered to, Ethan took care of other people. Where Jason did use his wealth and power as a weapon, Ethan used it to help out.

And where Jason was vindictive, Ethan took it on the chin....

So maybe where Jason couldn't be trusted, Ethan could be....

She wanted to believe that. She wanted it badly.

Because somewhere in the past few days she'd also realized that her feelings for Ethan were very different from her feelings for Jason. They ran deeper. They were stronger.

Too deep, too strong to deny any longer.

Yes, she'd tried. She'd fought them harder than she'd ever fought anything in her life.

But it didn't matter. The feelings were there and there was nothing she could do about them.

Feelings that left her wanting Ethan, wanting to be with him, so much that it suddenly didn't seem as if she really had any choice but to trust him...any choice but to try to make things work between them.

Because if she didn't, if she went on doing what Aiden had said—if she went on handicapping herself with what had happened in the past—she was never going to have Ethan. Hannah was never going to have Ethan.

And that was a very high price to pay. Too high a price to pay. Especially for safety from a man she'd misjudged, a man she was coming to believe she could be safe with.

A man she just might not be happy without…

So Paris mentally took her fears and all her misjudgments, and set them aside.

It was surprisingly easier than she'd expected.

And once she'd done that, she felt free.

Free to go after her real heart's desire.

And that was Ethan.

Ethan, who, she hoped, would forgive her for having denied him all she'd denied him in the past fourteen months.

Ethan, who, she hoped, really had come to the point where he wanted a family….

Chapter Eleven

There were worse times Paris's car could have broken down than that night, just after dark, on her way to Ethan's Cherry Creek house.

But not many.

At least, not many Paris could think of as her car began to sputter its now-familiar sputter and she eased it off to the side of the road, shrieking, "No! No! No!" at the top of her lungs.

And then it died. Deader than a doornail.

"Don't do this to me," she said to the car as if it would help, turning the key in the ignition—off, then on again—pumping the gas and hoping it would surprise her and start.

It didn't.

It just sat there, giving her not so much as a click or a chug.

She tried the engine again and again, but it didn't make any difference. And she knew it wouldn't. When the car stalled, it stalled for good.

"So what now?" she asked herself on a disgusted and frustrated sigh.

She took a look around her, not reassured to find nothing but darkness and a lot of evergreen trees.

She'd made it into Cherry Hills Estates where she'd been with Ethan that first night fourteen months ago. But the area was heavily wooded, and since miles separated one mansion from the next, she wasn't sure how much farther Ethan's house—or any house—was.

She didn't have a cell phone to call for help, and that didn't leave her many options.

Either she got out and hiked and hoped she'd come to a house before too long, or she sat there and waited for someone to pass by.

Not what she'd expected to be doing when she'd decided to go looking for Ethan tonight.

But just then her decision was made for her.

A car marked Security Patrol pulled up alongside her.

The uniformed officer who got out was an older man who didn't look the slightest sympathetic as he came up to the passenger side and pointed to her window so she'd roll it down.

Paris scooted across the bench seat and obliged him.

"Somethin' wrong?" he asked in a way that sounded more like an accusation.

"My car's dead," she said. "I was on my way to Ethan Tarlington's house."

The man looked from her to the car's interior, then to the car's exterior, and she could tell he didn't believe her for a minute.

But he didn't say anything. Instead he moved out of earshot and used a cellular phone of his own, presumably to call Ethan.

It didn't help Paris's already-high level of anxiety to wonder if Ethan was even there, since she'd only assumed that if his brothers were in Denver, he would be, too, and that they'd all be at this house. It didn't help her already-high level of anxiety to wonder what his reaction would be if he was. Or to wonder if he'd just tell the security guard to call a tow truck and have her taken away.

The patrolman reappeared at her window without warning then, startling Paris and making her realize just how nervous she was.

"Mr. Tarlington says he'll be right down."

No clue in that as to whether Ethan was happy about it or not.

"He said he didn't need me to wait for him, but I will if you want me to," the officer offered, sounding less suspicious.

"No, thanks. I'll be fine."

The man nodded but didn't say anything else before returning to his car and driving off.

As Paris rolled the window up and slid back behind the steering wheel she almost wished she would have had him stay. Because once he was gone and she was alone in the dark again, her stress seemed to come alive with a new force.

This was hardly the way she'd envisioned Ethan setting eyes on her again. She'd hoped to make a grand entrance of some kind, in her black spandex micromini skirt and the silky black spaghetti-strapped tank top she'd worn over it. Her plan was to look so sexy he wouldn't be able to remember that a few days earlier she'd dumped him.

But now the element of surprise was completely ruined and she just felt like an idiot.

Headlights flashed up ahead just then, blinding her and causing her pulse to speed up.

But the car went right past.

Not Ethan.

Her heartbeat slowed back down to the nervous pounding it had been doing since she'd decided on this course of action.

Maybe he wouldn't come at all, she thought as more time went by. Maybe even though he'd told the security patrolman that he would, he wouldn't. Or maybe any minute the security officer would return at Ethan's request to have her towed out of there after all because once he'd had the chance to think about it he'd realized he *didn't* want anything to do with her.

And then what would she do? Go after him with a paternity suit just to get to see him again?

Headlights shone from a different direction than the last ones, abruptly cutting off her worrying and making her heart race once more.

Was this Ethan? Was this Ethan? Let it be Ethan....

The black Jaguar pulled to a stop on the opposite side of the road, and Paris's heart started beating so hard it was like jungle drums in her ears.

What if he'd sent one of his brothers rather than come himself?

It was too dark to tell who was driving the Jaguar until the engine was turned off and the driver's door opened.

But then, in the dome light, she saw him.

Ethan.

It was Ethan.

She realized she'd been holding her breath and she let it out. Taking in another deep one and releasing it slowly in an effort to calm herself down.

He looked incredible to her. As if he'd gotten even more handsome since she'd seen him last.

He was close shaven and his hair had that tousled look that was such a nice counterbalance to the innate dignity and confidence that seemed to radiate from him.

As he got out of the car she could see that he had on faded blue jeans and a bright red polo shirt, but the dome light wasn't bright enough for her to tell what his expression was, to let her know what might be going through his mind, if he was happy to see her or angry from Sunday or annoyed at having his evening interrupted.

Then he closed the car door, the light went out and she was just left guessing.

Guessing and listening to the almost panicked race of the blood through her veins.

Don't let me have blown this....

Ethan came around to her side and tapped on the window with the knuckle of an index finger.

Paris felt even more like an idiot for not having rolled the window down yet, but she'd been so lost in fretting that she hadn't thought about that.

Now she rolled it down in a hurry.

When she had, Ethan bent over, resting his forearms on the door's edge.

"*This* is your car?" he said by way of greeting, amazement tingeing his voice.

"This is my car," she confirmed, referring to the nearly twenty-year-old sedan that had been in the garage every other time they'd been together.

"It's a boat," he said. "An *old* boat."

"I know."

Ethan poked his chin toward the other side of the seat. "Move over," he ordered.

Paris slid across, farther than she'd gone to roll down the window for the security patrolman, and Ethan got in behind the wheel in her place.

"It won't start," she informed him.

But he had to see for himself.

And while he did, Paris watched him, feeling as if

she was all twisted up inside. Car trouble was *not* what she'd come to talk to him about.

"It'll have to be towed. When it does this there's no getting it started again," she told him in a quiet voice that she thought echoed with her insecurity about what she'd ventured out to do tonight.

After turning the key in the ignition a few times and getting no response, Ethan accepted that and gave up.

But rather than simply getting out of the car and suggesting they go back to his place to call a tow truck, he angled himself on the seat, stretched an arm across the back of it, and gave her a long look.

"So what brings you out here? Just passing by?"

It was obvious that wasn't the case. No one would just be passing by this remote section of Denver that was designed to be out of the way so that its wealthy residents weren't easily accessible.

"I came to talk to you," she admitted.

He nodded his head. "Talking is good," he said, this time sounding encouraging.

It helped.

"Do you want to talk here or go back to the house," he asked.

"Are your brothers at your house?"

"Yes. But in case you've forgotten, it's a big place. I think we could find a room where we could talk without them."

Still, this whole thing was awkward enough. The seclusion and privacy of the broken-down car suddenly seemed preferable to the thought of anyone else being around.

''We can talk here,'' she said.

''Okay.''

But that was it. He was leaving the ball in her court.

Paris found it difficult to just jump in, though. Horrible fear had forced her to keep this secret. It was no simple matter to expose it now.

But she knew she had to.

So after a moment she screwed up her courage and said, ''Hannah *is* yours.''

''I know. That's what I told you Sunday morning.''

''But I told you it wasn't true and it is. That's all I'm saying. And that you can have a blood test if you want to be absolutely sure, but—''

''I don't need a blood test to be absolutely sure.''

There was something comforting in that and in his matter-of-fact handling of this whole thing that allowed Paris to go on.

''I'm sorry I couldn't admit it before. But to me, after Jason, just the idea of you being in the picture seemed like the threat of losing her and—''

''I know that, too, Paris,'' Ethan said gently, patiently.

''I didn't do it on purpose, though,'' she said then. ''Get pregnant, I mean. I want you to know that, too. That night—''

''I know what that night was. I was there, remember? I did all the seducing.''

It struck Paris all over again that Ethan really was different from Jason because even though Jason's children had been conceived during his marriage, he'd still ranted about how his ex-wife had trapped him into having them so she could take him to the cleaners for child support if the marriage ever ended.

And yet here was Ethan, who could well have suspected she'd had ulterior motives, not doubting her at all.

"Anything else you wanted to talk about?" Ethan said then, as if prompting her.

She wasn't too sure if she could just blurt out the rest so she said, "I haven't been very...upbeat in the last few days."

"Neither have I."

"I'm not sure exactly where you were headed with what you were saying Sunday morning, but—"

"I was saying that I want the three of us to be together."

"Well, that's what I want, too. Whatever that means."

Ethan finally cracked a smile. A slow grin. "It means that I'm in love with you and I want you to be my wife and I want us to raise our daughter together and dance at her wedding and baby-sit our grandchildren and die holding hands when we're a hundred and seven. Is that clear enough?"

"Pretty clear." Paris couldn't help smiling, too.

"Clear enough for an answer?"

"I want us to be together. To be a family, too. I

want Hannah to know you're her father and not miss out on that.''

''And...''

''And I'm in love with you, too.''

''Finally,'' he said as if it had been like pulling teeth to get it out of her. ''So the answer is...''

''The answer is yes, I would love to die holding hands with you at a hundred and seven.''

''And the rest of it?''

She pretended to have to consider that before she said, ''Okay, yes to the rest of it, too. But only because you have a great body. It doesn't have anything to do with your money. Or your mind,'' she teased.

''It isn't because of my money?'' he said, feigning shock. Then, more seriously, he said, ''I actually knew it wasn't for my money because if you were Bettina and my brothers had gone to give you carte blanche for car shopping today, you'd be driving a Rolls Royce by now. Not that this low-rider isn't nice...''

''No shocks,'' she informed him, explaining why the car sat so close to the ground.

''No shocks. Really...'' he said as if it intrigued him. ''Maybe we should test that out.''

Ethan eased across the seat, nearer to her, staring at her so intently that she thought she could feel his eyes on her. And letting her know that what he had on his mind, now that they'd put everything else behind them was not something they should do in public.

''What if the local watchdog comes back?'' she asked as Ethan hooked a single finger under the strap of her tank top and pulled it from her shoulder.

''We'll have a lot of explaining to do,'' he said before he pressed his lips to that spot where her strap had been.

Paris glanced out the windshield, then out the rear window. ''We really shouldn't.''

Ethan kissed the hollow of her throat. ''We really shouldn't have fourteen months ago, either. But look how great that turned out.''

He kissed his way up her neck, and somehow her head fell back so he could go on kissing the underside of her chin.

''Besides,'' he said in a husky voice, ''this works for teenagers. Who knows, it might work for us, too, and Hannah won't have to be an only child.''

Paris laughed again, but this time it came out a sexy rumble.

Then Ethan took her mouth with his in a kiss that was full of urgency right from the start, and Paris decided in that instant that she didn't care where they were or who might happen by. That all she cared about was this man and what he could ignite in her just that quick. This man and the fact that he loved her, that he wanted her as much as she wanted him. In every way that she wanted him.

He tasted sweet, as his tongue came to romp with hers. His hands on her shoulders were warm and sensual, lighting her skin on fire with desire for more of his touch, as her nipples turned to tight, yearning knots, and all on its own her back arched to relay the message.

Ethan understood it, letting those wondrous hands glide down to her straining breasts.

But just as Paris was writhing beneath his fingers, headlights flooded the car.

Ethan abandoned her breasts, and they both turned from their kiss to see if they were about to be found out.

But the car turned off before it reached them and again Paris said, ''We shouldn't...''

But Ethan wrapped one arm around her to pull her to him once more, recapturing her mouth with his and slipping his hand under her tank top to her bra-less, engorged breast.

And she was lost again as that fire that had coursed across her skin now came to life inside her, burning a path to that spot between her legs that cried out for him.

''This is so bad,'' she whispered when his mouth deserted hers to replace his hand at her breast, to take it fully into that hot, wet cove where his tongue went to work to drive her even more wild.

Wild enough to pull his shirt not only from his jeans, but to also unfasten those jeans and plunge inside to that indisputable proof that he was as on fire as she was.

It was as if they'd been starved for each other for far too long. For so long that they could only push clothes aside while mouths plundered and hands ravaged and somehow they defied those cramped quarters for their bodies to come together. For Ethan to find his home inside her in a burst of passion and the overwhelming need to be one. To soar to heights greater than any they'd reached before, until they were both suspended in that blissful, explosive moment that truly bound them in a way no mere words ever could.

And when it was over, when the stars and the moon and the sun had all been reached, and they clung to each other as they floated back down to earth, Ethan kissed her once again and said, ''I love you, Paris.''

''I love you, too,'' she could answer then without any qualms.

''And I think we'll keep this car in the garage just so every now and then we can do this in it.''

Paris laughed. ''But will it be as good without the threat of the security patrol hanging over our heads?''

''Oh, I think what we have will always be good, no matter what,'' he said, holding her close for another moment before the headlights flooded the car again and they waited to see if it was the security patrol about to discover them.

It wasn't, the car went past them, but it was enough to prompt them to sit up and make themselves presentable.

As they did, Paris kept looking at Ethan out of the

corner of her eye, marveling at how much her heart swelled with just the sight of him.

And she knew without a doubt that he was right, that what they had between them *would* always be good, no matter what.

Because how could it be anything else when she loved him as much as she did, when she knew he loved her just as much, and when they had Hannah to share.

* * * * *

Next month look for
Her Lord Protector *by Eileen Wilks in*

ROMANCING THE CROWN:
DREW & SAMIRA

Only from Mills & Boon Spotlight™.

Turn the page for a sneak preview…

Her Lord Protector

by

Eileen Wilks

The chimes above the door rang. Rose tucked her hair be-hind her ear, turned to the door—and froze.

It was him. The man from the airport. The one who'd been with His Grace, Duke Lorenzo Sebastiani, nephew of the king and head of Montebello's intelligence service. His clothes were cleaner and more casual today, but just as ex-pensive. His face was hard, lean. Not a lovely face, but the sort a woman remembered. And the eyes—oh, they were the same, the clearest, coldest green she'd ever seen.

So was the quick clutch of pleasure in her stomach. "What are *you* doing here?"

"Rose." Her aunt Gemma was repressive.

"Your store is open, isn't it?" He had a delicious voice, like melted chocolate dripped over the crisp consonants and rounded vowels of upper-class English.

Gemma moved out from behind the counter. "Pay no at-tention to my niece. Missing a meal makes her growl. Did you have something specific in mind, my lord, or would you like to look around awhile?"

My lord? Well, Rose thought, that was no more than she'd suspected, and explained why he seemed familiar. Se must have seen his picture sometime. This man wasn't just rich, he was frosting—the creamy top level of the society cake.

She, of course, wasn't part of the cake at all.

"Quite specific," he said. "About five foot seven, I'd say, with eyes the color of the ocean at twilight and a sad lack of respect for the local police."

Rose lifted one eyebrow. "Are you here on Captain Mylonas's behalf, then…my lord?"

"I never visit a beautiful woman on behalf of another man. Certainly not at the behest of a fool. I asked you to call me Drew."

Ah. Now she knew who he was. "So you did, Lord Andrew."

His mouth didn't smile, but the creases cupping his lower eyelids deepened and the cool eyes warmed slightly. "Stubborn, aren't you?"

"Do pigs fly?" Gemma asked in a rhetorical manner.

"Ah—no, I don't believe they do."

Rose grinned. "Aunt Gemma has a fondness for American slang, but she doesn't always get the nuances right. She enjoys American tabloids, too. And Italian tabloids. And—"

"Really, Rose," Gemma interrupted, flustered. "His lordship can't possibly be interested in my reading habits."

"No?" Rose's smile widened as she remembered a picture of Lord Andrew Harrington she'd seen in one of her aunt's tabloids a few years ago. Quite a memorable photograph—but it hadn't been Lord Andrew's face that had made it so. His face hadn't shown at all, in fact. "I'm afraid we don't sell sunscreen. If you're planning to expose any, ah, untanned portions of your body to the Mediterranean sun, you'd do better to shop at Serminio's Pharmacy. They have a good selection."

"Rose!" Gemma exclaimed. "I'm sorry, my lord, she didn't—that is, she probably did mean—but she shouldn't have."

The creases deepened. "I'm often amazed at how many people remember that excessively candid photograph. Perhaps my sister is right. She claims the photographer caught my best side."

His best side being his backside? Rose laughed. "Maybe I do like you, after all."

The door chime sounded. Tourists, she saw at a glance—a Greek couple with a small child. She delegated them to her aunt with a quick smile. To her surprise, Gemma frowned without stepping forward to welcome their customers.

Her *zia* didn't approve of Lord Andrew Harrington? Or possibly it was Rose's flirting she didn't like. Ah, well. She and Gemma had different ideas about which risks were worth taking. She answered her aunt's silent misgivings with a grin, and reluctantly Gemma moved toward the front of the shop.

Lord Andrew came up to the counter. "Perhaps you could show me your shop."

How odd. She couldn't feel him. She felt something, all right—a delightful fizzing, the champagne pleasure of attraction. But she couldn't feel *him.* The counter was only two feet wide, which normally let a customer's energy brush up against hers. Curious, she tipped her head. "Maybe I will. But I'll have to repeat my aunt's question. Are you looking for something in particular?"

"Nothing that would be for sale. But something special, yes."

Oh, he was good. Rose had to smile. "We have some very special things for sale, though, all handmade. Necklaces, earrings—"

He shook his head chidingly. "I'm far too conventional a fellow for earrings—except, of course, for pearls. Pearls must always be acceptable, don't you think?"

"Certainly, on formal occasions," she agreed solemnly. "I'm afraid we don't have any pearls, however."

He looked thoughtful. "I believe I have a sister."

She was enjoying him more and more. "How pleasant for you."

''No doubt she will have a birthday at some point. I could buy her a present. In fact, I had better buy her a present. You must help me.''

''Jewelry, or something decorative?''

''Oh...'' His gaze flickered over her, then lifted so his eyes could smile at her in that way they had that didn't involve his mouth at all. ''Something decorative, I think.''

''For your sister,'' she reminded him, and left the safety of the counter. Quite deliberately she let her arm brush his as she walked past, and received an answer to the question she couldn't ask any other way.

Nothing. Even this close, he gave away nothing at all.

Rose's skin felt freshly scrubbed—tender, alert. Her mind began to fizz like a thoroughly shaken can of soda, but she didn't let her step falter as she led the way to the other side of the store, away from her aunt and the Greek tourists.

Here the elegantly swirled colors of Murano glass glowed on shelves beside bowls bright with painted designs. Colors giggled and flowed over lead crystal vases, majolica earthenware, millefiori paperweights, ceramic figures and crackle finish urns. Here she felt relaxed and easy, surrounded by beauty forged in fire.

A purely physical reaction. That's all she felt with this man. That and curiosity, a ready appreciation for a quick mind. She turned to face him, and she was smiling. But not like a shopkeeper in pursuit of a sale. ''What is your sister like? Feminine, rowdy, sophisticated, shy?''

''Convinced she could do a better job of running my life than I do.'' He wasn't looking at her now, but at a shiny black statue by Gilmarie—a nymph, nude, seated on a stone and casting a roguish glance over one bare shoulder. He traced a finger along a ceramic thigh. ''I like this.''

The nymph was implicitly sensual. Rose's eyebrows lifted. ''For your sister?''

''I have a brother, too.''

''No doubt he comes equipped with a birthday as well.''

''I'm fairly sure of it. I'm not sure I want this for him

though. I like the look on her face. The invitation.'' His eyes met hers then. There was no hint of a smile now. ''Any man would.''

What an odd thing a heart was, pumping along unnoticed most of the time, then suddenly bouncing in great, uneven leaps like a ball tumbling downhill. ''She's flirting, not inviting.''

''Is there a difference?''

''To a woman, yes. I think of flirting as a performance art. Something to be enjoyed in the moment, like dancing. Men are more likely to think of it as akin to cooking—still an art in the right hands, but carried out with a particular goal in mind.''

The creases came back, and one corner or his mouth helped them build his smile this time. ''I'm a goal-oriented bastard at times.''

So they knew where they stood. He wanted to get her in bed. Rose hadn't decided yet what she wanted, but thought she would enjoy finding out....

* * * *

Possessed by a passionate sheikh

The Sheikh's Bartered Bride by Lucy Monroe

After a whirlwind courtship, Sheikh Hakim bin Omar al Kadar proposes marriage to shy Catherine Benning. After their wedding day, they travel to his desert kingdom, where Catherine discovers that Hakim has bought her!

Sheikh's Honour by Alexandra Sellers

Prince and heir Sheikh Jalal was claiming all that was his: land, title, throne…and a queen. Though temptress Clio Blake fought against the bandit prince's wooing like a tigress, Jalal would not be denied his woman!

Available 19th September 2008

www.millsandboon.co.uk